April's Shadow

April's Shadow

Gary Mortimer

© Gary Mortimer, 2008

Published by Little G Publishing

http://www.garymortimer.com

March 2009

ISBN 978-0-956112-0-0-2

Cover design by Utd Studio

Prepared and printed by:
York Publishing Services Ltd
64 Hallfield Road
Layerthorpe
York YO31 7ZQ
Tel: 01904 431213
Website: www.yps-publishing.co.uk

Thinking of;
Marie Ireland, Mark 'Sparky' Froud
and Margaret 'Meg' Hartless.

I am deeply indebted to my family and friends, all of whom have helped support this book through various means, be it a supportive word, a cup of coffee at the right moment or a forgiving smile when I've missed yet another social occasion.

A special thank you to my mum, dad and sister, Andy 'Soot' Sutcliffe and 'me bird'.

To each and every one of you, a very big 'thank you', because none of this would have been possible without you.

Chapter One

The room was strangely familiar. I couldn't help thinking I'd been here before, and not so long ago. Perhaps it had something to do with the high ceiling and cold white walls. Or maybe it was the lingering smell, and voices in the distance. Whatever it was, it wasn't home.

My head hurt.

There was an empty glass, a jug filled with water and something that resembled a grey cardboard hat resting on top of a small cupboard to my right. A plain white curtain enclosed three sides of my bed. This was the closest I'd ever get to private health care.

I stared up at the ceiling and tried to tune into the day. A nurse leaned forward and pressed a hand against my face. She raised my eyelid with a finger and poked a light into my eye. Her breath was warm and soothing. Her chin practically rested on my lips.

"Have we been introduced?" I asked.

"How do you feel?" she said, ignoring my remark.

"A whole lot better if you'd cut out the foreplay and just got into bed!"

She straightened her back and looked down at me. She wasn't ugly and she'd probably heard the same line a hundred times a day, and everyday, but that didn't stop the faint smile from caressing her lips.

She walked to the end of the bed and checked my chart.

"Am I going to live?"

"Probably." She frowned.

"You sound disappointed!"

"I'll blow a trumpet next time!"

I liked her. She was a woman after my own sarcastic heart.

I touched my head and found it wrapped in bandage.

"What happened?" I asked.

"You were hit over the head."

"With a mallet?"

"There are two men waiting to see you," she said, and made a gap in the curtain large enough for her to leave and Inspector Walker and Superintendent Matthews to enter.

It wasn't the kind of swap I had in mind.

They were dressed in black. Like two Priests preparing to read me my final rights, one last desperate attempt to squeeze my soul into heaven.

Matthews was carrying a plastic cup with steam rising up from the rim. Walker was clutching his trademark cigar but it wasn't lit. Just how many doctors and nurses had been forced to abandon their duties in an effort to get him not to light it, wasn't worth considering.

"What, no grapes?" I moaned.

"How are you feeling Mahoney?" Walker asked.

I contorted my face into a thousand shapes as I tried to get comfortable, but getting comfortable in somebody else's bed was never easy, especially when there was nobody else in it to get comfortable with.

"I've been better."

Matthews pulled up a chair next to the bed and placed his cup on the table. He looked tired. He had bags under his eyes large enough to carry a weeks shopping. Even his tie was at an angle.

Walker remained standing.

I looked at the two of them in turn. "So who plays the bad cop? I need to know because my money's on Walker."

"We need to talk Mr Mahoney,"

I looked back at the, not so Superintendent. He didn't seem in the mood for fooling around. But, then again, who the hell cared?

"Have you got permission? I mean, I might not be well enough to talk, I'm tired, I've been through a lot!"

But if I was waiting for the nurse to return and rescue me, I was wasting my time. The curtain stayed motionless. Even the voices in the distance had silenced. Maybe they were listening in?

Matthews sipped his coffee and cleared his throat. "We'd like to know what happened to you last night."

"I bumped my head!"

"I know," Matthews said. "I mean, before you bumped your head. What were you doing on that boat?"

I looked at the Superintendent, coffee poised, frown deepening and I mumbled; "I can't remember, must be the bump on my head!"

Matthews got to his feet and looked across at Walker. I wasn't sure if he was expecting help. But the Inspector didn't budge. Matthews turned a finger on me.

"Well maybe it's time you started to remember." He snapped. "Because four people are dead, twenty thousand pounds is missing and I want to know why."

Four? I quickly recalled the highlights of the previous evening in my head, the boat, the smell of fish, the fireworks, the blind-man and his dog, but all I could remember was two dead bodies.

"Four?" I asked.

"Two policemen, plus Collingwood and his sidekick," Walker informed me

I nodded back at the Inspector as Matthews paced the floor and did his best not to spill his coffee.

"You won't have noticed yet," he moaned. "But there's a media circus out there, reporters and cameras from all over the country wanting to know how a quiet seaside resort suddenly turned into Armageddon overnight."

"But I thought all publicity was good!"

Matthews didn't look happy. I'd pushed him as far as he would go. My work was done.

"I don't care about the publicity, Mahoney. I care about those dead bodies and the fact that you're one of only two people who walked off that boat alive."

I shot a glance at Matthews. "Who was the other?"

The Superintendent stared back at me in silence.

"You really don't remember?" Walker asked.

I shook my head as gently as my wound would allow.

"Adam Keatley," he replied.

"Preacher?" I questioned.

Walker nodded.

"What the hell was Preacher doing on the boat?"

Matthews sat back down. "That's what we'd like to know."

"That's why we need to know everything that happened last night," added Walker.

I looked up at him. "Everything?"

"Everything." He answered. "Right from the very start."

Chapter Two

My feet were stretched out across the office desk. I was killing a morning viewing the local paper. The headline grabber was an article on the Sands Project, a major development that had finally been pushed through by Helen Fitzsimmons, the Mayoress of Scarborough. She'd promised to set the town alight.

Next to that was a picture of a man called Collingwood. He was a local low-life who enjoyed making the most of other peoples' misfortune. His brother had been killed in a fall and, for some reason, the paper felt compelled to include the burial on the front page.

The centre pages focused on a local vicar, The Reverend Keatley. He was about to be rewarded for all his hard work by becoming a Bishop. The whole town was set for one big celebration. Personally, I couldn't understand why being restricted to moving at only forty-five degree angles, was considered a reward.

I rolled up the paper and thought about doing anything but what I was meant to do. The driving rain against the windowpane was accompanied by the distant thud of a stereo that echoed around the lilac walls. It danced inside my head.

The world outside was as cold as hell but my office was colder. I had the electric heater full on. It rumbled in a corner of the room like an empty stomach, and with just enough energy to prevent my breath from freezing in front of my face.

A biting wind nipped in through a gap in the windowsill. Every so often, and never when I was expecting it, the wind brushed the curtain skywards. My hands and feet had turned to stone.

How it would have looked to anybody who entered the office to find me sitting at a desk wrapped in two pairs of socks, a thick woolly jumper, a pair of gloves and a deep frown cemented on my forehead, I don't know. But that's how it was.

Paperwork lay untouched on the desk imprisoned by the weight of the telephone. My coffee mug was empty and I was hungry. Yet, somehow, I tried to convince myself that I'd done the right thing.

The blast of a horn sounded out as a train rumbled into the station nearby. I thought back to when I was only a matter of seconds from departing on one of those trains, leaving Scarborough far behind.

But Inspector Walker had got me a job. He paid me to issue summonses for those who'd missed their court appearance. It helped because now I had a target in which to finish my novel, my masterpiece, the literary adventure that would enable me to retire to the Lake District, sip wine and watch the grass grow under my feet. I had six weeks work, but two of those had gone already.

* * *

A gush of wind rocked the windowpane. I tore off the front page of the newspaper, folded it a number of times and jammed it into the frame. It was nothing more than a temporary solution.

I wiped away the condensation with the side of my hand and looked out of the window. Scarborough was stirring like a spoon through treacle as the morning rush hour crawled to a halt. It was the same every morning. I wondered why anyone ever took this route. Perhaps they were lost or looking for an excuse to be late for work. A left and then a right brought them out onto the main street, then up towards, not so much of a bottle-neck, more of a thimble. God help anyone who stalled.

Slowly an open-top bus, with bright sunny advertisements alongside sodden seats, inched forward just enough for me to see a man standing on the other side of the road. He was dressed in dark green trousers and a thick blue jacket. His hood somehow clung to his head and fought against the elements. The wind and the rain didn't seem to bother him. He stared at the traffic as it ambled by before glancing up in the general direction of my office.

He looked like a lot of people, like someone who just happened to be in the right place at the wrong time, and that was enough for me to turn my back and click on the kettle.

* * *

To the hiss of steaming water, I surveyed the office. I'd made some improvements. Most of them were when I was meant to be writing. But somehow it was easier to paint the walls lilac, buy some comfortable chairs, fix the leaking tap and stick the letters, *'Ronnie Elliott, Private Investigator'* in full on the door. It was after all his office. I was just the lodger, a shadow, someone with a dream.

Ronnie was the owner, the big cheese, the main man, that nobody came to see. He was taking a well-earned break from looking after his old man. But I'd hoped that sitting in his office, would provide the inspiration I needed. If not, he'd end up with the cleanest office in town.

* * *

I'd also bought a plant. I had no idea what kind of plant it was. It didn't seem to matter a whole lot, not to me anyway. It lived near the window, but I couldn't help thinking it didn't help very much. It needed the sun, we all needed the sun.

* * *

The steam from the kettle had only just started to cling to the ceiling when there was a knock on the door.

"Yeah," I said.

I watched it open slowly and the man from across the street leaned his head inside.

"Mr Elliott?" he asked.

I should have known, who else was he going to ask for? Elliott's name was in lights, or at least on the door. He had a reputation, not a particularly good one, but a reputation all the same. Nobody even knew I existed. It got to me on occasions, I mean, there were times I dreaded looking in the mirror, just in case I wasn't there.

"No," I answered.

"Oh," he mumbled.

"He's not in."

He said, 'oh' again and appeared troubled, but that didn't surprise me. Why else would somebody come knocking on the door of a Private Investigator?

"Could you tell me when he might be back?"

I was still trying to spoon some coffee into my mug. That's what I wanted to do. What I didn't want to do was talk to him. He was a stranger with a problem. And a problem shared in this office became somebody else's problem, my problem. And I had enough problems of my own.

He needed a Private Investigator, a proper Private Investigator.

"Well that's just the thing," I said, "he's on a break."

"Will he be long?" The man asked, checking his watch.

"No, I mean, he's on a holiday. It could be a couple of weeks."

The man rubbed his temple and sighed, "That's really no help."

"Yeah well, everybody's entitled to a break." I growled.

The man looked across at me and pulled back his hood. His chin was hidden by a beard while the rest of his face was covered in cuts and bruises. Some of them still appeared fresh. He looked like someone who had to step into the ring, to realise that he should never have stepped into the ring.

"No, I didn't mean," he started apologetically. "I... I meant........."

But whatever it was he meant he couldn't quite find the words to clarify. Instead he just stared at the floor while I stirred my coffee.

When I looked back at the door, he wasn't there anymore. But he hadn't gone. He'd sat himself down in one of my comfortable chairs.

I didn't want to think about how that made me feel, because it didn't make me feel very good at all. I tried not to let it show, but sometimes I couldn't help it. Sometimes people need to know when they're being a pain in the arse.

"Maybe you'd like a coffee as well!" I snapped.

He took me seriously. "I don't suppose you have any cream do you?"

"No, I don't suppose I do."

"Just milk then please."

I took off my gloves, only because it made me appear slightly more professional, and filled another mug, slamming the kettle and the mug as I went. I didn't want him here but I had to be polite, for a while at least, after all I was a guest in somebody else's office. But if matters didn't improve, I'd throw him out the window.

I placed two mugs on the desk and sat down.

"The name's Mahoney by the way, Richard Mahoney."

I couldn't believe how easily that name slipped from my tongue now. It felt good, better than my real name and everything else that came with it.

But, good as it sounded to me, the words simply took flight the moment they left my lips and shot over his head, out through the window and danced to the beat of the stereo from across the park. He didn't even seem to notice the frown on my face. Perhaps he was too busy searching the desk for a memory.

"You got a name?" I asked.

The man looked at me as if he'd just woken from a dream.

"I'm sorry?"

"What's your name?"

"Oh, er, Mr, Storey, Adam Storey."

He rocked forward in his chair and I thought he was about to reach out and shake my hand, but instead he pressed his fingers to a scar on the side of his head and rubbed it gently. He spoke with a Scottish accent and he looked like he'd swum most of the way. Thankfully it wasn't a strong accent or I'd have needed subtitles.

"Well, Mr Storey, would you like to take your coat off before you drown?"

He shook his head.

"I'm afraid I can't afford to stay, I, I need to find someone."

"I wasn't asking you to move in, I just figured you might want it drying out."

Without saying a word he slipped the coat from his shoulders and handed it to me. The label on the inside read, Rockport, which probably meant something to somebody but not me. It looked expensive and I wondered if Mr Storey was somebody who thought he could buy his way out of whatever trouble he'd found himself in.

I draped the coat over the heater. Immediately it stopped dancing and I realised that the only heat in the office would now be lost.

Mr Storey picked up his mug and held it tight to his chest. I thought about apologising for the cold but then I hadn't invited him in and I certainly wasn't God.

"So, you were saying."

He stared across at me as I sat back down.

"You need to find someone?" I explained.

"Yes. Yes. I do. That's right."

It seemed like a straightforward question but Storey prolonged the stare as if he was struggling to digest every last word. I wrapped my hands around my mug and hoped he would explain himself before we both froze to death.

But he just sat there. And the silence killed me. The tick from the clock tocked like a hammer.

I knew what was coming, a stranger with a story to tell and he'd search all day if he had to just to find some idiot who was ready to listen.

"This could turn out to be the longest case in history if I'm going to have to second guess everything!" I said.

"I'm sorry, I didn't realise, do, do you work for Mr Elliott?"

"In a sense. Who is it you're looking for?"

He stalled on a shiver and looked at me long and hard before reaching inside his pocket and pulling out a photograph. He passed it across the desk towards me. It was a head shot of a young girl somewhere in her teens. She smiled back at me. Her hair was shoulder length and mousy coloured. I placed the photo on the desk and looked back at Storey.

"Is she your daughter?"

"Yes. Yes, she is. She's my daughter."

I sniffed and brushed my nose with the side of my hand. "What did she do, run away?"

Storey frowned and massaged his temple with a thumb and middle finger. It was getting to be a habit.

"It's, it's a complicated story." He whispered.

"They always are," I tried to reassure him.

"My wife, we, we've had our problems. We divorced. It wasn't easy, we didn't speak, we haven't spoken for years, so I didn't even know I had a daughter."

"That must be tough!" I assumed.

"Yes, yes it is."

More silence.

"So she won't tell you where she is?"

"Who?"

Is was like pulling teeth with a spoon.

"Your wife."

Storey's face reddened as though he hadn't thought of asking her.

"Er, no. I can't, I mean, she's dead. She died recently."

"I see. I'm sorry."

"Well like I said, we, we didn't even live in the same town," said Storey with a shrug of his shoulders. "I can't even remember the last time I saw her."

I picked up the photograph and glanced at it once again.

"Does she have a name?"

"My wife?"

"Your daughter."

He looked towards the picture in my hand. His eyes were sad. He raised his shoulders and said; "April."

"Is that it?"

Storey's face glowed again.

"She....., somebody thought they were doing me a favour, my wife, apparently, didn't want me to know about, about her, my daughter. But someone sent me the photograph anyway. I'm not sure if they simply wanted me to know or if they actually expected me to try and find her."

Storey looked across at me and said; "I have to try and find her."

I nodded. "Have you been to the police?"

"She isn't missing!"

"Of course. So how about putting a copy of this in the paper?" I asked, tapping the photograph with a finger.

Storey shook his head. "I don't know what she knows about me, but I have to presume she doesn't know anything at all. I have to be very careful, I just can't turn up on her doorstep one day and announce that I'm her father."

He had a point.

"But you know she's in Scarborough?"

He nodded.

"How?"

"It was on the note."

"Was there anything else on the note?"

He shook his head. "No. It just read, this is your daughter and she lives somewhere in Scarborough."

I got to my feet. The walk to the window helped me

think, unfortunately it wasn't a long enough walk. I pulled on my ear and looked back at Storey. He appeared lost and sad. He held the mug tight, but he hadn't taken one single sip.

"So somebody sends you a photograph and tells you that the girl in the picture is your daughter and that she's living in Scarborough. Don't you find that a bit odd?"

Storey lowered the mug. He appeared put out.

"I don't know what to make of it in all honesty, I don't suppose I've really thought of anything other than I'd like to find her."

I watched Storey get to his feet and reach for his coat.

That's when it all starts. I'm meant to tell him, look I'm sorry, I'd love to help but I'm not a Private Investigator, I'm a writer with a dream and that's no help to anybody.

But I didn't. Instead I looked out of the window. The traffic had cleared but the rain still fell. The world looked cold and uninviting but that had nothing to do with the weather.

Storey was busy buttoning up his coat.

"Where are you going?" I asked.

"As I said, I need..."

"...yeah, I know, you need someone to find your daughter,"

He seemed shocked by the sharp tone in my voice and, to be honest, it surprised me a little.

"But has it occurred to you that you could end up paying this someone a lot of money just to sit twiddling their thumbs all week and not come up with anything?" I continued.

Storey revealed his thoughtful pose for a moment as he stared down at the floor.

"Do you have an alternative?"

Now I could handle the look of anger and I could handle a smile, but that lost look got me every time.

Maybe I was just staring at a reflection of myself, looking at that someone in need of a break. Maybe that's why I said what I said next.

"Have you tried anybody else yet?"

"I rang another agency, but all I got was an answer machine. I started to leave a message, but I didn't see the point. As I said, I really would like things to happen as quickly as possible."

"All right," I sighed. "Look, give me forty eight hours and I'll see what I can come up with."

"Are you a Detective?"

"No, not exactly, but like I said, I work with Mr Elliott and I know some people, who know some people, but don't worry, I'll be discrete."

Storey hesitated and that surprised me. All right, so I suppose 'I'll see what I can come up with' wasn't the most convincing line ever, but what choice did he have?

I listened to the clock tock again as he fought the reservations.

"What are you going to do?" he asked, eventually.

"Show her picture around, ask if anybody's seen her, if that's all right?"

Storey eventually nodded but he didn't appear convinced.

"So where can I contact you?" I asked.

He looked across at me with a petrified expression.

"What?"

"Where are you staying?"

"Oh, I'm...., I'm not sure yet. Is it all right if I contact you?"

"Whatever makes you happy."

"Finding April, Mr Mahoney, that would make me very happy."

"I'll see what I can do."

He nodded, just as something else dawned on him.

He reached into his pocket and pulled out a roll of banknotes.

"How, how much do I owe you?"

"For what?" I asked.

"Your services."

"I haven't done anything yet."

"Don't you want an advance?"

I held up my hand. "If I find something we'll talk."

Storey appeared puzzled. "Why would you do that?"

"I don't know," I mumbled. "So don't ask."

* * *

Storey folded away the money and looked at me one last time with an expression that suggested he didn't even know what day it was. Perhaps it was the shock of finding somebody ready to do something for nothing, or perhaps it was the fact that I just didn't know what day it was.

Storey nodded at me and left the office, a whole lot colder than when he'd entered, but maybe a whole lot happier, and that was a start I suppose.

* * *

I sat alone for another ten minutes staring at the photograph and wondering if I could be bothered to make another coffee. April looked like a nice girl. Her fringe slipped down to just above her eyes. She was smiling and didn't look like someone who'd tell you to go to hell if you asked her to tidy up her room or finish her homework. Nor did she look a whole lot like Storey, and that was probably as well, given the square jaw and fur on his chin.

I switched on the kettle. It made a clicking sound and that was that. Silence. Just when I thought the day couldn't get any worse, the kettle blew a gasket.

* * *

I put on my coat and gloves and took a walk to the Police Station. It would be an excuse to get out of the office and the fresh air would do me good. It was possible Inspector Walker might be able to help and, more importantly, he had a regular supply of coffee.

Chapter Three

It was ten past ten and the town centre had settled into its daily routine. The few people on the street appeared relaxed, some even ventured a cautious smile. Shopkeepers took advantage of the momentary lull to re-arrange displays that no doubt infuriated someone who had their eye on something in particular one week, but couldn't find it this.

The rain had relented. The fresh morning air gave way to cigarette smoke and the glow of a sun that enticed people to sit outside street cafés and sip elaborate coffees.

"The sun is shining and the sky is blue, please don't forget your Big Issue," bellowed a young man on the street corner.

I promised myself a copy the next time.

I always promised a copy.

* * *

At the top of town I took a right past the theatre with its neon lights, taking a break from their evening ritual, and stepped across the road to the police station.

Times had changed. The dull grey shoebox of an establishment had been replaced by a bright brick Lego building with a pretty little mosaic on the outside wall that tried it's damndest to symbolise how the law and the community were working closely together.

I followed the ramp up to a set of glass doors that swished open into a nice warm lobby.

The young lady behind the screen pushed her glasses up her nose and greeted me with a cheerful smile

"Good morning."

"Yeah." I replied. "Is Walker in?"

She turned to view the rota and nodded.

I reached for the guest book. The pen was chained to the desk. There was just enough leeway to write my name. I signed it, Mahoney. It was easier that way, that's how most people recognised me now, in Scarborough anyway. That's how I liked it, leaving the real me, Tony Blake, and everything that came with him, far behind and somewhere else.

"Anything exciting happened?" I asked.

She laughed excitedly but my question went unanswered. Whether she felt it was unethical, or whether she didn't reply because she couldn't stop laughing, I don't know and I didn't wait to find out.

A door clicked open to my left leaving me the freedom to roam the station. This was my reward for helping Inspector Walker.

I took a lift to the third floor. Eventually the doors opened on a familiar scene, a long line of desks leading all the way up to an office at the far end. All but one of the desks was occupied. Everybody sat diligently in their chairs, either typing out reports or speaking on the telephone.

At least I knew where to find a cop when I needed one.

Two men stood in Walker's office setting up a computer on his desk. Walker was in a corner of the room watching them with a mixture of interest and dread. I tapped on the door.

"Don't tell me they're replacing you with one of those things!"

Walker raised an eyebrow. "Not until they teach it how to light a cigar!"

"It must be hell, I mean, for someone who's only just learnt how to operate the coffee machine!"

Walker stepped towards me.

"You're here for a reason right?" He asked with a cold glare that, as much as I practised, I couldn't quite perfect.

"I'm looking for a girl." I said.

The Inspector turned to collect an evening paper from his desk and handed it to me. "Try the personal column."

"I did," I replied "but all the women over twenty-one were either taken or divorced, or taken, divorced and taken again."

"Seriously!"

".... I might have a case!"

Walker's expression suddenly changed to one of intrigue. We stepped outside the office.

"Go on," he quietly prompted.

"A man came to me...."

"You?"

"Well actually no, not me, Ronnie. He said he was looking for a girl."

"Why?"

"Why?"

"Yeah, why is he looking for a girl?"

I suddenly realised that I hadn't prepared myself at all. I was talking to a cop whose very existence was to question. Question everything and everyone.

"She's his daughter, that's why."

Walker stared right through me, and I quietly wondered how often such a glare made people cave in and talk.

"Has she got a name?"

"April." I replied.

Walker frowned.

"It's a complicated story. But that's all he knows."

Suddenly the frown was replaced by a thundercloud. I was trying the Inspector's patience.

"And I have a photograph."

I held out the image and Walker studied it for a moment."

"You don't know anything else about her?"

I shook my head.

"Do you know anything about him?"

I shook my head again.

"I just wondered if you might have some ideas about how to go about this, that's all. You know, maybe you could stick her picture in your computer and see if it comes up anywhere?"

Walker let out a faint smile from the corner of his mouth as he handed the picture back to me.

"This isn't the FBI, Mahoney. The only way that would work is if we'd ever had reason to record her details."

"Like if she was missing?"

"Yeah, like if she was missing."

I looked back at Walker.

"Has he reported her missing?"

"No, she's not missing."

He sighed. "Then there's nothing I can do."

"Is there anything I can do?"

"I don't know. Why don't you run the picture in the paper and see if anybody recognises her?"

"I can't."

Walker frowned again.

"She doesn't know about him," I explained. "I have to be discrete. I promised."

"Then you're just going to have to pace the streets and ask a lot of people if they've seen her, or if they know her."

"I was frightened you'd say that."

There was a knock on the door. Sergeant O'Neal was standing outside with his 'Christmas has come early' face on.

"A car crash has just been radioed in, Inspector."

"So?" said Walker. "Let the traffic boys take care of it!"

O'Neal shook his head and whispered softly.

"They did, but now the 'Super' wants us to take a look."

The thundercloud returned and this time it threatened rain. Lots of rain.

"Why?" Walker moaned.

"It involves Preacher, or at least, it involves his car."

I looked at Walker. I didn't know much about police work but I couldn't help wondering why just one name suddenly made the place feel even less welcoming than normal.

"Was he in it?"

O'Neal shook his head.

Walker scratched his ear and sighed. "Will this be ready when I get back?" he asked the men fixing the computer.

One of them nodded.

"And it'll work properly this time!"

The same man didn't know whether to nod or smile, for fear that, if it didn't, he could end up in jail.

Hitching his jacket up and over his shoulders Walker looked at me.

"Want to take a ride, Mahoney?"

Chapter Four

Sergeant O'Neal didn't say much on the way, but then neither did Walker. That didn't surprise me. Anything that ever pulled the Inspector from the comfort of his office chair always seemed to bring out the other side of his charming, impassive nature.

We drove north out of town. The villages were colourful and peaceful. Friendly faces moving at a pace that was never going to have them breaking out into a sweat.

A sign showed Whitby ahead but O'Neal took a right down a country lane. There wasn't a whole lot to see apart from fields, farms and a solitary pub. For a while the road rose and dipped like a rollercoaster. Eventually the trees and hedges gave way to a clear view over green and yellow fields that swept down towards a bright blue sea. I stretched my neck back towards the town until I could see a ray of sunlight caressing the castle headland and I thought to myself, Scarborough doesn't seem so bad from a distance.

O'Neal tapped the brakes and we came to a halt behind

a parked police car with its blue flashing light. The three of us got out. Walker still looked like a kid being dragged to the dentist. A policewoman stood on the roadside guiding what traffic there was around a set of cones. The road was narrow and helped to slow the cars. Most of them sneaked a view, others parked nearby and stood straining their necks to get a better look.

Another policeman came towards us.

"This is Traffic Constable Merrick." said O'Neal. "He was first on the scene."

Merrick didn't appear all that young but he was fresh faced, maybe he hadn't seen a lot of dead bodies and tangled wrecks. I read a book once that made references to how cops were only ever meant to see so many dead bodies before it sent them over the edge. Often they were left with no choice but to quit, or submit to the dangers of alcohol, while others committed suicide. Merrick, on the other hand, looked like he'd just had a good breakfast and he couldn't wait for his tea.

"The car was being driven by a young girl," he declared.

"Do we know who?"

Merrick shook his head. "She wasn't carrying any ID."

"Just my luck!" Walker moaned as we followed a track of trampled grass down to a wooded area where a car had run headfirst into a tree. The tree didn't look too bad but the hood of the car had been folded almost in two and the windscreen was obliterated. There was blood all over the dashboard, like someone had dropped a tin of red paint from a great height.

"This is Preacher's car?" Walker asked.

"Actually it's his wife's," Merrick replied. "The incident was reported about an hour ago. But it would appear it happened sometime last night."

Merrick looked sharp. He spoke clearly and precisely. I

wouldn't have suggested that he got a kick out of searching cars for bodies necessarily, but he certainly appeared upbeat about his work.

O'Neal asked. "How is she?"

"Not so good." said another voice.

The four of us turned to see a man stand up on the other side of the car. He had a big red happy face like a lump of strawberry jelly stuck on a broomstick, and he smiled as he walked towards the Sergeant.

"A fractured left tibia, three broken ribs, a sprained wrist, numerous cuts and bruises," he explained, with a dramatic roll of his 'r's'. "She's in Intensive, she's lost a lot of blood. I'm afraid it's touch and go, whether she makes it or not."

His presence seemed to unnerve O'Neal, that much was obvious by the way the Sergeant took a quick step backwards, cleared his throat, pulled a hand out of his pocket, scratched his ear and a whole load of other things that he probably didn't need to do.

"Any idea how the crash was caused?" Walker asked.

Merrick raised his shoulders. "We're working on that, sir."

"And do we know if she was alone?"

"It would appear so," Merrick replied. "At this stage we haven't found anybody else. We're not even sure if any other vehicle was involved, or whether the driver just lost control and ran off the road."

Walker appeared bothered by the whole affair, three faint lines formed a frown as he looked up the hill and back at the car again. O'Neal was also bothered, not so much by the car, but by the fat man's roaming eyes. He'd put some distance between them by making his way to the front of the vehicle and pretending he was intrigued by what had happened.

"So what do you think, Mahoney?" Walker asked.

After the initial shock of Walker even asking me what I thought, I looked back at him and said; "Well I'd like to think women drivers, but then again, am I supposed to think something other than an accident?"

"I don't know," said Walker, still sounding mystified, "that's why I was asking."

"Oh hello," said Fletcher noticing me for the first time and straightening his cravat. "And who's your friend, Inspector?"

"Mahoney, meet Fletcher, out forensic expert... among other things."

"Pleased to meet you Mr Mahoney." said Fletcher taking my hand and shaking it politely. "Are you one of the boys by any chance?"

"No." I said, staring him straight between the eyes. "I'm a Private Dick and that's the way it's going to stay."

"Ho hum." he smiled.

"You might want to take a look at this though, Inspector," said Merrick as he led us to the boot of the car.

We took a peek at two framed paintings.

"Are they valuable?" Walker asked.

Nobody answered. Everybody just shrugged their shoulders and looked at one another.

"Well maybe you could check it out, Sergeant."

O'Neal nodded and asked Fletcher; "Was she clean?"

"You mean, sober?"

"Or drugged?" O'Neal added.

"At this stage, it's hard to determine. Although we did find this in the glove compartment."

Fletcher smiled confidently as he held out a small plastic bag for us all to see. It was filled with a white substance. O'Neal studied it closely. Walker frowned. The whole affair was turning out to be worse than a trip to the dentist.

"I take it that's not a bag of sugar!" he snapped.

Fletcher shook his head.

Walker stuffed his hands into his trouser pockets and barked. "I don't like drugs!"

A rush of wind scattered a flock of birds from the nearby trees. I watched them circle the sky a couple of times until one of them decided it was time to head out towards the sea.

"I want to know everything you've got on this car Fletcher," Walker growled. "Everything!"

For the first time since we'd arrived Fletcher stopped smiling and quickly returned to his work. Walker had spoken and the world had listened and the world had better obey.

The three of us struggled back up the hill."

"So who's Preacher?" I asked.

Walker was too busy cursing every time his foot gave way and forced him to press a hand to the damp floor in an effort to stop him from falling.

So O'Neal replied; "Just some local who runs a nightclub."

"Is he trouble?"

"To some people, yes."

The crowd had increased on the roadside. People with nothing better to do than stare at a car rammed up against a tree. There are those who would go as far as to suggest it was art, while others would want to know who was involved, if they knew them and, if not, maybe they knew somebody who did.

A hat appeared above the crowd, a silly black hat that I recognised and instantly regretted recognising.

The last time I'd seen Eddie Hartless he was lying belly-up on a conveyor belt crammed with fish and not looking a million miles from Heaven's gate.

Now he was here and hurrying towards me with his

notepad at the ready.

"M, Mr Mahoney, c...., could you tell me what happened?" he asked quietly.

"Yeah," I said, looking back down the hill. "A car drove into a tree."

Hartless looked up from his notepad. "I..I mean, was it an accident?"

I didn't like Hartless, not only was he a reporter but he'd played me for a fool. Maybe I was, but that didn't mean that he had to join the queue.

"Yeah." I snapped. "Yes of course it was an accident."

Hartless started to scribble something.

"She was aiming for the fence." I finished.

There was a gloat on my face as I turned to leave.

"So it was a woman driver?" Hartless quickly questioned.

The gloat had vanished before I could take so much as a breath.

I turned to face Hartless. He tried to disguise his worried look as I approached him. I took hold of his lapel. Pulling him close I whispered; "You print anything that doesn't come from the cops and I'll..."

"a.... an, and you'll what, Mr Mahoney?"

I looked at him for a moment, and then I let him go.

Chapter Five

We drove back into town a whole lot faster than we'd left it. The villages were now just a blur. I checked a couple of times for Indians riding on our tail, but I guess the bottom line was, Walker just couldn't wait to speak to Preacher.

By the time we reached town a woman had informed the Inspector that Preacher could be found at The Casino. O'Neal parked the car on a pelican crossing right outside the bright building with it's giant dice and glass windows. What power.

We strode across the shiny wooden floor to where a bouncer stood with his hands crossed in front of him proudly guarding his mother's pride.

"Do you gentleman have a membership?" he asked politely.

O'Neal took out his ID and Walker snapped.

"Is that good enough!"

The bouncer blushed and smiled and hurried to open the door.

I followed O'Neal and Walker inside. A large seating

area filled the view with soft leather sofas. It looked like a waiting room. A waitress pointed to our right and we started to climb a set of stairs. It was only then, I could spy the slot machines, roulette wheels and poker tables at the far end of the room.

There was a restaurant at the top of the stairs. The eating area was busy and arched round the casino below. Walker and O'Neal craned their necks above the crowd until O'Neal tapped the Inspector on the shoulder and pointed towards a table occupied by half a dozen people; four men, two women and all immaculately dressed. This wasn't a last minute get together. This was very much an opportunity for people to impress. Missing the boat, wasn't an option.

The conversation was quiet as we approached, a little bit of hand waving, one or two agreeable expressions and a lot of sipping wine.

Walker came to a halt behind one of the men.

"We need a word Preacher."

Everybody at the table looked up at Walker and then across at Preacher. He didn't seem overly concerned.

"Can it wait?" He said, barely glancing over his shoulder.

Walker ducked his head towards Preacher and whispered; "We can either do it here nice and peacefully or I can grab a van and have you hauled off to the station with a few of the press boys waiting to take your picture, it's up to you!"

Preacher forced a smile.

"Is there a problem Mr.........." one of the men started to ask.

Preacher raised a hand and said; "It's nothing. Please, take a seat at the bar and order yourselves a drink, I'll be with you in a moment."

Most of the group appeared perplexed, and some, a

little slow to move. So Walker announced; "The bar's that way!" and helped one of the men out of his chair.

Everybody else in the restaurant cast discrete glances in our direction, wondering what was going to happen next. They had no idea Walker and O'Neal were cops.

The Inspector sat down next to Preacher.

"This better be important," Preacher snapped.

The Inspector picked up a glass of wine and raised it to his nose. He seemed to know what he was doing.

"I am important Preacher, "Walker replied. "That's why I do what I do!"

Preacher sat back in his chair and tipped his hands into his jacket pockets. His shaven head was bronzed. He looked like someone who spent a lot of his time in the sun.

"So what's this about?" he asked.

Walker nodded at O'Neal.

"Does the registration TPY 493X mean anything to you?" O'Neal asked as he dropped a piece of paper onto the table.

"It's a red Ford Fiesta." He continued as Preacher eyed the paper.

"It's my wife's," Preacher quietly replied. "At least it was. I'd forgotten all about it. Why?"

"We found it." Walker said.

"Near Cloughton." O'Neal added.

"In a field."

It was fun watching Preachers eyes dart from Walker to O'Neal as they quickly revealed the information. It was either something they practised a lot or it just came with experience.

"It had been driven into a tree."

"At quite a high speed," Walker added.

"It doesn't look good."

Preacher pushed the piece of paper aside and picked up his wine glass.

"Did you know the car was missing?" O'Neal asked.

"I'd forgotten it was there. I'm not sure it's even fit for the road."

"Are you saying it was stolen?"

"Well nobody asked if they could borrow it, if that's what you mean."

"There was a girl driving it. You wouldn't happen to know who she was would you?"

Preacher shot a glance across at O'Neal. "What's her name?"

"We don't know. She wasn't carrying any identification."

"Then I don't know."

O'Neal started to scribble something he considered worthwhile into his little black book. Walker sat back in his seat and tapped a finger on the menu in front of him.

"Is that it?" Preacher asked impatiently.

"Not exactly," Walker replied and nodded at O'Neal.

The Sergeant dropped the small plastic bag onto the table.

"What's this?" Preacher asked.

"Why don't you pop it into your tea? I guarantee you'll be singing Lucy in the Sky with Diamonds for a week!" Walker sniped.

"You found this in the car?"

Walker stared at Preacher.

"And you think it has something to do with me?"

Walker continued to stare a moment longer before slowly turning his attention to the surroundings.

"You like gambling?" he asked.

"Sometimes," Preacher replied, as if wary that anything he said might land him in a heap of trouble.

"Are you any good?"

"Sometimes."

Preacher appeared all edgy as though Walker was

backing him into a corner. He fought back with a scowl, the same one that separated the boys from the men, the goodies from the baddies, the people with brains from the monkeys. But which one was Preacher exactly?

"What about art?" Walker asked.

"What?"

"Art?"

"What about it?"

"Do you collect it, buy it, whatever it is you're meant to do with it?"

"Not particularly, no. Why?"

"We found some paintings in the boot. We're having them checked out. I just wondered if they might have been yours, that's all."

Preacher shook his head. Walker turned his attention to the bar.

"So who are your friends?" The Inspector asked.

"What's that got to do with you?"

"Don't have a heart attack Preacher I was only asking."

"They're not friends, they're business associates."

"Very posh!" Walker said.

Preacher stood up. "Look, are you going to arrest me or......"

Walker raised a hand and stopped Preacher short. He got to his feet and smiled; "I'm sure there's a perfectly good reason for all of this. Now you have yourself a nice meal while me and the Sergeant work day in and day out trying to discover exactly what that very good reason is!"

A phone started to ring on the table. Preacher reached to pick it up but Walker held his arm tight.

"But what bothers me is that, you haven't even asked how the girl is."

"Like I said, I'd forgotten all about the car, and if it

was stolen, well then, I don't really care what happened to her."

Walker held on to Preacher's arm for longer than I would have dared, as the phone continued to ring. It was like the whole scene was being played out in slow motion. Something had to give, either the phone would stop ringing or Walker would let go. Eventually Walker let go.

"Let's hope she doesn't die though hey, that would be rather messy, for you anyway," the Inspector smiled.

* * *

I couldn't help thinking that's not how things should have ended. I mean, other than Walker getting up Preacher's back, nothing seemed to have been achieved. I was all set for the Spanish Inquisition, Preacher and Walker ready for a showdown, two gunfighters standing face to face in the street, eyes straining, fingers twitching, foreheads sweating, both ready for the clock to strike. It wasn't right that we should just leave the building with Preacher on the phone, but that's how it was.

* * *

Outside O'Neal was talking on the car phone while Walker paused at the foot of the casino and stared back towards the large dice high above the glass doors.

"Something on your mind, Walker?" I asked.

"There's always something on my mind, Mahoney, that's the trouble with being me."

He lit up a cigar as O'Neal approached the two of us.

"That was Superintendent Matthews, you're not going to like this."

Walker didn't ask 'what?', he just blew out a ring of smoke and waited for O'Neal to explain.

"He wants you to put some men on Preacher."

It was incredible to see that, no matter how much Walker was frowning, he always managed to frown some more.

"And where am I supposed to get these *men* from exactly?" he sighed.

"Have you tried looking behind all those computers?" I quipped.

Instantly the two of them looked back at me and made me wish I hadn't. I glanced around at nothing in particular but when I looked back at Walker he was still staring at me. Only now his expression had changed.

"What's the situation with this girl you're looking for?" he asked.

"As in what?"

"As in, how long have you got to find her?"

I shrugged my shoulders. "As in, however long as it takes." I replied.

O'Neal started up the car. He was eager to return to the sanctity of his office but something far more productive was forming inside Walker's head.

I looked back at him and knew that I was going to regret asking; "Why?"

"I'd like you to follow Preacher." He replied sincerely

"Oh no, no, no, no, not another one of your stakeouts."

Walker let a cloud of smoke drift between us.

"Why not? You did such a great job the last time."

I raised a finger at him and said; "That's not even funny!"

"It wasn't meant to be."

The two of us stood staring at one another.

"It would be a great help, Mahoney."

"Yeah, but like I said, I've already got….."

"…. then maybe you could make the time?"

"No!"

Walker bit his lip and took a moment to take in the street. As usual people were passing by in cars and on foot desperate to know why a police car was outside the Casino.

"Fair enough," he sighed.

And there it was, that helpless, little boy lost look again. First Storey, now Walker. Hell, twice in one day, could I really be that unlucky?

I had every reason not to follow Preacher considering how I'd been stitched up the last time. But then there was something about Walker that I either liked or respected, I couldn't tell which and I certainly wouldn't tell him if I ever found out.

"Look, I said I'd give it a couple of days," I moaned. "If I haven't found anything by then... well, I guess, I guess I might be able to help."

Walker stopped short of getting in the car and looked back at me, but he didn't appear all that grateful.

"That long?" he asked.

"Yeah," I snapped. "That long!"

The Inspector ran a hand across his mouth in a concerned fashion.

"All right," he said eventually. "if that's the best you can do."

Now he was trying to make me feel bad.

"Yeah, that's the best I can do."

I could hear him whisper, 'thanks Mahoney.' But for the life of me I couldn't work out just how sincere he was being, the tone left me hanging in limbo.

But it's not easy spending your days thinking you're doing someone a favour while inwardly wondering if you're nothing more than a pain in the arse.

I watched the car drive away and realized that, perhaps there was only so much I could do to find this girl. I could make a few calls and see a few people. If anything led anywhere I'd follow the lead, if not I'd just tell Storey that I'd done my best. At least I'd done something. After that I could concentrate on following Preacher, it might even make a good story.

Satisfied with my decision I looked back down the street and suddenly realised that I didn't have a lift.

Bloody cops!

Chapter Six

I returned to the office in the hope that I'd finally troubled the postman into delivering some mail before he forgot where I worked. Then I would speed upstairs to see if the little red number on my answer machine displayed anything other than a nought. It wasn't just the fact that nobody ever called but the patronising tone in the woman's voice as she happily declared; 'you have no new messages'.

Barbara was making herself busy dusting down one of the vacant offices. There wasn't a lot else for her to do since Ronnie's was the only office in the building that was occupied. But she'd been contracted for the year and that was good enough for her.

Talking to Barbara made me realise that she knew everything about this town and everybody in it. But she would never gossip, not unless you happened to conveniently place a packet of cigarettes nearby. I told her she'd make a great detective, but she swore blind that she was happy with the work she did and that she had a home and a hardworking man to look after.

* * *

"Any post?" I asked, already knowing what the answer would be.

"I'm afraid not." she replied quietly, as if that might soften the blow. "But there is a young lady waiting to see you."

"Me or Ronnie?"

"Er, I don't think she said. I can't remember. Anyway I asked her to wait outside your office. I didn't think you'd be very long."

Barbara was so excited at the sudden upturn in my popularity that she practically pushed me up the stairs.

"I don't think she's from round here though." she whispered. "She sounded American."

I stopped halfway up the stairs and looked back at Barbara. "Could you fix some drinks? My kettle's broken."

Barbara winked and pointed a finger into the air.

"Coffee, I suppose." She smiled. "Americans like their coffee don't they, it's what keeps them going."

I smiled at Barbara and headed upstairs.

Sitting on the leather sofa outside my office was a young woman. She was dressed in a white blouse under a narrow dark blue suit. Her fair hair was tied back and fell just below her shoulders. She was wearing dark-rimmed glasses and her cheeks were touched with faint freckles. She sat with an elbow on the arm of the sofa and a finger pressed to her cheek, looking pensive, as though she was about to start painting the Sistine Chapel.

And I couldn't help wondering what a nice girl like her was doing in a place like this.

"You're waiting to see me?"

The woman got out of the chair and stood in front of me. She was tall but not too tall. I held out my hand.

"The name's Mahoney, Richard Mahoney."

She shook my hand but her eyes had strayed to the sign on the door. She appeared confused.

"I'm Ronnie's partner," I quickly explained. "He's taking a break, a holiday."

"I'm so glad I've caught up with you, Mr Mahoney," she said.

Her grip was firm and she sounded anxious. I pushed open the office door and followed her inside.

"Please, take a seat. I've got some coffee on the way."

She sat in a chair and crossed her legs and rubbed the back of her hands and that was enough to remind me to turn on the heater.

"It'll take a minute to warm up." I explained.

She smiled politely as I sat down.

"Unusual weather for this time of year," I said, but I had no idea why, I wasn't really big on small talk.

She continued to smile.

"Some blame the environment," I went on. "But I just think it's nature saying, you can't control me!"

Any minute now I was going to reach for a gun and shoot myself, it might just shut me up. Her smile had started to wane.

"So, how can I help you?" I finally asked.

She pressed a finger to the side of her face. Her mouth was narrow, it must have saved on lipstick. Her eyebrows were a little darker than her hair. Her shoulders broad and I wondered if the suit came with padding.

"It's my sister." she said, softly. "My younger sister, I'm afraid she's missing."

Missing? Somebody else was missing. Hell, overnight, Scarborough had turned into the Bermuda triangle.

"Have you contacted the police?" I asked.

She nodded.

"Yes of course I have, but let's be honest Mr Mahoney, they really don't have the resources do they. If they did find her, and I very much doubt they will, it would purely be by chance."

I looked down at my desk and wondered how it was that for over a month only the cleaner knew of Ronnie's office. Now two people in one day had come knocking. I should buy a lottery ticket.

"Look, I'm sorry, I'd love to help…"

"… but?"

"If you'd come by last week, or the week before, maybe I could have helped."

"And how would you have done that exactly?"

Her accent was soft but the tone in her voice suddenly changed. It took me by surprise.

"I'm sorry?"

"I said, how would you have helped?"

I stalled for an answer, partly because I wasn't sure I had one and partly because I suddenly wanted to tell her to go to hell.

"How would you have helped locate my sister?"

Perhaps it was nothing more than her way of dealing with rejection. She'd come to me for help and I was politely refusing. But, then again, I couldn't help thinking that she was questioning my ability.

"Well….., I'd……" (Where's the coffee? Why don't I come in and start all over again?)

She got to her feet. "Call out her name on the sidewalk perhaps?"

"Sidewalk?"

"Street." She quickly explained. "Or wave a photograph of her in the hope that some guy might recognize her?"

Experience had taught me that in about three hours

time I would come up with an intelligent answer, or, failing that, something sarcastic, a classic put down, anything to make me feel a little better than I did right now. But, try as I might, my brain was out to lunch.

"You don't know the first thing about looking for a young girl, do you?" she continued.

This was getting personal and I couldn't help thinking this woman had a chip on her shoulder larger than a goalpost and she was happy to swing it in my direction.

"Hey look." I said, pressing the palms of my hands in her direction. "I didn't invite you in here, so if you don't think I can do the job then why don't you... "

"... what?" She was leaning across the desk and staring back at me. "Go somewhere else perhaps? Another Private Investigator? How about Jo Envy? Oh, trouble is though, as soon as they realise that, Jo Envy is in fact a woman, they come up with some crappy reason not to hire her."

She finished with a flourish, flicking her ponytail back across her shoulders and standing hands on hips in the middle of the office, just as Barbara entered carrying a tray. I'd never been so happy to see somebody in all my life. I might have rushed over and kissed her, if it hadn't meant spending the rest of my life explaining why.

"Here's the coffee."

Her announcement was met with an eerie silence, but that didn't deter Barbara.

"Everything alright?" She asked.

I looked at Barbara and nodded. She placed the tray on the desk and smiled at the woman.

"Nothing like a nice hot drink to help talk things over. I made you a coffee because I thought you were American, you are American aren't you?"

The woman nodded and said softly; "Yes. New York."

"That's nice. Are you here on holiday then?"

"Actually I work here."

"Oh that's nice. Well I'll leave the two of you to it. Nice meeting you."

It was perfection in motion, seeing the way Barbara softened the atmosphere.

"Thanks Barbara." I said.

I watched Barbara head towards the door. Part of me wanted her to stay. I wasn't keen on being left alone with an angry woman. The door closed. The woman returned to her chair and sat quietly inspecting the back of her hands.

"So you're Jo Envy!" I said.

She nodded.

"But there's no missing sister?"

"No!" Envy sighed. "I just wanted to know what it took to get a case round here. I thought it might be something special, that way I could live with myself, but.........."

She looked back at me.

"Hey, I can be special! You just caught me on a bad day."

Envy got to her feet again.

"Unfortunately it all comes down to that same old cliché, while everybody assumes it's a jungle out there, they want Tarzan to sort out their problems, not Jane. She's meant to stay at home and make the dinner."

She started to pace the floor.

"I've got a law degree. I've studied criminal behaviour. I've got a counselling certificate and I can be Tarzan when I want to be. Look......"

Suddenly she was flexing an elbow in front of me and insisting that I feel her arm. I could have been wrong but it was as if she'd just squeezed a tennis ball up her sleeve.

"That's very impressive." I said. "I mean, the degree and everything."

"Obviously not impressive enough though!"

"Look, if it helps, I wouldn't take all of this personally, I haven't had a decent case in weeks."

"Not until now anyways."

"What do you mean?"

"I know about Mr Storey, he left a message with me, said something about needing to look for his daughter, then it must have clicked that the voice on my answer machine was a woman's so he just gave up."

"He didn't give up, he's in a rush, he wants things sorting out as soon as possible."

Envy stared back at me with an unconvinced expression. It was then that I knew that anything and everything I said would be a waste of time.

"How did you know he'd come here?" I asked.

"You're the only other detective agency in town."

"Of course," I replied, as I watched her sip her coffee.

"Anyway," she continued. "when somebody calls into your office, they don't confuse you with the secretary, do they? You don't see the look on their face when I have to explain that I'm actually a Private Investigator and, all of a sudden, they go looking for excuses not to hire me. So, yes, I take it personally."

Watching Envy get herself all wound up made me wonder if I should tell her the truth about my real name. But that might have made her feel worse. Not only would she have lost out to a man, just because he was a man, but to a man who wasn't even a Detective. That would be a hell of a thing to swallow.

So I didn't say anything.

Envy slumped back in her seat and I was glad, it gave me the chance to do what I always do best in this situations, pull on my ear and wonder what kind of a mess I was about to get myself in this time.

"Look, maybe I can help," I said

Envy raised her eyes at me.

"I've just been with the police, they want me to tail someone. I told them I couldn't because I already had a case, but look, if you want to help find this girl and leave me to follow this man, then maybe we could work something out."

Envy's light coloured eyebrows burrowed into a frown.

"Isn't that a bit like a hand-me-down?"

I got a little cross and said; "You got a problem with hand-me-downs?"

"It's not quite what I had in mind," she said thoughtfully.

"Well then welcome to my world." I said, holding out my hands.

Envy stared at the mug in front of her before reaching out and taking a sip.

I listened through the silence until I could pick out the traffic and the breeze brushing up against my window. The stereo was booming again. It sounded like the same crap song.

Envy looked like a nice girl, perhaps not someone you'd have instantly noticed across a crowded bar, but definitely somebody you'd have noticed by the end of the night.

"So?" I asked, eventually.

"What's Storey going to make of all this?"

"He doesn't have to know, does he? You report what you find to me and........"

".....you take all the credit!"

"I'm not in this for credit."

"Money then?"

I looked across at Envy. It was a look that gave everything away.

"You're not doing it for the money either?"

"I...I told him he was running the risk of being ripped off, that a PI could sit around all week and not find anything but still charge him a small fortune. So I told him to give me two days to come up with something, if I did, then he could start paying me."

"Are you some kinda English knight in shining armour?"

"No, just something special!"

Envy took another sip of coffee. It seemed to meet with her approval, and that was the first time I'd been able to make that assumption since she'd stepped into the office.

"Why would you want to do that?"

"Because I'm nice, or an idiot, you can make up your own mind."

She looked at me for a moment.

"So?" I asked

Envy put down her cup and let out a sigh.

"It still feels as though I'm working behind someone's back," she said. "And that's not going to change people's perceptions of me."

"I don't agree, in a small town like Scarborough it's all word of mouth, when somebody hears that you've done a really good job they'll come to you and they won't give a damn what you look like."

The expression on her face suggested that I might have a point.

"Besides." I added. "What have you got to lose?"

In-between taking a moment to gather her thoughts Envy would cast a glance every so often in my direction. Suspicion by nature was the number one rule of a Private Investigator, even I knew that much.

Eventually she asked; "So what have I got to go on?"

"Not a lot." I said, taking out the photograph and handing it to her.

"She looks like a nice girl. What do we know about her?"

"She's called April."

Envy flipped the photograph over as if she'd missed something important. It reminded me of when people search the inside of a card for the punch line when it was on the cover all the time. She passed her puzzled glance in my direction.

"Is that it?"

I nodded. "Her old man didn't even know he had a daughter until that picture was sent to him in the post with a note saying that she was here in Scarborough."

"That's quite a haystack."

"He doesn't want her picture in the papers either."

Envy crossed her legs. She seemed relaxed, maybe working on other people's problems had that affect on her.

"So what have you got in mind?" I asked.

"Well, I'll start by waving her picture on the street, and asking if anybody recognizes her!"

I smiled. She got to her feet and I followed her to the door.

"I presume you want to keep this?" she asked, waving the picture at me.

"It might help if I see her around. Why did you want a copy?"

Envy took out a gadget and aimed it at the photograph. A light flashed.

"Got one," she said.

She showed me the picture of April she'd just copied.

"Pretty impressive." I said, with as much sincerity as I could muster for technology.

"Have you got a cell phone?" she asked.

"A what?"

"A mobile?"

"Not since I grew too big for the cot."

Envy frowned impatiently.

"What kind of Detective doesn't have a cell phone?"

"The only other one in town!"

"So how am I supposed to get in touch with you?"

I looked back towards the desk.

"You could try the old fashioned telephone way, or the not so old fashioned answer machine."

"I've never worked with anybody old fashioned before!"

"I guess that's what happens when you're a knight!"

She looked at me for a moment but I couldn't work out what was going on inside her head.

"I'll get you one. It'll come in handy."

I didn't like the idea much, even if I figured how to work it out I would only lose it somewhere. But Envy was insistent, so I didn't bother arguing, it was easier.

"So how long have I got?" She asked.

"I told him a couple of days, but then again, if you don't find anything, where else is he going to go?"

Envy straightened out her jacket and offered me an all-knowing look.

"That might depend on why he's looking."

I frowned.

"Are you always so suspicious?"

"Everybody has their dark side."

"Even you?"

"Especially me!"

Chapter Seven

I needed a drink. I needed to finish my book. I needed to go on holiday somewhere far away. But all I had was a dream, an itch in my pocket and somebody else's problems.

I thought I was strong. At least I thought I was a whole lot stronger than I felt right now.

I sat alone at the bar, holding out some money in my hand. The face in the mirror stared back at me. He knew I was only delaying the inevitable.

I ordered a whisky. The barman asked if everything was all right? I looked at him and nodded, but he could tell I was lying. I watched him turn and wipe down a couple of wet glasses. He would have listened and he might have even found an answer because that's what he did, that was his real job. Most people who entered his bar were accompanied by family, friends or partners. Some were happy. Some got by. Others simply drifted through routine.

But it was the lonely ones, those who dared not look

at themselves, they were the ones who appealed to the barman. They were the ones who were so afraid of what they might find, they didn't even talk to their friends. They preferred a stranger, a compassionate voice trapped behind a bar. He'd heard it all before and probably would again before the night was through.

Perhaps we had something in common, the barman and me. We're sought by strangers in need of answers and we're lulled into thinking we might be able to help. Hell, sometimes we even consider ourselves valuable. Trouble was we were only as big as the problem. And we were only ever needed as long as the problem existed.

After that we become nothing more than a distant memory. A face people can't quite put a name to. A figure who just happened to say the right thing at the right time.

I picked up the whisky and looked at it in my hand. I thought back to that first night in Ronnie's office when I found a whole bottle of the stuff in his bottom drawer. It was just meant to get me through the night. Little did I know the nightmare I would wake up to.

But that's what followed.

I hadn't touched a drop since that evening with Walker, when I almost left town for good. But what was the alternative? Was there an alternative?

Helping people was a nagging itch. Not just because I liked to, but because I thought it might make a good story, and because I thought I could.

But that's not even heroic, that's just plain stupid. Who was I to help anybody, when I couldn't even help myself?

My hand shook, not much, just enough to set the alarm bells ringing inside my head.

The face in the mirror nodded as the whisky raced down my throat. It burnt inside my chest. My body shivered. I placed the glass back onto the bar very deliberately. The Barman asked if I'd like another.

I nodded and the face smiled.

Chapter Eight

I rang Walker and told him that I'd sit and watch Preacher for him. He was happy or at least as happy as he was ever going to be. I also told him that I needed a car. He said he'd see what he could do.

An hour later the office door opened and Ronnie Elliott shuffled in.

He looked like he always did, as if getting dressed was an inconvenience. His chin was supporting a patch of stubble that appeared all set to rendezvous with his nasal hair. Most of his shirt was buttoned up at an angle and some of it was tucked into the top of his trousers. The bottom of his coat was hunched over a newspaper that had been rolled into his back pocket. He scratched his belly as he glanced around the room and his little round eyes narrowed still further.

"Christ, kid, what have you done to the place?"

"I thought it could do with a tidy up."

Elliott pointed a finger at me.

"There's nothing wrong with an untidy office, an

untidy office is a working office. It also gives the place a little character and don't you forget that!"

He went over to my plant and lifted a leaf with his index finger.

"You turning this place into a jungle?"

It's true, there was never anything that would satisfy him. Ronnie lived to criticise, it's what made him happy.

"So is this business or pleasure?" I asked.

Ronnie looked at me with a puzzled expression.

"Oh yeah, I nearly forgot," he growled. "Follow me, I've got you some wheels."

I followed Ronnie outside. He led me across the park with its sprinkling of grass and withered trees and surrounding boarding houses with Vacant displays in the window. The boom of the stereo increased. It sounded like it had been composed by some git trapped in an empty can while having an epileptic fit. I tried not to let it bother me, because I didn't want to think I was turning into my dad. But it did bother me, that much was obvious from the way my left eye flickered. I looked up towards the flats, and promised myself a visit, in the not too distant future.

Ronnie whistled as we walked and not very well at that. It was as if he'd lost his spare teeth in a wind tunnel.

I hadn't seen him much apart from when he popped in to see how I was doing and to check that I hadn't burnt the place down. So we had never really built up much of a conversation. I would ask how his father was and he would tell me how his horses had done and that would be that. I knew as much about him now as I did the first night I'd slept in his office, when I'd stumbled into town on a train in search of a dream. I had nowhere else to go and no money to get there with.

"So what do you think? He asked, rubbing his chin.

I presumed he was referring to the stubble.

"I think you need a sharper razor!"

"It's called a goatee, it's the fashion, you should be up on these things."

Ronnie, a fashion icon? Now those were four words I never thought I'd use in the same sentence unless someone were to add, 'never in a million years.'

Just as I thought we were about to run out of universe, Ronnie stopped behind the rear of a parked car and held out his arms.

"There you go." He said.

I didn't say anything. It crossed my mind that I might gasp in horror only for him to laugh and say he was only joking and then hand me the keys to the really nice black BMW looking thing close by. It was only when he pressed the keys into the lock and opened the door that I realised I was going to have to gasp.

"Is this it?"

"Take that tone out of your voice kid! This is a classic car."

"It's....... it's......"

But it was hard for me to describe exactly what *it* was, except I couldn't imagine chasing any criminals in it, unless they were on a tricycle. And no attractive girl in her right mind would ever beg for a lift in my....... *it,* that was for sure.

"It's a 1955, Series 2, split windscreen, Morris Minor."

"Can you get it fixed?"

"Can I get what fixed?"

"The windscreen?"

Ronnie looked up from caressing the wing with his fingers and snapped; "It's meant to be that way, you idiot!"

"That's what I should have told the cops the night my headlight went!"

I watched Ronnie slump into the passengers seat and

open up the driver's door. I got in. The steering wheel was larger than a dustbin lid and the dashboard reminded me of a mantle-piece with a speedometer instead of a clock.

"So what do you think?" Ronnie asked, but not in a pleasant manner. More of a, think yourself lucky kid, kind of way. I got the feeling that, on the day he was born, the doctor decided not to pat his backside but punch him in the face, and he'd felt aggrieved ever since.

"Well naturally I'll ask the criminals not to run too fast..."

"Hey, this is Scarborough you moron, where the hell are you going to chase anybody? Pretty soon they'll either come to a dead end or a set of lights."

"You really do nothing for my romantic illusions of a Private Investigator, you know that."

Ronnie frowned across at me. "So do you want to borrow it or what?"

"Sure." I replied.

I watched as Ronnie pulled open the glove compartment and studied it closely like someone does when they pass on a pair of old trousers or a jacket, he wanted to make sure he hadn't left anything valuable inside.

I played with the steering wheel.

"It does forty miles to the gallon and the engine's in better condition than when I bought it brand new."

"You bought it brand new?"

I tried to picture the scene, it had to be in sepia.

"You got a problem with that?" he growled.

I shook my head.

Elliott rolled out of the car. I quickly followed. He handed me the keys then poked a finger into my chest.

"I want it back exactly as I left it, clean, scratch less and with a full tank of petrol. Is that clear?"

I nodded and reminded myself of that moment in the film when a soldier shows a picture of his family just as they're about to go to war and you know for a fact he's going to head-butt the first bullet that comes his way. So it was that Ronnie had practically sent an open invitation to the world to come and wreck his pride and joy and leave me totally responsible.

There didn't seem a lot else to say after that. Ronnie pulled out his newspaper and I thought he would be on his not so merry way. But for some reason he stalled and looked across at me.

"So how's the book coming along, kid?"

I stared back at him. "The what?"

"The book. You know, that thing about the Private Investigator. The reason why you came here in the first place remember?"

"Oh yeah," I said, in a vain attempt to avoid discussing my life's ambition with a tub of lard.

"Well 'Oh yeah', doesn't sound too promising!"

I shrugged my shoulders. Writing a book was personal, but Elliott wouldn't know that. There were certain intricacies, delicate details that had to be resolved before I could move on. It was like discussing a health issue and that wasn't something you would do with someone you didn't know all that well. And I didn't know Elliott all that well.

"I'm working on it!"

"So it's not finished then?"

I shook my head and Elliott appeared disappointed. What was that all about? What did it matter to him whether or not I finished the novel?

"So what's the delay, I mean, you solved the case, right? So the police are happy, everybody's happy. End of story, right?"

So much for not wanting to discuss something personal with someone I didn't know very well.

"Have you ever written a book?" I asked, with slightly

more venom than I'd intended.

Elliott smiled and spread out his arms.

"Do I look like someone who's written a book?"

Interesting. Are authors meant to have a certain look in the way that bookworms are generally associated with small round glasses and no life? Maybe that was it, maybe I wouldn't be an author until I'd discovered 'the look', whatever that was, a pipe perhaps or some kind of hat?

"I'm still in it though right?" Elliott asked as he waved his rolled up newspaper at me.

I nodded and wondered what vegetable might play his part if ever it got to the screen.

Elliott paused to look at me and I couldn't help thinking he appeared concerned.

"My old man's always telling me that everybody's got a talent, it's just that some have to delve a little deeper than others to find it. If yours is writing, kid, then you shouldn't let it go to waste, and if it isn't, then you shouldn't waste your time writing."

I concentrated my gaze on the newspaper as it was stabbed into my chest a couple of times before Elliott retreated back across the park.

"And what's yours Ronnie?" I asked. "What's your talent?"

Elliott turned and waved his newspaper into the air.

"Always backing the wrong horse, kid. Always backing the wrong damn horse."

* * *

A pile of A4 pages sat on my desk. Somewhere under all the dust was my first attempt at a novel.

How all the words appeared neatly arranged on the paper, but nobody ever seemed to appreciate all the anxious re-writes, the sleepless nights, the wondering was it all worth it, and all the characters who made fleeting appearances but never quite made it to the finished product.

And I couldn't help pondering over how I'd been set up the last time. There I was thinking I was the man in control, pulling the strings, when all the while I was nothing more than a puppet. That's what made it hard to finish the book.

* * *

I opened a Writer's Guide and thumbed through the pages. Unfortunately none of the publishers or agents reached out and begged me to forward my work. One seemed pretty much like the other and I wondered what their ultimate goal was. Jump on a popular bandwagon and sell millions or put everything into a classic that might just make their money back?

My life had come down to selling my soul, and for what? Was it just the money or did it mean more to me than that?

It had to mean more to me than that. This book felt like a part of me, posting it would have been like stuffing a leg or an arm into an envelope and wondering how a complete stranger would receive it.

There was always the Writer's Circle. Perhaps all I needed was a helping hand. Maybe their lack of inspiration might inspire me. And with the Writer's Circle came Trish. It would be nice to see her again. She quoted Chandler and she could brighten up a wet weekend in Scarborough with just a smile.

But that would have to wait. I had another job to do. Another stakeout.

I picked up the pile of A4 papers and put them back in the bottom drawer to gather a little more dust.

Chapter Nine

Walker asked me to meet him at the end of Preacher's road. Darkness was creeping in as the Inspector pulled up behind me. He got in the passenger side without saying a word. He was holding onto his customary cigar. I looked across at him. He was smiling. I knew full well why and I was ready for an argument.

"Nice car!"

"Hey, if you want somebody else to do your dirty work!"

"I just said, nice car, that's all!"

"Yeah I know, I heard you. And don't think you're lighting that thing in here."

Walker glanced at the cigar and appeared momentarily mortified.

"Any news on the girl?" I asked.

"Yes, and it's not good I'm afraid. It doesn't look like she'll pull through."

I looked across at Walker.

"What?" he asked.

But it was too good to be true. There was no way on earth it could be April, but I had to be sure. I took out her photograph and showed it to the Inspector.

"It's not her is it?"

Walker rolled his bottom lip and shook his head. "'No," he replied.

I put away the picture and wondered just what it was I was meant to say in such situations. I mean, somebody was very badly injured and that was sad, but I didn't know her. Did that make it all right? And while she continued to be injured she couldn't help Walker. Did that make me totally unreasonable?

"So how is it you're not looking for this girl anymore?" Walker asked.

"I didn't say I wasn't, but I've got some help."

"Who?"

I looked at Walker. "Somebody called Jo Envy."

"And who's he when he's at home?"

"I'm so glad to hear you say that."

"What?"

"Because, he's a she!"

Walker frowned. "I don't understand, why are you happy to hear me say that?"

"Because I wouldn't put it past you setting this whole thing up just so I'd be free to do your work."

Walker took my remark as a compliment and stretched out a smile. "So," he said, "is she good looking?"

"What's that got to do with anything?"

"Everything if you want to go out with her!"

"I never said anything about going out with her! We've only just met."

"She's not attractive then?"

"I didn't say she wasn't attractive either!"

"So why don't you want to go out with her?"

"I can't believe I'm listening to this."

Perhaps I was over reacting but Walker was enjoying every second.

"I'm just thinking of you that's all. You're a lonely man in a strange town. It can't be easy."

"What can't be easy?"

"Meeting a woman."

Walker was good, very good. I got the feeling extracting a confession was child's play the way he could wind people up.

"And you'd know all about that, I suppose?"

"I'd know if I wanted to go out with someone. It's what you do, you look at someone and you think.." Walker rolled his head to one side and curled his lip. "... yes, I'd like to go out with her, or, never in a million years."

"Has nobody ever grown on you?"

"Of course. But by then it's too late, you've become friends and you can't have both."

"You're all heart!"

Walker let out another smile and stared up at Preachers house.

"So, what's the deal with Preacher?" I asked.

"I'm not sure. Some people upstairs seem to have it in for him. Unfortunately I don't see why that justifies getting half a dozen of my men to follow him."

"So I could be sat here twiddling my thumbs all week?"

I watched Walker frown.

"The accident bothers me," he mumbled.

"In what way?"

"I can't see why she'd take that particular road."

"I thought it was the Whitby road?"

"If she was going to Whitby, she'd have taken the main road, it's quicker."

"Maybe she preferred the scenic route?"

"Not at that time of night." Walker continued. "All

61

you see is trees and hedges and other people's headlights."
He let out a yawn. "We're checking out some of the places
along the way, see if anybody can shed some light."

"Of course, if she was on drugs, she might not know
where she was going."

"I suppose," he sighed

"And you want me to report anything suspicious?"

Walker nodded and we both looked out at Preachers
place.

"So what does he do again?"

"He runs a nightclub in the town centre, The Mission
club." Walker turned to face me and the faint smile
suggested he was about to add something that would
amuse him and only him. "You might enjoy it!"

"The music?"

"There'll be some women there."

"Yeah, all dancing round their handbags and discussing
who's going to get divorced next!"

The smile slipped from his lips.

"You've got the wrong impression about this town,
Mahoney."

I felt slightly concerned, possibly because there are
some opinions that I value and even though I didn't know
Walker that well, I valued his. For some reason it was
important that he either felt the same way about me or at
least saw where I was coming from. So I made ready with
an excuse to justify myself.

"I guess that comes from sitting in a car all day following
slightly suspicious people while everybody else is either
crammed in a jam or sheltering under a bus stop!"

"So what else would you be doing if you weren't doing
that?"

"Writing my book. That's what I came here for
remember!"

Walker started to light up his cigar.

"Maybe you can help," I started.

The Inspector looked across at me.

"That computer you were chucking out of your office the other day?"

"What about it?"

"Why don't you let me have it, as a kind of a favour? I could type my stuff up then."

Walker sat back and flicked his match out of the window.

"I can do better than that," he said, pausing to take a drag on his cigar. "I'll get my wife to type it up for you."

"I can't ask her to do that!"

"Don't be stupid. She's bored at home. She's got another six weeks before she goes back to work. Besides, she's always wanted to know what I got up to at work. I am in it aren't I?"

Everybody wants to be in it!

"There's only one problem," I mumbled.

"What's that?"

"It's not finished yet."

Walker shrugged his shoulders. "So she can write up what you've got so far."

He made it sound so simple. So convenient. I let out a gentle nod.

The Inspector smiled. "So do you want it on a floppy or CD?"

I saw Walker's lips move but I didn't have a clue what he was talking about.

"How do you want it saving?" he explained.

"Couldn't you just print it out for me?"

Walker got out of the car. "Whatever. Just drop it into the office sometime."

I watched Walker stand proudly for a moment, hands on hips blowing his cigar smoke into the night sky and staring up at Preacher's house. Then he tapped on my window. I wound it down. He leaned forward.

"Be careful, Mahoney."

"Are you worried about me now?"

"Of course I am. If anything happens to you I'm going to have to turn off a computer and get one of my boys to follow him."

Chapter Ten

Night finally arrived with a twinkling of stars and a thin stretch of silver grey clouds that caressed the tip of a bright full moon. My car was only slightly warmer than the office. I draped a blanket across my lap and kept the thermos flask between my legs.

A double glazing van had just pulled away from Preacher's house. That's about all that had happened.

I ran the dial across the radio from left to right and left again, but all I could find was the local station. Not a lot had changed since I'd last listened to it. There were the same furniture ads, carpet ads and car ads. And the same DJ's who did their best to sound bright and cheerful but remained nothing more than annoying. Every now and again the constant chat was broken by a record. I hoped and prayed it was one I liked, because it would be so damn long before they played another.

Out in front of me stood Preacher's house. Lights lit up every room. Even the small front yard was dotted with electric podiums. None of the curtains were drawn.

Preacher was an open invitation to anyone who cared to look into his world and that got me thinking that this could be just a waste of time.

Just after nine the front door opened and Preacher emerged from the house. He checked his watch but nothing else. Aliens could have hovered above his rooftop but Preacher wouldn't have noticed. He pointed a hand out in front of him and I could hear a bleeping sound. Car lights flashed momentarily just down the street and Preacher got into a big black one. What a useful device I thought, if ever I lost my car. Not that I could ever lose this thing!

He turned on the engine. I was cold but comfortable enough not to want to move. Screw Walker, I thought. I could just sit here, roll up in my blanket, go to sleep and tell him that nothing had happened. But then it would just be my luck to wake up tomorrow to find that Preacher had taken over the police station and was holding the whole world to ransom. The nice warm blanket was ditched onto the back seat. I turned on the engine and got that old sinking feeling that this was going to be a long night.

* * *

Preacher's car was easy to follow. It had a large tyre attached to the back window with the words, *Mission, The Experience of a Night-time*, emblazoned all over it. And he never got out of third gear or threaten so much as an amber light. He pulled up at every junction and even waited for an old lady to cross the road. I followed him into the town centre and most of the way down North Street till he took a right. The road was a dead end. From there I knew where Preacher was heading, so I reversed into a nearby car park.

I walked the rest of the way until I caught my reflection in a shop window. Something was wrong. I was dressed in a raincoat, a t-shirt and jeans. Never did anyone look less like they were heading for a nightclub and I wasn't meant to stand out.

It crossed my mind to try and get in anyway because hopefully the bouncers would turn me away and I could go home and let Preacher hold the world to ransom safe in the knowledge that it wasn't my fault. But that wasn't going to solve anything. I had to make an effort.

I went home, searched the bedroom for a shirt that was slightly pressed and slipped on a pair of trousers. I combed my hair and checked my look in the mirror. A face smiled back and asked what the hell was I up to?

Chapter Eleven

An irritating thump boomed out from the blacked out windows of the club high above the street and already I wasn't happy.

There wasn't a queue outside, just two large bouncers, nodding and smiling at one another. They hopped from one foot to another swinging their arms in front of their stomachs. I could have sworn I'd seen them both a long time ago on a visit somewhere with lots of other caged animals.

I got all set for a hard time. The club advertised itself as a classy joint with a 'Strictly over eighteen' sign on the door but somehow I couldn't help thinking that had nothing to do with the IQ.

"Can I help you?"

The voice came from a polite face behind four silver bars. She was either the smallest woman I'd ever laid eyes on or she was sat on the floor.

"Yeah. I'd like to go in please."

"That'll be ten pounds."

I couldn't remember the last time I'd been to a club, but I could remember it didn't mean buying shares in the place. And not so much as a *please* to go with it.

I handed her the money and asked; "Do I get an escort with that?"

One of the bouncers, sensing trouble, meandered over to me.

"Can I help?" he grunted.

"No, I'm sorry," I said, taking my change and looking back at him, "You're not quite what I had in mind!"

* * *

I headed up the carpeted stairs towards the noise. The thumping sound increased with every step. It was driving me nuts. The only time I got this close to such a pounding was when I woke up with a hangover and that was hell.

Eventually the stairs came to a halt and a corridor took me into an open area with a dance floor and a bar. The room was like a cavern. The air, a mixture of essences but all overpowered by the tinge of sweat and cigarette stained clothes. I was a stranger trapped somewhere between cellulite city and cancer corner. Most of the people looked as if they should have been doing their homework. The blokes dressed like they'd just got up and I wore more clothes in bed than the women had on.

Nobody appeared comfortable. The girls danced but to nothing in particular. The blokes drank but only because it was something to do.

* * *

Preacher was standing next to the DJ, barking out some instructions. It gave me time to buy a drink. It was the only thing that was going to get me through the night.

But the bar was a pig trough. People jostled, shoulder to shoulder waving their money in the air and hanging out their tongues to dry. I took my place behind a girl with a tattooed back. It was like she'd fallen into a printing press. The 'inside of a cave look' may well have appealed to her now but what the hell was she going to look like when she turned fifty?

The wail of the DJ's voice through the speakers instantly summoned the herd to the dance-floor. There followed an obscene demonstration of hand waving and hip gyrating. Not that I minded, it left a gap at the bar.

The staff were all dressed in white shirts, bow ties and black waistcoats, even the girls. One girl in particular caught my eye. She appeared older then the rest. She had bright blue eyes, shoulder length auburn hair and a smile that cut me in half, especially when she caught me staring.

Unfortunately she was serving somebody else, so a much younger and not so attractive bloke stepped in front of me and ask what I wanted. 'You to go away, and her to come and serve me.' is what I wanted to say, but instead I asked for a whisky.

The guy was all action; he juggled the bottle, filled a glass, tipped the ice bucket, operated the till and buttoned a sleeve all with the one hand. If I'd been a girl I might have been impressed.

I handed him my money and sipped the whisky. It wasn't the best I'd had, but it would do for now.

I rifled through my pockets and picked out the photograph of April. In the pale light I looked out across the wave of sweaty bodies. She could have been almost any one of them. If only Storey had come looking for a girl eight foot tall with bright purple hair and a carrot growing out of her ear, I might have got lucky.

Above the wave Preacher was talking to a man in a dark suit. He led him away to another bar that was separated from all the noise by a large glass panel. A bouncer stood at the entrance. The room was a whole lot quieter inside, just some people who'd overdosed on Grecian 2000 and Brut in an attempt to stay as young as possible for as long as possible.

At the far end of the room Preacher opened another door and the suit followed him inside.

Out of sight there didn't seem much point in sticking around. My glass was empty and the music was too loud. I decided to spend the rest of the evening out in my car. Old age had finally arrived. The coffee in my flask tasted so much better than the liquid in here and at least I could control the volume on my radio.

* * *

Preacher went home around 3.15am. He went to bed about 4.20am. The lights went off fifteen minutes later. I pulled up my blanket till it cradled my neck and tried to sleep. Half an hour later I rolled to one side and caught my head on the window. It was only then I realised how cold I was.

"Bugger this." I moaned.

Following Preacher was one thing. Freezing to death was another. I checked the darkness in the house one more time and drove home to my nice warm flat.

* * *

In the dim of the streetlights I fixed myself a drink. It was possible that the late hour would be enough to make me sleep but I wanted to make sure.

I sat at the window and waited for the whisky to weave its magic. It didn't take long. I thought about writing a chapter. It intrigued me the kind of stuff that came out of my head at four in the morning when I was tired and intoxicated. I've come up with some classics over the years, works of art that would put Colin Dexter to shame.

I think it had something to do with the logical side of my brain saying, go ahead, make a fool of yourself, but you'll see it all for real in the morning and you won't be so cocky.

I found a piece of paper and a pen, poured another drink, sat at the table in the window and fell asleep.

Chapter Twelve

I was up early the next morning but I hadn't slept much. Falling asleep at the table had left me with a sore neck and a stuffed nose. I drew back the curtains and looked out across Peasholm Park. A stream of water trickled down the roadside from the early morning rain. Children dawdled to school and a bright sun filled the world with clear green, yellow and blue colours. On any other day I might have thought how lucky I was to be alive, but this wasn't any other day. I'd just had three hours sleep. I was tired and hungry so, as far I was concerned, the world could go screw itself.

I got dressed and looked down at my belly. My shoes were fast fading out of view. I had to lose weight but that wasn't easy. Walker had fixed me up with a flat directly above a café and breakfast came free. The owners were relatives of Walkers and that seemed to suggest that they could never do enough for me. The supply of bacon and sausages was endless. Resistance was futile.

Unfortunately, by the time I'd slipped the last slice of

bread over the remains of my runny egg, I was ready to explode. I heaved my stomach out through the door and headed back upstairs to the toilet. This was going to be a long day.

* * *

Half an hour later I was staring at the office phone and wondering if I should ring Walker. But considering all I'd done was follow Preacher to his club, drink some whisky and fall asleep at the table, there didn't seem much point.

So I packed a flask and some cheese rolls into a shopping bag. I'd buy a paper on the way up to Preacher's place and possibly even treat myself to a book, something like The Loneliness of a Private Investigator.

I took my plant over to the sink and ran some water into the earth. The green leaves had yet to flower and I wondered if they ever would. Maybe I'd bought something that was just permanently green. Maybe I could take it back and swap it for one with flowers?

A neon light flashed a clear bright red zero on the phone. I picked it up and rang Envy. She didn't answer. I left a message and got all embarrassed when I mentioned where she could find me if she needed to, outside Preacher's house parked in a car with all the charisma of tumble dryer. It wasn't so much killing the romantic illusion of a Private Investigator as burying it six feet under and throwing away the spade.

Chapter Thirteen

I got a parking space someway down the road from Preacher's house. His car was just ahead.

I made myself as comfortable as possible and read the paper a couple of times. I even jotted down some ideas for an ending to my book. It wasn't easy. I needed something that didn't have the main character screwed by the cops. But all I got was a list of names, contrived endings and a headache.

The cheese rolls hadn't lasted long enough either. I was forced to take a short walk to a nearby takeaway and treat myself to a pizza. All the toppings.

Down one of the back alleys I came across an old man in an old suit crouched next to a car parked on the pavement. He was mumbling to himself and, even though I knew nothing about cars, I asked if I could help. There was a loud gush of wind as the car rocked and a tyre went down. It was only then that I noticed all four of them were flat.

"Is this your car?" He asked.

I shook my head.

"Wouldn't mind if it was," he continued. "These people need to be taught a lesson, always parking illegally and nobody does anything about it, wouldn't have happened in my day, but it's hell if you've got a pushchair or wheelchair, so bloody inconsiderate."

He was still mumbling as he made his way down the street. I looked at the car and smiled. So clever. No damage had been caused, but what a pain in the arse to pump them up again. Serves them right.

I would love to have stayed around just to see the owners face, but I had a pizza to eat and a man to follow.

It was eight-fifteen and I was thinking of all kinds of things and none of them were about work. Somebody could have stolen my tyres and left me on a pile of bricks and I wouldn't have noticed. I was too busy wondering, should I have tried harder at school? I wonder what Australia's like this time of year and, what would I do if my book ever got published? That was never going to happen of course. All I was going to get was polite replies from publishers and agents saying how much they liked my work but that it was so difficult selling anybody new to the public. I needed a name just like the music world needed a face, talent wasn't an issue anymore. It all came down to selling as much as possible, as quickly as possible and as cheaply as possible.

* * *

A light came on in Preacher's house as night made its customary appearance. Two months on and life hadn't moved an inch. I was sitting in a car watching somebody else's life go by.

But the saddest thing of all was the lie I tried to sell myself that, one way or another, I was going to come out of this a better person.

* * *

There was a tap on the passenger window but to somebody with their mind a million miles away it sounded like a hammer. I sat up startled and saw Jo Envy peering in through the glass. I opened the door. She flopped onto the passenger seat. She was wearing a tracksuit. Her hair was tied in a ponytail and she was breathing heavily.

"I didn't see you pull up." I said, glancing up at the rear view mirror.

"That's because I didn't pull up," she panted.

She glanced down at her outfit as if that explained everything.

"You walked?"

"Ran"

"Ran?"

She nodded.

"Were you being chased?"

"I've been stuck in my car all day, I needed the exercise."

I didn't say anything; I was too busy trying not to look like someone who couldn't believe anybody would want to run anywhere.

"Anyway, I got you this," Envy said as she reached into a pocket and held out a gadget that wouldn't have looked out of place on the Starship Enterprise. She pressed a button and a light came on.

"It's easy to operate; you just press this button to find my name and this to dial my number."

There was a ringing sound and Envy pulled out another phone.

"See," she said. "It's easy."

"I'm not really very technically gifted!" I argued. "In fact.....,

"... a five year old could operate this, Mahoney."

"But I don't know any five year olds!"

Envy ignored my protests and handed me the phone.

"What would you rather do, run to a call box every time you need to contact somebody?"

"Do you run everywhere?"

"Well, you've got it if you need it. There's a ten pound credit that should last you a while."

I looked at the phone in my hand in the same way I might have looked at a baby in my lap, as though it should be anywhere else but where it was.

"Anything else?" I asked reluctantly.

"Well, not a lot," Envy replied, making herself comfortable. "All I've done, I say all I've done, it's taken me all day, but I've called into numerous shops and café down the main street and showed April's picture around.

"And?"

"And a couple of guys thought they recognized her, but they couldn't be sure. However this one girl thought that she'd seen April go out with someone called Smudge."

"Smudge?"

Envy nodded.

"Sounds like somebody we shouldn't have too much trouble finding."

"What makes you say that?"

"Well, he'll either be climbing up somebody's drainpipe in the middle of the night or hanging out on a street corner being a pain in the arse."

"You don't know that for sure!"

Envy was right or at least she could have been right. But I still had my instinct, that was mine and it kept me from being like everybody else.

"Don't you have a nice word for anybody?" she asked.

"Only when I'm carrying a dictionary. Do we know anything about this Smudge?"

Envy shook her head.

"Nothing."

I watched Envy as she looked out through the windscreen and I thought how different she looked without her glasses. Everything about her seemed to stand out that little bit more, her roman nose; strong and forthright, her skin; a rich creamy colour, her green eyes and I wondered if I was asking myself if I fancied her or not.

'I'd know if I wanted to go out with someone. It's what you do, you look at someone and you think..' I quickly tried to clear Walker's philosophy from my head.

"So what's your gut feeling?" I asked.

She rolled her bottom lip up across her top lip in a moment of contemplation.

"My gut feeling is that, hopefully we're on the right track and that April is here somewhere."

"And what does your head say?"

She looked across at me.

"I don't know, I haven't asked it yet."

Envy started to get out of the car.

"So what do you want me to do?" I asked.

"Haven't you got enough on?" she replied, glancing up towards the house.

"I could spare a few minutes, I mean, Preacher didn't get up much before twelve today. He spent a couple of hours at the club and then relaxed at home before the night shift."

"Well then, maybe you could ask around, there can't be too many people with a name like Smudge. Or, better still, put an ad in the paper."

I nodded.

Envy ducked her head back inside the car and asked; "So when are you seeing Storey again?"

I shrugged my shoulders.

"I'm assuming he'll ring tomorrow. Why, do you want to meet up with him?"

Envy shook her ponytail a couple of times.

"I don't think that'd be such a good idea right now. Let him believe you're doing all the work. When he's happy that we might be onto something then you can mention me."

I looked at Envy and said OK. She nodded and turned her attention to the backseat. I had no idea what was going through her head until she said; "Is this what you've been eating all day?"

I glanced at the empty pizza boxes and then at her.

"No." I replied. "I had sausages and black pudding for breakfast."

Her expression was a picture. It was like somebody had taken a chainsaw to her prize marrow.

"We really need to talk."

"I thought we were doing."

"About your health."

"Yeah fine, as long as it doesn't involve having to eat anything I can't pour brown sauce over or lifting anything heavier than a shoe-lace."

"Who's going to look after you Mahoney if you don't?"

"I don't get a lot of time for romance!"

"I was talking about your body. You're cholesterol must be going through the roof."

I had no idea what she's talking about!

"The rate you're going," she continued. "You won't be able to run for after a bus let alone a crook!"

"There you go with that running thing again!"

"You have to look after yourself Mahoney!"

"I thought all you Americans sat around eating burgers and chips all day!"

"Fries!"

"What?"

"We eat fries. Chips are crisps."

Why was everything so complicated?

"What time do you get up on a morning?" she asked.

"Nine, ten. Depends what time the bacon fumes hit me"

"Where do you live?"

I couldn't help thinking I was getting myself into something I was going to regret.

"Up above a cafe on Columbus Ravine. Why?"

"Fine, I'll call for you tomorrow morning."

"Why?"

"We're going for a run."

"A run?"

"Or jog if you prefer."

"How about a walk or a quick amble?"

"A Jog!" she insisted.

"But I thought we were supposed to be looking for somebody?"

"They'll be plenty of time for that afterwards," she replied.

"But I'm going to have a late night here!"

I sounded like a kid being forced to do his homework.

"All right, we'll make it the following morning. If you've seen Storey by then you can bring me up to date."

She shut the door and disappeared down the road.

"That won't be the only thing I'll be bringing up," I said to nobody but the car.

* * *

I watched Envy jog out of sight in the rear view mirror. And I thought about how, in the space of twenty-four hours, I'd let myself be talked into a stakeout and a run, neither of which I had planned or really wanted to do. Hell, I wasn't even sure I wanted to be in Scarborough.

But as much as I wanted it to aggravate me and, as much as I wanted to tell people to leave me alone, I couldn't.

I thought about lying to myself, I thought about

suggesting that deep down I had a heart of gold. That I just wanted to help. Then a car appeared in the street. Its headlight lit up the windscreen. It was enough to reflect my image. Unfortunately the image was very clear and it wasn't one of someone with a heart of gold. It was one of somebody too soft to do anything other than go with the flow and see what comes out at the other end.

Chapter Fourteen

Two hours later and with a blank page still at my mercy, I followed Preacher to the club. I paid my money at the front door. I still didn't get my escort. I climbed the stairs and immediately wished I hadn't bothered.

The music sounded the same and all the people looked the same, only more, a whole lot more than the previous night. I couldn't find Preacher and I wasn't in the mood to look.

I took out April's photograph and glanced around the room. I'm sure it crossed the empty shell, that most of the girls here called a mind, that I was looking at them because I found them attractive. Make-up, it's one per cent appliance and ninety-nine per cent vanity.

I asked a few if they recognised April. Some answered but most either grunted or shook their heads. One simply smiled forever, and I wondered if she really should have been let out this late and all alone. But nobody asked why I was looking, and that bothered me.

Twenty minutes later and as if by magic, I found myself

at the bar. Feeding time had reached a frenzy. The animals appeared so desperate for refreshment that most appeared willing to sacrifice any and all change for instant service.

I caught the eye of the barmaid from the previous night and smiled my best smile. She smiled back and, much to everyone's annoyance, breezed over to ask what I would like.

"Well, a whisky would do for starters," I shouted. "With a little ice."

She repeated my request in an accent that intrigued me.

"Interesting." I said.

"What?"

"Your accent."

She raised an eyebrow as she prepared my drink. Another 'come-on' and how would this one go, she wondered.

"You're not from round here, are you!"

She laughed. Her eyes danced.

"You're not even English?"

She shook her head.

"Give me a clue."

"Hey, how about just getting a move on!"

I looked to my left. A kid stood trying to stare me out. He had cropped hair, narrow eyes and a head full of dreams. He tried to appear tough but only as tough as the beer he had been drinking would allow. Trouble was, he hadn't had enough.

"Don't get hysterical kid; it's bad for your heart!"

I looked long enough for him to swallow his Adams-apple and turn away.

The barmaid recovered her smile. "Latvia."

"Latvia." I said, quickly trying to picture it on the map. Now I have no trouble pinpointing Australia or The United States, even Singapore, but Latvia was killing me.

I didn't know the first thing about it.

"I'm sorry; I don't know a whole lot about Latvia, other than how to spell it."

She smiled. She was nice, very nice. The kind of nice that would have had me booking a holiday in Latvia if they'd stuck her picture on the brochure. The name 'Alana' was written in black letters on her gold badge and the blouse she was wearing was one size too big. It looked as if it had been folded a dozen times into her short black skirt. But what stood out a mile was the faint purple line beneath her left eye.

She took my money and headed for the till. I turned to check on the youth next to me. I was ready to give him a confident smile but a crash of glass drew my attention back behind the bar. There was a tray of glasses on the floor. Alana appeared petrified. A man was staring at her, hands on hips and wearing a look that could seriously wound, if not even kill. It was just one of those things, but Alana looked like she'd been cornered by a bear. Her shaking hands caressed the side of her face as the man picked up a brush and pressed it against her. She started to sweep the glass.

"I'd like my change now please!" I yelled.

The man glanced over at me. He was wearing that same, not very nice, expression and pointing it at me.

"She'll be a minute." He snapped.

Perhaps the regulars had no problem being spoken to as if they had just crawled in through a cat flap. But I wasn't one of the regulars. I reached out across the bar, grabbed his jacket and pulled him over towards me by the lapel.

"How about you pick up the glass and the girl gives me my change!" I insisted, loud enough to grab everybody's attention.

He looked at me as if the last thing on his mind was

doing anything for anybody. Trouble was, my drink was warming and I couldn't help thinking how his narrow white face would look good under my shoe.

"Is there a problem, Bob?" A voice boomed out.

I turned to see Preacher and one of his sidekicks.

"No problem," I said, gently tapping Bob on the side of his face. "This nice girl was just about to get me my change, wasn't she Bob!"

It's possible that Bob hadn't looked so angry in a long time, and it's possible he would have liked to have taken that anger out on me right now. But, to his credit, he took a breath, dipped his shoulders, smoothed his lapel and retrieved the brush from Alana. She quickly handed me my change.

"Thanks." I smiled.

I was kind of hoping she'd smile back, but the whole episode seemed to bother her. She turned away and hurried off to serve another customer.

I tucked my change into a pocket and took a sip of whisky. All the while Preacher was looking at me with a frown.

"Don't I know you?" He asked, pointing a finger in my direction.

I looked back at him without answering.

"You're one of the cops who was with Walker the other day at the Casino."

A whole lot of people at the bar turned to look my way. I tried to make out like it didn't bother me.

"Wrong." I said.

"I saw you." He argued.

"Maybe you did, but that doesn't make me a cop."

"You were with Walker."

"That still doesn't make me a cop."

His frown grew deeper.

"I don't understand."

"It's simple. My name's Richard Mahoney. I'm a Private Investigator."

His frown slowly turned to a smile, a very cautious smile.

"Interesting!"

"That's what everybody keeps telling me," I mentioned.

"So what are you doing here?" he eventually asked.

I sipped my drink. All this yelling was tingling my tonsils.

I said. "I heard the whisky was good!"

Preacher laughed and so did everybody else. But I was lying, the whisky tasted dry.

"So you're not a cop?" He asked.

"You take a lot of convincing!"

Preacher glanced a couple of times to his left and right before letting out a big friendly grin and dropping an arm across my shoulder.

"Well, in that case," he started. "Why don't we go somewhere quiet and top up that drink of yours."

It didn't seem like such a bad idea just as long as getting to this 'somewhere quiet' didn't involve me having to walk down a dark alley with two blokes built like Rhinos carrying crowbars.

I followed Preacher to the Cocktail Lounge, the room with the large glass panel that looked out over the dance floor. Here the music was soft and more akin to a place where somebody like me could have a drink in peace.

The customers inside were few and older then those sweating outside. Men with less hair than they'd be comfortable with, smiling their false teeth at attractive young ladies in the hope that they'd get laid before the expiry date ran out on their condom.

Preacher spread himself out on a large grey sofa while one of the barmaids prepared our drinks. I sat nearby and watched the youngsters dance behind him. Two minutes later we had our drinks. I had another whisky, Preacher a bottle of water.

"So the police haven't sent you to spy on me then?" he asked in a manner that suggested he really didn't give a damn even if they had.

"And why would they want to do that?"

"Oh, I was just thinking of that business the other day at the Casino that's all. It was obviously meant to ruffle some feathers. Any news on that girl?"

I shrugged my shoulders. "Not that I know of."

"Pity."

He sounded sincere.

"So the cops think you're up to something?" I asked.

"They always think I'm up to something," he laughed as he unscrewed the lid on his bottle. "Usually its dealing, judging by the number of raids we have in here. Either that or serving under aged drinkers."

"Are you?"

Preacher appeared impressed by my boldness, it was possibly something he didn't come across very often. He smiled.

"I run a club, Mr Mahoney. People will naturally think the worst. Even my brother refers to it as a den of in, iniq....., a not very nice place. So if I told you no, you'd probably think I was lying."

"On the other hand, you could just answer the question."

Preacher looked up from the bottle and stopped smiling. Perhaps he realised that I was a pain in the arse and that I wasn't just going to go away. He got to his feet and stared out across the dance floor with his back to me

"When I first laid eyes on this place it was a right dive, there were under-aged kids, druggies, smackheads, dealers, the lot. I wondered how anybody would knowingly let a child loose in here. You get the picture?"

I nodded even though he didn't turn his head far enough to see me.

"I suppose, well in fact, I know, I was lucky. My parents always wanted to know where we were and what we were up to and, God forbid, we ever got into any trouble. I suppose that's the difference, that was the big difference, they cared."

I sipped my whisky and wondered if I should have been taking notes.

"So I took a gamble," Preacher continued. "I decided to buy the place and clean it up. It wasn't easy. I had to have the whole place refurbished. Then I hired completely new staff, staff I knew I could trust to turn things around for the better and who wouldn't take money on the door to let in the floaters."

"That still doesn't explain why the cops would want to pick on you."

Preacher returned to his seat and smiled across at me.

"Have you any idea how much money was coming in and out of this place Mr Mahoney, and I don't mean on the door or behind the bar?"

I stared back at Preacher and I think I knew exactly what he meant.

"This club was a prime location. All kinds of people had a piece of the action. So what I've done hasn't made me very popular."

"So you think somebody wants you out of the way?" I presumed.

Preacher nodded. "Possibly."

And suddenly I found myself siding with him. That's how gullible I was. Two minutes into a conversation and I was backing the underdog. He might have been telling me a pack of lies for all I knew but that didn't seem to matter just as long as he was up against it. I'd be there fighting his cause and making a fool of myself once again.

I finished my drink and placed my glass on the table.

"So," he started slowly. "What are you really doing here?"

I stumbled on an answer. I couldn't tell him I was following him. I might have ended up at the bottom of the fire escape wearing a size twelve imprint on my head. So I quickly weighed up just how much trouble it might be letting him know about April. When I couldn't think of anything I reached into my pocket and pulled out her photograph.

"Have you seen this girl before?"

Preacher studied the picture closely and my gut feeling was that he had. His eyes were curious, like when you see someone in the street you think you recognise but you're not completely sure. But then the curiosity faded and he shook his head.

"No." he replied. "I can't say I have."

"Funny, it didn't look that way for a moment."

"That's because she looks like a lot of the girls that come in here. They all dress the same, they all look the same and they all want the same thing. I'm sorry I can't help."

"Any idea where I might look for her?"

"That might depend on what she wants."

"What makes you say that?"

"This is quick fix town, Mr Mahoney, that's all most people want. Instant tans, instant cash, instant food. Nobody cares if it doesn't last, most don't expect it to, not their job, not even a relationship. It's what they're used to."

"But I haven't got a clue what she wants or where she is, I just need a start."

Preacher studied the photograph a little longer.

"Well she's good looking." He said, very matter-of-factly. "And, being a good looking girl can get you a lot of things, work, boyfriends."

"So what about work? Where do young girls look for work round here?"

"I'd start with the retail shops, especially the fashion shops, or even down on the sea front."

I looked at Preacher and nodded as he handed me back the photograph.

"Is she your daughter?"

"What makes you ask that?"

"She's someones."

I looked at Preacher. He was smarter than he looked and therefore it was a pity if he'd got mixed up in anything that wasn't good.

"What about a kid called Smudge?"

"Is that his real name?"

"I doubt it, but it's all I've got."

Preacher shook his head and then pointed towards the photo in my hand.

"Let me have a copy," he said, "I can look out for her. Chances are she'll end up in here anyway."

April smiled up at me. I took that as an expression of hope and not resignation.

I turned on a heel. "Not just yet," I replied. "I'm kind of banking on the long term fix."

* * *

I left Preacher smiling down at his bottle of water and went back to the bar. It was an excuse for another drink. But Alana was nowhere to be seen. I asked the kid behind the bar but he just shrugged his shoulders and hurried away to juggle another bottle.

I took my drink to the edge of the dance floor.

High above me a young girl cavorted in a cage. She wasn't wearing a whole lot and that was meant to make her look sexy. But wearing less can sometimes look very un-sexy and this was one of them. The cages were everywhere, each one holding either a half-naked boy or girl. Perhaps they weren't very good dancers or maybe they hadn't paid for their drinks? Years ago it used to be stocks. Either way it was equally embarrassing. When the strain of looking up got to my neck I glanced across the room and spied Bob. He was standing alone on the other side of the floor. He looked like someone in need of trouble. I decided to oblige.

"Where's Alana?" I yelled into his ear.

"Who?"

"Alana. The girl behind the bar."

He shrugged his shoulders, but I figured that wasn't because he didn't know. He just didn't really care.

"That won't do Bob!"

"Look, she's probably just left, that's what they do."

"And why would she just leave halfway through the night?"

"Probably because she couldn't hack the work."

"Or maybe if you hadn't been such a pain in the arse she'd still be here!"

Bob looked at me for the first time. It was a challenging look but whether he wanted to go outside, take off his jacket, roll up his sleeves and obey the Queensbury rules, or simply have a game of cards, I couldn't quite tell.

Eventually he started to walk away. I caught hold of his arm and stopped him dead.

"If anything's happened to her, I'm going to come looking for you!"

Chapter Fifteen

I wasn't sure what to expect Sunday morning. I was used to lying in bed, thinking about buying a paper and wondering what to have for breakfast. But that probably didn't apply to Preacher.

Reluctantly I threw back the covers, showered, bought a sandwich and a coffee and went up to the office.

The good news was there was a red number 'one' shining brightly on my answer machine.

I pressed *play* and a voice said; 'Mahoney, it's me, Walker. Give me a call when you get a minute.'

Another voice, in a much happier tone, said, 'to hear the message again, press one, to save the message, press two, to delete, press three.' I pressed the third option.

The excitement had lasted a hic-up.

* * *

I didn't bother ringing Walker back. I went one better, I called in to his office. It was an opportunity to take him at his word and drop in my novel. He smiled when I placed the pages onto his desk. It was like I'd offered a part of me, an arm or a leg and I wasn't much use with the two I had!

"Are you sure this is all right?" I asked.

"She was delighted when I told her."

"I'll have to get her something, a bottle of wine or something?"

Walker shrugged his shoulders. "A signed copy will do."

I was shocked. "You have that much confidence in me?"

Walker sat back in his chair and smiled. "So, what's new?"

There was an optimism in his voice that concerned me.

"You mean, have I got anything on Preacher yet?"

"Actually I was thinking more about, how are things going at the club? Have you met any nice women yet?"

"You really are a pain in the ...."

"........ I was only asking!"

I allowed the silence to answer for me.

"And how's Jo?" he continued.

"Jo?"

"Your partner."

"She's fine. How's that girl?"

His dark expression had already given him away. "She didn't make it," he said, softly.

"Oh," I muttered.

"We got a name though, a Jenny Munro, just in case you hear anything."

"Right."

"And there was no trace of substance abuse.

I nodded. "Maybe she was just carrying?"

"Maybe," Walker agreed. "So, any joy with that girl you've been looking for?"

"No."

"Well don't worry. Most children return home sooner or later and usually when they've run out of money or need their washing doing."

"You sound like you're speaking from experience!"

"My dad always told me, you can love your children all you want but that doesn't stop them from thinking they're better off somewhere else. In the end all you can do is be there for them."

"He sounds like a nice man, were you adopted?"

"Just keep me posted, Mahoney."

Chapter Sixteen

I couldn't help thinking how Walker didn't seem all that bothered about Preacher. He almost appeared more preoccupied with whether or not I could land a woman.

The sun was lighting up the day with a bright smile. It seemed to suggest that, sitting in a car all day, would be such a waste. I rang Envy.

"What's wrong?" she asked.

"Nothing. I just thought I might spend a couple of hours looking for April."

"That'd be nice. I'm going down Trafalgar Square and North Marine Road. I thought I'd talk to some of the landlords. It's a chance in a million but there's a lot of bedsits and cheap flats down there. Why, what were you thinking?"

"I might try the seafront."

"Yeah, well, just keep away from all those fish and chips shops!"

"You spoil all my fun!"

* * *

I parked the car close to Preacher's flat. It was only a short walk down through the valley and onto the seafront. The rush of waves, the bleep of bells and the sound of peoples' laughter greeted me as I made my way under the cliff bridge.

* * *

The Grand Hotel rose high above the beach. There used to be a building at the foot of the hotel where I stood for hours looking at a world of model railways and planes. Unfortunately those memories had been replaced with a line of rotting benches and weeds protruding between cracks in the hotel wall.

* * *

I reached the first big arcade, it wasn't particularly busy. The sun was hot and the tide was out so the Pilsbury dough families had laid claim to their spot on the beach. Close enough to park a big toe in the water and near enough to roll into the cafés at every urge.

The salt air was a mix of candyfloss and chips. It made me feel hungry and I'd only just had a big breakfast.

An assortment of cuddly toys stared out from their glasshouses and a silver crane swung silently above them. To the clank of the arcade a couple of old ladies poured pennies into slot machines as raspberries, strawberries and yellow bells took turns to appear in the glint of their eyes, but never when they really needed them.

A young girl stood propped up against the entrance. She was dressed in a thin white top that slipped off her left shoulder and blue jeans that finished just below her knees. Her presence unnerved me because she was staring in my direction.

I turned my back on her and went over to a cashier pressed inside a little glass box. He wasn't doing anything other than reading a magazine but it bothered him all the same that I might need assistance. I showed him the photo of April.

"Have you seen this girl before?"

He looked at me and shook his head.

"How about a kid called Smudge, have you heard of him?"

"No." He replied, dying to get back to his small print.

"Thanks," I muttered.

The girl was still looking at me.

* * *

And that was pretty much how it was as I strolled the rest of promenade, past the harbour and finally to the waffle shop at the far end of the foreshore. I'd invited myself in to every chip shop, ice-cream parlour, bar, café and restaurant and nobody had seen April or heard of Smudge. But what bothered me more than anything was that nobody seemed to give a damn. Nobody wanted to know what some middle aged man was doing with a picture of a pretty young girl in his pocket. If they assumed I was the father then they didn't appear all that concerned that my daughter was missing. And, if they presumed I was a Private Investigator or a plain-clothed cop, then they cared even less that somebody else's daughter was missing. It probably all came down to the fact that it wasn't their problem. That somewhere down the line somebody else would take care of it. How easy it was to pass responsibility.

I checked my watch. It had taken nearly two hours to achieve the nothing that some people spent a lifetime doing.

* * *

I needed to get back to see Preacher but I was hungry and my feet ached.

There was an endless choice of cafes and restaurants. I plumped for the one with the mock Tudor exterior and dark tanned furniture. Most of the tables were occupied, people happy at last that the summer had arrived, but not stupid enough to believe that it would last forever.

I checked the menu. The sausages and bacon were appealing but Envy's voice nagged inside my head. I plumped for scrambled eggs on toast and a coffee. Bloody healthy people!

* * *

I'd only just finished wiping my plate clean with a slice of bread when the waiter pounced ready to whisk my plate away. I pulled the photograph from my pocket and held it up for him to see.

"Have you seen this girl before?"

It didn't seem to matter who or how many times I asked the routine was always the same. They look at the picture, then at me, pull a face and then shake their heads.

I laid the photo down on the table and stirred my coffee.

"Why are you looking for that girl?"

I glanced up. It was the girl from the arcade. She was staring back at me and chewing gum. She'd sat herself down in the chair opposite and pointed a finger at the photograph. Something, I have no idea what, prevented me from telling her to mind her own business.

"I'm not," I replied.

But she wasn't just going to go away. She continued to stare at me.

"I'm looking for a friend of hers," I continued.

She tilted her head to one side.

"A kid by the name of Smudge," I explained.

"Smudge?"

"Yeah."

"Why?"

"Because I need to speak to him."

"Are you like, a policeman or something?"

"No. I'm like, a Private Investigator."

"That's funny," she laughed but not very sincerely.

"The kid's name or the fact that I'm a Private Investigator?"

"I just didn't think they existed that's all, only on the telly I mean."

"Well I definitely existed the last time I looked in the mirror."

"What do you need to speak to him for?"

"You ask a lot of questions!"

"You have to if you want to be a Private Investigator."

"Is that what you want?"

She shrugged her shoulders. "Is it good money?"

"That depends." I replied.

"On?"

"On who's got a problem and whether or not they can afford to have somebody take care of it."

"You don't look rich."

I smiled. "That's because I have to blend in."

She sat back in her chair. Her confidence unnerved me. She didn't look any older than sixteen. I never spoke to anybody that way, not when I was that age.

"You're cute!" she said.

"Cute!" I almost choked on my coffee. "Nobody ever called me that before."

"It was meant to be a compliment."

"I'm sure it was."

I checked the room to see if anybody was eaves dropping. It wouldn't look good to have somebody think

I was being chatted up by a schoolgirl, especially when I was also carrying a photograph of a young girl around.

I dropped a couple of pounds coins onto the table.

"What's that for?" she asked.

"A tip, what do you think?"

"Why would you like, leave a tip?"

I shrugged my shoulders.

"It's what you do."

"It's what you do if you've had good service, but this place is mingin'."

A couple of customers on a nearby table turned to look in our direction. But I didn't mind if they overheard her criticism. At least she wasn't chatting me up.

"Shouldn't you be at school?" I asked out of the blue.

She shrugged her shoulders.

"Does that mean, yes?"

She dipped her head to one side and mumbled: "Nobody cares if I am."

"What about your parents?"

She looked at me and laughed, sincerely this time.

"You don't have any parents?" I presumed.

"Course I do. But they're always like arguing. They do my head in. My old man beats my mum. I hate him but she won't do anything about it."

I felt my hand roll into a fist. There were women who drove men nuts for all kinds of reasons, I know because I've met some of them. But no woman ever deserved to be hit. I would quite happily have spent the rest of my life beating the crap out of every coward who hit a woman, if only somebody had the guts to make it law. So much for 'cute'.

"I'm sorry to hear that," I said as I got to my feet and started for the door.

The girl followed me outside and I wondered if I was going to have to tell her to get lost.

"What would it be worth if I knew where Smudge was?"

I looked back at her.

"A place in Heaven, if you believe in such a thing."

"What's wrong with Heaven?"

"I don't know, I've never been."

She tugged at my arm.

"But what if I knew where Smudge was?"

I looked at her. "Do you?"

"I might."

I started to walk away.

"Don't you want to know?"

"You know I do."

"So what would it be worth?"

She was still chewing. By the end of the month she'd have the jaws of a Rotweiler.

"Do you know where he is?" I asked again.

"No," she mumbled. "But I probably know somebody who does."

I waited for her to continue but all she did was look back at me and chew, and all I heard was the noise of the arcades and traffic and kids laughing.

"Who?"

"I can't tell you."

I set off down the street again.

"I'll have to like, speak to him first," she yelled as she ran after me. "See what he says." She added.

"You do that."

"So how will I find you?"

I stopped and checked my watch. I didn't really think for one minute that she'd find out anything worthwhile, but then again, what if she did? She was the only person I'd spoken to in the last two hours who'd shown the least bit of concern.

"All right. We'll meet here again at the café, tomorrow

at the same time. And don't be late!" I added, pointing a finger at her.

"So what's your name?" she smiled.

"Mahoney, Richard Mahoney."

I started on my way again.

"Mine's Debbie."

"I'm pleased to hear it."

"Tomorrow at one then?"

"Yeah."

She smiled and skipped down the road. I tried to recall the last time I'd ever skipped anywhere but I couldn't remember. Come to think of it, I couldn't remember the last time I'd smiled. Bloody growing up!

Chapter Seventeen

Preacher spent most of the day in a café close to his home. He read a newspaper and ate scrambled eggs on toast. And I wondered if he had a personal trainer by the name of Jo Envy? After that he topped up his tan in a town centre salon before walking to a corner shop and buying a bunch of flowers. Things were looking up, maybe he had a date?

Around six o'clock he drove to the Casino. I watched him go inside. I tried to follow but a bouncer stopped me.

"Do you have a membership?" he asked.

"I'm a Private Investigator and I'm following somebody."

"I still can't let you inside without a membership."

"Then find me someone who can!"

It took ten minutes and a phone call to Walker before I was finally allowed inside. It would have been easier to get a membership but it was the principle. Once I had a membership I had an open invitation to return here any time, any day, and lose what money I had.

The place was colourful and bright. It had large screen televisions showing music videos and cricket matches. And it was packed with the kind of people I wasn't expecting to see. When I thought of casinos I pictured toffs in tuxes' and women in revealing dresses losing the kind of money that would make people like me weep, but they wouldn't bat an eyelid.

But this place had an air of desperation. It was full of everyday people who bought lottery tickets, shopped at TK Maxx and wondered how they were going to pay next weeks bill.

* * *

Preacher was at a roulette table. He had four piles of chips in front of him. I watched from a safe distance as he placed a pile on number twenty-six. The Croupier called 'last bets' then flipped a tiny silver ball against the spin of the wheel. It circled forever. People stood and sat and watched intently with fingers, legs, arms and toes crossed. Eventually the ball dropped and skimmed the numbers. Eyes widened and necks straightened as the ball finally came to rest.

"Nineteen, black," The croupier announced.

Nobody sighed or jumped for joy or shot themselves. In fact, nothing happened at all, except the croupier collected and divided all the chips and the game commenced again.

There wasn't so much as a whimper.

Preacher put another pile of chips on number twenty-six. Maybe he figured it had to come up sooner or later. Something to do with all things equal perhaps?

The wheel span. The people watched. The ball hurdled and landed. Number twenty-seven. Preacher didn't even wince.

He went on number twenty-six for the third time and

number twelve came up.

The croupier cleared the decks and Preacher pushed the rest of his chips out across to number twenty-six. Personally I'd have put my dough on the red section, considering black had come up six times running. At least that way I'd have doubled my money. But what did I know?

Preacher took a couple of chips from the pile and handed them to the Croupier. He said 'thanks' and Preacher started to leave. It looked like something of a routine. I hurried across to the table and put down a tenner. The croupier handed me my chips. I put them all on the red section and stood back.

Preacher headed for the exit. He didn't even look back.

"No more bets, please," The croupier announced.

The wheel span. The ball sped in the opposite direction.

My throat tightened. What the hell was I doing? I never gambled.

Preacher had left the building by the time the ball started to hurdle the numbers again. I cast a glance at the people watching the wheel spin. They stared intently like they were frozen in time. I could have picked their pockets and they'd have never known.

The ball sank and the wheel slowed.

"Green zero."

Well who'd have guessed that?

Chapter Eighteen

I picked up Preacher as he made his way out of town. He stopped outside a house and pipped his car horn. A minute later a little old lady appeared from the front door and got into the car. Some date!

I followed the two of them as they drove into the countryside. In my rear view mirror the town lights slowly dropped out of sight like stars twinkling a million miles away.

We drove so far the fields and hedgerows and houses gave up trying to accompany us, and we were left with just heather and sheep.

We were practically the only cars on the road, which meant I had to stay quite a way back. But Preacher's car was easy to follow with its Mission advertisement looking back at me.

Eventually they came to a halt outside a pub miles from anywhere. I pulled up a little way back. The car park was heaving. I watched as the two of them walked past the pub and up a little hill towards a monument. Preacher laid the flowers under a stone cross. The two of them stood in silence for a moment as the wind howled and shook my car.

This was a hell of a place to come.

Ten minutes later Preacher and the old lady entered the pub. Two hours after that they drove back to Scarborough. It was fast approaching ten thirty when Preacher dropped off the old lady and saw her safely to the front door. He kissed her on the cheek. She waved him goodbye and he went home.

Chapter Nineteen

Monday morning Preacher was back at work. I figured he'd be there for a couple of hours so I decided to visit his brother.

* * *

He ran, or owned, or whatever it is Vicars do, a village church on the outskirts of town and not far from where Walker had invited me to the car crash.

It was like most churches on a sunny afternoon, very English looking with leaning gravestones, sheep baa-ing in the fields and crows squawking high in the surrounding trees.

The air was filled with the scent of recently cut grass and freshly laid flowers.

But the church itself was under going some major repairs. Scaffolding had been erected around three sides of the tower. But there was no sign of men in paint splashed overalls, scratching their bums and checking their watches, just someone in a dark overall nipping the earth with a trowel and filling a bucket with weeds.

I stepped up close to him. "Is it me, or is the whole of Scarborough held together by scaffolding?"

The Rev. Keatley arched his neck and looked up at me through curious eyes. No doubt he was quickly trying to decide, was I a mad man in search of somebody to listen to my insane mutterings? Or somebody he could lure into his flock?

"It could be that the town needs a lot of support right now."

"Would that be financial or moral?"

"A little of both perhaps."

"Must help to have friends in high places then!" I suggested with a rueful smile.

"I would agree if God were a roofer or a plasterer, but even I'm forced to get on my knees and pray that the contributions continue the way they have."

The pictures in the papers hadn't done the vicar justice. He was a lot taller and stronger looking. He wouldn't have looked out of place on a rugby pitch. And he didn't talk in that awful drone I'd heard before, the one that made you think, I don't care what sins I've committed, just get me out of here!

He got to his feet and he was even taller.

"In answer to your question though, I suppose we're all in a constant fight to keep up with change, or in our case, to keep that change in check for a while."

"You don't think it's good to change?"

"What I mean is, we've had to keep people away who wanted to buy this land and build a supermarket here. There was a time when the congregation wasn't large enough to fill the pulpit and I was concerned, but now we're thriving. Unfortunately that doesn't stop them coming back with their offers."

"I guess you've got to resist the hand of temptation then!"

The vicar smiled. "Are you a religious man, Mr....?"

I shook his hand. "Mahoney. I went to church once, the vicar tried to drown me and made some strangers make promises they could never keep."

"Pity."

"Oh I'm sure he didn't mean it. He was just following tradition."

"No, I mean, it's a pity you were put off."

I shrugged my shoulders and said; "I doubt there's a place in heaven for people like me anyway!"

The vicar studied me for a moment.

"People like you?" he asked. "But there's a place in heaven for everyone."

"That's my gripe."

"I'm not sure I understand!"

"Well, you see, I've always had a problem with the idea that all you have to do is say 'sorry' for being a pain in the arse all your life and that gets you a free ticket into heaven."

"You think it's wrong for God to forgive people?"

"That's up to him, but I couldn't be up there mixing with the kind of scum bags I've come across. I'd have to leave or kick them all to hell!"

The vicar gave me a long stare. It's possible he feared a giant thunderbolt might fall from the sky and wreck his church. It's even possible that he may have wanted to continue the conversation, but a van pulled up outside the church gates. It was full of youngsters.

He waved a hand towards the van and looked back at me. "Net practice," he explained.

"Net practice?"

"Yes, we're putting together a rather good cricket team. Keeps the youngsters motivated. Do you like cricket Mr Mahoney?"

"About as much as I like religion!"

The vicar took a moment to condense my comment before breaking into a smile. He took off his robe and suddenly he appeared as normal as anybody else. A very imposing anybody else.

He held out his hand and I felt obliged to shake it.

"Why don't you pop along to one of our services?" he asked. "I promise not to drown you!"

"I'll think about it."

Chapter Twenty

Preacher had arrived home by the time I returned to town. I watched his house while I scribbled some lines into my notepad. I had a possible ending, something that may satisfy my ego. If it looked as good on paper as it did in my head anyway.

An hour later I decided to call into the office and then grab something to eat. I had a long night ahead.

I parked the car in my usual spot and headed for the front door. I was busy searching my pockets for the keys when a figure blocked my path. He was wearing a dark suit and dark shades. He held out an unlit cigarette. "Excuse me pal, do you smoke?"

"Only when I'm on fire," I replied.

He wasn't amused.

"Well maybe you wouldn't mind getting into the car anyway?"

I looked at the car. It was big and silver and driven by another man wearing a suit and shades. Maybe they got two for the price of one.

"I don't need a lift either!" I replied.

"My boss would like to speak to you."

"Who's your boss?"

"The sooner you get in the sooner you'll find out."

* * *

I could have tried running. The men looked cool but that didn't mean they could run. But the more I considered it, the more I really couldn't be bothered. The day was hot and, besides, I wanted to know who their boss was and why he'd sent a big car to fetch me. The only other time I'd get to get to ride in such luxury would be when I was wearing a wooden suit and wishing I'd spent more time believing in God.

* * *

We drove in silence down to the foreshore. The place was heaving but then the tide was in. That meant people squeezed into the arcades, cafes and shops. How the owners must have wished the tide would stay in forever.

The car came to a halt outside a rowing club, people were partying on the balcony, drinking beer and waving at passers-by. They didn't pay much attention to the car and they paid even less attention to me as I was lead across the pavement and into the building below. It was an ice-cream parlour but we weren't stopping for a Ninety-Nine. A hand guided me to the end of the room, up a narrow set of stairs and into a long narrow office.

There was a desk at the far end of the room with a high leather chair facing a view of the harbour. A tune was playing on the stereo.

"Mr O'Riley?" said one of the men in shades beside me.

A finger pointed up from the other side of the chair and that meant silence. I stood and looked at the many photographs that lined the walls. Some were of Scarborough but most were of a large round guy with thin black hair and beady eyes. The shots detailed the man performing a number of civic duties such as cutting a tape with a pair of scissors, eating a plate of fish and chips, standing proudly outside an ice-cream parlour, offering presents to kids in a hospital and shaking hands with a woman with a chain around her neck and not looking unlike Helen Fitzsimmons.

Eventually the music came to an appropriate lull that was long enough for the chair to swing round and allow me to see a large round guy with thin black hair and beady eyes smiling back at me.

The office was as hot as hell but he wore a suit and none of the windows were open. So I guess he liked it that way.

"Mr Mahoney," he said, stroking a black cat in his lap, "I've been expecting you!"

He prised a pair of headphones from his head and, with the flick of a wrist, waved the men away back down the stairs. He pressed a remote and the neon lights on the equaliser instantly died.

"Pink Floyd, Mr Mahoney." He said with a certain sense of satisfaction in his voice, a voice that seemed to take up most of his breath. "I find their music so invigorating, so moving."

I shrugged my shoulders. "Like a laxative you mean!"

His left eye flickered and his large cheeks wobbled as if he'd never heard anything so insulting. But the day was still young.

O'Riley held out a hand "Please, take a seat."

I did as he asked.

He ran a finger over his top lip. "So you're a Private Investigator."

"And you're an ice-cream salesman!"

He shifted his bum a couple of times and placed the cat onto the desk. And I couldn't help noticing that it didn't move. It didn't even breathe. O'Riley sensed my curiosity.

"Sooty," he whispered sadly. She was killed last week."

I tried to appear bothered but in truth I couldn't care less. As far as I was concerned, one less cat just meant a whole load of fleas would have to find somewhere else to play.

O'Riley slipped a finger inside his shirt collar and allowed the stale air to feel his neck. He carried a couple of suitcases under his eyes for company. His stomach heaved and his voice wheezed when he spoke and I figured he didn't get out very often.

He sat back in his chair and crossed his legs. It's possible that's the closest they ever got to any exercise. And I thought I was bad.

"She was run over," he continued, with a deep breath. "But the cowards didn't even have the decency to report it. I don't think that's a very nice thing to do, do you?"

I looked at the stuffed remains, at the cold bright eyes staring out into the distance and I shook my head.

"But think of the milk you'll save!"

O'Riley got to his feet. It didn't make much difference, he was the shape of a cube.

"Are you always this rude?" he asked, mopping his sweaty brow with a handkerchief.

"Listen, ten minutes ago I was walking down the street minding my own business, I didn't ask to speak to you and I certainly don't give a damn about your cat."

O'Riley looked at me for a moment before forcing a smile and settling back into his chair.

"But I needed to speak to you." He said.

"You could have just asked!"

"In private."

"You could have just asked."

He held up his hand.

"I appreciate that, Mr Mahoney, but this is a matter of some concern to me."

"It always is. I think that's supposed to make me feel better and you feel good about yourself."

O'Riley held up his hand again as if to apologise but it didn't help.

"Look at me," he muttered, "Where are my manners, I haven't even offered you a drink."

He pointed towards a tray and it's possible he could have found anything I wanted. But I didn't want anything other than not to be here any longer. I shook my head.

"So this matter," I questioned. "Is that the reason for the beef?"

"Beef?"

"Your boys outside, wearing the Burton suits and Wilkinson shades."

"Oh," O'Riley mused. "Let's just say, they're protecting my assets."

"So what is it you want from me?"

O'Riley took a moment to stare at me. I got the feeling he was looking for answers, something that might reveal if he could trust me or not. But whether he got his answer or if he just thought, to hell with it anyway, I'm not sure. He just got out his handkerchief and mopped his brow again.

"I hear you're looking for something."

"We're all looking for something," I replied. "It's what get's us out of bed."

"I mean, someone," he quickly corrected himself. "A girl?"

I guess the pause that followed was for me to look across in awe at his obvious talent for knowing everybody else's business. But I let him down.

"I hope you're not getting personal!"

"I'm not in the mood for games. You and your partner have been looking for a girl called April."

O'Riley crossed his hands in front of his chest and interlocked his chubby little fingers.

"Why? Do you know her?" I asked.

He shook his head. I stood up.

"Then I'm wasting my time and yours."

"Please," he said, waving one of his chubby fingers at me. "Don't be so hasty."

One of the suits stood guarding the exit. It's possible I could have taken him but I didn't want to damage my knuckles. Besides, I wanted to know what O'Riley was really up to. It couldn't be that he'd invited me down here just to show how good he was at sticking his nose into everybody else's business.

I sat down.

"I like to make a point of knowing what goes on in this town Mr Mahoney, it helps when you have assets to protect."

"Well I doubt you have to worry about April getting her hands on your ass...."

"...it's not so much April herself, it's why she's missing that concerns me.

"Who said she's missing?"

"You're looking for her aren't you?"

"I still didn't say she's missing."

O'Riley nodded and picked up his cat. He started to stroke it and I wondered if the damn thing had perhaps jumped in front of the car on purpose.

"Did you know that the ChildLine organisation speaks to over 3,000 children every year?"

I looked back at O'Riley without answering.

"They deal with children who have either run away or

been kicked out of their home. And they're the ones who actually contact somebody. There's probably twice as many as that that nobody knows about, because nobody cares."

I pulled on my ear as O'Riley continued his sermon. It was obviously something close to his heart.

"There are all sorts of issues involved of course, bullying, family problems, physical abuse," O'Riley continued. "It's not a pleasant business."

O'Riley slowly squeezed his frame out of the chair once again and waddled across to the window."

"Am I supposed to be taking notes?"

He turned to face me and gritted his teeth. "Were you also aware that 11 girls have been reported missing in Scarborough alone this past year?"

I shook my head.

"That may not surprise you, it may not even concern you, until, perhaps, you come to realise that they are all attractive, all orphaned and all under eighteen. And nobody can vouch for them."

O'Riley allowed his words to sink in before asking; "Is April an orphan?"

I shook my head."

"You're a professional and you need to keep your clients details confidential, I appreciate that, but something's going on here Mr Mahoney, young girls are disappearing without a reason and I want to know why."

"Why?"

"Why?" he asked, sounding surprised.

"You're not a Private Investigator and you're not a cop, so yeah, why?"

He smiled. "As I said earlier, I like to keep an eye on this town; it pays to keep one step ahead. If people go missing, then there's usually a reason for it and it doesn't necessarily have to be a legal one."

I stood up and this time I was going to leave.

"Well, like I said, April isn't missing. Somebody just wants to get a message to her that's all."

"Well then that's a relief," said O'Riley with a genuine sense of sincerity.

He stepped up close and shook my hand.

"I assume that 'trust' is a dirty word in your line of work, Mr Mahoney, but, I can't help thinking that, somewhere down the line our paths may cross again and, if they do, I'd like to think that, perhaps, we could help out one another. I'm not a man to cross you understand."

* * *

There was a message from Storey on my answer machine. He wanted to meet me at ten o'clock. It cut into my stakeout a little but, not having to put up with that noise at the club for a while, suited me just fine.

Chapter Twenty-one

Nix Bar was something new, something special and something refined. A place where people with a little more class than the average punter could have a drink in peace, maybe even a cocktail. Well that's how the ad in the newspaper read anyway.

* * *

Storey was sitting in a quiet corner of the bar with his head resting in the palm of his hand. His face was shielded from the crowd. He didn't have a drink and he didn't see me approach.

"Storey?" I said.

He didn't look up.

"Storey!" I said a little louder.

He looked up sharply.

"Oh, I'm sorry," he apologised. "I was miles away."

"Do you want a drink?"

"Er, no, I, er, I'm going to get back to my room, I'm a little tired. But you go ahead."

I shook my head and sat down. "I've got a long night ahead. If I drink anything else I'll spend most of it asleep."

Storey politely smiled. He looked tired. His cuts and bruises were taking their time to heal.

"Have you any news?" he asked.

I didn't appreciate the optimism in his voice. I didn't appreciate it because I had to douse the flames. I wanted to help. I wanted to be the bearer of good news. But I didn't really have any and there was always the chance I never would. I spoke quietly as if it might help.

"Well the bad news is, we haven't found her yet, but..."

"We?"

"What?"

"You said, 'we', you said, 'we haven't found her yet'!"

First mistake and I hoped that my face didn't give me away.

"I'm sorry, I was giving it the Royal we, as in you and me, we're both looking for her right?"

Storey nodded and appeared convinced. Which either made him a fool or me a very good liar.

"Well, it looks like she may well be in Scarborough."

"What makes you say that?" he asked.

"Some people recognized her photograph and somebody thought she'd been out with.........." How would I like to be told that my daughter was going out with a kid called 'Smudge?' ".........some friends only recently, so it looks promising."

I wasn't expecting a hug or a kiss, after all I'd only just started to make inroads into the haystack, but neither was I expecting Storey to go all cold on me.

"What's the matter?" I questioned.

Almost without thinking, he started to fumble with a

napkin. He worked on it tirelessly. If he'd have been any good at origami, I'm sure I'd have witnessed the creation of a dinosaur at any moment.

"Storey?" I prompted.

He looked across at me.

"I thought you wanted her finding. I mean, I don't expect you to go all gooey on me but I thought you might be happy at least."

He dropped the napkin. Both of us watched it fall to the floor but neither of us bothered to retrieve it.

"How can I be happy Mr Mahoney?" he asked.

I raised an eyebrow and allowed him the time to explain.

"Relieved perhaps, but I can't be happy, not until I know what the situation is anyway. I mean, there's so much running through my mind at the moment,"

"Such as?"

"Well, who on earth is she for starters!"

"She's your daughter!"

"Perhaps, but will she be happy to see me? Will she even want to see me?"

"Well you've got a choice. You can walk away now and spend the rest of your life wondering or you can let me find her. I know which one I'd prefer."

"You're right; of course, it's just a little difficult that's all."

"Yeah, well, we've got to find her first."

"Of course. I'm sorry."

Storey edged his finger across his forehead again. He looked old enough to know that life was all about raising hopes and then have them taken away from you at a moments notice. It's how you deal with the result that matters, how soon you get over all the crap, how you bury it deep in your conscience, tell yourself that it really doesn't matter and then prepare yourself for even more.

"Let me find your daughter and you keep your worries in a bag for the time being?"

"I can't tell you how much I appreciate your help Mr Mahoney."

"Yeah." I said, not looking him in the eye, and quickly leaving just in case he suddenly found the words.

* * *

I checked my watch and thought how dark it was considering it had just gone six o'clock. Then I realised that the damn thing had stopped. I shook it once or twice and wondered if that would ever work on someone who'd had a heart attack and, if it did, would they sue me for whiplash?

* * *

The clock above the railway station gave me the usual three alternatives, 9.35, 9.40 or 10.03. Bloody town! All I knew was it was late.

* * *

I drove to the club but I didn't get out the car. I sat there for about half an hour just watching the windscreen fill with condensation. My senses lulled to the sound of the local radio station. The darkness grew heavy on my eyes. Images of Envy striding around my office and flexing her arm started to fill the darkness before it was replaced by a picture of April smiling back at the camera and Storey in my office with his broad frame, cuts and beard. Life was full of strange people.

* * *

It had just gone six o'clock when I woke up, bloody watch.

I entered the club. It was practically empty. I asked the

girl in the cloakroom what the time was.

"1.30!" she yelled.

Preacher was nowhere in sight. I didn't feel clever. I was supposed to be following him. I checked out the Cocktail lounge. The people there looked familiar but none of them were Preacher. I looked around the rest of the club at people who'd reached that stage of denial, when they'd swear blind they weren't drunk but most obviously were. The way they meticulously put one foot in front of the other and then staggered three steps left and into a wall. The way the table kept moving every time they went to put their drink down. And the way they spat and shouted into everybody's ear when they spoke. That's the problem with being sober in a place like this.

* * *

But there was no sign of Preacher or Bob or Alana. I started to panic. I was letting Walker down.

I asked one of the bouncers where I might find Preacher. He spoke into some gadget on his lapel and told me I might find him at the Casino.

* * *

Sure enough he was at the roulette table sticking a pile of chips on number twenty-six. I kept my distance. He didn't see me. Number thirty-two came up but Preacher didn't bat an eyelid.

It was time to grab a drink.

* * *

It had just gone four o'clock in the morning. The moon was thinking about retiring as I aimed my key into the front door. Preacher had gone home and that was good enough for me. I needed my bed. My eyelids were heavy and my shoulders hunched from sitting all day in a car. I flicked on the lights and reached for a hook with my coat. It fell to the floor. I left it there. By the time I reached the bedroom there was a trail of clothes behind me.

Rain leapt at the window. I pulled the curtains tight and got into bed. Sleep would bring dreams of writing my third best selling novel in a tiny thatched cottage somewhere in the Lake District and walks to the post office to buy the morning paper and chatting to villagers who cheerily looked my way and said 'good morning', like they really meant it. The sun would always shine and my coffee would never go cold.

Ten minutes later there was a knock at the door. Not so much a knock, more of a gentle tap that I almost missed. It crossed my mind that it could have been someone somewhere else so I let it go. A few seconds later the knock grew louder and quicker. There was no mistake, it was my door.

"Shit!" I said, throwing back the bed covers.

If this was one of Walker's dawn raids he was going to regret it.

I reached the door and realised I was only wearing a pair of boxers. I traced the trail for my trousers and a vest and opened the door an inch.

Out on the landing, shivering and wet and looking at me with begging eyes was Alana.

"Please, can you help me?"

Chapter Twenty-two

I didn't get to sleep much that night. The sofa was two sizes too small and my mind kept wanting to know why an attractive girl was sleeping in my bed while I was out here on the sofa?

Around about seven the bright sun got too much for the paper-thin curtains. I rolled back my excuse for a blanket and started towards the kitchen.

I switched on the kettle. Apart from the odd grimace, I hardly made a noise but, two minutes later, Alana was stood in the doorway. She was wearing what appeared to be one of my shirts and not a lot else. And I couldn't help thinking how it never looked that good on me.

She ran her fingers through her un-brushed hair. She probably thought she looked a mess, but she looked a whole lot nicer than most women did after a complete makeover.

"Fancy a coffee?" I asked.

She pouted her lips and nodded.

"How do you like it?"

"Milk, no sugar please."

Her voice was croaky, probably as a result of her night in the rain.

I handed her a drink and we made our way into the room. I left the curtains drawn, it was bright enough already. I relaxed in a chair while Alana sat on the sofa and crossed her bare legs underneath her body. She hugged the cup with tight fingers and slowly sipped her drink.

"Is it all right?" I asked.

She nodded.

I glanced at the radiator. "Your clothes should be dry now."

She nodded.

"Did you sleep all right?"

When she nodded again I realised that I was going to have to change my line of questioning. There were things I needed to know but I didn't want to scare her, or me.

Unfortunately before I got a chance to ask anything there was a knock on the door. To me it was just a knock on the door but, by the look on Alana's face, it was hell calling and she didn't want to be in.

We both got up. I headed for the door. Alana retreated to my bedroom.

"Who is it?" I asked.

"Jo! Come on Mahoney, we're going to be late!"

I opened the door and found Envy stood outside and decked in a tracksuit.

"Jesus, can't you sleep?" I asked.

"We're going for a run remember?"

I lifted her wrist and checked her watch. It was 7.20.

"I don't recall anybody saying anything about delivering milk at the same time!"

"This way we get it over and done with and it's a beautiful morning."

"How can you tell?" I asked, still wiping the sleep from

my eyes. "God hasn't even turned the lights on yet."

Perhaps it was the shock of not expecting to see Envy so early or perhaps it was the fact that she wasn't at work but there was something about her, something different, something that couldn't stop me from thinking that, beyond her stern expression and the dark-rimmed glasses and the, I could beat you in an arm-wrestle with my eyes closed, was someone who wasn't the slightest bit unattractive.

"Come on, hurry up." She smiled. "Or do you want me to come in there and dress you as well?"

I suddenly realised how that might complicate things.

"Er, look, can you give me a few minutes?" I asked.

Envy smiled and I dreaded to think what was coming next.

"Who is it?" She asked.

I glanced back inside the room and then back at Envy.

"How........, it's not, it's not anybody! Well, it's not like you think anyway."

"Don't be so modest."

"No..., I......"

"Look, I'm getting cold. I'll grab some water at the shop. Meet me on the corner in five minutes."

"Can you make it ten?"

Envy was standing at the bottom of the stairs smiling up at me.

"Now I'm impressed, Mahoney?"

And then she disappeared.

I went back inside and found Alana sitting on the edge of my bed. She looked up at me and inched the shirt down her legs as far as it would stretch.

"What are you frightened of?" I asked.

"Nothing."

I sat down next to her. "All right, so who are you frightened of?"

She brushed her fringe away from her face and stared down at the floor without saying a word.

"Look, I've got to go," I explained. "But I won't be long. You're welcome to stay. You know where the shower is and your clothes are on the radiator."

She looked at me and said "Thank you."

I smiled.

"Are you going to be all right?"

She reached forward and kissed me on the cheek.

* * *

Something was wrong. I was out with a smart, attractive woman dressed in tight leggings and there was another half-dressed young girl sitting on my bed. Yet, here I was, running! That's not how it should have been.

* * *

Envy didn't ask any questions and I didn't tell her anything. All she wanted to do was run. But it was obvious from her pace that she was taking it easy. We'd only just got to the bottom of Columbus Ravine and already I was on borrowed breath.

"We'll take a right onto the foreshore," she said, as easily as someone who was sat at a desk tapping words into a computer and drinking a cup of tea. "The sun should be coming up over the sea, it's a beautiful sight."

"Can't I just take your word for it?" I panted.

"Force yourself Richard, you never know when you might need to go that one step further, and then you'll thank me."

I wanted to reply something sarcastic, a put down, but my breath was no more. My head span. The words were all there but I wasn't capable of putting them in any order.

Every step was a strain and that was understandable

considering the only time my body ever moved at a pace faster than walking was if I'd just fallen down the stairs.

Knives dug deep into the top of my legs and my calves as my muscles were stretched to the limit. Envy bounced along the pavement. I dragged my body.

Slowly we passed the mass construction that was the Sands project. It was fronted by colourful advertisements that suggested everybody who was anybody should get a piece of this wonderful future.

We turned onto the drive and the sea opened up in front of us, a blue, heaving mass that swooshed up onto the beach and played tag with the seagulls.

"We'll head for the castle." Envy said.

She had to say that, it was the only point to aim for apart from a small café and a bus stop, both of which appealed to me a whole lot more.

A strong breeze carried a salty spray over us. It was refreshing and camouflaged my perspiration.

Out on the waves a group of surfers patiently waited for the ride that would make their morning quest worthwhile.

The castle inched nearer, one step closer and three steps back. My lungs were almost at breaking point when Envy finally led me up a narrow path towards the castle walls. We zig-zagged for a few minutes between thorny branches and overgrown bushes. Tourists could have been lost for weeks in the undergrowth.

When we reached the top I decided to call a halt.

"Give me a minute here." I panted.

Envy turned and studied me impatiently. She wasn't out of breath. She wasn't even sweating.

"Are you enjoying this?" I moaned.

"It's like anything, the more you do, the better you become at it."

"Yeah, well, I'm really sarcastic." I mumbled.

"Your health's important, Mahoney."

Envy took a moment to go about her stretching exercises while I took a moment to check out her legs.

"It's a lovely view," she said, referring to the sea below.

"I couldn't agree more," I replied, referring to her legs.

Envy caught me staring. I didn't mind. And I appreciated her look of contempt. After all, what person in their right mind didn't appreciate somebody admiring their talents?

"We ought to keep moving," she insisted. "It won't help standing around."

"Yeah," I agreed. "We might get a parking ticket!"

* * *

But I was adamant that we walked. At least it wasn't standing and it was still a form of exercise, like running but in slow motion.

We passed through a gap in the castle wall. The pathway dipped between a set of trees before the South Bay came into view. Immediately the air was filled with the smell of shellfish and the hollow sound of a, once booming, harbour.

"So how's the stakeout going?" Envy asked.

"Slow, I replied between breaths. "Even the cops don't seem to know why I'm following Preacher."

"His brother's far more interesting."

"I met him."

"He's a nice guy isn't he?"

"It was hard to tell, he was weeding a graveyard at the time."

"He's like a local hero."

"Because he likes cricket?"

"Because he's transformed that church and tripled the congregation. He's also fed, housed and found work for a lot of ex-cons and immigrants."

I suddenly recalled the paper I'd been reading the other day.

"Is that why they want to make him a Bishop!" I asked.

Envy nodded. "Together with the prestige it would bring the town and the fact he's a darn good vicar."

We took a right and headed back into town.

Envy finally got round to asking: "So what did Storey have to say for himself?"

"Not much, I mean, we haven't got a whole lot to go on yet have we."

"But you mentioned that some people recognised her?"

I nodded.

"And what about Smudge?"

I paused to view the red roof cottages that sloped down towards the sea and I didn't bother to answer. Instead I allowed my thoughts to recall the day I first met Helen Fitzsimmons. My first case and every bad feeling that came with it.

"You didn't tell him did you?"

I shook my head.

"How come?"

"I'm not sure it'll do any good."

"He might have recognised the name?"

"I doubt it." I replied.

But all the while Envy felt I had something else on my mind.

"And what else, Mahoney?"

"Nothing. That was it. I didn't even bother having a drink."

"No, there's something else on your mind." She said as she took my arm and pulled me round to face her. "You're holding out on me!"

"No. Not you," I replied. "Him."

"Storey?"

"Yeah."

"But why? He's our client."

I stalled on an answer. Envy tugged my arm.

"It's just that, I don't know. It's just that I've been played for a sucker before and I don't want it to happen again."

"I don't understand."

"We don't know the first thing about Storey. He's a middle aged man looking for a young girl and we don't know why."

"I thought you said he was her father?"

"But we don't know that for sure do we!"

"You think he might well be up to something?" she asked.

"Isn't everybody?"

Envy allowed a frown to dampen her features. "So what do we do?"

"We go on looking. But we keep some things to ourselves for the time being, at least until we know what's going on. If that's all right with you?"

Envy looked at me and smiled. But deep down maybe she was wondering if that included her. Maybe she thought I didn't trust her. And maybe she was right.

Chapter Twenty-three

Envy instructed me to do some stretching exercises when I got home. She assured me that they would help, otherwise my legs would seize up.

All I could think of was taking a shower, getting into some clean clothes and wondering what line of questioning to take with Alana. But I needn't have bothered. She was gone and she'd taken her clothes with her. I guess I was kind of lucky considering my wallet was still in my jacket. And I never even got to ask how she found me.

* * *

I waited an hour to see if she might return. I showered and shaved and hoped she wasn't in any kind of trouble.

When she didn't show I headed up town. It was still early. Up above the bricks and windows, chimneys, scaffolding, seagulls and tiles the morning sun was crawling into action.

The town responded with the bleep of cash points, the tap of heels and the boom of engines. Pedestrians dodged traffic on the precinct while pigeons chased litter scattered from the brushes of the mobile council vacuum cleaner. Patches of chewed gum and bird dung lit up the precinct. Already a queue had formed outside the Post Office. There was still another thirty minutes before it opened and most of the people looked like they had nothing else to do for the rest of the day, but still they queued.

A breeze nipped down the street bringing with it the smell of freshly baked bread and coffee.

As if in a trance I headed straight for the vendor. It was impossible to pass within a hundred yards and not be trapped by the hypnotic fragrance of hot Brazilian beaches.

"Morning Mr Mahoney."

"So it is." I replied.

The vendor turned to pour what may have looked like jet oil but was in fact the best coffee I'd ever tasted. His name was Lee and he always wore the same look of shock whenever I saw him, the kind of look that suggested his wife had just run off with the Avon lady when all the time he'd suspected it was the milkman.

"Anything interesting," he asked.

"Maybe."

My reply took him by surprise. He did well not to drop the cup as he handed it to me.

"It's a little delicate though," I continued. "If you know what I mean!"

Lee tapped the side of his nose and then pointed the same finger in my direction. I've never questioned that response and maybe I should have. I mean, who's to say it didn't mean, 'here's your change and now wait a minute while I hire a plane and write whatever you're about to tell me all over the bright blue sky in clear white letters'?

I waited a moment as Lee turned to serve a young woman in a business suit and assured her that the housing decline wouldn't affect the town just yet. When he was through I took out the photograph of April and showed it to him.

"Pretty girl." He said.

I nodded. "Her name's April, but like I said, it's a delicate situation, I can't have people asking around after her. But maybe if you spot her or hear someone mention her name......."

Lee nodded back at me.

"Can I keep the photo?"

"I'll get you a copy. She might also have known somebody by the name of Smudge. "

"Smudge?"

I nodded again. "You can ask about him if you like, tell him I'm looking for him, but don't scare him."

"Naturally."

I started back down the street as Lee began to explain to his next customer how, all being well, Scarborough Football Club will soon be able to play their home matches here again instead of having to travel all the way to Bridlington.

In short, Lee not only knew, but talked to, everybody in town, including those who'd only just arrived. He was that kind of person, confident without being pushy and chirpy without being a pain in the arse. I felt happy knowing he would be looking out for April and, whoever the hell Smudge was.

* * *

The Evening News office was a hive of activity. A lorry was parked on the main street unloading giant toilet rolls into a press ready to print the groundbreaking stories that would at best send shock waves around the nation, or at worst, cause a ripple across the pond that was Scarborough.

An array of headlines lined the office windows; *Gun Drama: Men Held, Family caught up in bomb mayhem, Drunken yobs attack cashier* and *Couple Gassed and Robbed*, nothing like a trip to the seaside to escape your troubles.

I pushed back a little black gate that guarded the entrance to the reception area. A young girl busied herself behind the counter. She didn't speak when I approached. She simply raised her head and half smiled. She was blonde, or at least that was the impression she wanted to give. Her skin was smooth, she had green eyes, high cheekbones and black eye liner that met at the edge of her eyebrows and curved back towards her ears.

"I'd like to place an ad please."

"OK, if you'd just like to fill out this form over there and then leave it with me when you've finished." She spoke with a croak in her voice and I couldn't help thinking she wouldn't be much help with the crossword.

I took the form to where I'd been ordered, placed my coffee on the desk and stretched the pen as far as it would go. I tugged on my ear and wondered what I was meant to write in such situations. I wanted Smudge to contact me but I couldn't tell him why. So in the end I just wrote down that I had some important documents for him to collect, so if he, or anybody who knew him, could contact me, I would appreciate it.

I handed the form back to the girl. For some reason she read it. I mean, I wasn't even sure it was her job. It took a while and I hadn't used any big words.

She looked at me with a strange expression. "That's an unusual name."

"Mine or the kids?"

"Smudge."

I nodded again.

"Is there a reward?"

"Don't people do anything for nothing anymore?"

She tilted her head to one side as if her brains cells were about to commence a lap of her head

"I think it would help."

I went back to the desk and added that there would be a reward. Then I handed her the form and left before she talked me into writing how much.

I was halfway to the office before I realised I'd forgotten my bloody coffee.

Chapter Twenty-four

I caught sight of a pair of polished shoes and a neatly pressed suit relaxing in a chair at the top of the stairs.

A young man was whistling a tune and twisting a gold lighter between his fingers. I've always wanted to do that, the twisting, not the whistling thing. I figured it would be a good attraction at a party or in a bar. I had to get out more.

He looked to be somewhere in his early twenties. He had thick fair hair brushed back tight to his head and covered in gel. And despite the fact the sun struggled to pierce the walls, he had on a pair of sunglasses.

He got to his feet and slowly removed the glasses when he saw me reach the final step. My legs ached. That stretching hadn't worked. All I wanted was to sit down. I was never going to run, ever again.

The kid shook the creases from his left trouser leg and held out a hand. A gold watch slipped down his wrist and into view.

"Mr Mahoney?" He assumed.

I nodded sharply and just the once. It was more than I wanted to do. But the fact that I didn't shake his hand didn't seem to bother him.

"The name's Ricks."

"I'm glad to hear it." I replied.

"I work for the Evening News."

"That's great kid, but whenever I need a paper I just go to the corner shop."

His confident smile suddenly evaporated. "No, I mean, I'm a reporter!"

I unlocked the office door and glanced back at him. I think he was hoping that, somewhere along the line, his words would have some effect on me other than generating the usual sarcastic response.

"I was wondering if I could have a quick word?"

A strange request I thought. Nobody ever asked a Private Investigator for a quick word. Beating on your soul and searching your conscience for the slightest ounce of integrity took time and courage and a whole lot of words.

I stepped inside the office and tried to appear as if I had a ton of things to do, when in fact I couldn't think of anything, except stare at the kettle. But that was broken and I already had a drink.

Ricks parked himself in the middle of the office and looked around the place like someone with a view to buying it.

"I've never seen a Private Investigator's office before."

I sat down and placed my polystyrene cup carefully onto the desk.

"So just how different from low down and dirty were you expecting?" I asked.

Ricks smiled. It lifted the fuzz on his chin a little. "No, it's the character, this place has life."

I cast a quick glance at the walls and carpet and then

back at Ricks and I couldn't help thinking that I'd let a mad man into the office. How was I going to get him out again without damaging the furniture?

"So, are you going to tell me what this quick word is about, or am I going to have to dust around you?"

Ricks looked at me apologetically and then crouched into a chair. He left his glasses on the desk and pressed his trousers with the tips of his fingers.

He spoke in no more than a raised whisper and every phrase was emphasised with a hand movement. He either karate chopped his way through a sentence or measured it like fisherman might a prize catch.

"Can, I be blunt, Mr Mahoney?"

"Is there supposed to be another way?"

Ricks twisted his lighter. "The thing is, when I said I was a reporter....,"

"You lied!"

"No. No, I am a reporter, it's just that, and don't get me wrong, I like my job....."

"But?"

Ricks cast a quick glance over his shoulder as though he expected to find somebody sat behind him taking notes.

"Well really, it's not enough, if you know what I mean," he continued. "All I ever get to do is cover some story on a charity event or plans for this and that, stuff that never seems to go anywhere."

"I guess that's the price of working in a small town!"

"Exactly, I knew you'd understand," he finished by curling his finger and thumb into a little round O shape.

Understand? I was just being flippant.

"What I need is something more challenging, Mr Mahoney. I mean, it's all right for most people I suppose, but I'm not most people. I feel like a big fish in a little sea."

"Pond."

"What?"

"It's big fish in a small pond."

His face momentarily reddened. "Well, anyway, what I'm looking for is a meal ticket, something I can sell to the majors and get me a job there."

I tried to picture a meal-ticket as I flipped the lid of my coffee. Steam spiralled into my face, encasing me with images of sandy beaches and tanned bodies in bikinis.

"So what's all this got to do with me?" I asked.

The kid shifted in his seat and stopped twisting his lighter.

"Well, it's just, you know, I thought we might be good for each other that's all. I mean, me being a journalist...,

"A would be journalist!" I quickly corrected.

"And you being a Private Investigator," he continued.

A would be Private Investigator, I thought to myself.

I sat back in my chair as if to contemplate what Ricks was telling me.

"And in what way would we be good for one another?" I asked.

"Well, you know, I sort of speak to people, I hear things and stuff, just like you do."

Ricks glanced up from his lighter and pointed his chin at me. "There must be something going on that maybe I could write about!"

I looked at my coffee. All I wanted to do was drink it in peace. But, in order to do that, I had to take care of Ricks.

"Is that it?" I asked.

"Yeah," he replied. "It's either that or writing stories about people planting trees for the rest of my life!"

I got to my feet and ran the chair back across the floor with a shriek.

"One," I said, pointing a finger at Ricks. "Don't go knocking people who plant trees! And two, what is it with you lot over there?" I said, waving at thumb in the general direction of the Evening News but probably pointing it more towards the police station. "You think you can come in here and take me for a ride any time you feel like it?"

I started round to the other side of the desk and suddenly Ricks appeared uncomfortable.

"I don't understand!" he whined.

I looked down at him. "Well you've got a choice, you can either leave by the door or I throw you out of the window."

"I don't ...."

I grabbed Ricks by his lapel and pulled him to his feet.

"And I know which one I'd prefer!" I suggested.

"All right! All right" He moaned. "I'm going."

I let go of his jacket. He squinted his eyes and straightened his lapel. He still appeared puzzled, not that I gave a damn.

"I, still I don't understand why you won't help."

"Because the last time somebody from your office suckered me into a job I was left out on a limb with the cops beating down my door and two goons trying to beat the crap out of me. I'm not about to let that happen again, OK!"

I pushed Ricks to the door. The lighter dangled in his hand. He still hadn't worked out anything. He looked at the door and then at me.

"What, are you talking about?"

"Ask Hartless."

"Hartless?"

"Yeah, he works with you right."

"Yes, but he's just...., what's he got to do with anything?"

"I'm sure he'll explain."

I opened the door and waited for Ricks to leave. He

went back for his sunglasses. He pressed them to his face and offered me his best disgusted expression.

"I thought, I thought you'd like….."

"Look, I'm not your meal ticket kid, you want to leave town, then take a train like everybody else. It might even run on time."

I closed the door and went back to my desk. I picked up my coffee. But it was cold.

Bloody reporters.

Chapter Twenty-five

I headed for the foreshore. I was late but I didn't rush. The afternoon had turned hot. Very hot. But at the back of my mind I couldn't help thinking that Debbie wouldn't be there anyway. What had seemed like a bit of fun yesterday would have disappeared in the reality of actually doing something about it.

People crowded the pavements. The sun had brought them out in their hoards. On days like these who needed the stress of booking flights, packing suitcases and standing crossed legged, asking for the toilet in a foreign language?

I reached the café and checked my watch. I mumbled a swear word because it still showed six o'clock.

Much to my surprise, Debbie was sitting at a table.

"I saved you a seat," she said.

She was holding onto a menu and wearing the same clothes as yesterday.

"You're late!" she said.

Part of me felt the instinct to apologise. The rest of me wanted to tell her not to be so rude.

I sat down. "I've been busy!"

She handed me a menu. "What do you want to order?"

"I'm not sure I've got time for anything."

A twinkle formed in her eyes. "But I've got some important information for you."

"Good."

"Actually we should have met in some like, deserted warehouse or something," she added, with a sense of excitement. "Late at night!"

"This isn't a game."

"I know!"

She leant across the table and whispered; "But somebody might be following us."

A waiter suddenly appeared and broke my glare.

"I'll have a coffee please," I said.

He repeated the order as if there might be some confusion. Then he looked at Debbie.

She picked up the menu. "A diet coke for me please. And I'll have the fungi pasta with side salad but no onions. I don't like onions," she added with a glance at me.

The waiter repeated the order once again and left.

"You look crap." She observed.

"What a lovely way you have with words."

"No seriously, are you all right?"

I shook my head. "Somebody thought it would be a good idea to drag my body around the sea-front at a pace faster than walking. There should be a law against it."

The girl frowned. But I couldn't be bothered explaining, because it wasn't that important.

"So what have you got to tell me?"

Her eyes widened and she held her hands up as though she was about to start some happy clappy church song.

"Oh my God you're going to be like, so excited!"

"Are you sure?" I mumbled.

She nodded as a coffee appeared on the table. It was quickly followed by a glass of coke. Diet coke, complete with a straw. Debbie clutched at the straw and pressed her lips to the top. I grabbed her hand.

"Do you know where Smudge is?"

She frowned at me. I allowed her to drink. She let out a breath and sat back in her seat.

"The girl in the picture, who is she?"

"I can't tell you."

"You *can't* tell me?"

"It's confidential."

"But I'm your partner!"

She was testing my patience.

I clenched my teeth. "No," I said. "You're not my partner. You're just somebody doing somebody else a favour."

She appeared momentarily disappointed.

"Does that mean I don't get anything for telling you?"

"It means if you don't tell me, I'll go straight to your school and tell them where you are!"

She covered her mouth with the back of her hand and started to laugh. "I'm not really supposed to be at school," she said. "I left last year. I'm seventeen."

"And I suppose you lied about your parents as well!"

She continued to laugh. Almost any other time I wouldn't have minded. It's nice to hear people laugh, most of the time. But most of the time wasn't right now. I was ready to walk out and the only thing that stopped me was the fact that she really might know something.

"Aren't you hungry?" she asked.

I was about to take hold of her hand again and let her know I was through with her games, but the waiter appeared with a plate of food.

I sat back and watched and waited as she picked up

her fork and went to work on the pasta with side salad. No onions.

"He was seeing a girl, somebody called April," she said eventually. "Is that the girl in the picture?"

I didn't answer and I tried not to look as though the name meant anything to me.

"Anyway," she continued. "Apparently they were like, shacked up together someplace, but nobody's seen them for a while."

"What's, 'a while'?"

"That's what I asked. But they didn't say."

"Who's 'they'?"

"Just people."

"Did you find out where he lived?"

"Are you married?" she asked, completely out of the blue.

I tried not to appear either shocked or agitated. But I definitely felt one of them. I just couldn't work out which.

"Would it help if I was?"

She smiled as she slowly slid the fork out from between her lips.

"You really are cute, especially when you're angry, you like…"

"… where does Smudge live?"

"8 New Queen Street. Flat 4."

I made a mental note of what she'd told me. Then I wondered if I should have written it down. Image was such a vital ingredient, but then so was time, and I didn't want to waste most of mine walking up and down New Queen Street, simply because I couldn't remember the number of the flat.

So I collared the waiter for a pen and wrote down the details on a serviette.

"Have you been there?"

"No," she shrieked as if I'd just accused her of stealing

the church collection.

I concentrated a glare on her young pale face. "Have you been to the flat?"

"No!"

I sat back satisfied that she was telling the truth.

Debbie put her fork down. "Why would you ask?"

"Because I don't want to put you in any danger, that's why. I'm not even sure I should have asked you in the first place, and no, that doesn't make me cute!"

"I can take care of myself!" she smiled confidently.

"That's what most people think till they realise they can't."

But she was too young to realise what I was talking about. Right now her world was full of music and clothes and romance.

"How did you find out all this anyway?"

"This boy at my old school, he like organises drug deals, he knows most people."

"You know people who do drug deals?"

I was starting to sound like her father and she knew it. She leant across the table towards me.

"He used to well fancy me, he probably still does. He'll do anything for me. Besides, it got you what you wanted didn't it!"

I reached for my wallet and placed two ten pound notes on the table.

"What's that?" she snapped with a curled up lip.

"It's called money! Consider it your payment."

"What am I supposed to do with it, buy an ice-cream?"

I looked at the money. "That's a bloody big ice-cream!"

Debbie slumped in her chair. She didn't look happy.

"Looks like it's about time you learnt to appreciate the value of money," I said, tapping a finger into one of the notes. "There's more money there than I earned in a week at your age."

"Er, so help me here, am I supposed to like, feel sorry or proud of you?"

I stood up quickly and a pain shot through my legs.

"It's not what you get," I winced though the remains of my run. "It's how well you use it. And that goes for most things."

"Are you sure you're all right?"

"I'll live." I moaned.

I picked out our waiter and handed him a ten pound note. I didn't wait for the change. I wanted to get away from here as quickly as possible. I hurried out of the door as fast as my aching legs would allow, which was pretty much a shuffle.

* * *

I'd got what I'd come here for but I wasn't happy. Why did that happen?

I took out a couple of pedestrians with my shoulder and didn't even apologise. I heard them tut. It wasn't a nice thing to do and maybe sometime later I'd chastise myself, but not right now.

I reached the junction to the main street. The traffic poured out onto the foreshore. I was tempted to stride out in front of them regardless of the consequences, but a voice beside me said; "I don't want the money."

I turned to see Debbie holding out the two ten pound notes in my direction.

"Why not?"

"I want to be your partner."

"You can't."

She almost stamped her foot as her face took on an expression of frustration.

"Why?"

"First of all it's not my business and secondly………."

I looked at Debbie as I reminded myself of the dangers I might have put her in.

"And secondly, what?"

"And secondly, things happen."

"You mean like I could get into trouble?"

I didn't answer. I didn't have to.

"But people get into trouble all the time!" She argued.

"They're not my responsibility!"

Debbie calmed herself as if my words suddenly meant something.

"See, I said you were cute."

I almost smiled and so did she.

"But I still don't want the money." She insisted.

I was reluctant to take it back and even more reluctant to ask her why. But curiosity got the better of me.

"So what do you want?"

"I want to be a Private Investigator."

This time I smiled and then I laughed. Not at her ambitions but at the way she said it.

"What do I have to do?"

"I'll talk to Ronnie."

"Who's Ronnie?"

"He runs the business. He'll know what to do."

Much to my surprise Debbie reached out and hugged me.

"Thank you," she said.

And continued to say it another three or four times before I managed to slip away.

Chapter Twenty-six

The climb up through the old town to New Queen Street didn't thrill me. Almost every muscle in my legs groaned and pulled. I never knew I had so many. So much for the stretching exercises!

I took a breath at the top. The tide was coming in, bringing with it a cold, grey fret. The fog horn was already booming out.

* * *

I dragged my leaden feet the rest of the way. New Queen Street was a hundred yard stretch of guest houses that were no longer guest houses. Most were boarded up with an array of 'For sale' notices outside. The rest looked like they should have been.

A group of youngsters were sitting on the bottom steps near to where I needed to be. Whatever it was they were talking about wasn't as interesting as watching me approach. I looked at them long enough to realise that they weren't about to sell me insurance.

These were the boys who drank from tins cans concealed in brown paper bags, who sniggered at the cops and who spat without ever disturbing the roll-ups that lived in their lips. I could smell their breath ten yards away and I wasn't even down-wind.

One of them stood up and pressed his back to a wall. He was nodding his head to some tune nobody else could hear. He started to laugh. I think it was meant to show me and everybody else just how confident he was. He pressed a hand into a back trouser pocket and clicked the fingers on his other hand. The others laughed along with him.

When I passed he said. "How you doing?"

His face was mean. It's hard to imagine someone so young looking so mean. What the hell could have happened to him I wondered? But there he was, standing in front of me, carrying all the meanness anybody could never wish for.

I stared back at him, deep and into his pale grey eyes, and long enough for him to appear slightly uncomfortable.

I said; "Fine."

They laughed, but I couldn't see the joke.

* * *

I climbed the steps to the flat. It was littered with bin bags, some of which had been ripped open. Pizza boxes and beer bottles slipped out onto the steps. The air smelt damp and uncomfortable. It just didn't go with the whooshing waves and golden sands.

The front door was open. People could come and go as they pleased. Free papers, charity bags, unopened envelopes and leaflets for loans lined the hallway. I went up the wide-open staircase and stood outside number four. The door was shut but it wasn't locked. I pushed it open. The room was huge and high. It must have cost a fortune to heat. There was an unmade bed in the corner, a sink, oven, wardrobe and a set of drawers.

What was most notable though was that, either Smudge had left in a hurry, or somebody had taken the time to go through his stuff. The place was a mess. Posters had been ripped from the wall and CDs were piled up in the middle of the floor. Most of the artists I didn't recognise. I was so far behind the times that I didn't even know what music people listened to anymore.

The smell of unwashed clothes rotting in the corner of the room and boys odour finally got to me. I didn't want to be here any longer than I had to. I hurried through the rest of the room, looking for something, anything significant. I found a framed photograph sticking out from under the unmade bed. It was a montage of a young man, a boy in a variety of poses with young girls. His hair was blonde and if he wasn't kissing a girl, he was holding one close, in a manner that suggested they would be kissing the moment the picture had been taken. I looked at the girls. A couple of them could have been April. They looked similar. The same fresh face and the same innocent smile. One in particular was a shot of a boy and a girl sitting on a railing in front of an amusement arcade. He was in shorts. She wore a bikini top.

I unclipped the back of the frame and took out the picture.

"Looking for anything in particular?"

The voice made me jump. I turned to see a man in the doorway dressed in a white shirt and black trousers. He had a pen and a notepad stuffed into the top pocket of his shirt. I wanted to punch his lights out for making me jump. But I also needed some answers and he might be the encyclopaedia I was looking for.

"Aren't we all?" I replied.

"Are you the kid's old man? Cos if you are let me tell you he's behind with the rent."

"How much?"

"A couple of weeks, it might not seem a lot but hey, you know, I've got bills to pay like everyone else. Normally I kick them out, I've got plenty of people looking for somewhere to live, you know what I mean?" The man stepped inside the room and scratched his head as though doing so might propel a thought or two. "Christ, look at this place. How the hell can these kids live like this?"

"You know Smudge?"

"Smudge?" he frowned.

"Yeah, the kid who lives in this mess."

He got out his notebook and scratched the back of his head again.

"Number four," he said, checking the door. "I've got Alex Smith down here, who the hell are you anyway?"

"You should have asked that in the first place."

He tried to get tough. "I can call the police, just as easy like."

"You can," I agreed, stepping up close to him. "And why don't you get the Health Inspectors down here at the same time. I'm sure they'd have a field day. No fire escape, no..."

"Hey, I was just looking after the kid that's all; we get all sorts in here." He said, waving his arms around.

I handed him the photograph I'd taken. "Is this him?"

He screwed his face into a ball until his eyes almost disappeared. "Yeah, it looks like him."

I took back the picture. "Has anyone else been here looking for him?"

"You mean like friends?"

"I mean, like someone who didn't look like they had a friend in the world."

The landlord went quiet. I looked across at him. He scratched the back of his head and struggled for an answer.

"Look I, I don't live here like. I just call to collect, you know, the rent, you know what I mean!"

I turned my back on him and scanned the room one more time. On a bedside cabinet I found a couple of passes. One to a place called Murrays, the other was Saltys. I put them in my pocket then took the notepad from the Landlord and wrote my name and number down.

"If you see or hear anything suspicious, you give me a call OK?"

I stuffed the pad back into his pocket and took out my wallet.

"How much is the rent?"

The sweat gathered on his forehead as he drooled over the money in my hand.

"Eighty a week."

"For this dump?"

"Hey, I can't help how they treat the place now can I!"

"Maybe if you made it a little more respectable, they wouldn't treat it so badly."

His pained expression looked for excuses but I didn't have time to wait. I pressed some money into his sweaty palm.

He checked it and grinned back at me.

"Is there anything else I can do for you?" he asked.

* * *

I was halfway down the stairs when I felt a strange tingling sensation in my chest. I didn't think anything of it at first, but it continued. I held on tight to the railing and considered the possibility that I was having a heart attack. I wasn't too young too die and I hadn't been eating well for a long time. Maybe that run had taken more out of me than I thought. Shit. This was embarrassing. I didn't want to die here. They'll pick my pockets before the thought of calling an ambulance ever crossed what was left of their tiny little minds.

I took a deep breath, I don't know why, and pressed a hand to my chest. I hoped to feel a still beating heart but what I found was my bloody mobile phone. I pulled it out of my breast pocket and looked at it in the palm of my hand. I had no idea which button to press, so I pressed any. The phone stopped ringing. I put it to my mouth and yelled, "Yeah." Then I put it to my ear. Nothing.

I'd pressed the wrong button, but at least I wasn't having a heart attack.

I stepped outside just as the phone rang again. I didn't have a clue what I was doing. I got to the bottom of the stairs and stared at the youths still dreaming of Brooklyn.

"How do you work these things?" I asked, holding out the phone.

The cocky one stepped up close and looked at the phone and then at me. I'm sure he considered snatching it from me and running like hell. But he needn't have bothered, I couldn't be arsed chasing him and, deep down, he probably knew it.

He pointed at the phone. "Press the button with the little green symbol on it."

"That one?" I asked.

He nodded. I did as he said and raised the phone to my ear.

"Mahoney?"

"Jo?"

"Yeah. Where are you?"

"Wishing I was somewhere else." I replied. "Why?"

"I've got some news about April."

"Really? What?"

"I think I've found her but it's not good news."

"What do you mean?"

"I need to confirm something first. Can I meet you at your office?"

"Sure."

"I'll be there in about ten minutes."

"Good. I'll see you there."

The phone went quiet. I looked at the kid.

"What do I do now?"

"Press the red button."

Simple. I was now in the twenty-first century. I felt complete.

"Are you a cop?"

I shook my head.

"A Private Investigator."

"Cool," he replied.

"Is somebody in trouble," another one asked.

"What makes you ask?"

The kid shrugged his shoulders and mumbled; "I dunno."

"Any of you know somebody called Smudge?"

Instantly they took on the role of four naughty schoolboys summoned to the Headmaster's office. They looked at one another and then at the floor and, only momentarily at me.

I decided to take out my wallet. This was turning into an expensive day.

"We don't really know him. We just see him from time to time," one of them replied as he stared at the money in my hand.

"But you haven't seen him lately?"

He shook his head.

I started to count out some notes.

"Has anybody else been asking about him?"

Nobody answered so I pushed the notes back inside my wallet.

"There was this bloke........"

I looked up as one of the youngsters was rapped on the shoulder by a mate. He rubbed his shoulder as though he'd been struck by a thunderbolt. He was thin and pale and I wasn't sure what he could tell me. It wasn't that he couldn't remember what he'd had for breakfast because he didn't look like he'd had anything for breakfast.

"Look, I know it's probably not 'cool' to help the good guys, but I think this kid could be in trouble."

I held out the money. The one who'd helped me with the phone took it.

"There was this fella, he came by asking about Smudge. He went through all his things,"

"Yeah and he pinned Jordan against the wall."

"He didn't pin me!" Jordan snapped.

"He did!"

"He took me by surprise that's all. Anyway, we didn't know where Smudge was at, so he just went away like."

"If you see him again," I began as I searched my pockets for a piece of paper, "would you ring me?"

They all nodded in turn.

"Except I don't have a pen or a piece of paper."

"Your number, it'll be on your phone." One of them said pointing towards my chest.

"What?"

"Your mobile. It should have your number on it."

I was totally confused. I just handed him the phone and watched as he pressed a couple of buttons. He worked it like a secretary on a typewriter. It was all very impressive, if only I knew what he was doing.

"There," he said, holding it up for me to see, "Are you Mahoney?"

I nodded.

"That's your number."

"I still can't write it down anywhere."

He smiled as he took out his own phone. He tapped a

few more buttons then held it up for me to see.

"Now we can ring you."

"Cool," I replied.

Chapter Twenty-seven

It took me ten minutes to get back to the office. I called into a photo shop on the main street and got a couple of instant copies of April. I handed one of them to Lee and bought a coffee. He hadn't heard anything about April or Smudge. He put the photo away in his top pocket and tapped his nose again.

* * *

Storey was waiting outside my office when I arrived. He appeared anxious. He was pacing the creaky floorboards backwards and forwards a dozen times at least.

"I wasn't expecting to see you," I said.

"I was wondering if you had any news?"

That's the trouble with people, they expect things and they can't always wait.

"Well you'd better come in before you wear the carpet out."

The office was cold. It was always cold.

"You want a coffee?" I asked.

Storey shook his head and it was a good job, considering the kettle was broken. He was now pacing the office and chewing a finger.

"Have you found anything out yet, Mr Mahoney?"

There was a slight strain in his voice as if he was developing a cold. It was the kind I used to try on my mother when I didn't want to go to school. But it never worked.

"Only that April isn't where I've looked so far."

"That doesn't sound very hopeful."

I looked across at Storey. "Look, we're doing everything we can to find her right."

Storey shot a glance at me. "We?"

It was obvious what I'd said and I felt stupid. It was as if nobody could ever trust me with a secret.

"You said *we*!"

"I meant........," I struggled. "I meant, you and me, you're looking for her as well right?"

But Storey wasn't convinced this time and I couldn't blame him. I'd landed my size nines right where they shouldn't have been, and I was struggling for a way out.

Two things could have happened next, Storey might have believed me or he might have punched me on the nose and walked out. But what I didn't expect was a third thing, a knock on the door.

I hoped it was Barbara with a cup of coffee. That might have just given me enough time to dig my way out of a hole. I was about to go searching for a spade when Envy waltzed in. In the space of a minute, things had gone from pretty crap to very bad. All we needed now was an earthquake.

She was wearing her glasses again and that, presumably, meant business. They made her appear professional. She wore a black jacket, she liked black. It slipped all the way to the top of her knees. It was buttoned tight, hugging her frame. Her black trousers and black heeled shoes added height to what her wide shoulders tried to conceal.

She looked at Storey and then at me. "Is this our client?"

Storey's eyes were bulging with rage.

"Who the hell is this?" he yelled, waving a hand at Envy. "What the hell's going on, Mahoney?"

I was about to explain that things weren't quite how they looked. That they were perhaps a whole lot worse. But I couldn't help noticing that, while I searched calmly for the panic button, Envy stood firm. She didn't appear the slightest bit concerned. In fact, she looked quite at home standing in the middle of the room with one hand on her hip and a glare fixed on Storey.

"That's what I'd like to ask you, Mr Storey." She said, in a tone that you wouldn't want to argue with, unless you were backed by a room full of Marines and a Sherman tank.

Storey looked at me. "Who is this woman?"

I pulled on my ear in a desperate attempt to stall for time and, the hope that I might come up with a suitable explanation. But, try as I might, I couldn't come up with anything other than;

"This is Jo Envy, Mr Storey, she, she works with me."

Storey's eyes narrowed as he asked; "I hope you're not about to tell me she knows....?"

I tried not to nod but I couldn't help it. I sat down. I felt bad. I'd betrayed the first rule of a Private Investigator, the trust of a client. When the world and everybody in it doesn't give a damn and there's nobody else to turn to, not even a bartender, then there's always the Private Investigator. That stranger in an office hiding a bottle and a whole heap of feelings in his bottom drawer. A figure ready to lend a compassionate ear to the next problem that knocked on the door. They were supposed to be the last throw of a dice, not a poke in the eye. And maybe, most of the time, they did or said the right thing, just as long as they weren't called Richard Mahoney.

I sat there feeling less than happy with myself and about two feet tall. The office appeared huge and ready to swamp me.

Storey started to leave and there was nothing I could do or say to stop him. He strode past Envy.

"I'm also good at my job, Mr Storey, very good."

But Storey didn't appear to be listening. He got to the door and reached for the handle. He couldn't see the bombshell that was fast approaching, but come to that, neither could I. After all, there was no air raid warning, no blackout signal, no whirring of engines. In fact, the world was pretty much as it was meant to be, at least in this little corner of the world anyway. Right up until the moment Envy turned to Storey and said, "So good in fact, that I know who the girl in the photograph is."

I fixed a gaze on Storey as he paused at the door. He looked back in the general direction of Envy.

"And I know for a fact that she isn't your daughter," she added.

Suddenly the office shrunk in size as I focussed my gaze on Storey. He was still angry and he had every right to be, but now he was intrigued, and that stopped him from leaving.

I'd been in that situation myself, many a time, you really want to do one thing but something else stops you, and all you do is end up hopping from one foot to another like a child who's too scared to tell anybody he really needs the toilet.

Eventually Storey let go of the door and took a couple of steps towards Envy. I wasn't sure what to make of his expression; it was all creased up, his eyebrows rolled like a ship on the crest of a rough sea. His frown deepened and his lip twitched. If he was about to confront Envy she didn't appear the slightest bit concerned. She stood tall with both hands on her hips staring back at Storey and I couldn't help thinking that she didn't need a Sherman tank or a room full of Marines.

"She isn't?" he whispered.

Envy shook her head politely.

"So, so who is she?"

Envy held out the newspaper and explained; "Her name's April Dawes and she died in a fire here in Scarborough just over a month ago."

I watched Storey as his eyes scanned the newspaper, his lips mouthing the words, but his tongue silent. I glanced across at Envy.

"It was an accident," she explained. "A gas explosion in a flat she was renting. Nobody else was involved."

Storey lowered the paper and stared out across the room. He appeared lost, like someone who should have been told yesterday that they only had twenty-four hours to live.

"This isn't right," he said, quietly.

Storey was instinctively following the natural reaction to bad news.

"Are you sure this is her?" he asked, waving the paper at Envy.

"There was a police investigation for God's sake!"

Storey tapped his temple with a finger until the tapping became a hammering. It seemed to trigger the rest of his body into slight convulsions. Most of the blood circulating his large frame suddenly appeared hell bent on taking a fast trip up to his head, as his face turned red, either from rage or embarrassment. For a moment I thought he was going to explode, and how was I going to explain that to Barbara; *yeah, here's an empty coffee cup. Oh and by the way, there are bits of Storey all over the wall.*

He dropped the paper onto the desk and pointed a finger at me. "I came to you in confidence," he groaned.

"I needed some help that's all," I argued. "I thought you wanted her finding and quickly."

He stared at me for a moment. I hoped he would believe that I was being sincere and not that I wasn't particularly good at my job. But his eyes were cold, not sad, just cold.

He cradled his forehead. "Something's not right here."

"What do you mean?" I asked.

"This isn't April," he said, tapping a finger into the headline.

"But....." I tried to argue.

He raised the same finger back at me. "Are you going to find her?"

"With all due respect Storey, that won't be too hard, all we have to do is find where she's buried!"

"This isn't April I'm telling you!" His finger drilled into the headline as the perspiration gathered on his brow.

"As I said, there was a police investigation." Envy snapped as she prowled up behind him.

But Storey didn't appear interested in anything she had to say.

He gritted his teeth. "Something's not right here, Mahoney,"

"What's not right, exactly?" I asked

He looked at me without saying a word but his troubled expression bothered me. If I had been a betting man, I'd have put my shirt on him slumping into a seat and telling us what was really on his mind. What else could he do?

"If it's money you're after," he said, reaching into a pocket and pulling out a roll of notes.

I waved my hand at him. "What do you want me to do, dig up her grave?"

Storey reluctantly returned the money to his pocket and continued to stare back at me. I wanted to offer him a handkerchief so that he could wipe the sweat from his head. He turned to leave. "If you won't look for her, then I'll find somebody who will."

He opened the door and looked at the two of us in turn.

"And when I find her," he continued, wagging a finger up at the ceiling, "I'll make sure that the two of you never work again."

* * *

The two of us watched in silence as our client stormed out of the office, leaving Envy perplexed and me shirtless.

The fog horn sounded as the door slammed. The dust in the office took time to settle. For a moment everything was silent. I looked across at Envy. She could sense I had something to say.

"What?" she asked.

"I was just thinking, how that won't be too difficult."

"What?" she asked.

"Him, making sure we never work again!"

"He scares me," Envy said, casting a look back towards the door as if to check Storey hadn't crept back inside. "There's something not right about him."

I went to the sink and filled a mug with water and fed it to my plant.

"The girl's dead!" she continued.

"I know, you said."

"So why does he want us to keeping looking for her?"

I watched the water slowly seep into the earth. It left a shiny wet surface but I wasn't really sure what difference it made, because I wasn't really sure what to expect. Was my plant suddenly about to grow a foot or turn a different colour? Something, anything, would have been nice, some kind of response to show that I wasn't wasting all this water.

"Do you know anything about plants?" I asked.

"What?"

"Plants." I said, pointing at my, not so, prized exhibition.

Envy shook her head.

"Pity."

"Are you mad at me?" she asked.

"Why would I be mad?"

"For losing the case."

I took the mug back to the sink and hovered over the desk like a bee on heat in the middle of the summer. But I didn't sit down. There was something else I wanted to do, trouble was, I couldn't think what it was.

"You didn't exactly lose it did you."

"I know but, you know." She sighed.

"Maybe we could have been a little more discrete."

"What do you mean?"

"Well, for a start Storey had no idea I was sharing the case with you, and then we hit him with fact that the girl he's been looking for isn't his daughter and that she died in a fire sometime ago. Stoning him to death might have been more preferable."

"Do you think he's going to be all right?"

I shrugged my shoulders. "I'm not sure what is 'all right' in his case."

And then I realized what it was I wanted to do. I reached for my coat.

"So what are you going to do now?" Envy asked.

"What I do best in these situations," I said, looking back at her and slipping on my coat. "Have a drink."

Chapter Twenty-eight

Envy also decided to do what she did best in these situations. She worked out and I pitied the weights.

I went to the pub, a place on North Marine Road and somewhere I'd familiarised myself with. Somewhere I felt comfortable drinking alone. It was small and snug, with wooden floors and bare walls, a place that spent its money on decent beer and not fancy furniture. The customers were mixed, a cross section of students, office workers, shop-keepers and domestics. Everybody was served by a landlord who kept a smile on his face no matter what time of the day it was.

A small black man sat still at a piano in the fire place. There was never any sound and the customers seemed to like it that way.

I sat on a wonky stool at a wonky wooden table and stared out across the room.

The beer was as perfect as ever, and by that I mean it was chilled and not too expensive. I could have happily spent the rest of my life sitting here, if only I could talk the Landlord into including Bed and Breakfast on a never-ending tab.

I sat thinking about Storey while the man in the mirror frowned back at me.

I took the photograph of April out of my pocket and placed it on the table next to my drink. Try as I might, I couldn't stop asking myself why Storey had been carrying a picture of a young girl around in his pocket and asking someone to find her, if he wasn't the father.

I also wondered if I'd see Envy again. Without a case there didn't seem any reason to meet up with her, apart from the fact that she was good to have around, especially if I needed my furniture moving. There were even times when I found her attractive. That's what happens when you drink alone in a bar.

The man in the mirror smiled.

* * *

Five minutes later a shadow stretched over my table and didn't go away. I looked up to see Hartless peering down at me.

"Of all the bars........." I mumbled.

"You,... you're a h...., a hard man to find, Mr Mahoney."

"Obviously not hard enough!"

He pointed a finger at my glass. "Would,... would you like another?"

It was tempting. I never liked to refuse a drink, especially when somebody else was buying. Unfortunately there were two reasons why I had to say no, firstly I had a job to go to and, secondly, Hartless was offering.

"No thanks."

Hartless disappeared to the bar and I wondered if that would be the last I'd see of him. I had nothing to say and I wasn't in the mood for polite conversation. I'd just lost a case. I drank some more beer. Hartless reappeared chewing his inside lip. He sat down. I tried not to look like it bothered me.

"If you're going to bug me about that crash, you're wasting your time," I groaned. "I don't know anymore than I did yesterday, and that was nothing at all."

"N..., no, I'm not," Hartless replied. "We're still waiting on the police report, we,... we'll take it from there."

I was shocked. Perhaps we were heading for polite conversation after all.

"So what do you want?" I asked.

"A,... a young man by the name of Ricks, I believe you know him."

"I've seen him, I don't know him,"

"You told him he had to ask me w...why you wouldn't help him with his article."

"And what did you tell him?"

"Well, to be honest Mr Mahoney, I.., I haven't got a clue."

I put down my drink.

"Well how about you start with the night you asked me to meet you down at the harbour because you had something important to tell me, but when I got there you were nowhere to be found. I hunted high and low until I eventually found, who I thought was you, playing dead on a conveyor belt with a ton of dead fish?"

"Th..that was a dummy!" Hartless protested.

"Well I'm sorry if I couldn't tell the difference!"

Hartless's expression folded into a hurt look. Not that I minded. He drank some of his drink then wiped his lips.

"I still don't understand w...what any of that has to do with Ricks!"

"It's simple. You came to me for help. Hell, you followed me all over town for two days before coming up with this cock and bull story about Elliott committing suicide, only you didn't think he could have because you knew him so well. So you made me think it was us against the world, when all the time in you were in with the cops right from the very start. You must all think I'm some kind of mug."

Hartless cut me a glance. "Is the, that what you think?"

"You want to tell me differently?"

"Would you listen if I did?"

I picked up my glass but it was empty. I'd worked myself into a frenzy. That's what reporters do. I needed another drink.

"I need another drink."

Hartless sat at the table and tore into his lip while I went to the bar. The Landlord was busy with a couple of customers. But I didn't mind. It gave me the chance to calm down. I ordered another pint and a whisky chaser. I downed the chaser. It shook my head like a rattlesnake.

I took a deep breath and went back to the table. Hartless tipped back his hat just enough to wipe his brow with a finger. We shot each other the odd, not very welcoming, glance, until Hartless leaned over the table and said quietly;

"I w... was on my way down to the harbour that night, just as we'd arranged, but I was pulled over by the police. T.., they told me that Superintendent Matthews wanted to see me. I went to the station and the, that was the first I knew of anything. Matthews told me that things had got out of hand and that my life could be in danger. The, they wanted to protect me and keep an eye on you."

"So that was it, you went and hid?"

Hartless raised his hands and then his voice. "I didn't have any choice! They placed me in protection. I lived in a cottage in Robin Hoods Bay for three days living off pizza and coffee and sharing a room with somebody I'd never even met before. I wasn't allowed to make any calls, not even to work and I..., I don't even like pizza!"

I stood up and buried my hands into my trouser pockets. I don't know why, but being on my feet and taking a deep breath, might help me think a bit clearer. I was wrong.

"I, I didn't like what was going on any more than you did Mr Mahoney."

I looked out across the room and gulped my beer.

"I thought you knew what was going on," he continued.

I sat back down. My thoughts were still playing catch-up.

"D...didn't the police tell you?" he asked.

I shrugged my shoulders.

"I can't believe Inspector Walker didn't say anything."

A memory slipped into view, something about Walker trying to tell me something, but I didn't want to listen. The picture was very dark, black almost. Walker talked and I drank whisky, because I didn't want to know.

"I seem to recall he tried to explain something," I mumbled. "But I wasn't really listening, I didn't really care."

"Bu, but you did such a great job."

"So everybody keeps telling me," I moaned.

"S, so what is the problem?"

"You mean apart from the lies?"

Hartless chewed his lip and stared back at me.

"Apart from the lies, it's the people you think you know," I explained. "The people you think you're helping. When you don't know who to trust anymore, then what else is there?"

Hartless looked down at his drink.

"L...like I said, Mr Mahoney, there, there wasn't a lot I

could do, I was as much in the dark as you, were."

I nodded. "So they used the both of us!"

"It would appear so."

I tried to wonder how that made me feel. Was it that I could share the burden now or did it make me feel worse that somebody else had been involved?

I looked at Hartless. "Well, then I'm sorry for snapping at you the way I did," I confessed.

Hartless offered me a very curious expression. "I'm sorry?"

"You know, the way I spoke to you the other day, it wasn't nice."

The reporter smiled. "Bu, but that's how you always speak to me!"

"No it isn't!" I frowned.

But Hartless just stared back at me while I tried to recall the various conversations we'd had. It was like that moment when a film catches you out in the final scene. You quickly piece together each scenario in your mind because you're sure they must have made a mistake somewhere along the line. But all I could remember was Hartless finishing off my ice-cream and lying dead on a conveyor belt.

I'd misjudged him, simply by what he did for a living, and not for what he was as a person. Sometimes there's a difference, and, even if there wasn't, it's probably worth finding out first, before releasing the slings and arrows.

I said. "I'm still not sure I can do anything for Ricks."

"Actually, by the sounds of it, I think it's more like what he can do for you."

Bugger! There was the bait again.

"Such as?"

"W.... why don't you ring him and f...find out?"

Chapter Twenty-nine

I took a shower, dipped my face into a sink full of cold water and filled my stomach with coffee. I was tired and not in the mood to follow Preacher all night. Something had to happen, something that would keep me from falling asleep at the wheel.

Just as I was about to leave, my jacket started to make that buzzing sound again. I pulled out the mobile.

"Hello."

"Mahoney?"

"Yeah."

"It's Walker. Where are you?"

God, he's checking up on me.

"Just on my way to Preacher's place. Why?"

"I need to see you."

"When?"

"Now?"

Chapter Thirty

"I'm here to see Walker." I said to a policeman who stood guarding the entrance to Paradise Alley and trying his best not to freeze to death.

"Walker?" he repeated.

"Yeah, Inspector Walker."

The policeman ducked his head into his jacket collar and asked for Inspector Walker. A muffled voice asked; "Is it Mahoney?" I nodded at the policeman. "Yes sir," he replied.

"Let him through," The voice said.

"You wouldn't happen to have a tall blonde hiding down there as well would you?" I asked.

* * *

The concrete archway that guided people down along the footpath was shrouded in overgrown bushes and weeds. It looked like a scene from an Edgar Allen Poe novel.

Fog drifted up the narrow walkway hugging the trees, clutching the archway and choking what was left of the warm air. All that was missing was a raven and the echo of thunder.

The damp grey walls of the veranda were stained with graffiti. 'Steed wuz here.' Apparently so, but why? Who cares? So what? And wouldn't you rather be somewhere else?

I headed down into the fog as a voice called out from the shadows. A deep voice with just a hint of an Irish accent.

"Yer always sticking yer nose in!" the voice yelled.

I quickened my pace.

* * *

A blue flashing light from a parked ambulance momentarily disturbed the fog and blinked across a small area that had been cordoned off with special tape. Beyond that, uniforms diligently searched the undergrowth. Ten minutes ago they were probably wondering what to have for tea, now they were crawling around on their hands and knees in mud.

Walker was surveying the scene and talking to a couple of important looking people. One of them was Superintendent Matthews. The Inspector appeared anxious. He saw me approach and pointed a finger into the air. I waited.

A stretcher was lifted into the ambulance. I glanced up at the giant bridge supports as far as the fog would allow.

Walker stepped over the tape and walked towards me. He tipped his head in one direction so that I would follow him.

He stopped a few yards from the scene and looked at me. He was still anxious. He tucked his hands into his trouser pockets.

"What's the matter?" I asked.

The ambulance pulled away.

Walker let out a sigh and a cloud of cold air rose up from his lips. "Look, I'm not checking up on you or anything Mahoney, but, I need to ask you something."

The Inspector sounded hesitant and that wasn't like him.

"What?" I asked.

"Were you following Preacher last night?"

"Last night?" I stalled.

Walker looked at me and nodded.

"Yes." I lied, and inwardly wondered how convincing I sounded. "Why?"

"Have you spoken to him at all?"

"A little, yeah."

"But he doesn't know you're following him?"

"I told him I was looking for April, that seemed a good enough reason to spend all night in his club drinking his whisky."

The Inspector let out another sigh and turned to view the scene behind us.

"Why all the questions?" I asked.

"The body we just found, it looks like he'd been following Preacher."

"Following him?"

Walker nodded, just as one of the men he'd been talking to called out to the Inspector. Walker waved back at him and looked at me.

"The thing is Mahoney, and don't take this personally, but you don't need to follow Preacher anymore. The police are going to be crawling all over him now. It's what the Superintendent wants."

I stood there not knowing how not to take what he had just told me personally.

"You think Preacher killed him?" I asked.

"I don't know." Walker spoke like somebody tired and badly drawn.

"What happened?"

"Inspector!" the voice called out impatiently again.

"Look, I'm sorry, Mahoney, I've got to go. I'll try and speak to you later, OK."

I didn't nod because it wasn't OK. I'd just been fired. If only I'd been doing my job properly I might have been able to defend myself.

I watched Walker return to the group of uniforms searching the undergrowth and suddenly I felt cold. I'd lost two cases in one day, that had to be a record. Maybe I should apply for a job in Lost Luggage.

I wasn't happy at all. I'd also lied about following Preacher and now somebody was dead. How soon was that going to come back to haunt me?

* * *

I went back to my car. The cop at the entrance informed me that it was 6.50pm. I could have gone back to the office but what for? I could have gone for a drink but why? I no longer had a case to work on. All I had left were the pages of a novel I was struggling to complete.

I sat in my car and stared out of the window. Why was fate always hiding down a dark alley ready to slap me round the face, and just when I thought I had things all worked out?

I turned on the engine and finally decided that it was time to look up some old acquaintances, those other perspiring pen pushers. I needed a pick-me-up.

I headed for the library.

Chapter Thirty-one

The books in the main hall groaned as I made my way upstairs. If this had been a nightmare they would have slipped from the shelves one by one and pursued me relentlessly through the cold stone hallway. An eerie chant would have echoed all around asking why I wanted to waste my time working on new material when there were so many wonderful pages left unread downstairs?

* * *

Everybody glanced in my direction as I tapped on the door and made my way inside. I expected to recognise a few familiar faces, Ms 'I'm a fluffy bunny' Simms, the humming Aussie, Gerald with his head still buried in the tool shed and Trish. I mean, where else were they going to go?

But sitting in Ms Simm's chair was a man with a cheery smile and bright red face. He wore a pair of small silver rimmed glasses and a roller neck sweater that sported a logo of some kind.

"Arh!" He exclaimed, like someone falling from a bridge, "another budding author I presume, good to see you, good to see you!"

He held out his hand as though he was about to commence the Sand Dance and pointed to a chair.

There was no sign of Gerald or the Aussie. I recognized one of the men but I couldn't remember his name. He'd never read out any of his stuff and he never went to the pub. I just thought he was lonely and this was as good a place as any to come and pass the time away.

More importantly Trish was there. She'd cut her hair but that was the only obvious change. She still looked dangerously gorgeous. I sat down opposite her and waited for her to offer me the faintest of smiles.

The tutor opened a file in front of him and asked if he could take my name.

"Richard," I replied, without thinking.

Trish frowned and I realised what I had said. But it was too late to go back now. How could I admit to a bunch of strangers that I'd got my name wrong?

"Mahoney." I added.

The tutor marked it down in pen and concluded by slipping a red tick in the box next to it.

"Marvellous," he said, rubbing his hands together. "Now, my name is Mr Robinson but you can call me, Mr Robinson!"

He laughed out loud as did everybody else.

"Seriously though," he said, "You can call me Paul and, as I was telling the others, I've recently had my first novel published, it's a profile of new wave band in the seventies, early eighties and their political influence on society. I've also written a couple of scripts for television."

The fact that Paul had put pen to paper would have been enough to elevate him to the status of Superstar in this room. But knowing that he'd actually had a book published and worked on television scripts had him sitting next to God.

He thought it was a good idea to have everybody else introduce themselves to me and mention what they'd been working on.

Most of them were setting out for the first time. They all had the right words they just needed to put them in the right order. Some, including the bloke I couldn't recall, hadn't written anything. The exception was a woman called Georgia, she was three quarters of the way through her first novel. She was very clear about the plot and the characters. She even made up diaries for them, this was important to her, it made the characters feel real. I wanted to argue that, if they were real then not all of them would have had a diary. And even if they did, some would forget to write in it.

But I didn't say anything because I'd already placed her in my 'didn't like' box.

Mr Robinson was infectious. He had charm and energy in abundance. He asked if I would say a few words about myself. It may not have seemed like a lot to him but it was quite a challenge for me.

"Well, I'm actually a, Private Investigator, working here in Scarborough," I began, and that seemed to grab everybody's attention. "And I thought it might be a good idea to write about some of the things I've been involved in."

"Marvellous, marvellous," Mr Robinson chipped in.

The group continued to stare across at me, anxiously waiting to feed on my next word. But that was it.

"And that's it," I said.

"Well that's marvellous." Mr Robinson concluded with a clap of his hands. "Now, I believe Dorothy was about to kick us off."

Everybody turned to view Dorothy. She sat twiddling

a pencil between her fingers. Her father had recently passed away. Someone had suggested that a good way of dealing with the loss was to write about it. Luckily she hadn't asked me. I'd have just told her to drink a lot of whisky, it would have had much the same effect. Drink stirs emotions, helps you pour your heart out to a stranger and then you get a headache. It's dearer than a pencil but at least you don't hold out thinking it'll change your life for the better.

The circle moved at a pace. Mr Robinson had everybody involved, even the guy who never spoke, which was good because it helped to know what was going on inside that head of his.

And then he called it a night. Everybody looked at one another and generally agreed how productive the whole evening had been. Trish was slow to put away her stuff. I hoped it was a deliberate attempt to allow me the time to move next to her.

"Hi." I said.

She looked back at me. She didn't smile but, then again, she didn't frown either.

"Are you going to the pub?"

She waited as Mr Robinson made his way across the room and forced me to promise that I'd be back next week. I nodded. What the hell else was I going to do?

Trish looked at me. She was gorgeous. "What are you doing here?"

I wasn't brave enough to say, 'Because I wanted to see you'. I was never sure if a woman would take something like that as a compliment or a reason to call the police.

"I don't know," I mumbled. "I guess it's just nice to have somewhere to come and talk about your work."

There was a moments silence.

"So, are you going to the pub?"

Trish shook her head.

"I've got to go home," she said.

"Got to? Do you have a curfew or something?"

She picked up her bag and said, "Kind of."

I quickly followed her to the door. "I'll walk you home."

"I live in Ayton."

She studied the blank expression on my face and realised that, living in Ayton, meant absolutely nothing to me.

"It's four miles away." She added.

"I'll pack some lunch."

She checked a smile, it was better than telling me to go to hell.

"I've got a car."

"Great. I'll walk you to your car then."

* * *

The walk only took five minutes. At first all we managed was small talk, but by that, I don't mean we restricted ourselves to words consisting of just one syllable. We discussed the weather, Scarborough at this time of year and the high cost of living.

Her car was a creamy coloured, two door thing that you'd have trouble squeezing a family into.

"Thanks for walking me safely to my car!" she said with a hint of a smile. The kind of smile that made my hormones dance.

"So who lives in Ayton?" I asked.

"Lots of people."

"And do any of them come looking for you if you're late home?"

"I'm a big girl now!"

"So I've noticed, but would anyone worry if you were late home?"

"And why would I be late home?"

185

"Oh I don't know. What if someone was to ask you out for a drink?"

"I'd have to say, thanks, but I've got an early start in the morning."

"What do you do?"

Trish looked at me for a moment. "You ask a lot of questions!"

"I didn't think they were particularly difficult ones!"

She opened the door and dropped her file onto the back seat.

"I work at a Nursery on Manor Road."

"But you don't mean plants and trees do you?"

She shook her head. "No, I mean children."

"Oh." I mumbled.

"Oh? What does, oh mean?"

"Nothing, just, oh."

"You don't like children?"

"Let's just say we don't really get on, they're too loud and you can't take them back when they leak."

"What a strange perspective you have on life."

I nodded in the assumption that she was paying me a compliment.

"So how about another time?" I blurted out of nowhere. "For that drink I mean?"

"Why?" she asked.

"Because I'd like to see you again!"

"Are you asking me out on a date?"

I looked back at her without answering because suddenly I felt like someone else, someone who shouldn't have been here talking the way I was. My stomach churned, my heart stammered and my hormones no longer danced.

I forced a quick nod and her confidence increased. Her eyes smiled but her lips didn't move.

"And who'll be accompanying me on this date," she asked, stepping up close to me. "Tony Blake the would-be writer or Richard Mahoney, the would-be Private Investigator?"

I stared at her for a moment. My face reddened. A million thoughts passed through my head but none of them stopped long enough to make any sense.

"Forget I asked." I said, and hurried away.

* * *

I found myself half an hour later straining against a north easterly as I looked out over the bay. I was thinking of Trish and how I didn't like the way she made me feel. Apart from her name, where she lived, that she liked to write and how my hip pocket moved every time she smiled at me, I didn't know the first thing about her. I had no idea what music she enjoyed, if she was single, married or divorced, what food she liked and where she went on holiday. The kind of questions that came so naturally to most people, but not me.

Maybe I liked her for what she was and who she is.

But the thought that scared me most of all was, how I'd never felt this way about anybody, ever before.

Chapter Thirty-two

Getting out of bed was never easy. But it was even harder when I didn't have anything to get out of bed for. I was also troubled by the fact that I'd lied to somebody, somebody I respected, liked, and who had put their trust in me.

I'd let Walker down. And, no matter what angle I tried to look at things, I couldn't come up with a decent enough excuse as to why. That wasn't good.

My conscience had me showered, dressed and halfway to the police station before I'd wiped the sleep from my eyes.

* * *

Unfortunately Walker wasn't there. He was fighting the flab at the gym. I got there ten minutes later, but it wasn't much of a fight. Walker was peddling like fury on a bicycle and getting absolutely nowhere. I walked over to him.

He looked at me with a bucket load of sweat trickling from his shovel like facial features. "Come for a workout?"

"Is that what it is?"

"It'll do you good!"

"If that's looking good I'll stay the way I am!"

Walker glanced away with a look of contempt.

"I need a word." I said.

"That sounds ominous!"

"I can come back if you like?"

Walker slowed his pace and shook his head. "No. It's all right," he panted. "I need to speak to you anyway."

"That sounds ominous!"

Walker nodded. "So what's on your mind?"

"How come you were asking if I'd been following Preacher last night when you'd only just found the body?"

"It had only just been reported an hour or so before."

"It had been laying there all that time?"

Walker shrugged his shoulders as though it was no big deal.

"It's hardly surprising given the number of dropouts lying around there. It's just that this one started to smell a little more than the rest."

Walker slowed his reps even more. "Why?"

I hesitated because I was still wondering what the consequences might be of telling the truth and, if lying would be a burden to anyone, or anything, other than my conscience.

"Mahoney!"

I looked at Walker. "When I said I'd been following Preacher all night, I'd lied."

The look on Walker's face wasn't the kind of picture I'd want to paint too often.

"I had to see Storey," I hurriedly explained. "But I was only there for a few minutes, give or take an hour."

I knew I was in trouble the moment Walker stopped peddling. He towelled his forehead and turned in the saddle so that he could frown at me full on.

"Storey?" he asked.

"Yeah, the guy looking for his daughter."

"I thought Envy was dealing with that?"

"She is! She was. But Storey didn't know that. It's a long story but he'd hired me, so we just wanted to keep things simple until, or if, we come up with something. And then we did, or rather Envy did."

Walker squared me a glance. "She found the girl?"

I nodded.

"Well that's good."

"Not exactly," I replied. "She's dead. She'd died in a fire."

"And how did your client take that?"

"Well, for some reason he insisted it couldn't have been April. He went a bit manic to tell you the truth. Anyway, we're not working for him anymore. I told you it was a long story. The point is, I just wanted you to know I'd lied, about following Preacher. As soon as I left Storey I went to the club but Preacher wasn't there,"

Walker raised his eyebrows.

"He was at the Casino," I quickly explained. "And he didn't look like he'd just killed anybody!"

The Inspector sat in quiet contemplation for a moment as if trying to decide whether or not to throw me to the lions. I couldn't remember the last time I'd felt so uncomfortable, until I recalled the moment in the office with Envy and Storey. As things turned out I was making quite a habit of it.

"Sorry," I said.

Walker reached for a bottle of water and gulped most of it down in one.

"Are you angry?" I asked.

"It just makes things a little harder that's all."

"In what way?"

"If you'd been following Preacher we could have ruled him out of the equation."

Nice! Not only did I feel bad about letting Walker down but Preacher as well. I should have gone straight home and stuck my head in the oven. Only I didn't have one.

I ran a hand across my forehead and moaned; "I can't believe this has happened, I only took an hour out, nothing happened any other time. I can't believe he could have killed someone."

"Nobody's saying he did. Like I said, I was just hoping we could have ruled him out that's all. You know me Mahoney, I don't assume anything.

I nodded at the Inspector. At least we agreed on something. We liked to keep an open mind. It's my excuse for not having a clue as to what is going on. I mean, a character in a book called Tom Diddit, dressed in bloodstained clothes and carrying a smoking gun around in his pocket, would still leave me wondering.

"So what was it you wanted to talk to me about?" I asked.

At that point two men jumped on the bikes next to Walker. They were both wearing headphones so it's unlikely they could have heard or were even bothered by anything we had to say. Even so, Walker decided to move to a quieter part of the gym.

We sat in a couple of chairs and Walker drank his water.

"I want you to do something for me Mahoney," he said

"What?"

"I want you to keep your eye on Preacher."

"But you said, ..."

Walker held up a hand and cut me short.

"What I said was, The Super doesn't want you following

him, that's been taken care of, it's out of my hands."

"I don't understand."

"The body we found."

I nodded.

"He was an ex-policeman, doing something independently. I had no idea about it."

"That must make you feel good!"

Walker looked at me and then glanced around the room as though he was about to reveal the secret of life, and he didn't want anybody in ear shot dressed in a dark suit and smoking a cigarette, the kind of people who only seem to store any useful store in large vaults marked 'confidential'.

"Anyway, they've taken me off the case and I don't like that, I don't like having my hands tied. There's been a murder on my patch and I'm not supposed to do anything about it? I don't think so!"

"So?"

"So, I'd like your help."

"Well in the circumstances I guess I owe you!"

Walker let out a faint smile.

"So what do you want me to do?"

"You've got to know Preacher pretty well."

I nodded.

"Well let him feel that he can trust you, tell him that the police might be on to him, that they've made him their number one suspect."

"Am I supposed to be setting him up?"

Walker shook is head. "Just keeping your eye on him that's all so that, if and when something else happens, you'll be close at hand!"

Chapter Thirty-three

I went back to the office. It felt good to be needed again. At least it stopped me from replacing Ronnie Elliott's name with the letters M.U.G. on the door.

I watered my plant and considered working on the conclusion to my book. I had an hour to spare and, going to the Writer's Circle, was supposed to have inspired me. But all I could think of was Trish.

Bloody women!

The phone rang. It was Storey.

"Mr Mahoney?"

"Yeah!"

"I need to speak to you."

"I'm listening."

"No. Not over the phone. I, I need to speak to you in person. Can you come over? It's really important."

It always is, I thought to myself.

"Where are you?" I eventually asked.

"The Delmont Hotel. Room 44."

I paused to consider if I really wanted to meet Storey again, but then, what the hell!

"Give me half an hour," I said.

"OK. Oh, and one more thing, Mr Mahoney,"

"What?"

"Please come alone."

* * *

I didn't particularly like the idea of seeing Storey, especially alone. There was something about him that unnerved me.

I stood outside the office for a moment trying to think of a reason to avoid him. But when I couldn't think of one I started to unlock the car door. Just as I did, two men approached me from across the street. They were dressed casually in jeans and jackets and they were wearing mean faces.

"Mr Mahoney?"

"Who wants to know?"

The shorter of the two, and not by much, reached into his top pocket and pulled out a small leather wallet. He flipped it open. It looked like something he did a lot. A police badge shone back at me.

"My name's Sergeant Warne and this is Sergeant Lucas." He said.

Warne was smart looking and purposeful. Lucas, on the other hand, stood like a reject from the Flintstones. All brawn and no razor. He was too busy glancing up and down the street to even bother taking out his badge. He didn't so much as nod at me.

"We were wondering if you had a minute."

"That's about all I've got!"

"Would you take a look at this please?"

Warne tucked away his badge and pulled out a piece of paper.

"Have you seen this girl before?"

It was a photograph. I didn't have to study it closely.

"Her name's Alana Rubos," Warne went on. "She worked at the Mission Club."

Now there was a time when, if a cop came asking about someone you told them what you knew, simply because they were the good guys, and the people they were after weren't so good. But they were the good old days. The unshaven guy dressed in black at one end of the street was going to get one in the belly every time from the clean cut guy dressed all in white. That's how it was. Plain and simple.

But not anymore. Things, and especially people, were not so clear cut. Nowadays it was best to make up your own mind.

But I said 'yes' because I wasn't telling them anything they didn't know already.

"When?"

"The other night at the club. I bought a drink off her."

"Anything else?"

"No, just a drink."

"No, I mean, did you talk about anything else?"

I shook my head. "She was too busy."

"Well thanks anyway."

They started to leave.

"How come you're asking? Is she in some kind of trouble?"

For some reason, my concern gave Lucas a queue to step up to my face and smell my breath. "What makes you think she's in trouble?"

"Don't get hysterical. I was only asking!"

He carried charm by the bucket load. Trouble was, he'd left his bucket at the station.

He pointed a finger at me and growled. "Aren't you a bit long in the tooth to be strutting your stuff in a nightclub?"

"And didn't you know it's rude to point?"

Lucas looked at his finger almost apologetically and rushed his hand back into his trouser pocket.

"Besides," I continued. "I was only there because I was working for your boss."

"Our boss?" Warne asked.

"Inspector Walker."

Lucas practically scoffed at the name as Warne bundled him to one side and handed him a set of keys

"Why don't you put your feet up in the car and give your brains a rest?" He said to Lucas.

Lucas scoffed one last time before shuffling back across the street and into an unmarked car.

Warne offered me a smile. "I'm sorry about him. He's had a bad day."

"So about the girl?"

"We were just checking up that's all. There's been reports of illegal immigrants working in the pubs and clubs. Miss Rubos was on our list. Trouble is, we haven't got a lot to go on and nobody's seen her in a couple of days now."

I nodded. "So how come you're asking me?"

"I don't understand."

"There were at least two hundred people there that night, so why me?"

Warne shrugged his shoulders. "You were seen talking to her that's all."

I nodded again.

"Well thanks anyway."

Warne followed Lucas into the car. I watched them drive away.

It took a lot to grab the attention of a cop. Not even a beating or a robbery was usually enough to prise them away from their desks. Now I had them greeting me in the street and for nothing more than a girl who'd found a job behind a bar.

But what got me most of all was the change in their attitude the moment I mentioned Walker. Warne couldn't have been nicer if he'd started handing out Christmas presents. It was as though he didn't want to cause any trouble.

That had to be worth mentioning the next time I graced the Inspector's presence.

Chapter Thirty-four

I knocked on the door of room number 44. A moment later a voice said.

"Who is it?"

"Mahoney."

The door inched open and an inquisitive eye peered out at me.

"Are you alone?"

"It's how I work best." I said

The eye continued to peer out at me and not a lot else happened. I started to feel uncomfortable like a mouse caught in a rat-trap.

"Are you going to let me in or am I going to stand talking to the door all night?"

Storey retreated and left the door open. I followed him inside. It was like walking into a cave. The curtains were drawn and the lights were operating on dim. There was a tray with an empty plate and an empty dish lying next to the unmade bed. Thankfully a window was open; it helped keep the place from going stale. The television was on but the volume was down.

I turned to look at Storey. He was pressed up against the door holding onto an expression that pained me just to view it. His hair was unbrushed and his beard untrimmed.

He started to massage his temple almost as if on queue.

"What's going on, Storey?"

Storey forced himself away from the door and held out an arm.

"Please, take a seat," he said.

I did as he asked; anything to get this over with as quickly as possible.

"You look like hell." I said.

But Storey didn't bother arguing. He sat on the edge of the bed and looked across at me.

"I wanted to say sorry about the other day," he said quietly.

"You could have done that over the phone." I frowned.

He nodded. "But I have good reason for behaving the way I did."

I crossed a leg and waited for him to explain. He stroked his beard a couple of times and looked back at me.

"I'm sorry," he apologised. "But this isn't easy."

"What isn't?" I asked, suddenly wondering what I'd invited myself into.

"Telling you what I have to tell you."

"Well, how about you start from the beginning?"

"That's just the point." he winced. "I can't."

I was fast running out of patience and Storey looked like he could sense as much. He quickly got to his feet and tried to explain.

"I have no idea who I am, Mr Mahoney."

He looked down at me as if that was that. The missing link. The final piece of the jigsaw. As if I was meant to yell out, 'well why didn't you just say so, it's all so clear now?'

But I didn't.

"Just the other day," he quietly continued. "I found myself lying up against a tree out in the middle of nowhere and I have no idea how I got there."

"I've had a few nights out like that myself!"

Storey shook his head.

"No, I mean, I have no idea about anything right up to that moment. I don't know my name, where I live, whether I'm married or not. I have no memory at all."

I watched him pause to rub his head a couple of times and immediately my sceptical personality reared its ugly head.

"So where did the name come from?"

"I saw it on the front page of the evening paper when I booked into this other hotel."

"Didn't they ask for any ID?"

"I paid in cash."

"You had nothing on you at all?"

"Just the money and the photograph."

"So how come you didn't go to the police?"

Storey looked across at me as if the idea was totally ridiculous.

"I can't." he mumbled.

"Why?" I asked, and immediately began to imagine a hundred and one reasons such as; he's a serial killer, a paedophile, a rapist, hell, the things I get caught up in!

He tapped his head with his fingers. If his temple were a keyboard he'd have made one hell of a pianist. He looked at me for a moment. It was the calm before the storm, the silence before the revelation, the moment you realise you should get out now before it's too late, but you never do. Curiosity may well have killed the cat but it also took quite a few people along with it too.

"I'm not sure but I think I may have been attacked. I mean, I was pretty beaten up. I was bleeding all over. I went to the hospital. They stitched me up."

"Didn't they want to know who you were?"

"I discharged myself during the night."

"It could have been an accident!"

"Out in the middle of nowhere and why has nobody reported me missing, my wife, my family, my friends? I've checked the paper every night, but there's been nothing."

I thought about what O'Riley had said, about the missing children having nobody who cared enough to report them missing. But he hadn't mentioned anything about a man somewhere in his forties with nobody to care for him.

"Are you OK?" I asked.

Storey, or whatever his name was, nodded gently and let out a faint laugh.

"It's funny," he said. "I mean, I don't even know what kind of a person I'm supposed to be. Am I meant to be happy or grumpy? I picked up a broadsheet today, but is that supposed to mean I'm intelligent? And then, for breakfast, I had bacon and eggs but what if I'm supposed to be a vegetarian?"

"I'm sure the pig will forgive you!"

Storey tried to smile, but not knowing who he was was probably playing on his mind. He went to his jacket pocket and picked out a mobile phone. He held it up for me to see.

"I thought this might help but there are only a couple of names on it and nobody I recognise."

He put the phone away.

"So how come you didn't tell me all this before?"

Storey stifled a laugh with the back of his hand.

"Oh come, come, Mr Mahoney. You're an intelligent man, I can see by the look in your eye that you're not completely convinced I'm telling the truth now. So a father looking for a daughter seemed far more believable don't you think? Besides, you put most of the words in my mouth when I came to your office."

I quickly thought back to the rain on the window, the kettle boiling, my gloved hands; my big mouth. And then it suddenly dawned on me.

"So where did April come from, if you've lost your memory I mean?"

"Her photograph was all I had in my pocket, that and the money-belt."

"So you could have been robbed and they just didn't know about the belt?"

"I could have been."

But, true to from, I felt a 'but' coming on.

"But?"

"There's something else."

"What?" I asked.

"I had a card, for this place, The Delmont Hotel" he said quietly. "It had the number 44 written on the back. I didn't think it meant anything till yesterday, when you told me you weren't going to look for April anymore. I booked myself in."

"And?"

Storey took a moment to walk a few paces across the room. He stopped at the phone and pressed his hand on the headset.

"There was a phone call this morning," he said, quietly. "I picked it up thinking it was Reception, but this voice, a man's voice said, 'Machin?' I don't know why but I said, 'yes' and he said 'have you got the package?' and I said, 'yes' so he said, 'be at the old Zoo and Marineland tonight at ten.' That was all. He hung up."

"But you have no idea what the package is?"

Storey waved his arms and started to laugh.

"I have no idea about anything. I don't know why I said what I said, I suppose I was just clinging to the hope that these people might know who I am."

"They also might want to throw you in the harbour if you don't turn up with the package."

Storey gazed at me through a look of fear. "But they can't kill me, I don't know anything."

"You wouldn't be the first."

Without thinking, I'd wound Storey up like a clockwork toy. He started to pace the floor again and tap his forehead. And for a moment I thought he was going to explode, literally.

"So what am I going to do?" he panicked.

I stood up and pulled on my ear.

"Nothing," I replied.

He waved his arms around frantically. "Nothing? But, you said….. "

"I know what I said. But the point is, they're expecting somebody to turn up tonight and if you don't, then they'll come looking for you, and that won't be very nice either."

Storey started across the room towards his coat. "I've got to get out of here!"

I took his arm and held him firm. "I thought you wanted answers?"

I'm not sure I'd ever seen someone so frightened.

"I do, but I don't want to die getting them!"

"You're not going to die. We're just going to talk to them, or rather I am."

Storey frowned. "You?"

"I'm guessing they don't know you from Adam, or Storey at least!"

I checked my watch. Then I asked what time it was.

"Quarter past seven. Why?"

"I'm just trying to work things out that's all."

"But what if they do know who I am?"

"Then I'll ask if you're meant to be a Veggie!"

"I'm serious!"

I shrugged my shoulders. "I'm going to have to stall them, aren't I? Maybe this way I can find out who they are and what they're up to."

Storey bowed his head and quietly confessed; "I don't like this. I don't like it at all."

"Neither do I!"

"Even if you do speak to them, then what? You still don't have what they're looking for?"

I pulled on my ear and headed for the door;

"Well hopefully by then, I'll have come up with a better plan than I've got right now."

Chapter Thirty-five

I sat in the car. Rain pelted the windscreen. I still didn't have a plan, I was just taking each minute as it came. But I had an itch, a nagging feeling that wasn't going to go away. I wanted to see Trish, I didn't like how I'd reacted the other night. How I'd, over-reacted. She was about the best thing that had happened to me in ages and, even then, nothing had happened.

* * *

I pictured bumping into her and saying sorry and her smiling and telling me it was fine. I'd invite her out for a drink and I'd wonder why I'd made such a big deal out of something so pleasant. It was that easy. All I had to do was talk to her. If only things were so easy in real life.

* * *

I turned on the engine. A young couple walked by hand in hand, they didn't seem to mind the rain and I hated them for looking so happy.

Chapter Thirty-six

I left the car outside my flat and walked the hundred yards or so to the old Zoo and Marineland. Storey couldn't have agreed to meet in a worse place.

I stood at the top of the dilapidated theatre steps and looked out across the baron waste that was once a thriving park. All that kept the place from total darkness was a moon that skipped between soft grey clouds and the intermittent beam of a lighthouse just beyond the castle. A cool wind nipped in from the sea bringing with it childhood memories of dolphins and sea lions, mini-golf, spitting lamas and pretty girls with bright smiles lighting up the popcorn stands.

The zoo was still here but it wasn't the kind of attraction you'd want to bring your children to.

The security fence had been bashed to the ground and sometime tonight druggies and drunks would congregate and litter the giant ant heaps and graffiti covered entrance towers with their syringes and cans and tough talk.

* * *

I walked a dozen or so paces and stopped. The wind shook the moon and momentarily stirred the litter and bushes. A car came up the hill and stopped. Two men got out. Two smartly dressed men. One of them carried a torch and shone it in my face.

"Where's the girl?" He asked.

I hid my face behind my hand as I stared into the light. The girl? The package. The package was the girl. Did he mean April? Why didn't I know anything?

"She's got a cold," I replied, through a squint. "I told her to stay at home. Didn't want her spreading her germs everywhere, did I?"

The two men stepped up close but the light was still blinding. It left me talking to a couple of silhouettes.

"You were supposed to bring April!" Declared the voice.

"I know."

"I presume she's safe?"

Interesting. He didn't know what I knew. He didn't know that she was dead. But was that a good thing or a bad thing?

"Yes. Yes of course she is."

"So why didn't you bring her as agreed?"

How could they not know April was dead? It had been in the papers ages ago. Not headline news I know but, hell, this is a small town and sooner or later everybody gets to know everything

Something was wrong. I had to stall for time.

"Because I didn't like the odds," I said.

"The odds? What odds?"

"The odds on me walking out of here alive."

The voice kept the light on my face. "Have you lost your mind?" The obvious answer was 'possibly' but I kept that one to myself.

"We're not the slightest bit interested in you, all we

want is the girl. That's what you're paid to do, fetch and deliver, it's your job, it's what's given you such a high reputation."

His voice was mocking now, but that didn't bother me half as much as the light in my face.

"Well maybe I don't like the idea of handing over a young girl to a bunch of, to a bunch of, whatever you ares."

The man stepped behind me and whispered. "Are you trying to bribe me, Max?"

Max? Max Machin? What a crap name. Made him sound like some comic book hero. There's no way Storey looked like a Max.

"No, I'm just trying to make sure I sleep soundly at night."

There was a crack to my kidneys and I fell to my knees.

"You're messing with the wrong people, Max."

I took a moment to recover my breath before stating; "All right, look, there's a problem."

The voice stayed close to my ear. "Problem?"

"He's lost her!" Suggested the other man.

"No! No, I haven't lost her!" I snapped. "I know exactly where she is."

"So?"

"The problem is, I can't get to her for a couple of days."

"Why? Where is she?"

"I'm hardly going to tell you that am I? You'll just put a slug in my back and walk away."

"What makes you so sure we wouldn't do that anyway?"

"Because it would take far more than two days for you to find her and I'd have thought that would be a waste of your valuable time and resources!"

There's nothing like a little flattery to get you out of a hole, I find.

The man without the torch went back to the car. I could hear him talking, but I couldn't hear what was being said, or even see who was doing the talking. At least it gave me the chance to massage my kidneys.

Thirty seconds later he made his way back over to me. I was still on my knees.

He bent down. "Looks like it's your lucky day, Machin."

"Try telling that to my kidneys!"

He gripped my hair and shone the torch into my eyes.

"You've got two days."

"Two days?"

"That's right."

"Then what?"

"We'll call you. What's your mobile number?"

"I don't know."

The man behind me quickly searched my pockets and pulled out my phone. He pressed some buttons then read out a number, it was longer than my bank account. The other man wrote it down on the back of his hand.

"Two days, Machin. And no funny stuff!"

"I don't do funny stuff." I growled.

"Good. We get the girl and you get your money!"

He helped me to my feet. I stood up slowly but not all the way. It was impossible to straighten my back.

"Are you all right?" he asked.

"What a dumb question!"

"We just want to get things right."

And I want to kill you, but that'll have to wait.

"So how did you get here?"

"I walked," I replied. "Why?"

"Good, we wouldn't want you trying to follow us."

There was a second crack to my kidneys and I fell to the

floor again. I cried in pain as a couple of doors slammed and the car pulled away.

Chapter Thirty-seven

I went straight back to the hotel. Every step was hell. My legs had only just recovered from the run and now my kidneys were ready to desert me.

It was late but I figured Storey would be tapping his temple and wearing a hole in the carpet with wonder. He opened the door as far as the chain would allow. He didn't seem happy to see me.

"Let me in Storey before I bust the door down."

He rushed the chain open and stood back. He waited at the door as if expecting a party of people to waltz inside. When he realised there was only me, he pushed it too.

I staggered across the room and leant up against the wall in the hope that it would ease my aching back.

"Are you all right?" Storey asked.

I glared back at him and didn't bother answering.

"You're name's Max Machin," I declared.

"What?"

"Exactly."

"I think I'll stick with Storey," he mumbled.

"I'm glad to hear it. Oh, and by the way, you're a delivery man."

Storey became confused. "I don't understand."

"You fetch and carry. It's a bit like working for the Post Office only people don't need stamps and you guarantee delivery, except in this case of course."

"This isn't something official is it?" he asked.

I shook my head as I slowly eased my aching limbs into a seat.

"Have you got any pain killers?"

Storey shook his head.

"How about something alcoholic and strong, or just alcoholic?"

"I could ring reception?"

I waved a hand to suggest he didn't have to bother. He sat down opposite me.

"Am I a bad man?"

"It looks like you work for some bad people. Somebody wants somebody finding, you find them, and they pay you to deliver them."

"The girl?"

I nodded. "It looks like it."

"I was putting her life in danger?"

"Yeah."

It wasn't what Storey wanted to hear. He'd gone from being a caring father to an unsympathetic mercenary in a matter of minutes. Suddenly, wondering what paper he was supposed to read, seemed the least of his worries.

"This is terrible." He moaned, tapping his temple. "How did I ever get in this situation?"

"Let's not worry about that right now," I said. "Let's worry about how we're going to get out of this mess."

"Why, what did you tell them?"

"To give me a couple of days."

Storey sprang to his feet. "A couple of days, what

difference is that going to make, the girl's dead, remember?"

"But what if she isn't?"

Storey cut short his frantic walk across the room and stared back at me.

"But it was in the paper," he argued. "There was a police report and everything."

"I know. But then people make mistakes, even the cops. Especially the cops. Besides, you said there's something not right about all this."

Storey's fingers sank deeper into his temple. "I know but, I know. If only I could remember!"

I got to my feet. I needed a drink.

Storey followed me to the door. "So, what are they going to do?"

"Ring me."

"And then what?"

I opened the door and looked back at Storey. "I don't know. I'm still working on that part of the plan."

Chapter Thirty-eight

Somehow I'd managed to get two cases, lose them both and then have them thrown back at me, all in the space of forty-eight hours. It was worse service than an airport carousel.

And, as much as I appreciated the work, I really didn't know which way to turn next. I'd gone from looking for material for a book, to getting waist deep in a whole load of trouble and without so much as a spoon to bale me out.

I needed something on April, something I could feed the lions. But that wasn't going to be easy considering she was dead.

* * *

Apart from all that, I still had a job to do for Walker. He'd thrown me a lifeline and I wasn't about to let him down. I also felt I owed Preacher. I don't know why, I just did. He didn't look like the killing type, not to me anyway.

* * *

I went to the club because that's where I expected to find Preacher. Each of the doormen greeted me with a nod as I made my way past the queue outside. It was like something out of Saturday Night Fever, without the white suit, the dancing shoes and the razor nick. But Preacher wasn't in.

"He's at some private function over at the Royal Hotel," they told me.

"Will I get in?"

"You can try."

* * *

I got through the lobby without a problem but a doorman was standing guard outside the function room and he was all ready to play the tough guy.

"Any chance I can have a word with Mr Adam Keatley?" I asked.

"Have you got an invitation?"

"Do I need an invitation just to speak to him?"

"This is a private function!"

"That's not what I asked."

We were stood nose to nose. That's how he wanted it. Maybe he liked it that way. Maybe he was just having a quiet night. But before things could get out of hand, Preacher spied me through the open door. He dropped some money into the doorman's pocket and pulled me inside.

"You seem to turn up everywhere, Mr Mahoney."

He waved a hand into the air and, as if by magic, a waitress appeared. She was tall and blonde and wearing a very small uniform. The short skirt and tight blouse made it hard to notice she was actually carrying a tray of glasses topped with champagne.

I took hold of a glass and watched the waitress slip back into the crowd.

"What's going on?" I asked

Preacher nodded towards a crowd of important looking people. "Various proposals for The Sands project, the people and the Council in particular want to know what the investors have to offer."

"And you're an investor right?"

Preacher momentarily shrugged his shoulders.

"I'm considering it, but I'm up against some big wheels."

"Such as?"

"Such as Jack O'Riley," he said, pointing a finger at the large ice-cream salesman drinking from a glass in the corner of the room. "Nick Collingwood." (Who couldn't be seen.) "And Mark Pitman." A wild haired, bearded figure with milk bottled bottom glasses, struggling to get served at the bar.

I'm sure they were all very interesting characters in their own right, but the figure that caught my attention the most, was the newly crowned Lady Mayoress. She was talking to a group of people and, unlike everybody else who looked like they'd been thrown into a room full of strangers, she appeared confident, totally at ease. Her name was Helen Fitzsimmons, somebody else from a recent past that I wasn't too excited about revisiting.

She caught my gaze and offered the faintest of smiles.

I turned to face Preacher. "Look, I need to speak to you about something,"

"Can it wait? I've just got to do a little more socia, er, bullshitting. But I'll be straight back. Enjoy your drink."

Preacher disappeared into the crowd. I started to wonder if there were any cops in disguise watching his every move.

Helen Fitzsimmons meanwhile was bending an ear to what somebody was saying, but she never took her eyes off me. I turned to view the room but all I saw was a lot of people I didn't want to talk to.

I sipped my champagne. It filled my nostrils with bubbles. It was like drinking washing up liquid. I swapped it for a beer the next time the waitress passed within arms length. Then I took a moment to study the cardboard cut-out in the middle of the room.

This was the Sands project, the multi-million pound scheme designed to rescue a dwindling seaside resort and make a few people very rich. The run down chalets were to be replaced with up to date en-suite units. The current open-air pool, that was only used twice a year, was to be replaced by an elaborate indoor leisure centre, and the giant ant hill and syringes up at the Zoo were finally going to be replaced by upmarket flats. Next to a council sign advertising that Scarborough was the place to *work, rest and play,* was the expected bill for this lavish development. It had just reached £150 million. It may well have been cheaper to buy everybody a Mars bar, but then again, I couldn't help thinking how impressive it all looked. The whole town was really buzzing.

"Quite a sight, don't you think?"

I turned to find Helen Fitzsimmons standing next to me.

"Yeah, and the project's not too bad either!"

She smiled and not very reluctantly. As ever she was dressed in money and it would have been a waste of time hanging around for the change. I couldn't help noticing her chains of office. "Nice necklace!"

She smiled. "Thank you. Weren't you even going to say hello?"

"It crossed my mind."

She tried to appear hurt. I remembered how good she was at that. "I thought we were friends?"

"And what made you think that exactly? The fact that you threw a lot of money my way? The fact that you got drunk and kissed me? Or the fact that I think you've got nice legs?"

She paused a moment to revel in the compliment. I didn't mind, because I was quietly complimenting myself at the same time. I don't think for one minute, that there was anybody else in this room who would dare talk to Helen Fitzsimmons the way I had.

The fact that she'd somehow elevated herself to Mayoress didn't bother me either.

Fitzsimmons pressed her red lips together. "I see you haven't changed in the slightest!"

"Well I wouldn't want to disappoint you now would I!" I said.

She raised a perfectly manicured eyebrow before turning to shake a couple of hands that passed nearby. It was all very polite, but totally insincere. I couldn't help thinking how refreshing it would have been for someone to say, 'so how did you get this title Helen, and were you horizontal most of the time?'

"So what are you doing here, apart from enjoying the free drink?" I asked.

Fitzsimmons glanced back at me without her cool, elegant expression for once.

"You're not going to try and slap my face again are you?" I asked.

She smiled. "That wouldn't look very good in public would it," she assumed.

"So why are you here?"

"It's my duty."

"Just like it was your duty to play dead?"

Fitzsimmons threw me a sharp look. "Is that what bothers you?"

"A lot of things bother me. That's just one of them."

A band started up on the stage. They began with a tune that everybody recognised but me. It just meant we had to raise our voices.

"I'd hate to ask what's going on in that mind of yours Mahoney."

Her dark brown eyes were challenging me and, for a second, I thought about responding. I just wasn't sure how, so it was probably as well that Preacher returned and put his arm around the pair of us.

"You two seem to be getting along?"

I looked at Fitzsimmons and allowed her to answer.

"Mr Mahoney was telling me that he's a Private Investigator, isn't that fascinating."

"Only I'm not the kind you'd normally find on television!" I quipped.

It was a reference to a conversation we'd had a while ago and to which she allowed a slight nod of her head.

"Yeah, well let me tell you, I've only known this bloke a few days but I can assure you he's pure quality."

Preacher was patting my shoulder so hard I feared losing my drink.

"If ever you need a good man, Your Ladyship," he continued. "You need look no further than him."

"I'll bear that in mind," Fitzsimmons replied, as only she could.

"Talking of being a 'good man'," I motioned to Preacher. "I need to speak to you a moment, in private."

"Oh," Preacher laughed, "don't you know that always means bad news."

"Well I'll leave you boys to it," Fitzsimmons said and slipped elegantly away to receive more compliments.

Preacher looked at me. He appeared anxious. "So what is it?"

"When you said you thought the cops, or someone at least, might have it in for you?"

Preacher nodded

"Well I think you might be right."

His eyes narrowed. "How come?"

"I don't know what was going on before but now, they think you've killed someone."

"Killed someone?" He said.

And loud enough to grab almost everybody's attention. He placed his bottle of water onto the bar and ran a hand over his tanned skull.

"Killed someone?" he questioned again, only far more quietly. "When?"

"Two nights ago."

"Wow, they're really going for me big time. I mean, I could just about handle the under aged drinking and drugs raids, but now I'm supposed to have killed somebody?"

All I could do was nod and hope this wouldn't go any further. But then he took a breath and drank some water and asked;

"So what did you tell them?"

I tried to look surprised. "I'm sorry?"

"Well you've seen me round the club most nights haven't you. I mean....," he started to laugh, "When did you see me kill anybody?"

I looked down at the floor and then back up at Preacher. He was still laughing at the suggestion, and well he might, if I'd have been doing my job.

I didn't really know how to tell him what I had to tell him, so I just told him.

"Unfortunately, on that particular night, I didn't get to the club till late."

Preacher's lip quivered but he didn't say anything.

"I had to see a client," I explained.

"And, let me guess, it was just then when I was meant to have killed this, whoever?"

I nodded.

Preacher let out a sigh so loud that almost everybody in the room turned to view. He recovered a smile and waved back at them.

"But you'll have cameras at the club right?"

I watched Preacher take a sip of water and shake his head.

"We only keep them for a couple of days, then we record over them. But If I'd have known I was ever going to be suspected of murder, I'd have kept them!"

He was turning sarcastic.

"I'm sorry," I said, weakly.

Preacher smiled again. "So why are you telling me this?"

"Because I'm not meant to."

He frowned back at me.

"There's something not quite right about it," I explained. "There's not going to be anything in the papers. This person was working undercover."

"He was a cop?" Preacher gasped.

"Ex-cop. He was following you."

"Wow. They really have got it in for me."

"Any idea who?"

Preacher stared out across the room for a moment before slowly shaking his head. But I couldn't help thinking he wouldn't have told me even if he had. I might have been a 'good man' but that didn't necessarily mean he could trust me.

Eventually he held out an arm and shook my hand.

"Thanks, Mahoney."

"For what?"

"For coming all this way to tell me."

"It was a five minute walk!"

"Even so, you didn't have to and I appreciate that."

I watched Preacher walk slowly back to the crowd. It was a calculated move that gave him just enough time to recover his smile and pretend that he was, once again, having the time of his life.

In the meantime, I stood alone, knowing full well that nobody was ever going to invite me to their party ever again.

"You boys finished with the macho talk?"

I looked up to see Helen Fitzsimmons standing close by. She was holding out a glass of champagne.

"I thought you had to wear some kind of uniform to pass those things around?"

"Is that what you'd like?" she asked.

I paused to consider Fitzsimmons in a uniform, in any uniform, and I wondered if she had the same affect on all men.

"Quick, take it," she insisted. "Before I tip it all over your head."

We stood side by side and surveyed the scene. People were politely watching the band and inwardly thanking them for the fact they no longer had to make such an effort to talk to one another.

"You seem pretty friendly with Preacher," Fitzsimmons observed.

"Is that a problem?"

"Do you question everything?"

"Isn't that my job?"

Fitzsimmons smiled.

"So what are you doing here in your official capacity?"

"The Sands project is very important to the development of this town. There are some major investors here, some genuine, some not so."

"Not so?"

"Quite."

"And what happens to the 'not so'?"

"I'll do what I can to make sure they stay at the back of the queue."

It was then I recalled how powerful Fitzsimmons was. She liked to get her own way, and it was probably better to let her have it, if you wanted a peaceful life.

I went to sip my champagne then realised how much I disliked it. Even Fitzsimmons looked to be struggling.

I nodded at her. "Would you prefer a proper drink?"

She glanced at her glass and then at me.

"Only if you promise to wear a uniform!"

I tried my damndest not to smile but it was a cute remark. I went to grab the barmaid's attention when Fitzsimmons suddenly said; "Actually I'd rather go home, I've got an early appointment,"

I felt slightly disappointed and perhaps it showed.

She widened her eyes. "Perhaps you can take me?"

"Don't you have a driver?"

"Of course I do, but I don't fancy sharing a night cap with him!"

* * *

I waited out on the street while Fitzsimmons picked up her coat and told her driver that he could go home without her. I rang Envy on my mobile. She sounded sleepy.

"Did I wake you?"

"Nearly. What's up?"

"I was just wondering what you were up to that's all?"

"Nothing much, why?"

"No new cases?"

"No."

"It's just that I might have something."

"Business?"

"Yeah, but it's always a pleasure," I replied as I saw Helen Fitzsimmons approach. "I'll call you tomorrow OK."

"OK."

"I'm not coming between anything or, anyone am I?" Fitzsimmons asked.

"Just my, my partner my, my working partner."

* * *

We started down the street. Already the town was packed with people who wouldn't recognize themselves in a mirror. Staff in the fast food outlets struggled to comprehend what customers were trying to order as they shielded their eyes from the bright neon menu and wished it came with pictures. And sometime tomorrow most would look back on the evening and recall how great a night it was.

* * *

"Do I know him?" Fitzsimmons asked.

"Who?"

"Your partner."

"Obviously not, because he's a she.

"Oh."

"What do you mean, oh?"

"Just, oh."

"Nobody ever means just, oh."

"I do."

* * *

We reached the car and I unlocked the passenger door and Fitzsimmons was wearing much the same expression as I had the first time I saw the car.

"What?" I asked, impatiently

"This is your car?"

"No, I just got lucky with the keys."

I started to unlock the door. But Fitzsimmons still looked like someone who'd got a plate of fish and chips when she knew full well she'd ordered caviar.

"Get in," I insisted. "It'll be good to see how the other half lives."

"Just as long as I don't have to peddle!"

Chapter Thirty-nine

Helen Fitzsimmons lived in what was generally described as a leafy suburb, and it probably was a while ago. But the hedgerows had been replaced by fences, trees chopped to the roots and gardens either concreted or paved and dotted with sandstone. It was all as ugly as hell. Nowhere for the rain to run and pretty soon sparrows would arm themselves with boxing gloves in an effort to defend the last leaf of sanctuary.

Fitzsimmons pointed a finger towards one of the houses and I pulled up in the driveway.

* * *

There was no butler to greet us at the door and I followed her into the lounge.

"Why don't you make us both a drink, while I slip out of this simply awful dress?"

I watched her leave the room and I looked at the dress. It didn't look that bad to me. It hugged her still narrow frame and exaggerated the sway of her hips. And somehow I couldn't imagine Helen Fitzsimmons spending valuable shopping time trying out everything that caught her eye before finally contenting herself with something 'simply awful'.

The drinks cabinet was easy to locate, it was lit up in the shape of a boat in the corner of the room. It was covered with bottles and glasses from every country you could think of. I plumped for something that had already been opened. I didn't want to be held responsible for corking a vintage bottle worth thousands just because I liked the look of the label.

From next door I could hear the sound of muffled voices as Fitzsimmons played back her answer machine. Nobody seemed to get the time to say as much as, Hi I'm.., before being fast forwarded into the future.

All of which gave me time to survey her room. The carpet was burgundy and the walls light red. It gave the room a nice warm glow and that was something I wouldn't have associated with Helen. Above the fireplace sat three framed pictures of a lighthouse caught in various stages of a storm. And these weren't the kind of photographs that had been captured by some bloke using a throw away camera while out walking his dog one Sunday afternoon. They were special.

Fitzsimmons returned to the room with a gentle sigh. It forced me to turn and view her. She liked making an entrance. She caught sight of the glass in my hand with an eager smile as she made her way across the room, hips swaying, legs showing, breasts heaving. From twenty feet away she looked like a million dollars. From two foot away, I could count every penny.

I'm sure men all over the world have paid a lot of money to see a whole lot less.

"Thank you," she said.

She took the glass and looked me in the eye, as though

I was supposed to thank her for the view.

"You like the pictures?" she asked.

I looked back at the lighthouse.

"As a matter of fact I do."

"Why?"

"Because they remind me of me."

"You?"

I nodded.

"Don't tell me you lived in a lighthouse?"

I looked back at her. "I was just thinking of all the crap that washes around you when you're a Private Investigator."

"So why do you do it?"

"Because I don't like having crap on my doorstep!"

Fitzsimmons smiled and sipped her drink.

"Come, let's sit down and have a chat," she said as she made her way towards a sofa, that she probably referred to as her chaise-long. "I do miss our little chats, don't you?"

I remained standing, the view was better.

"By little chats, do you mean, how you enticed me to follow your husband, knowing full well it wasn't him who'd been blackmailing your father and then thinking that by throwing money at me I'd always be at your beck and call?"

She tried to look hurt again. Those Bette Davis eyes were working overtime.

"You really can be rather harsh at times."

"Really?"

"Yes, really."

"I guess it comes with the job."

"Nevertheless, you seem to like it."

"The job or the being harsh bit?"

"Both."

"Yeah," I smirked. "I guess I do."

"You're still unhappy because of what happened to Hebden?"

I sipped some drink. It was sharp. It raced straight to my brain, did a tango and took a bow.

"You shouldn't be," she continued, rising to her feet and stepping towards me. "Hebden was a selfish, conniving, horrible little man who used people to get exactly what he wanted."

"Isn't that what usually makes people successful?"

Fitzsimmons gritted her pearly white teeth.

"When the police first informed me of what they thought was going on, I was very sad. Hebden and I had been friends for a long time, my father treated him like a son, but all that counted for nothing in the end. I'm just sorry his body was never found."

"I wouldn't worry about him ever surfacing again."

"Did you ever see what was in the caskets?"

I shook my head.

"I was too busy wondering if Hebden was going to shoot me before I drowned."

"It must have been awful for you!"

I looked at Fitzsimmons and tried to measure her sincerity. She was good, I knew that, I just didn't know how good.

"Actually the *awful* thing was never being told what was going on. I may be a lot of things but I'm always honest. I followed all those wild goose chases and blind alleys, only to discover the cops had set me up all along."

Fitzsimmons stopped short of taking another sip of her drink and looked up at me with a curious smile.

"Is that what they told you?" she asked.

"Is what, what they told me?"

"That they'd set it all up?"

I thought back to the night in the bar with my arm in a sling and a whisky in my hand. I was heading for a train out of Scarborough, when Walker caught up with me, and mentioned that he hadn't wanted to go along with the plan. He hadn't said anything else, but only because I hadn't allowed him to.

And when I looked back at Fitzsimmons, she wasn't exactly smiling, she was glowing.

"Well who else could it have been?" I asked.

Fitzsimmons returned to the boat with all the bottles. She was now lighting up the room and saving on enough electricity to last a week.

"No way!" I winced

"Why not?"

She brought a bottle over to where I stood, still trying to work things out, and topped up our glasses.

"Because I'm a woman?"

"Because," I snapped. "... because!"

"Superintendent Matthews and I go way back."

I watched her place the bottle on the table and look back at me. I was lost for words.

"You didn't really expect the police to be behind all that, did you?"

I didn't like the tone in her voice, it was condescending. It reminded me of the teacher at school who couldn't believe I didn't know what a certain capital or multiplication was, especially when it was so obvious to everybody else.

But, try as I might, I couldn't bring myself to say, *of course not.*

"Weren't you suspicious of the fact that only O'Neal and Walker turned up most of the time?"

I didn't answer.

"You'd just reported a murder but there was no armed police surrounding the flat."

I still didn't answer.

"Or when you found that reporter chap in the warehouse, didn't you find that the least bit curious?"

I managed a nod, but I was lying.

"I just thought that was Scarborough, everything done on the cheap!"

Fitzsimmons stepped towards me and cupped a hand around the side of my face.

"My poor little Private Investigator, I thought they'd told you."

I wanted to take hold of her fingers and squeeze that patronizing tone out of her voice. All this time I thought I'd been done by the cops.

"Is there anything else I should know?" I asked, as I brushed passed her and took another view of the lighthouse.

"Not really, no?"

"So why the elaborate set up with your ex and that girl?"

"You appeared nervous. It was as though you knew what to do, you just didn't know how to do it."

I glared at Fitzsimmons: "So you thought you could buy me!" I snapped.

She smiled. "What does it matter, the police said that you did a very good job, they couldn't have done without you, isn't that what's more important?"

"It's important to me, but what's important to you? That you found out who was blackmailing your old man or that Frank Hebden is now out of your way?"

I wasn't sure how Fitzsimmons would react but I didn't expect her to press a hand onto my shoulder and step into my face.

"I like it when you get angry," she whispered.

She reached forward to kiss me but I held her shoulders tight.

"So what is important to you?" I asked.

Her eyes danced backwards and forwards for a moment as if to test the sincerity of my question.

"That I get to turn this town around," she said, smoothly. "I'm rather fed up with it being the butt of people's jokes."

"What do you expect; it's a small English seaside resort with under-developed lodgings and overpriced food?"

"But I'm going to change all that, I'm going to raise the profile of this town starting with the Sands project. I'm also going to rid the streets of those grubby little criminals. This, is going to be the place to come again, you'll see."

She was serious.

"And I'll tell you what else is important to me."

"What?" I asked.

"That I get my own way!" she smiled.

I thought at first Fitzsimmons was going to kiss me but instead she bit my lip. It hurt like hell. I pressed the back of my hand to my lip and held it up until I could see blood. I looked at her. She started to laugh. I wanted to hit her but I've never hit a woman. I almost convinced myself that maybe there's a first time for everything but then I did the next best thing, I pulled her close and pressed my tongue deep into her mouth. We danced backwards across the room. At first we struggled to keep in step and it's probably as well that we came up against the chaise-long or we might have danced all the way to Whitby. She tore at my jacket and nearly dislocated my shoulder. It was hard to think when I'd had a worse beating that I enjoyed so much. I pulled her hair as we kissed, she laughed at the pain. She ran a hand up the back of my shirt and dug her nails deep between my shoulders blades. I could feel the skin being sucked beneath her fingernails.

My hand reached out and probed one of the legs I'd admired so much from afar. She let out a groan. I ran my hand all the way up her knee to the inside of her thigh. She chewed on my ear. Her breathing was loud as if she hadn't eaten for a week but I didn't care, not until my conscience started to fight back the testosterone. I opened my eyes and looked at her and realised, they weren't Trish's eyes. These weren't Trish's lips. She wasn't Trish.

What the hell was I doing here?

I got to my feet in a panic and pulled myself away from Fitzsimmons's flailing legs and arms.

She looked up at me, still breathing heavily, half laughing and half frowning.

She ran her fingers through her messed up hair. "What's the matter?"

All I could do was look at her and shake my head.

Suddenly she was concerned. She rose to her feet and straightened out her dress.

"Richard? What's the matter?"

"I'm sorry," I mumbled. "This isn't right."

She smiled. "But everything looks just fine from here."

She held out a hand. I pushed it away.

I inched my jacket back over my aching shoulder. "I've got to go."

"Don't tell me the big Private Investigator is still fighting his feelings?"

She was mocking me again. I turned and headed for the door. That's when she realised I was really leaving.

"Richard? Richard."

I ignored her.

"You come back here right now," she yelled. "You can't do this to me!"

I opened the door.

"Have you any idea who I am?" she screamed.

"Yeah," I replied. "And that's the problem."

I closed the door and heard the sound of glass smashing on the other side. It was a hell of a shot and one I wouldn't risk again for a long time.

Chapter Forty

I didn't sleep very well that night, but it had nothing to do with the case, or young girls turning up in the middle of the night and forcing me to sleep on the sofa. It was all about upsetting somebody as powerful as Helen Fitzsimmons. She wasn't somebody to mess with. That's what had me twisting relentlessly between the sheets, and I kept seeing her face whenever when ever I closed my eyes. And when I finally lulled myself into a deep sleep, the shattering glass turned into the sound of gunfire.

I woke up startled. Sweating. Panting.

Bloody nightmare case.

I checked my watch. Bloody watch.

Chapter Forty-one

I fixed a coffee and paced the flat and wondered how it was that drinking whisky had become far easier than picking up a pen and writing.

It wasn't meant to be that way. 'Writer's block' was supposed to be nothing more than just another avenue to explore. I expected to love the challenge of a blank piece of paper and thrill in the mass of jumbled words that would soon take on a life form of their own.

But that final chapter had become a curse. The moment never seemed right. The words hard to fathom. Something would always come up and, if it didn't, I would reach for the whisky bottle and pour another glass.

* * *

I strolled down to the foreshore. The sun had only just squeezed clear of the horizon but already life was in full swing.

Petrol fumes, freshly baked doughnuts, coffee and waffles stirred my senses. Traffic buzzed along the foreshore. Families laden with carrier bags, buckets, spades, windbreakers and lunchboxes crowded the beach and chalets.

Three canoeists paddled with clockwork precision, riding the rollercoaster of waves just behind the Regal Lady, as it headed out towards Jackson Bay.

A couple of open-top busses with bright advertisements waited patiently for passengers. One of the drivers patrolled the pavement enticing the public on board by yelling; "It's nice on top, ladies". I couldn't help thinking that sometime, in the not too distant future, I'd be reading a story about a bus driver who was sacked after thirty years service for sexist comments.

* * *

I bought a coffee and picked out a table overlooking the beach. I searched my wallet for the two business cards I'd found in Smudge's room, and placed them on the table. Then I rang Hartless.

"H... hello, Eddie Hartless s.... speaking."

"It's me, Mahoney."

"Oh h... hello."

"Ever heard of a place called," I held out the card in front of me. "Saltys?"

"Yes, yes of course, I have. Why?"

"Do I need a pass or a membership or something?"

"No. No, you just, you just pay at the door."

"What is it?"

"Just one of those clubs, you know."

"You mean a nightclub?"

"No, more of a," Hartless was being incredibly coy. "You know, one of those lap dancing kind, kind of places, I think."

"You think?"

"W .... well no, I...., I mean it is."

I was shocked.

"They have places like that here?"

Hartless got all defensive. "Oh, and I, I suppose y..., you're about to suggest that there aren't enough p...., pretty girls in Scarborough to warrant having such a place, are you?"

I tried to sound hurt. "I can't believe you'd think I'd say such a horrible thing."

The phone fell silent. Hartless was sure I'd have been chomping on the bit to make such a remark, if he hadn't have suggested it first. But he was too polite to labour the point.

"So what are you doing later?" I asked.

"I,.. I'm not sure, why?"

"I thought I might buy you a drink."

"A drink?"

"Yeah, you know, alcohol!"

"Where?"

"Saltys!"

"W...well, it's just, you know......"

"It's a long shot Eddie, but I might find a lead."

"You...you don't normally ask!"

"I know, but I thought we might go in the guise of a couple of reporters, so we can poke our noses around. Tell me you're up for it."

"I, I'm not up for it," he replied. "B... but I'll go anyway."

"Fine, I'll meet you outside at eight."

"Oh, by the way, h... have you spoken to Ricks yet?"

Ricks. No I hadn't because I hadn't had time and because I couldn't be bothered. But mainly because I couldn't be bothered.

"I was about to," I lied.

"Well he's r... right here if you, if you want to speak to him."

"No!" I yelled. "Look, tell him to meet me outside that café at the top of town around one. OK."

"OK."

And if I get run over by a bus in the meantime, I'll be more than happy.

* * *

I put away the cards and replaced them with my notepad. The blank pages stared back at me. They appeared cold and uninviting. They dared me to write something, anything, but nothing helped. Nothing encouraged. I feared the pages would just scoff at my attempts and, in about an hour or so, a member of staff would complain about the amount of paper I'd thrown into a ball under the table.

* * *

In the reflection of the window I could just about make out my features. Maybe that was it. Maybe that was the problem. Mahoney was no longer a figment of my imagination, an illusion that flowed from my pen. Now he was real. Mahoney knew me. He could see into my dreams, share my thoughts and feel my misery. He lived the danger.

I used to wonder, if the characters could talk, what would they say, what they might ask. But I couldn't even think that anymore, because now they talked and walked. Now they even demanded.

I was no longer writing something fictional but actually responding to people who needed answers.

The tide rolled up its sleeves and charged the beach in its relentless quest to scatter gulls, squash castles and bathe the sand in salt.

My novel was no longer mine and, if that was the case, then maybe that was the reason I couldn't finish it. Maybe that was the reason why it was easier to reach for the whisky bottle. At least I still found the freedom to dream in whisky.

* * *

"Are you Mahoney?" A voice asked.

My view of the beach was suddenly impeded by a man cramped into a donkey jacket. He had thick red hair, a squashed nose and a faint blue spot tattooed in the middle of his forehead.

"The Private Investigator?" He added

"Who wants to know?" I asked.

The man sat down in a chair opposite me and pulled out an envelope.

He pushed the envelope across the table towards me. "This is for you."

"Hey, a brown envelope, just what I always wanted!"

He pressed a finger on the envelope, just enough to stop me from picking it up. I looked back at him.

"There's two thousand pounds inside." He said, but not like a game show host might have done, but, as if he was giving away every last penny he'd saved.

"I take it there's a catch?" I suggested.

"You stop looking for the girl!"

I sat back in my chair and studied the man. He had a gap in his teeth that stopped him from smiling too much and light blue spots on his knuckles. His frail frame suggested he might struggle to stand tall in a strong wind. But he thought he was tough.

"What girl?" I asked.

He twitched his nose like a rabbit and lifted his finger from the envelope.

"You're asking the wrong person, I'm just delivering a message."

I pushed the envelope back across the table.

"Well you can tell your boss that I'm a Private Investigator and my customer comes first."

He stared straight back at me. "I can't do that."

"Why not?"

"Like I said, I'm just the messenger."

"So deliver my message!"

He shook his head.

"I just get a call, it's what I do. They give me a box number." He pointed down at the envelope, "That's what was in there, along with the message. I never get to see who I'm working for and that's the way I like it."

"Does it pay well?"

"I get by."

"Your family must be very proud of you!"

The man shifted on the chair and turned his knuckles into a fist.

"I can just picture your headstone now," I continued. "'Here lies a complete waste of space!'"

He wanted to argue. I could see the hate in his eyes. Nobody wanted to be told their life had been a waste of time, even if it was true. But there was nothing he could say because that's not why he was here, and that's not what he was being paid to do. All of which gave me the license to say whatever I wanted to.

"So how much do you get?" I asked.

"What?"

"For delivering the envelope. How much?"

"None of your business!"

I leaned across the table towards him and smiled.

"You don't really mean that!"

He avoided my gaze by staring out of the window.

"Maybe you don't want to tell me because you're scared."

He tried to stare me out. "I ain't scared of nothing."

But it didn't work. He didn't even get to ten seconds

before he was looking back out of the window.

"So what happens if I don't do what they say?"

"I don't think you need to ask that!" he replied, smiling ever so slightly at the window.

"Well, I mean, am I going to spend a few months in hospital recovering from a broken knee-cap, or worse?"

"That's not my decision."

"Of course not, you're just the messenger boy."

I sat back and finished my drink.

"And what happens to you if I don't take it?"

The man looked back at me as if he'd never contemplated the idea.

"Nothing." He tried to sound convincing, but fell well short. "I've given you the money, that's all I have to do."

"And what if I tell, whoever, that I never got it, that I never even saw you."

"Who says you'll get to speak to them?"

Good question. I mean, I had no idea what, or who, I was up against. Maybe they'd just bump me off in the middle of the night while I slept.

The man could sense my hesitation and it forced him into another weak smile. He pushed the envelope as far across the table as it would go.

"If you're as smart as you think you are Mr Mahoney, you'll take the money, treat yourself to a nice holiday and you'll forget this girl ever existed."

* * *

The man left me with my blank page and an empty cup. He'd soiled the atmosphere and ruined my day. At least I had a good excuse not to finish my novel this time.

* * *

Outside the tide was at its highest. It crashed high above the cobbled road that swept out around the castle and onto the South Bay. It rained down on cars and scattered passers-by. If it got any worse they'd stop the traffic, but not the people. Think about it, keep the cars safe but the people can keep coming, daring the waves, flirting with danger, tempting nature to do its worst.

Sometimes it was hard to feel sorry for people because, sometimes people got exactly what they deserved.

Chapter Forty-two

It was early afternoon but that didn't stop the town from rushing off as fast as it could towards the end of the day. The sandwich shops were running down on stock while the tills ran out of change. It was an art the way staff made customers feel bad when all they held was a twenty pound note in their hand.

Cigarette fumes clung to a breeze as people grabbed a quick smoke in cramped doorways and bus shelters. Inside the buildings the air was clear and clean. Outside the place was turning into Los Angeles.

* * *

Ricks was sitting at a table outside a café on the high street. He was twisting the lighter in his hand and staring down at an A4 sized file covered with scribblings and doodles.

I pulled out a chair. He sprang to his feet and tugged at the lapel on his jacket.

"Mr Mahoney. I really appreciate you seeing me again."

"Yeah, well you've gotta thank Hartless for that."

Ricks looked down at his shoes and then at the table.

"I will. I will. Look, would you like some coffee?"

He reached for a pot and, without waiting for an answer, poured another cup. I sat down.

"Help yourself to, you know," he said, pointing at the milk and sugar in an exaggerated fashion.

I poured some milk and dropped a spoonful of sugar into my cup. And all the while Ricks remained silent. I looked across at him. He didn't appear so full of himself anymore and that pleased me. He sipped his coffee and waited for me to speak. When I didn't he said; "I'm, sorry about the other day, my approach was all wrong."

"And you think a nice cup of coffee will help?"

Ricks stared back at me and curled up his lips into a fake smile. He probably considered telling me to go to hell, but he couldn't because, for, whatever reason it was, he needed me.

"I, just wanted to clear the air that's all."

"Hartless said you might have something for me?"

Ricks put a hand over his mouth and coughed but it was nothing more than an opportunity to think his words through carefully.

He leaned forward and went into his whispering routine again. "You've been working pretty close to Preacher haven't you!"

Ricks must have seen the look in my eye, because he quickly waved a hand in my direction and cut in; "Look, I'm not asking for details or anything, I know you wouldn't tell me anyway, it's just….,"

"It's just what?" I snapped.

"Well, you know about this body the police found under the bridge?

I drank some coffee and angled a stare at Ricks without answering. Maybe he was just being rhetorical. Maybe he was calling my bluff. Either way I didn't want to tell him more than I had to.

"The police seem to think he might have been following Preacher."

"Is that what they told you?"

Ricks toyed with his cup. "Well no, not exactly. I mean, they wouldn't, would they, without any proof or anything. But that's what's being suggested, off the record, so to speak."

"Is that what this is all about? You want to sit here and discuss rumours?"

Ricks panicked when he sensed my impatience. He quickly replaced his cup in the saucer and grabbed my arm. At least it stopped him karate chopping his way through a sentence.

"No, not at all, in fact," he paused. "In fact, I'm actually coming at this from a different angle."

"What angle?"

He squared me a glance. "I don't think the man was following Preacher at all."

The reporter waited an age for me to say something. But I wasn't going to make things easy for him. I sipped my coffee, checked my shoe laces and waited for a breeze to cool the afternoon air.

"You don't think he was, or you know he wasn't?" I eventually asked

Ricks pulled his chair a little closer. It was as though I'd finally invited him to a party he'd been waiting all year to join.

"I've, done some digging around," he said, enthusiastically. "Turns out this bloke was an ex-police officer. He'd retired a few months ago on medical grounds but he worked in a department that helps with unsolved crimes, you know, once a cop.........."

I remained unmoved by what Ricks was telling me. I

didn't want to fan his flames of enthusiasm.

"So?"

"So, I think he was onto something."

"You mean, you don't think he was just here enjoying the delights of a wet weekend at the seaside?"

"No."

I sipped some more coffee. And when I'd finished Ricks was still looking at me as though I was meant to congratulate him or something.

"Is that it?" I asked.

"Well no, not exactly."

"Then what?"

"Well, I kind of need to know if he had anything on him."

His approach was cautious. It made the lighter spin faster than ever in his hand.

"On who?"

"What?" he frowned.

"On who?" I repeated.

"No, I mean, I need to know if he was carrying anything on him, you know, such as names, documents, anything like that."

I waited until his hands finally came to a halt.

"Is this official?" I asked. "I mean, have they even released his name yet?"

Ricks held out a copy of the evening paper. I checked my watch. It was wrong but I knew it was still early.

"Hell what time does this thing come out?"

"Eleven-thirty."

"So is it a late morning edition or an early evening one?"

Ricks shrugged his shoulders. I studied the headline.

DEAD BODY FOUND UNDER BRIDGE. The body of Daniel Reece was found last night under the Valley Bridge. Police are treating the incident as suspicious.

"So go ask the police!" I suggested.

Ricks laughed for all of ten seconds.

"You know, they're not going to tell me anything. This is more than likely going to be a murder investigation after all."

"And what makes you think I want to help?"

"Do you think Preacher did it?"

I put the paper down on the table and didn't answer. So Ricks pointed at the paper and spoke for me.

"There are people who seem to have it in for him, and I don't know why. And, something like this certainly doesn't help."

"The police haven't charged him or anything," I argued.

"Not yet."

I stared at Ricks. He picked up his file.

"I, just thought you might want to be in the loop that's all, especially if he's innocent."

He was throwing me a line, the old guilt-trick line. Ricks didn't give a hill of beans whether Preacher was guilty or not, he was just looking for a meal ticket. Only trouble was, I did care.

"So what are you expecting to find on Reece?" I asked.

Ricks paused to glance down the street.

"I'm not sure. I mean, I've got an idea, but until I can come up with something concrete, I don't want to be wasting anybody's time."

"Since when did reporters give a damn about facts?"

"Because, if this is what I think it is, then I have to be right."

I looked down at my coffee and then at Ricks. I had my reasons for wanting to help Preacher, I liked him, I felt sorry for him and, I'd let him down, when I should have been following him.

So maybe going along with Ricks for the time being wouldn't be such a bad idea. But it would be only as far as I felt I could trust him.

I finished my coffee. "So what do you want from me?"

"Anything you can get on Reece."

I got to my feet and nodded. "I'll see what I can do."

"Thanks Mr Mahoney," he beamed. "You won't regret this."

"You're damn right I won't, because I promise you this, you try to make a sap out of me and it'll be the last thing you ever do."

Chapter Forty-three

Walker was chewing on a cigar and staring out of his office window when I approached. I tapped on the door and stepped inside. The Inspector craned his neck and spun his chair round to face me.

He stubbed out the cigar in an ashtray next to the 'no smoking sign'. "Mahoney, I wasn't expecting you."

"I need a favour."

"Oh."

"Yeah," I continued. "I was wondering if you could tell me anything about Reece, apart from, you think he may have been following Preacher?"

Walker stared at me for a moment. I couldn't be sure what was going through his mind, it could have been what he was going to have for tea tonight, it might have been, have much longer do I have to put up with this crap until I retire?

But eventually he said; "Such as?"

"Did he have anything on him, you know, like a notebook or a diary perhaps?"

Walker continued to stare before reaching for the intercom.

A voice said, "Yes Sir."

"Would you bring me everything we have on Daniel Reece."

"Reece?"

"Yeah."

"Yes sir."

Walker released the button and looked at me.

"Would you like to share what's going through that head of yours with me Mahoney?"

"It's just something that Ricks brought up, it might not be anything."

"Ricks?"

I nodded. "He's a kid reporter with the evening paper."

But Walker didn't appear convinced.

"He seems to think that Reece might not have been following Preacher after all," I explained. "It's just a lead he's working on."

"And you want to help?"

"He's keen."

The Inspector cupped his square jaw with a left hand and tapped the desk with the other. It was his thoughtful pose.

"You also want to protect Preacher!" he suggested.

I didn't answer.

"You seem to be doing everything but finding this girl?"

I shrugged my shoulders. "Well one more blind alley isn't going to hurt!"

A man walked in and handed the Inspector a box file. Walker waited for him to leave before opening it up. He looked inside.

"This is all he had on him," he said, handing me the file.

There were a number of newspaper cuttings. At first glance they just appeared to be reports on people who'd avoided sentencing for various crimes. There were also a couple of police case notes and a filo-fax complete with names, addresses and telephone numbers. I looked over at Walker.

"Can I keep any of this?"

"The case notes you'll have to leave behind, this is still a possible murder enquiry. The rest you can borrow, but I want them back, asap, and just as you found them."

I took out the filo-fax and press cuttings and handed the rest back to Walker.

"Anything interesting?" he asked.

"You'll be the first to know."

"Somehow I doubt that!"

Chapter Forty-four

"What is it?"

"An envelope!"

Envy let out a sigh. "I can see that!"

She momentarily glanced at me before opening it up and looking inside. Suddenly her eyes widened and she blew out a whistle.

"There must be..."

"Two thousand pounds." I assured her.

Envy fanned the money in her fingers like a deck of cards.

"What did you do, win the lottery?"

I sat down opposite her. "A man gave it to me."

"Just like that?"

I shook my head. "He insisted that I stopped looking for the girl. I assumed it was April, but it could have been Alana."

"Alana?"

Boy this was getting complicated I thought to myself. I scratched my head.

"A girl from the club, she stayed over one night, she was frightened."

"Of what?"

"I don't know and I didn't ask. But the police were asking about her. I'll probably just end up sweeping it under the carpet like everything else."

Envy paused as though she was trying to take in everything I'd said.

"So, this man with the envelope?"

"What about him?"

"Who was he?"

"He didn't say, he was just the messenger boy."

She straightened the edge of the money by tapping it on the desk a couple of times. Then she placed it carefully back into the envelope.

She sat back and contemplated life for a moment. "Didn't you tell him?"

"Didn't I tell him what?"

"That we weren't looking for April anymore!"

My eyes shifted from her gaze.

"You did tell him we weren't looking for her anymore!"

"Well that's what I wanted to talk to you about," I ventured.

"Mahoney!"

I looked back at her. "Storey phoned me the other day. He told me this story about waking up in the middle of the woods and having no memory."

"That still doesn't bring April back from the dead!"

"He was meant to deliver a package to some people, some not very nice people."

"A package?"

"Yeah."

It didn't take long for her to realise what, or rather who, the package was meant to be.

"April?"

I nodded. "Storey is some kind of delivery man."

"Nice!" she said.

"Anyway, I went in his place, to see what they wanted."

"You did what?"

"Well he couldn't go!" I argued.

"You could have been killed!"

"Not without delivering the package."

"You should have called me."

She was right, but doing the right thing didn't always come naturally to me.

"I know," I replied.

So what happened?"

"I told them I couldn't get April for a few days, so they punched me in the kidneys a couple of times and then they said they'd ring me."

"I'm sorry to sound repetitive Mahoney, but April's dead."

I took a walk to the window. The view never seemed to change all that much whatever the weather. The sun was shining, stretching a bright yellow glow across the park, but the trees struggled to bloom and the church continued to bake in neglect.

"There's part of me that's not so sure anymore." I said to the reflection of Envy in the window.

"Well obviously it's not your head, I mean, she's lying in a grave somewhere!"

"Don't you think they should have known that? I mean, it was in the papers and everything."

"You know it was."

"And this is a small town Envy, everybody ends up knowing everything, eventually."

"Well obviously not them!"

I shook my head. "No, something's not right."

I walked back to the desk.

"Do me a favour, would you" I asked.

"I don't like the sound of this."

"Just see if anyone actually made an official identification?"

"Oh my God, you're not suggesting it might not be her?"

"Think about it Envy, somebody offers me two thousand pounds not to find her, while somebody else is ready to kill me if I don't deliver her. They're too many people who seem to think she's still alive."

"And if it's not her body lying in the morgue then what?"

"Well we've got a choice, we either pretend we've never heard of her and split the money," I said, looking back at the envelope on the desk.

"Or?"

"Actually I don't have an 'or'!"

"You're playing a dangerous game."

"I know."

"If that's not her body then we're just back to square one!"

"I know."

"Which means we're going to have to look for her again!"

"I know."

"Because if you don't deliver her........"

"I know."

Chapter Forty-five

I called in at the Evening News offices and asked to see Ricks. Thirty seconds later he bounded down a set of carpeted steps and pulled me outside onto the street.

"Did you get anything?" He huffed.

I handed him the cuttings and the filo-fax.

He scanned the pages like someone who'd just discovered the Dead Sea Scrolls.

He pulled back his lips. "Boy, I didn't think people used these things anymore!"

I poked the filo-fax with a finger. "I need all this back, just as it is, or the Evening News will be looking for another reporter!"

Ricks looked at me and nodded.

"Now I've got something to work on," he beamed.

I wanted to tell Ricks not to get his hopes up, because that's what happens in this job, you see a light at the end of the tunnel but, most of the time, it just turns out to be just another shot in the dark.

But in the end I didn't say anything. After all, there

would be plenty of other people ready to burst his bubble.

"Anything else?" He asked.

I shook my head

Ricks started back inside. I grabbed his arm.

"You tell me everything you get!" I insisted.

He nodded. I gripped his arm tighter.

"Everything!"

Chapter Forty-six

Hartless was dressed in a suit but no tie. His shirt was unbuttoned at the collar and just enough to reveal a small gold cross.

I pointed at his pale white neck. "Is that for protection?"

Hartless instinctively gripped the cross and nervously asked; "W.... why, am I going to need it?"

"That might depend on the women in there!"

As always Hartless wasn't sure how to take my comment. He almost smiled and chewed his mouth a little.

"I,... I wasn't sure if I should wear this," he said, tipping back his hat.

"I wasn't sure you had a choice!"

"I took it off once," he said, like a naughty schoolboy caught behind the bike shed selling cigarettes. "Bu,... but everybody called me, Hatless. So I never bothered again."

I smiled and then I laughed. Eventually Hartless began

to laugh as well. It was the funniest thing I'd heard in weeks.

"Be, besides," he said, pulling himself together. "I was worried we might stand out."

I pressed a hand onto his shoulder. "We're going into a club to ask a lot of uncomfortable questions, so we're going to stand out." I looked at his hat. "So you could have worn a bath tub on your head, it wouldn't have made the slightest bit of difference."

* * *

Saltys stood on the corner of Bishop Street and smack bang in the middle of town. But there was nothing Godly going on around here, just a sense of what some people might consider liberation but what I called desperation. The Casino, the banks, even the very different kind of salvation going on inside the lap dancing club.

* * *

We squeezed our way between a set of burly, balding bouncers. They must have made the dancers feel safe because I got the feeling that not just anybody got inside.

The club was a lot smaller than I was expecting, nothing more than a bar with a small stage at one end, and half a dozen round tables at the other. No wonder they called it lap-dancing, that's about all there was room for.

The tables were full. Smartly dressed middle-aged men sat round drinking from bottles. Three girls wriggled on the stage in g-strings, while another wriggled in the lap of a young man, who appeared more than a little uncomfortable with the situation. It could just be that he wasn't used to having a pretty young girl dance naked in his lap while his best mates looked on.

"How about you pick your chin off the floor and tell me what you want you to drink?" I asked Hartless.

"Oh, er, w... what are you having?"

"A whisky."

"Oh, I think, I think I'll have a pint then please."

I ordered the drinks while Hartless went back to staring at the girls.

I was served by a young man in a pressed white shirt, waistcoat and tie. When he handed over my change I showed him the picture of Smudge that I'd taken from the flat.

"Ever seen this kid before?" I asked.

He looked at me inquisitively. I straightened the picture. He shook his head.

"Are you sure?"

"I only started here last night. You could ask Amy, she's been here longer."

Amy was wearing a similar shirt, tie and waistcoat but she was busy serving a group of men. I decided to wait and enjoy my drink. Hartless was chewing his lip and staring out across the floor. I pressed a finger to his chin and closed his mouth.

"So how come you don't stutter all the time?" I asked.

He rolled his bottom lip in a thoughtful manner.

"I only, I only stutter when I'm nervous," he replied.

"I thought you chewed your face when you're nervous?"

"No, that's just a habit"

"It's also something you do when you're nervous."

He shook his head.

"No, i..., it's something I do when I've got a lot on my mind."

"So what makes you nervous?"

He looked thoughtful for a moment

"Or, all kind of things I suppose, b... but people generally."

"What about work?" I asked.

"No, work is when I chew my mouth. Die, dying."

"Dying makes you nervous?"

"No, scared. Do, doesn't it you?"

I looked at the back of my hand. There was no reason for it other than I could see the scar from when a splintered piece of wood pierced my hand. It reminded me of lying in the mud with water quickly filling my lungs, and I remembered that I was scared because I didn't know where I was going next. I could live with not knowing while I was alive, I'd been used to that most of my life, living from day to day, place to place. But wondering what came after death bothered the hell out of me.

"No." I said. It was the easy answer. "Just as long as it's quick and not halfway through sex."

Hartless chuckled. I wanted to clarify whether he was laughing at what I'd said, or if the idea of me having sex was so ridiculous, that it was laughable, but the barmaid was free.

I held up the picture and asked; "Ever seen this guy before?"

She took the picture and studied it for a moment.

"He has an eye for attractive girls," I continued. "Maybe he spoke to you?"

"If he had an eye for attractive girls, he'd be looking in the other direction." She had a challenging manner. Maybe she should have got a job on the door.

"What's the problem Amy?" said a voice.

"Nothing Mr Malone."

I turned to see a lump of lard dressed in a suit standing next to me. He reached for the photo and took it from the girl.

"Who's this?" He asked.

"What's it to you?" I said.

"I'm the Floor Manager and I don't like seeing my staff hassled."

"Since when was asking somebody a question hassling them?"

"Since when they were too busy!"

But before I had chance to count the number of customers at the bar on one hand, he'd straightened his frame in front of me and was standing in my face. It was a threatening pose he'd borrowed from The Beano. It came free with the rolled up lip.

"Are you a cop?"

I sipped my whisky. I'd become an expert. It was cheap and nasty.

"Why, would it bother you if I was?"

He let out a laugh. It was nothing more than a short sharp, scoff that was meant to tell me how nothing bothered a big strong boy like him, not even the law.

"I think you and your friend should leave."

Hartless nodded and gulped back his beer.

"And I think I should finish my drink first," I said.

He pressed a large hand on top of mine in an attempt to stop me from raising my glass. Hartless was already in his starter blocks. The door wasn't close enough.

I looked the man square in the eye. "The last person who got that close to me ended up with my name tattooed on her shoulder. You wouldn't want the same thing to happen to you now, would you?"

He did the laugh thing again, only not so confidently this time. He angled his head and thought about staring me out. Then he let go of my hand and stepped away to view me from the end of the bar.

"I, I, I don't think that was so clever Mr Mahoney," Hartless eventually said.

"Neither do I, but I didn't like his attitude."

"I, I wasn't thinking about his attitude, I was more worried about the s, the size of his fists."

I nodded and finished my drink. I caught one last glance

at the barmaid. She smiled.

"My name's Richard Mahoney, I'm a Private Investigator," I informed her. "If you remember anything about Smudge give me a call. It might just save someone's life."

She nodded.

* * *

Hartless and I walked up town without saying very much until we reached the end of the street.

"S..., so what now?"

"I don't know," I replied. "But I'm hoping we've ruffled a few feathers. Maybe somebody will come out of the woodwork and ask what we were up to."

"As long as they only a... ask."

I looked back at him.

"Don't worry, you don't know anything OK. If they want any answers then they're going to have to come to me."

"And the, then what?"

"And then, I'd better come up with some."

Chapter Forty-seven

I got home tired and dirty. I turned on the hot water tap and waited as the sink filled and the mirror disappeared behind a film of condensation. I wiped it clear with the back of my hand and stared at my face. It was someone I didn't recognise. I wasn't ageing well, there were grey hairs and wrinkles round my eyes that had multiplied overnight, some called them laughter lines, but they must have been somebody else's laughter. I picked out a razor and scratched the foam from my chin. I showered, towelled myself dry and slipped on a pair of boxers, only they didn't exactly slip on. I hopped backwards and then sideways across the room. After bouncing off the wall and almost back into the bathroom, I settled into a chair and looked up to see Alana standing with her back to the wall and trying not to laugh at me.

She was wearing a short skirt, a long sleeved blouse and not a lot else. Not that I minded, but it didn't do a whole lot for her goose pimples. Her arms were wrapped tight around her waist as though she was clinging to life itself.

I wondered how she'd got in. I'd checked the door a dozen times, because it's what I do, but then I realised it didn't matter a whole lot when you've given somebody a spare key.

"You look frozen."

She nodded. There wasn't much point in arguing.

I went to the bedroom and found her a jumper. She slipped it over her head and offered me a tired smile.

"Would you like a drink?" I asked.

She nodded. I sat her down in front of the gas fire and made us both a coffee.

I took my place on the sofa. "So where have you been?"

"I tried to see some friends but they are not there. I am too much trouble?"

"No! No, not at all, but you *look* like you're in trouble."

She went all quiet and stared down at the floor. I'd had better reactions when I'd asked women for a date and most of the time that was hell.

"Talk to me." I said.

She shook her head and stood up, but where she was heading I don't know, because I didn't give her the chance. I got to my feet and took hold of her shoulders and held them tight. She looked at me as if she'd been there before, somebody being rough with her and I didn't like the fact that this time it was me. But I wanted to help and I needed some answers.

"Look Alana, you might have a very good reason for keeping quiet and normally I would respect that, but some men came looking for you the other day."

"Men?"

"Yeah two cops, policemen, I mean."

She looked worried like most people do when they hear that the cops are asking after them.

"Did they say why?"

I couldn't help thinking that Alana wasn't being totally up front with me, so I decided to keep a few things from her. For the time being at least.

I shook my head.

She started to cradle my face with her hand.

"So what did you tell them?"

"That you served me a drink in the club but that I haven't seen or heard from you since."

She looked at me for a moment as though she was expecting something more. Then she started to kiss me, full on, wrapping her tongue around mine, and they seemed to get on fine. Twisting, probing, caressing teeth, tonsils, the lot. Her hand pressed my chest and started to claw at the buttons on my shirt. There was a time when I would have died for a moment like this, except that, right now, I could die because of a moment like this.

I took hold of her wrists and gave us both some air.

"You don't like me?" she frowned.

Two women in less than twenty-four hours, both throwing themselves at me, but it would have been wrong to think of busses. Either it was my new aftershave, or a lack of blokes in Scarborough.

"Yes, I like you, but if kissed every girl I liked, I'd need a new set of lips."

She didn't understand, her deep frown and a tear gathering in the corner of her eye told me as much.

"But this isn't right."

She appeared hurt by my remark so I tried another approach.

"Look, if you're in trouble I want to help."

She pulled free of my grip and wiped her eye with the back of a hand. She stood motionless in the middle of the room like someone who wasn't really sure what they were doing here. I sat in a chair and invited her to do the same.

"Why don't you drink your coffee?"

She took a moment to accept my offer, and an even longer moment to speak, but I was in no rush.

"I am worried," she said eventually.

"I know you are, that's why I want to help."

She stared back at me without saying a word and sipped her coffee.

"Why did you come here Alana?" I asked.

She frowned at me.

"I mean, why me?"

"Because..." she whispered. "Because you are kind."

"All I did was buy a drink! Normally it takes a whole lot more than that to have a nice girl turn up at four in the morning asking if she can stay the night. How did you even find me?"

"Somebody overheard you tell Mr Preacher your name and that you are a Private........., thingy."

"Investigator," I corrected, although 'thingy' might have been more appropriate in my case.

"Yes. And you stand up to that man," she continued. "He isn't nice."

"Did he hit you? Is that where you got that bruise from?"

It wasn't there anymore but Alana instinctively touched her face with a finger and looked down at the floor again.

"No!"

"Because if he did," I started to pull on my big American macho hat again, and then wondered how soon it would be before I regretted it.

"He didn't."

"So what's going on Alana?"

Alana sniffed and took a deep breath that came out all prolonged and edgy. She looked at me and then at the floor. I hoped I wasn't going to have to ask her again.

"I saw what happened to Jenny."

"Jenny? The girl in the car crash?"

Alana slowly nodded. "She is my friend. I saw what happened."

"I don't understand, you saw what happened? You mean, you saw the crash?"

Alana shook her head.

"No, I mean, before. We were at Mr Preacher's house. Jenny needed somewhere to stay, she could not stay at her flat. I asked Mr Preacher if she could stay at his house. He has helped before. I stayed with her."

"And?"

"We were talking, you know, and listening to music, when we hear a noise."

"A noise?"

Alana nodded. "It is like breaking glass, like a window breaking. We couldn't see anything. Jenny went to call Mr Preacher at work but the phone is in the hall and before she can pick it up …"

Alana paused as she relived the moment. Her hands shook as she pressed a finger to her mouth and placed it between her lips.

"Take your time." I said.

"Some men came in, two men, and they both grabbed her and shouted at her," she continued. "One of them hit her on the face."

Alana took another deep breath as her eyes started to water.

Her tears were now in free-fall. I searched the flat for a handkerchief but gave up. I grabbed a roll of kitchen towel. She wiped her face and then blew her nose and put her finger back into the corner of her mouth.

"I didn't help." She whispered.

I took her hand.

"You couldn't help."

"I did not understand what they were saying. They hit her again and she fell."

She took a moment to wipe her eyes.

"Then what?"

"One of them dragged her outside and the other stole some pictures."

"Pictures?" I questioned.

Alana nodded. "From the wall," She explained, and raised her arms to clarify somebody taking something from above.

"What did you do?" I asked.

"Nothing," she cried. "I just watched."

"But you went to the police?"

Alana stared back at me, her tears were flowing.

"You didn't go to the police?"

She shook her head.

"You couldn't go to the police?"

Her lips moved but the words struggled to break free.

"I'm, I was, frightened. I didn't want to get in any trouble."

"What kind of trouble?"

The room filled with silence as Alana took a moment to reply.

"I do not have a visa to work," she mumbled. "I am supposed to be just a student. But I like to work. I like the money. It is easy to get job here."

"Careful, you'll give some people down the Dole office a complex!"

"Now I am scared they will send me home!"

I wanted to tell her that it wouldn't be a problem, that the system wasn't really that good. Even if she confessed everything they'd probably just lose all the details.

But, just as I wanted to tell her everything was going to be all right, Alana started to cry again. I was fast running out of kitchen roll. I handed her what I had left and she squeaked a *thank you*.

"I do not want to go home, but Jenny is dead."

I patted her shoulder. "Nobody's saying you have to go home."

"But it is not safe for me anymore."

"Then we'll have to find somewhere that is, until I figure out what's going on at least."

Alana sat back just enough to get a good look at me. Her eyes were sparkling and red.

"How will you do that?"

Here we go again. The lies. And not only that, but I'd be doing it for free again.

"I'm a Private 'Thingy' remember. It's my job to find out things."

Her brief smile quickly gave way to a frown. "But I have no money, I cannot pay you!"

"I didn't ask you for any money did I?"

She grew increasingly puzzled.

"But how...." She started.

I held up my hand and stopped her from asking too many questions I couldn't answer.

I got to my feet and did what I did when I was in the office, I walked to the window. It was dark outside. Lights lit up the park across the way and kids gathered outside the corner shop.

I thought it might help, thinking on my feet, but in truth it didn't make a whole lot of difference I'd have probably thought the same thing after four pints and a curry. I wanted to protect Alana. She was scared. She'd been dragged into a situation she didn't belong to and none of it was her fault. Trouble was, who the hell was I to protect anybody from anything? It also seemed a little more than coincidental that Warne and Lucas should suddenly turn up asking about her.

"I don't know," I eventually replied. "But that's how I

work. I know I've got to do something, I just never know what, until I get either punched or shot, and that's when I realise I must be getting close."

"You're funny," she said softly.

I offered her a frown. "You're not talking about my looks now are you?"

Alana stood up and walked over to where I stood scratching my head. She straightened her hair and wiped her eyes with the last of the kitchen roll. She pressed a hand on my chest. I was worried she might feel it was beating must faster than normal.

"No," she whispered and kissed me gently on my lips. "I wasn't talking about your looks."

I stepped away.

"I am causing you trouble, yes."

"Yes."

She appeared slightly confused. It wasn't the answer she was expecting.

"But I like trouble!"

"You are a very kind man." She smiled.

Well that's one way of putting it, I thought. Truth was, I'm just plain stupid, and a sucker for women with brown eyes.

* * *

It didn't take long for me to realise I wasn't going to get any sleep. The sofa was it's usual uncomfortable self. So, I promised myself that, first thing in the morning, I'd go to the police station and squeal on Alana. Anything to get my bed back.

A storm the size of Texas was on display outside. I pulled back the curtains, listened to the thunder and watched as the lightening stretched out across the sky and highlighted the greens, yellows and blues of Peasholm Park. It was a truly amazing site.

And as the thunder rumbled and the lightening crackled I thought about finally submitting my work to agents and publishers. It would be nice to let somebody in London feel good about themselves as they dismissed my work. All that power had to mean something, the opportunity to speak on behalf of the reading public. The bastards.

A pale white face appeared in the lightening above my sofa. A soft, cold, white hand gently pressed against my lips and stopped me from screaming. As the lightening slipped away I adjusted my eyes to the darkness and saw Alana kneeling down beside me.

"I am frightened." she whispered. "I do not want to sleep alone."

She took my hand and led me towards the bedroom. For some strange reason I started to wonder how old she was and if I'd cleaned my teeth. She got into bed. I laid down next to her. She pressed her body close to mine and wrapped an arm across my chest and snuggled her lips to my face. Her breath was soft and warm and tickled the end of my nose.

And then she fell asleep.

Chapter Forty-eight

When I woke the following morning I found Alana lying on my arm. It took an age to free myself and even longer for the blood to start circulating again.

I dragged my arm out of bed and into the kitchen. I needed a coffee.

I left a note for Alana. I told her I was going out for a couple of hours. She was welcome to stay at the flat. It was probably safer if she did. I signed my name, 'Private Thingy', and left.

* * *

Preacher had already arrived at the club by the time I caught up with him. I sat in his office and waited as he helped unload a delivery.

Twenty minutes later he strolled in looking like he'd just taken his last breath. He slumped into a chair.

"Don't you have people to do that kind of work for you?" I asked.

He glanced across at me. "Three mornings running my

Bar Manager has rung in late. Well today I told him not to bother anymore. Unfortunately I'd forgotten about the delivery. I should have made him unload it, then sacked him."

"Welcome to Quick-fix city!" I smiled.

"Very funny," Preacher said. "So what brings you here, the bar doesn't open for another eleven hours?"

"I know, I checked."

I sat back in my chair and suddenly wondered if I was doing the right thing telling Preacher what I knew. After all, somebody had ended up dead. But then I figured I still held the trump card.

"I was just thinking about the other night that's all, the night of the accident."

"What about it?" Preacher asked.

I watched him walk to a hip high cabinet and pick up a coffee perculator. He waved it at me. Never being someone to refuse a free offer, I nodded.

"Well I can't help wondering why you never told the cops about Jenny being in your house that night?"

Preacher paused over one of the cups. "I wasn't sure it was any of their business," he mumbled and went back to filling the cups.

"The girl's dead. I think that kind of makes it their business now."

Preacher placed the cups on the desk and sat down.

"Dead?"

I nodded.

"I'm sorry to hear that."

He sounded sincere. I reached for my cup.

Preacher looked over at me. "So how did you know she was at my house?"

"Because I'm a Private Investigator."

"Alana," he suddenly blurted out, as though I'd been holding the answers to a quiz the wrong way round.

"She's been speaking to you?"

I nodded.

"I wondered where she'd gone."

"So how come you didn't report it to the cops?"

Preacher casually looked at me and smiled.

"Because, they'd have just laughed at me, I'd invited Jenny in remember! I'd said she could stay. But I had no idea she was going to take anything."

I drank my coffee in silence before deciding to tell Preacher what really happened.

"Jenny didn't take the paintings," I announced.

"What?"

"Two men broke into your house, they smacked Jenny around and took off with the paintings."

"I was robbed?"

"Well that's how it was meant to look," I suggested.

"What do you mean?"

"Because if it was a robbery, it would have to go down as one of the worst ones ever. Breaking into a house, stealing a couple of paintings and then leaving them in a car with a dying girl, that's just plain stupid."

Preacher momentarily buried his head into his hands.

"Did Alana get a look at any of them?"

I shook my head.

"But I don't understand," he sighed. "If it wasn't a robbery then what were they up to?"

I stood up. "I'm afraid you're going to have to figure that one out for yourself."

"But I don't have any idea," Preacher moaned.

"Well maybe it was payback time!"

"For what?"

I stood back in the middle of the room and pulled on my ear. It was becoming a habit but it never seemed to do any good.

"You said yourself you've put a few faces out of joint

with your club."

"But is that a good enough reason to kill a girl?"

"Personally I don't think there's ever a reason to kill anybody, but that's just me and I'm not the one who broke into your house."

"So?"

"So maybe you ought to ask, who would, why, and, more importantly, what have they got planned next!"

* * *

It was difficult to assess exactly what Preacher did or didn't know. For a start he had to know that something was wrong that night. Even if he'd accepted that Jenny may have stolen some of his possessions, that didn't account for her breaking a window.

And if he did know something was wrong, then why hadn't he done something about it?

It was time to pay his brother a visit.

Chapter Forty-nine

The church was quiet. The only noise came from the village hall just beyond the graveyard. From a distance I could hear music and see the heads of people spinning and ducking and weaving very strategically as they passed the narrow windows. I stepped up close until I could see a group of people ballroom dancing. They moved with elegance and style. The women smiled and raised their arms gracefully while the men followed with anxious faces, fearing to tread on their partners toes.

I opened the main door and stepped inside. Most of the faces caught a fleeting glance at me as they span into a another position. The Reverend was in a corner of the room playing the music and looking more than happy with himself. He waved a hand at me and tapped his watch and stuck five fingers into the air.

* * *

I went back to the church. It gave me time to ponder on what I was going to say and how I was going to say it. All of thirty seconds later I realised I didn't have a clue what to do or say. I would just have to wade in with my size nines as usual. It was the only way.

* * *

I found myself staring down at a gravestone when the Reverend finally appeared.

"Mr Mahoney isn't it?" He beamed.

"What a good memory you have for names."

The Rev brushed my comment aside with a wave of his hand.

"I recall my Headmaster remarking how he only ever remembered the names of pupils who had been either very good or particularly bad."

"Isn't there a bit of both in all of us, otherwise there wouldn't be much point in coming here?" I questioned, nodding back at the church.

The Rev. smiled. "I take it you haven't got to one of my services yet?"

I shook my head. "I figure this is as far as I'm ever going to get."

I looked back at the grave. The Rev followed my eyes.

"But hopefully not so soon," he remarked.

The gravestone read; *Sophie Keatley, beloved wife of Adam. Too soon, so missed, forever loved..*

"What happened?" I asked.

"Poor thing. She was involved in a hit and run. My brother sat up with her for two whole nights. Unfortunately, she never recovered."

"Preacher?"

The Rev. nodded and asked; "You know him?"

"You could say that."

The Revs intrigue multiplied as the two of us turned and headed towards the church.

"I've been following him," I continued.

"Following him?"

I nodded.

"May I ask why?"

"Because I'm a Private Investigator."

* * *

I'd chosen my words deliberately for affect and that doesn't happen very often. It requires a skill, the art of thinking before speaking. It's a bit like someone with a gun taking aim before firing. Whereas I was more of a, squint my eyes, shoot from the hip, and face the consequences later, kind of person.

But I wanted to test The Revs reaction. But he was careful, maybe even prepared, because all he did was cast a frown for a moment and gently nod his head.

* * *

The Oldies Disco was coming to an end so the Reverend was able to let somebody else wind things up. He lead me to the vestry. The room was a whole lot warmer than I'd expected and far cleaner. The furniture wasn't lined with cobwebs, and bats didn't flap hurriedly to the ceiling when we stepped inside.

A large desk occupied the middle of the room accompanied by two chairs. Up against the wall was a cabinet lined with pictures of children all with smiling faces. Some of them were playing football, some were playing cricket, but most of them just smiled.

"Please, take a seat," said the vicar.

I did as he requested.

"So what is it you want to know about Adam?"

"I think he's in trouble."

The Rev. started to laugh. He raised a hand in an attempt to stop laughing, but all he did was laugh some more.

"I'm sorry," he said, slowly pulling himself together, "But if I had a pound for every time I'd ever heard that, well, I probably wouldn't be a vicar anymore."

"You're not surprised then?"

"Oh Mr Mahoney. Adam's been getting himself into trouble ever since we were at school. I've lost count of the number of times I've covered for him. It was never anything serious of course, simply answering back or sticking up for himself, the kind of things they'd turn a blind eye to now. But our parents wouldn't have approved, which was why we'd have to lie about why he was late back from school because he'd either had detention or was answering questions down at the police station. Would you like a coffee by the way, or some tea perhaps?"

I was going to say 'no', because I didn't feel comfortable sitting in a church talking to a man of God, but the vicar was already standing over a kettle and flicking on a switch.

"Yeah," I answered. "A coffee would be fine."

"So you must be the same Private Investigator Adam spoke about the other day," he said as he pressed a couple of mugs together on a tray.

"He mentioned me?" I sounded surprised because I was surprised.

"He said that you were looking for a young girl."

I nodded.

"I take it you've been to his club then?"

"Yeah, his den of iniquity."

A cloud rolled out of sight and allowed the sun to highlight the bright colours of the stained glass window behind the Reverend's desk. But Jesus didn't look happy. He was staring down from a cross with an expression that wondered, was it all worth it?

The Reverend placed a tray complete with milk, spoons and a sugar bowl on the desk.

"Despite always getting into trouble my brother is quite a clever man, Mr Mahoney," he continued. "I just wish he would turn himself to something far more useful than running a night club."

The kettle boiled and the vicar filled the mugs and sat down.

"So, what's Adam got himself mixed up in this time?"

"Well the truth is, I'm not sure."

I topped my mug with milk, added some sugar and sat back in my seat.

"A week or so ago a young girl was involved in an accident. She had been staying at your brother's house when two men burst in, beat her up and took off with some of his possessions. She was found sometime later badly injured in your brother's wife's car. She never recovered."

"Yes, I remember reading about it," he replied with a soft sigh. "But what makes you think my brother may have been involved?"

I shrugged my shoulders. "Because I'm from the old school of detectives, I believe everybody's guilty until proven innocent, you don't make many friends and it might cause a lot of paperwork, but if you point the finger at everybody you're bound to be right sooner or later."

"An interesting philosophy," the vicar observed, as he reached for his cup and took a sip of coffee.

"What bothers me, is that he didn't say anything to the police. In fact, he didn't say anything to anybody."

The vicar smiled. "That doesn't surprise me," he said assuredly.

"And why's that?"

The Rev paused to look at me.

"Because Adam doesn't have a lot of time for the police. In fact, he doesn't have a lot of time for authority full stop."

This was something new.

"Our father was attacked some time ago."

I raised an inquisitive eyebrow.

"He was beaten up, apparently for nothing more than the change in his pocket. They left him to bleed to death. Nobody saw anything. Nobody was charged. Up until that moment Adam had set his heart on becoming a vicar just like our dad. That's how he got the nickname, kids used to tease him at school, that's how he got into most of his scrapes. But after the attack he gave up on everything. He didn't talk to anyone for over a month. Then he just upped sticks and left. I didn't see him again until he turned up a couple of years ago out of the blue with his wife."

I paused over my coffee as I tried to digest everything that had just been thrown at me. It was times like this I realised I should have carried a notepad around.

There was a knock at the door.

"Come in," said the Rev.

The door squeaked open and a young boy leaned his head inside.

"There's a man from the BBC here, Mr Keatley."

The Rev immediately checked his watch.

"Good Lord! I'd lost all track of time. I'll be right out."

The boy left and we both stood up.

"Harry Graystone," The Rev. explained, as if I should know. "Come to get some background on the big day."

I frowned.

"I'm being made a Bishop this weekend."

"Oh yeah," I nodded.

We walked towards the side door.

"You still look concerned Mr Mahoney."

"Only because I'm worried that your brother might try and take matters into his own hands."

"What makes you say that?"

"Because somebody broke into his house and took some of his belongings, and he's had the cops crawling all over him ever since, do you really think he's just going to leave it at that?"

We stopped at the door and the Vicar looked across at me.

"Look, I appreciate your concern, Mr Mahoney, but I'm sure Adam won't do anything stupid, if that's what you're worried about."

"Is that what you know, or is that what you pray?"

* * *

I drove back into town trying to unravel exactly what had gone on. If April wasn't dead, where was she? Was Preacher holding an ace up his sleeve and why? And what about this pain I felt every time I thought about Trish?

Maybe it was time to swallow my pride and talk to her. Make things up to her. I didn't feel good about just walking away the other night.

But before all that, I had to get Alana somewhere safe.

Chapter Fifty

"Why do you have a picture of this girl?" Alana asked as I returned to the flat.

She held out the photograph of April I'd left lying on the table.

"Oh that," I stumbled. "It's no, nothing, no, just a case I was working on."

I took the picture from her and popped it into my coat pocket.

"You were looking for her, yes?"

I glanced at Alana and wondered why the whole situation made me feel so uncomfortable. Was it that I'd left something confidential lying around? Or was it that I'd left a picture of a young girl lying around?

"No! Well, yes. Yes I was, but not anymore. She died. In a fire."

"I know."

Her reply took me completely by surprise.

"You know? You mean you know she died in a fire? How?"

Alana sat down. "She was a friend of Jenny's."

"Jenny's?"

She nodded.

"Did you know her, the girl in the picture?"

Alana took a moment to answer me, as if she was weighing up whether it was right to do so or not.

"No, not really, only because of Jenny. They shared a house with two other girls. Jenny was upset when she heard about April."

"Naturally."

"And it did not help when she went to see the others girls and they weren't there."

"How come?"

"She did not know. They had just gone away without saying anything."

I got to my feet and massaged my temple. All this thinking was giving me a headache and I was fresh out of aspirins.

"What were these girls called?"

"Petra and Natalie."

"But they're not there anymore?"

"No. And nobody has heard from them in a long time."

"Do you know somebody called Smudge?"

Alana went back to the nodding routine.

"Have you any idea where he is?"

"No. I haven't seen him for a long time," she replied.

I picked up Alana's coat.

"We need to get you somewhere safe," I explained.

"No!" she screamed.

Her reaction was slightly over the top and I let her know it with one of my best frowns.

"People are dying or missing and probably even both and you could be next!"

She stepped up close to me and put a hand on my face.

"But you can protect me!"

"Only when I'm here and I'm not here enough. You need proper protection."

"I do not want to go to the police!"

"Don't believe everything you hear, they're not all bad!"

"Please," she pleaded.

I was too soft for all this.

"You can't stay here, Alana, they might come looking for you."

"Then I'll find somewhere else."

"Is there someone you can trust?"

She nodded.

"I want their name, address and telephone number. And I want you to keep in touch."

Alana smiled back at me.

"I mean it!"

Chapter Fifty-one

Walker was in a meeting and couldn't be disturbed. I was told I could try him again in just over an hour. I bought a coffee and went back to the office and thought about what to do next.

The place was quiet, until I opened the window and heard the thump of the stereo. There were a lot of things I needed to do; I'd promised to find April, I needed to water my plant, I wanted to speak to Trish and I was supposed to be finishing my book, but none of them were easy with that bloody thumping sound going on all the time.

I started on the plant. I got as far as the sink but the pounding drove me back. I looked at my coffee and realised that it wouldn't take a minute to cross the park, break down the door, throw the stereo out of the window and still get back to a luke warm drink.

The beat continued.

I strode across the park. The door to the apartments was open. I walked inside and strolled up the stairs. The music increased. I knocked on the door. A slug somewhere in his early twenties opened it. Quite honestly I couldn't have cared less if Hercules himself had lived there. He raised his head at me.

I pushed him to one side and headed for the stereo.

"Hey," he shouted.

When I didn't respond he shouted even louder.

"I'll call the law!"

The stereo was like nothing I'd ever seen before. I couldn't begin to find the volume button, so I did the next best thing. I pulled the plug out.

"I am the law!" I said, relaxing in the peace and tranquillity of a silent room.

"You can't do that!"

"I just did. And the next time I hear your noise, it'll be going out the window. Some of us have to work!"

"You could have just asked!" he yelled after me.

"I didn't think you'd hear!"

I slammed the door behind me.

* * *

One down, three to go.

I don't know why it was so important to see Trish, maybe it had something to do with the fact that I could die any minute and if I did die, what was I going to have to show for it? For somebody in his thirties I didn't have a whole lot to brag about. I could pack all my worldly belongings into a matchbox and still have room for the sink.

In short it was sink or swim time. Those men would be calling again wanting to know if I had April. The fact that I was as close to her now as I was two days ago, didn't help.

If I was going to die I was going to die fighting.

* * *

I drove to the north side without the slightest touch of Dutch courage. It was three o'clock. There was no plan. I had no idea what time Trish finished work or even if she was at work. It might have made more sense had I gone inside and asked to speak to her. But I didn't do sensible, not when it came to women anyway.

* * *

I was sitting in a car again watching life go by. Just as my backside started to fall asleep, Trish stepped from the nursery holding a young girl by the hand. I got out of the car. She looked across in my direction as I shut the door.

I made my way over to her.

"Hi." I said.

"Hi." She replied.

I looked at the young girl and then at Trish. "Do you get to keep one for good behaviour?"

Trish smiled but it wasn't an action that made me think, had this been Groundhog Day, I probably wouldn't use that line again.

"Who's the man, mummy?" The girl asked.

Trish bent her head towards the girl.

"This is Mr...," she looked up at me. "Mr..."

"Richard." I said. "Please call me Richard."

"Hello Richard."

"Hi... "

"Amy." Trish said.

"Hi..., Amy." I said.

I don't recall a time I'd ever felt so uncomfortable and I'd had some uncomfortable times. I'd been pinned to a lump of wood, beaten to a pulp and shot at, but standing here not knowing whether to shake this little girl's hand, pat her on the head or throw her a ball, beat the lot.

Trish stood straight and waited for me to speak.

"Sorry." I said, glancing back at the car. "But I didn't

know how else to get in touch with you."

She nodded and I realised that she was going to make me grovel all the way to wherever it was I was going.

"I just wanted to say sorry, for the other night, you know, I was an idiot. I..."

She nodded again and the uncomfortable feeling increased. There was two pair of eyes focussed on me instead of just the one pair of green ones I'd prepared myself for.

A group of women emerged from the house with other children. They said their goodbyes to Trish. It gave me time to realise that I'd made a big mistake coming here. Perhaps I should have thought it through at least. Instead of simply following the American example of barge in, shoot a lot people and then ask if you've got the right address.

The women disappeared down the street. I blew out a mouthful of air and tried to start again.

"I was just wondering if you were free one night? I thought, maybe we could just have a drink, you know, and talk a little and I'll be whoever you want me to be, Blake, Mahoney, it doesn't matter to me."

"But it might to somebody else!" she quietly suggested.

"To be honest, I'm not sure what the difference is anymore, we're both underachievers."

"You really know how to sell yourself!"

I felt my face blush. Next time I'm just going to shoot myself, it'll be easier.

A door opened and another group of people emerged from the nursery.

"How about tomorrow?" Trish asked quickly.

"Tomorrow?" I was shocked.

"Is that a problem?"

"Well, no."

"Seven o'clock at The Lodge in Ayton. It's easier for me to get to. It's on Moor Road. Take a right at the school, you can't miss it."

Had a leaf tumbled from a nearby tree and brushed my head it would have knocked me to the floor.

"Right," I said.

"See you then," she smiled.

* * *

"Put away the gun, Mahoney, you're back in business," I said to myself as I got back into the car. There's no need to shoot yourself after all.

I jammed the key into the ignition with thoughts of how wonderful life was all of a sudden

"And stop talking to yourself!" I said as I started up the engine.

It roared.

Chapter Fifty-two

April and the girls had shared a flat on Castle Road. The place was easy to find, there was a pile of furniture that over ran the yard and spilt onto the pavement. Men in sweat-stained T-Shirts wiped their brow with the back of a hand and frowned at the heavy workload that didn't appear to be diminishing.

"Either of you the landlord?" I asked.

Instantly they jabbed their heads in the general direction of the hallway and towards a middle aged man inspecting a clipboard.

I squeezed past the furniture and over to the man.

"Are you the landlord?"

"Yes," he replied defensively and with an air of suspicion. "Why?"

"I was just wondering what you could tell me about the two girls who used to live here."

"Could you be a little more specific? I've had a lot of girls live here," he half laughed.

"Petra and Natalie."

"Oh yes," he smiled. "Very nice girls. Foreign, but very nice all the same."

I paused to allow the two men to inch past us with another load of furniture.

"We're just getting the place back in order," he explained. "There was a fire here a few weeks ago. Poor girl died. Only just got round to letting it out again."

"About the girls," I said.

"Yeah, why do you want to know?"

"I'm a Private Investigator. I've got to issue them with a summons," I lied.

"A summons? What did they do?"

"I'm sorry, that information is strictly confidential."

"Well I'm sorry, like I told the police, there's not much I can tell you."

"The police were here?"

"Yeah, just the other day. They were asking about the girls as well."

"What did you tell them?"

"Not a lot really, I mean, they kept themselves pretty much to themselves. I never had any problems with them and they always paid on time."

"Did they leave a forwarding address?"

He shook his head. "I'm afraid not."

"How come? I mean, what about any outstanding mail?"

"They said it didn't matter, that I should throw it away, which is a blessing considering the amount of junk we get. Bit of a fire hazard I reckon."

"Is that it?"

He looked at me as though I was expecting him to pull a rabbit from a hat when he didn't even have so much as a hat.

"And the cops, they didn't get anything either?"

"Just a note," he replied.

"A note?"

"Yeah, a note somebody had stuck through the letterbox, but the girls had already gone."

"And you gave it to the cops?"

He nodded.

"Did you happen to see what was on it?"

"No!" He snapped. "It was folded in two with the girls names on the front."

I looked at the man for a moment and I wondered just how close I'd come to actually getting a break.

"I don't suppose you can remember anything about these two cops can you?"

"Such as what?"

"Such as their names or what they looked like?"

"Why, are you suggesting they weren't who they said they were?"

That's exactly what I thought, but I wasn't about to tell him that.

"No, I just want to see if they've got a lead that's all."

The man rubbed his chin for a moment and really looked like he was making an effort but some how I couldn't help thinking he was about to come up blank, especially when he started to shake his head in a forlorn manner.

"No, I'm sorry. I know one of them showed me his badge, but I really didn't take any notice, you know how it is."

"But the other one didn't look too bothered did he!" I suggested.

The landlord look at me. "No, not really no."

It had to be Warne and Lucas. The Gruesome Twosome.

"Thanks," I said, and hurried back to the car.

* * *

It's possible the girls were working illegally. Their names sounded foreign after all. Maybe that's why Lucas and Warne had been sniffing around. But something told me there was more to it than that. There had to be more to it than that, otherwise Private Investigators would soon go out of business.

Chapter Fifty-three

Walker was sitting at his favourite table in his favourite bar reading his favourite paper with his favourite pint in front of him. He looked like a man content with the world. His shift was over, it was somebody else's turn to clean up the streets. He wasn't going to appreciate me turning up out of the blue.

I placed my pint onto the table and sat down opposite him. I watched as the Inspector's eyes looked down at my glass and then up at me.

"This isn't good news is it?" he scowled.

"Maybe I've just come for a drink?"

Walker shook his head as he replied; "You've got that look."

"Look? What look?"

"The look that always brings bad news. It's the same look people carry around in the force. I see it whenever they have to tell a parent that their child won't be coming home tonight. You try to hide it. You hope, in time, it'll go away with, but it never does."

"Well nobody's died," I quickly reassured him. "Not that I know of anyway."

"I'm glad to hear it! So what's on your mind?"

"Have you ever heard of two cops called Warne and Lucas?"

Walker thought for as moment before shaking his head.

"I don't think so, why?"

"It's just that their names keep cropping up that's all."

"In what way?"

"First of all they came by the office asking if I knew a girl called Alana who worked at the Mission Club. Apparently they're looking into illegal immigrants working in the bars and clubs."

Walker nodded.

"Then they were asking this landlord about two girls who just happened to have disappeared off the face of the earth a few weeks ago."

Walker sipped his beer. "Were all these girls foreign?"

"I believe so."

"So what's your problem? They were investigating illegal immigrants. It's hardly surprising the girls skipped town, better than being deported."

"I know. It's just that."

"It's just that what?"

"These girls all knew one another, and they all knew Jenny."

"The girl in the crash?"

I nodded.

"That still might just be a coincidence."

"I know." I mumbled.

Walker folded up his newspaper and pressed it onto the table.

"But?"

"I think there's something else going on here."

"Even though I finished my shift over half an hour ago and I'm in a pub drinking my beer because it's what I'm entitled to do, I suppose I'm going to have to ask you to elaborate on that 'something' aren't I?"

I looked at Walker and knew he wouldn't like hearing what I was about to tell him. But I didn't have a whole lot of choice.

"I know that Jenny wasn't alone in Preacher's house that night."

The Inspector shuffled forward in his seat and offered me an inquisitive glare.

"She was with Alana."

"The girl at the club?"

I nodded. "Apparently two men broke into the house. They slapped Jenny around a bit and then they took her away."

"Did Alana see any of this?"

"She was hiding."

"They didn't know she was there?"

"It doesn't look like it."

"Did she see them?"

"They were wearing balaclavas. She wouldn't know them if they walked in the room and shook her hand."

"How do you know all this?"

"She told me."

"When?"

"A little while ago."

"Why?"

"Why?" I frowned.

"Why would she tell you?"

I shrugged my shoulders. "I'm not sure. She said it was because I stuck up for her at the club. She came round to my flat. I suppose she didn't have anybody else to turn to."

Walker picked up his drink and finished it. He wiped the froth from his lips with the back of his hand. He looked ready to leave.

"Where is she now?"

"Alana?"

He nodded. I shrugged my shoulders again.

"You let her go?" he asked anxiously.

"She said she wanted to stay with friends, she's scared."

Walker leaned across the table and pointed a finger at me. He spoke through clenched teeth.

"She could be an important witness Mahoney!"

"But she didn't see anything!" I argued.

"She saw something. And you'd be surprised how the little pieces of information add up into one big clue."

Walker got to his feet and I followed him outside. The night was cool. The air was fresh. It was the kind of evening to spend sitting in gardens breathing in the fumes of a barbecue and drinking a bottle of wine. But now we had more pressing issues.

"Have you no idea where she is?"

I shook my head. "I don't think she even has a mobile."

The Inspector sighed and brushed a hand through his hair and stepped from side to side for a moment.

"I told her to keep in touch."

"You think she will?"

"I'm not sure where else she's got to go."

"Good," he said, aiming a finger at me. "And you let me know the moment she does."

I nodded.

"You know, this wouldn't be so bad if you hadn't have thought that there was something suspicious going on," Walker moaned.

"So now it's my fault?"

Walker rubbed his side.

"What's up?" I asked.

"I think I've got an ulcer coming on."

"It's probably just wind!"

"Not knowing my luck."

He took a deep breath and stood up straight.

"You let me know the moment she calls you, OK!" he said, poking a finger into my chest."

"I'll try, but she really is scared."

"She could have every right to be, her life could be in danger!"

"But who else knew she was there?" I asked.

Walker buttoned up his jacket. "Don't forget, this is a small town Mahoney, and people talk. If one person knew she was there then, chances are, by the end of the week, everybody else knows. We've just got to hope we get to her first."

* * *

I walked back to my car and turned the keys to the ignition. The engine started first time. It was about the only thing I could rely on at the moment, things were that bad.

It was back to the drawing board. I checked the rear view mirror, I expected to see a face frowning back at me, wondering what the hell I was doing leading everybody from one blind alley to the next, including myself. What I didn't expect to see was a stranger pointing a gun at me.

He calmly ordered me to drive.

I must remember to lock the door next time.

Chapter Fifty-four

I didn't get much from the guy with the gun other than directions. I followed them to the letter. We drove for about ten minutes until we arrived at a disused barn.

The man with the gun pushed me along a straw sprinkled path and up to a barn door. He nodded his head just the once. I pushed the door open and stepped inside. The place was dark and smelt of hay and manure. There was a table in the middle with a couple of empty chairs either side. Two other goons, waiting inside, grabbed my arms and bounced me into one of the chairs. They strapped my hands tight behind my back.

There was a time when people had a reason to die. It could be old age, disease, famine or war. It wasn't necessarily a nice way to go but at least people knew why. But the same couldn't be said of today. Nowadays somebody would happily cut you down to size just for the fun of it, the prestige, just because you happened to be walking down the right street at the wrong time.

Thankfully these guys appeared old school. Professional.

They wanted something, so they weren't about to ice me just for the fun of it. I hoped!

So I tried to remain relaxed. I looked at the bare table and then at one of the goons standing with his arms across his chest.

"Mind getting me a menu?" I asked, tugging at the straps. "I'm kind of tied up."

He didn't answer. I stared at the empty chair.

"Looks like I've been stood up!"

One of the men cracked his knuckles, one after the other and smiled at me. I would have clapped if I could have.

Almost immediately another figure entered the room, a smart looking figure in a smart looking suit. He sat down and clicked on a light in the middle of the table. It half blinded my vision

"I suppose you think you're tough Mr Mahoney!" said the man in the suit.

His voice was soft.

"Tough enough to worry you."

He laughed.

"I've seen people like you come and go. They think they're big when they're nothing really. They want to set the world alight but they can't even find a match most of the time, and before you know it, they're sleeping in the gutter and begging for change."

"Well I'm five foot ten," I snapped. "If that's big then I'm sorry but don't worry, I don't even carry a match, so what's really eating you?"

"I want to know what you were doing in my club the other night?"

Saltys! So that's what all this was about. I really had rattled somebody's cage.

"So you're Collingwood?"

The suit didn't answer.

"Tell me, do you put all your customers through this?" I moaned.

"You were asking a lot of questions."

"I find it helps when you need to buy a drink!"

Collingwood paused to tap a finger on the table but I didn't recognise the beat.

"You were asking about some kid?" he said.

"Smudge."

"Right. Why?"

"Because it's my job!"

"You're not a reporter! I checked."

"No, I'm a Private Investigator."

"Really!"

He sounded impressed. I should have told him not to bother.

"So, why were you looking for him? Did somebody ask you?"

"That's confidential and you know it!"

Collingwood laughed politely and stood up. He walked towards me and sat at the edge of the desk. He looked down at me. A lot of people seemed to look down at me.

"And what about the girl?" he asked.

"I wasn't asking about a girl!"

"But you have been?"

"What's that to you?"

"I was only asking."

"Like I said, I'm a Private Investigator."

"Do you know her?"

I shook my head. I needed to keep April out of this.

"She was just a lead that's all. It's Smudge I need to talk to."

"Why?"

"Like I said, that's confidential."

"I see," he said, and retreated to the other side of the table. "So you're a hero!"

"I've been called worse."

"But are you a foolish hero?"

His question took me a little by surprise and therefore I wasn't ready with an answer.

Collingwood took a couple of steps towards me. "For the last time, Mr Mahoney, who are you working for?"

"Just good old me."

He smiled. And I didn't like the way he smiled. I mean, I don't think he was about to congratulate me on passing the initiation test and rewarding me with a Government contract to infiltrate a terrorist organisation operating here on the East coast.

He sat back down in his chair as another figure made his way over to the table.

I looked to my left and straight into a silhouette.

"Mr Mahoney, meet Dr Peterson," said Collingwood. "He's a dentist by trade."

I watched Peterson heave a black bag onto the table and open it up. It revealed an array of instruments all very silver and sharp. It was like some kind of medieval torture display.

"And I thought there was a problem finding a dentist in this town!"

"It pays to have contacts, Mr Mahoney," Collingwood laughed for a moment, before adding; "Unfortunately though, Dr Peterson lost his licence some years ago."

"Have you tried under the sofa, I always find that's a good place to look!"

"Everybody has a vice, don't you think, Mr Mahoney?" Unfortunately Dr Peterson's was, and no doubt still is, the soft, delicate skin of young girls, isn't that right Mr Peterson?"

Peterson nodded and drooled, he was far too busy rummaging through his instruments to speak.

"Well I'm afraid you won't find any soft delicate skin

on me, it's all thick and scarred."

I was trying to think positive thoughts but that wasn't easy when I noticed one of the goons stretch an extension lead across the floor towards the table. I started to worry. Unlike the men up at the Zoo, this lot meant business. Something about April bothered them but I had no idea what that something was.

"Now, if you have nothing more to tell me, Mr Mahoney then I'll leave you in peace. I detest the sound of screaming."

Collingwood opened a door and left. Peterson pulled the light closer and lit up my mouth. He rolled what looked to be a bit of silver paper up and, considering what else he had on view, it didn't seem the most obvious choice.

What the hell was I doing? I hated dentists, even nice dentists. All I had to do was tell them what they wanted to know. So why the hell didn't I speak up? Was it the medal I'd receive? Was it the front page news? Was it the so called promise of a welcome in everybody else's heaven? Or was it simply the satisfaction of doing my job to the best of my ability?

No, it was the fact that I hated people who just thought they could come along and get what they wanted, when they wanted it and bollocks to anyone who stood in their way.

Peterson looked into my mouth and licked his lips.

"Now, what have we here?" he asked in an accent not a million miles from Liverpool. It was slow and droll and a very effective anaesthetic.

"Open wide."

"Go to hell!"

It was the best I could do. A fist snapped into my ribs and I yelled out in pain. A figure helped Peterson grip my jaw and force a rubber cube inside my mouth. It was too large to dislodge and it strained my jaw until I thought it would snap. Now I was worried. I gulped a swallow and I gulped many more as a film of sweat gathered on my temple. What the hell was I doing?

"Now," said Peterson. "Any fillings?"

My neck was held tight as Peterson closed in on my mouth. I had never felt pain like it. The silver paper touched my tooth and my head exploded. The force of the explosion flipped me to the floor. I was still sitting in my chair but with a view of the ceiling. It was one thing feeling pain, but quite another not being able to cry out and touch it.

"Hold him still you idiot!"

The idiot levered me upright again.

Peterson reached into his bag and pulled out an instrument and attached to the lead. "Now, if you thought that was painful!"

He switched on a drill. If I was going to die I wanted it to be quick. A gun to the head was a possibility but certainly not drowning or being burnt to death or having my teeth drilled.

Peterson held up the instrument and smiled. The buzzing sound filled the room. Even the goon to my right decided he couldn't watch anymore. He stepped out of sight. What the hell was I doing?

"Now, is there anything you'd like to say, Mr Mahoney?" Peterson asked.

I stared back at him.

"Good," he said with another lick of his lips."

I took a mental note of his sad grey eyes, the nasal hair, the birth mark on his cheek and I swore there and then that if it was with my dying breath, I'd kill the bastard.

Chapter Fifty-five

When my eyes eventually focussed on the world around me, I found myself surrounded by trees and the soft sound of running water like chips sizzling in a frying pan.

The car sped away. It was too quick for me to clock the number plate.

My mobile phone was lying on the floor. I picked it up. It didn't look too good. I pressed a button. Nothing happened. So they didn't like mobile phones either!

I got to my feet and dusted myself down. My head felt like it had been hit with a hammer. I could only take so much. My tooth and my jaw hurt like hell.

I'd told them that I was working for a screwball called Storey who was looking for his daughter and staying at the Grand Hotel. I didn't think I was putting him in any danger considering that wasn't his real name or where he was staying.

But, more importantly than that, it bought me some time.

I assumed that dumping me out here gave them the

opportunity to check out my story. They weren't going to be very happy, but you can't please everybody.

* * *

I stood at the side of the road. It meandered to my left and to my right. Either direction could have got me lost forever. I had no idea where I was or where I was going. I flipped a coin and set off to my right.

The sun cut through the branches and warmed my tired limbs. Birds nestled high in the trees whistling the kind of tune that only they could sing and there was never a bum note.

Why hadn't they killed me? Right now I wouldn't have cared. I was fed up with being beaten and shot at and spoken to as though I wasn't worth the luxury of a cat-flap.

A car came into view. It was heading in the opposite direction but I didn't mind, it was still a lift. I held out a thumb. It drove on by. Think about it Mahoney, look at the state you're in. I was a tramp. Even I wouldn't have picked me up right now.

* * *

The sun was glowing a bright orange colour by the time I reached a road that stretched round a mere where nobody fished. Another car passed me by. I carried on. The road widened until a large ugly building came into view, a silent school and then a college and then a busy main road. I was back in civilisation with all its noise and greed and backstabbing. I wasn't happy.

Chapter Fifty-six

It took me an hour to find a taxi and locate Ronnie's car. Thankfully it was OK. I really wouldn't have wanted to inform him that his four wheel classic had just been set alight or driven off a cliff.

It brought a smile to my face when I finally found the car waiting patiently where I'd been ordered to leave it. Perhaps for the first time I'd noticed a certain appeal about it. The shape, the colour, the fact that it was like nothing else any other detectives drove around in. A 1955, Series 2, split windscreen, Morris Minor.

I ran a hand along the wing and patted the headlight. I was going soft.

I checked the barn. It was clean, like nobody had been there in months. These guys were good.

* * *

I returned to the sanctity of the office, poured a whisky and stretched my aching feet out across the desk. For a moment I sat in silence and ran a finger over my tooth.

I thought about ringing Envy but a tap on the door distracted me.

Debbie walked in and offered me a big bright "hi."

I didn't reply. I couldn't be bothered. But that didn't seem to deter her.

"So this is your office!" she beamed.

I stopped short of a sarcastic remark. I wanted my whisky and I needed a rest.

"You came all this way just to see my office?"

"Maybe."

She made her way over to the window before spinning on a heel and staring back at me.

"Have you spoken to your partner yet?"

I had completely forgotten about talking to Ronnie and it was probably as well. It wasn't fair to leave wild animals alone in a room with him let alone a young girl, especially before breakfast.

"No." I said.

She didn't try to mask her disappointment. "Pity."

"I will!"

"When?"

"I've been busy."

"You're still looking for that boy?"

"Maybe."

"It said in the paper there's like, a reward."

"You've been reading the paper?"

"Somebody told me."

I sipped my whisky.

"What's that?" she asked.

"The devil's poison."

"Oh my God, you never give me like, a straight answer do you!"

"I'm sorry," I replied. "I'm tired."

"I just thought you might want some good news that's all."

I looked at Debbie but I didn't dare consider the possibility that her good news could, in any way, match my expectations.

"Yeah, you're right," I smiled. "I would really appreciate some good news."

"So how much is the reward?" she asked.

"I didn't think the money mattered?"

"I have to live on something don't I? Till I become like a Private Investigator anyway."

She was serious. And who was I to discourage her? Besides, she'd probably do a better job than me.

"Forty pounds."

"Make it fifty!" she said.

"Are we just making up numbers?"

"Fifty's a real number!" she quipped.

"Do you know where Smudge is?"

Debbie shook her head. I got all ready to boot her out the office when she suddenly started to smile.

"I've done better than that," she said quietly. "I've found April."

Chapter Fifty-seven

I rang Storey and told him that it looked like I might be on to April. He appeared relieved and so was I. The men would be calling soon. I was about to ring Envy when I decided to wait until I had the good news in my hand.

* * *

Apparently April had been hiding out in some deserted chalets over on the south side.

In all honesty it would have been quicker to walk from the office. A ten minute stroll over the Cliff Bridge and then down past the Spa and onto the chalets. The fact that it was raining shouldn't have deterred me, it was exercise and a whole lot better than getting stuck in a jam at the top of town and having to put up with Debbie humming along to a tune that only she could hear through a music system that was attached to her ears.

Half an hour later I double parked at the far end of the Spa and we walked the rest of the way. The smash of the waves against the high wall didn't subdue the tinny beat from her headphones.

"Do you have to play that thing?" I shouted.

She aimed her chin at me and plucked the headphones from her ears. "What?"

"You have to be alert if you want to be a Private Investigator."

She turned the music off. Peace at last.

We continued past the Spa and came to a halt outside a dull grey two storey building with a dozen chalets below and a dozen chalets above. It didn't look like it had been used in over a decade, maybe even more. Every one of the doors downstairs had been either smashed or smothered with graffiti. There was a talented artist going to waste in this town

"Wait here." I said to Debbie.

"Why?" she moaned.

"Because I said so."

"But that's not fair, I found her!"

"I know, but she might be scared and she's not going to want half a dozen people suddenly turning up out of the blue."

"All the more reason not to have like, some big oaf like you, knocking on the door either."

I was shocked. "Oaf?"

She looked away coyly.

"You know what I mean," she whispered.

She had a point. I mean, if I was locked up in a chalet I'd rather see Debbie standing there than some strange bloke, oaf.

But I also had a job to do. Finding April was my responsibility. I had to take charge. I put a hand on Debbie's shoulder.

"Look, you might be right. But this is what I'm paid to do, this is my job. I'm the one who's meant to bring her in. If anything goes wrong then it has to be my fault, not yours."

I waited for Debbie to eventually nod and force a reluctant smile.

"You stay here and keep an eye out OK."

"OK."

* * *

I checked the downstairs chalets first. They stank of seaweed and salt and leftover food and urine. But there was no sign of April. I shrugged my shoulders at Debbie and went round to the side of the building. A wooden door barely hung on its hinges. I kicked it open and took the stone steps upstairs to the second floor. The chalets there were much the same as the ones below.

I looked down at Debbie. She was propped up against the railing and staring back towards the Spa building.

I checked the first chalet. It had been gutted by fire. The second came equipped with empty beer cans and syringes. The third one appeared locked. It was only then that I started to wonder what I was going to say to April. I knew somebody who wanted to meet her because he thought he was her old man, but it turns out he's nothing more than somebody who was shipping you as cargo in exchange for money and actually your life is in danger, but you probably know that already, which is why you're hiding.

Maybe I ought to let her do most of the talking.

I took a breath and tapped on the door. Nothing happened.

"April," I said softly. "April are you in there?"

Still nothing happened and for a minute I wondered if this would just go down as another wasted moment in my life, something to add to the endless catalogue. Then a voice quietly asked; "Who is it?"

"My name's Richard Mahoney, April. I'm a Private Investigator. I've come to help you."

Once again there was silence. I watched the door for

a moment until it slowly opened. A young girl appeared on the other side. A tired, pale young girl who looked nothing like the one I'd seen in the photo. It was as though she hadn't eaten, slept or even washed in a week.

I prepared my warmest smile. But, much to my surprise, she put a hand over her mouth and let out a scream. That was quickly followed by a whooshing sound and a crack over the back of my head.

A pool of darkness opened its arms and beckoned me inside. Not that I had much choice.

Chapter Fifty-eight

I could hear the faint whistling of birds in the distance, the crash of the ocean and muffled voices as my eyes strained open. I was lying on the floor. Debbie was busy trying to press a coat under my head.

"Oh my God, you're like, bleeding."

"What the hell happened?" I asked.

"I think somebody hit you."

I rubbed my head. "You don't say! Did you see who?"

Debbie shook her head. "I was downstairs like you said. I got worried, you were gone so long."

I focussed my eyes into the chalet. It was empty. My head started to spin. Blood seeped from a wound just above my ear. My hand was covered in a bright crimson colour.

"Somebody's taken her," I moaned.

I tried to get to my feet but the world was spinning far too fast. I knelt back down.

"None of this would have happened if you'd let me see

her!" Debbie argued.

I looked at her as best I could in the circumstances. "How do you know? There might have been a gang of them for all you know and then we'd both have been lying here wondering what day it was."

She started to point out something. I could see her lips move but I couldn't hear a word because my head started to roll to one side. I was all out of blood and the darkness opened up again.

Chapter Fifty-nine

The nurse had lied when she said it wouldn't hurt because it did. It hurt like hell. She just accused me of being a baby, that was her way of dealing with this situation and she was sticking to it. She had thick, permed hair and bright blue eyes. And she didn't look like someone who'd have a lot of difficulty attracting attention on a night out.

I tried to focus on the white walls as the needle scratched my head and slipped in under my skin. It took forever.

"Are you enjoying this?" I asked.

"I wasn't the one getting myself beaten up." She replied.

"I didn't do it on purpose!"

Another scratch, another pull. I really had to finish my book and get out of this mess.

She flipped off her little white gloves. "There, all done."

"That's it?"

"I'll get you a little morphine for that tooth, but you really ought to change your dentist!"

"Not even a lollipop?" I asked.

"Blame it on the cut backs!"

I followed her out the room.

"You can leave a tip at Reception if you like."

She took a right and left me feeling nothing more than an inconvenience. In truth, I probably was, grown men getting hit over the head in the street! Whatever next?

Out in the corridor Envy sat patiently waiting. The hospital had informed me that I would have to have somebody come and collect me, and she was the first person I could think of. I was pleased to see her. But Debbie had disappeared.

Envy tipped my head to one side and inspected the wound.

"Lucky it was your head," she smiled.

"So everybody keeps telling me!"

"Are you sure it was April?"

Instantly I checked my pockets and pulled out my wallet. I hadn't been robbed.

"It looked like her and nobody took anything. But I'm going to need another one of these," I said, holding out the damaged phone.

Envy sighed. "And now somebody else has got her."

I nodded.

"Any idea who?"

"No," I replied.

I checked the clock on the wall.

"What's the matter?"

"I was just thinking," I replied. "Those goons are supposed to be ringing me any minute."

"The ones asking about April?"

I nodded.

Suddenly Envy got all perplexed. "You weren't going to give them her were you?"

"Of course not. I was just hoping that, with her, I

319

might know a little more than I know right now, which wouldn't be too difficult, considering I know absolutely nothing at all!

Chapter Sixty

We went for a coffee. I'm not sure it was a good idea considering I still had a headache, but it gave me the chance to bring Envy up to speed.

"So," Envy began on reflection. "In the past twenty-four hours you've had somebody drill your teeth simply because you were asking questions about Smudge and then somebody hits you over the head when you think you're about to meet April?"

"I've certainly had better days!"

"Why you though?"

Her question took me by surprise.

"What?"

"Why you? I mean, we're both looking for April. In fact I've probably spoken to far more people about her than you have, why haven't I been hit over the head or had my teeth drilled?"

"I'll be sure to ask that the next time I'm tied to a chair or walking down a dark alley."

Envy reached forward and touched my hand, but not

in a sexual, if nothing else works out we still have each other, way. More of a friendly, trying to work things out, protective manner. At least that's how it looked to me.

"I think you've got too close to somebody," she said. "One of these people, Preacher, Collingwood, maybe even O'Riley, has something to hide or something to gain from what you might know."

"But I don't have anything and I certainly don't know anything!" I argued.

"But they don't know that, not until they start torturing you!"

I took a sip of coffee. It wasn't as nice as I'd hoped. I sat back and touched the side of my head. The stitching was prominent. Everything felt so uncomfortable.

"How did you get into all this?" I asked.

Envy eyed me over the rim of her cup and raised her eyebrows.

"The detective stuff," I added.

She smiled and stared down into her cup.

"A few years ago I met the love of my life, a guy who walked into my world and swept me off my feet. We met in the States, near to where I lived. He said all the right things and pressed all the right buttons. Unfortunately, what I didn't know at the time was, he was a confidence trickster. He took me for every penny I had, and I mean every penny, the loan on my apartment, everything."

Envy paused to look across at me. "Do you know what it's like to put all your faith in someone and have them betray it?"

I shook my head. It was the easiest thing to do in the circumstances.

"Everything about him had been a Goddamn lie. All I knew was that he was English. I moved here with the promise that, whatever it took, I'd track him down."

"And?"

She sighed. "Well it was hopeless. The police wouldn't help because I hadn't gotten anything to go on except for a vague description. So I ended up paying a Private Investigator to look into it for me. After four weeks of taking my money I realised he hadn't even set foot outside his office expect to visit the bar. Well, you now what they say, if a jobs worth doing......"

"Did you find him?"

"Not yet," she replied in a way that suggested that one day she would, and you wouldn't want to be in this guy's shoes when she did."

"But if there's any justice in this world!" she added.

I nodded. "So what's with all the counselling and working out stuff?"

Envy stared out across the room.

"I suppose that was all a kinda reaction to what had happened, a sort of re-inventing myself, if you like. I never want anybody to do anything like that to me ever again."

I looked at Envy for a moment as she finished her coffee.

"You're pretty good," I started. "I mean, I don't know that much about being a Detective but, if I ever wanted one, I'd probably come to you."

Envy smiled and blushed.

"You've got heart and determination and I reckon they must go a long way in this line of work."

"But I still haven't found the guy who broke my heart and I still haven't found April, so I can't be that good."

"I reckon it's only a matter of time!"

"Do we have time? I mean, does April have time?"

I let out a sigh and slumped in my seat. Reality had come calling once again. Building up somebody was one thing, but finding somebody else was proving quite another. I didn't have a clue where to look for April and my head was aching. I stood up. The room span. I grabbed a chair to support myself. Envy got all concerned.

"Are you all right?"

I nodded.

She smiled. "You ought to lie down."

"I know, but I need to find Smudge, he's all we've got now. Maybe he knows something about April."

Envy grabbed my arm.

"I'll find him. You need some rest."

I didn't argue because I couldn't argue.

"It's my turn to get hit over the head," Envy said with a wink.

Chapter Sixty-one

I had just about made it to the sofa when the phone started to ring. I ignored it. Thirty seconds it rang again. I walked across the room and snatched it up.

"Yeah!"

"It's me, Walker. I need to see you."

"Now?"

"Now."

So much for my rest. I must be really wicked!

* * *

Our shoes echoed around the corridor as we made our way along the tiled floor towards the beat of a song from the next room. The place smelt like a hospital, but only the staff ever left here alive. Sunlight warmed the narrow passage way.

Walker pushed on a door and we entered a room with wall to wall cabinets. Fletcher was standing behind a desk and scratching the back of his neck. He was dressed in a long white coat. He pulled on his cravat and greeted us with a smile. Walker nodded back at him. Fletcher turned down the volume on his radio but left it loud enough to continue clapping his hands and singing along to the chorus of a George Michael song. He was far too happy to work in a place like this.

We waited next to one of the cabinets. Fletched checked the name and pulled on a handle. It swung open. A figure appeared, all horizontal and covered in a white sheet.

Walker looked across at me.

"You ready for this?"

I nodded, but I wasn't really sure.

Fletcher pulled back the sheet. I lowered my eyes and saw the face.

"Shit!" I announced.

"Is it her?" Walker asked.

I looked up at him and nodded.

"How did, how was she....?"

Fletcher pushed the drawer closed. "Strangled."

* * *

Walker and I retreated to the corridor.

"Who else knew what you told me?" The Inspector asked.

I stopped walking and looked at the wall behind Walker. There was nothing particularly special about it, just clean, plain tiles, but it helped delay what I had to say.

"Mahoney!"

"Just Preacher," I answered.

Walker twisted his mouth to one side in silent contemplation.

"Funny isn't it," I continued.

"What?"

"I mean, how conveniently the finger of suspicion always seems to point at him!"

"If you think so."

"Well that's where this is going isn't it?"

"Don't get so defensive, Mahoney, I was just asking a simple question that's all. I had no idea who knew what."

He had a point. I was over reacting.

"Maybe you ought to speak to those coppers, they might know something?"

"I will," Walker replied.

But somehow that wasn't good enough.

"I said I'd take care of her!" I moaned, as a rush of guilt washed over me.

"I'm sure you did what you could!"

"Well obviously it wasn't enough was it, because now she's dead."

"You can't blame yourself, Mahoney, you didn't ask her to come to you and you had no idea what she might have been mixed up in."

I looked at Walker, but the guilt refused to go away.

"That's just the point," I argued. "The harder I look the less idea I have. I've become a liability. All I know is, it wasn't me who killed her and I'm pretty sure it wasn't you!"

"I'm glad to hear it."

"That just leaves everybody else!"

Walker suddenly appeared a little apprehensive. "What are you going to do?"

"Maybe it's time to put the squeeze on a few people."

"Careful Mahoney. I don't want to have to come down here and identify you."

* * *

It's possible I could have been mistaken, but Walker almost sounded sincere!

Chapter Sixty-two

Preacher couldn't have killed Alana because I'd only just spoken to him about her. Nobody was that stupid.

But the who's and the why's and the where's kept rattling around my head and getting louder all the while.

It was time to look over some old ground and see if I could come up with something new.

I rang Hartless and told him to meet me in twenty minutes down on the foreshore.

The place was packed, wall to wall people and cars. But I found a parking space opposite O'Rileys ice-cream parlour and stuck Elliott's disabled sticker in the window and waited.

The day was hot. The sun poked its head between the clouds and looked down on Scarborough. It's possible it might have sighed and wondered why it ever bothered to pay a fleeting visit, because nobody ever seemed to appreciate it that much. They either talked about how the summers were always so much hotter in the good old days, or that it was far too hot to do anything, and how the gardens could do with a bit of rain before they were concreted over.

Those who didn't moan took to the beach and covered themselves in oil or toasted their skin before a mad rush to the nearest medical unit and a fortnight off work.

Every so often I would catch a glimpse of O'Riley at the window. The rest of the time he was out of sight and I wondered what anybody could do all day alone in an office with a dead cat. And then I stopped wondering because, with O'Riley, it was more than just possible.

* * *

Next to the ice-cream parlour was Madame Marlene, the Tarot card reader. Business was brisk, but then she would have known that from the moment she woke up this morning. Personally I never dared ask what my future might hold, just in case they told me it was all used up.

Out on the beach the donkeys trudged wearily through a gap in the crowd. Each one of them looked like their latest request for an increase in carrots had been rejected.

And then, right on queue, Hartless appeared with a shopping bag. His hat failed to hide the kind of expression that most people wore when they had to work on a day like this.

He opened the car door and slumped into the passenger seat.

"Y..., you wanted to see me?" he chewed.

I nodded.

"What's the matter?"

"Lots of things."

"Oh dear."

"For instance, I was wondering if you might know why somebody would want to bash me over the head, drill my teeth and kick me in the kidneys a couple of times. Am I really that nasty?"

Hartless looked at me for a moment without answering, so I brought him up to speed with what had happened. He did a lot of wincing and groaning sounds as he followed my route from the barn to the hospital and to the morgue.

"Th,.. that's not good news," he concluded.

"I know."

"And have, have you any idea who's got April?"

I looked out of the window. The world was full of people, but it could have been anyone of them. All I needed was a reason and a lot of luck.

"No."

"So how, how can I help?"

I looked at Hartless.

"Envy came up with this idea that, despite the two of us working together, it's only ever me who got the knocks."

"M….maybe you're just unlucky?"

"I'd already figured that one out for myself," I quipped. "But she also thought that maybe I've rattled somebody's cage and it possible you might know why."

Hartless got all nervous about what he might be getting drawn into.

"W…, what would I know?"

"Well, for instance, what do you know about O'Riley?"

Hartless paused to glance up at his office.

"Mmmm interesting," he replied.

"How, mmm, interesting?" I asked.

"W…., well there are two sides to O'Riley, the, the public and the private side."

"And let me guess, the public side isn't half as mmm interesting as the private?"

"Well, in public he runs a chain of er, of ice-cream parlours, he was also town Mayor and he, he does a lot for charity."

"Sounds like a nice man. Now get to the interesting bits."

"The, this is strictly off the re, record of course!"

"Of course."

"Well, apparently he, he runs a protection racket throughout the old town, but it's not, it's not the kind that s....smashes up the place if you don't pay him anything. It's about protecting the interests of the old town, making sure people are trading legitimately, paying the right wages, that kind of thing, and er, keeping outside traders at bay."

I nodded. "Anything else?"

Hartless hesitated.

"Eddie?"

"He er, he also likes to keep the streets clean."

"I really can't see O'Riley pushing a broom!"

"Not the, that kind of clean," Hartless responded.

"I didn't think so."

"It's only a rumour of course."

"I can live with a rumour."

"Well, apparently anybody er, caught thieving or dealing in and around the old town, you know, usually f....finds themselves waking up on a fishing boat in the middle of the North Sea."

"Interesting and not something those dimwits in Parliament are ever likely to pass! What happens to them?"

"The rumours go, they can be out there for days at a time and naturally they're er, made to work for their keep."

I looked back towards the office and realised that I was beginning to discover a deep respect for O'Riley.

"But where's the money in that?" I asked.

Hartless shook his head.

"D...don't forget, this is only a rumour, but as far as I know he, he doesn't do it for the money. He just likes to protect the old town, it's his town and the people, the, they love him for it."

"What about the cops?"

Hartless shrugged his shoulders. "The, they don't seem to c....care one way or another."

"Just as long as nobody gets hurt, officially anyway?" I added.

"Y.., yes," Hartless agreed. "Just as long as nobody gets hurt."

"And what about Preacher?"

"W..., what about him?"

"That's what I was asking!"

Hartless shrugged his shoulders. "I r..., really don't know much about him. W..., why?"

"The cops seem to have it in for him that's all. But he seems like a decent guy to me."

"L.., like I say, I can't really vouch for him one way or another."

* * *

There was a tap on the window and I turned my head to see Envy looking back at me. I wound down the window. She propped herself up against the side of the car and handed me a phone.

"Try not to damage this one," she insisted.

I studied the phone. "Are you on commission?"

"Well I knew you wouldn't have gotten one for yourself and I figured that sooner or later somebody would need to get in touch with you."

"Yeah, but it's always bad news."

I looked at Envy and immediately I knew I'd struck a chord.

"It's bad news isn't it?" I said.

"Alex Smith, or Smudge as we knew him. His body was found yesterday in a disused mine up near Robin Hoods Bay. Sounds like he's been there sometime."

"P..., poor kid." Hartless muttered.

Envy bowed her head a little more to see where the voice was coming from.

"Oh, Envy, this is Hartless, Hartless this is Envy." I said as a way of a quick introduction.

"Actually it's Jo," said Envy, stretching in across my lap and shaking the reporters hand. "I'm afraid Mahoney isn't on first name terms yet."

"Er, Eddie," said Hartless.

"Hi, Eddie."

"H.....hello Jo."

"Well isn't this cute." I moaned.

"So what now?" Envy asked.

"I don't know, maybe the two of you should get married."

"I mean with Smudge dead and April gone?"

"I don't know."

"Have you heard from Storey?" she asked.

I shook my head. "I didn't have the heart to tell him I'd lost April."

"Do you want me to tell him?"

"No, he'll only get all nervous again."

Envy stood up straight.

"Well just give me a ring if you need me."

I nodded and the two of us sat in silence watching Envy slip back into the crowd.

"So, the, that's Jo!" Hartless said with a twinkle in his eye.

"Yeah, the, that's Jo. Why?" I asked, as if it wasn't obvious.

He shrugged his shoulders. "She seems n.....nice that's all."

"Nice as in pleasant or nice as in you fancy her?"

Eddie stared down at the floor of the car.

"I hardly know her!"

"So?"

"I, just said, the, that's she's very nice, that's all."

"And?"

"And, nothing."

"Eddie."

Hartless appeared increasingly uncomfortable.

"You want me to see if she'd like to have a drink with you?"

"No!"

"Dinner?"

"No!"

"Maybe just lunch then?"

"Mahoney!"

I'd never heard him call me Mahoney before. Mr Mahoney, but never just Mahoney.

"What's wrong with her?"

"N.....nothing."

I stared across at Hartless.

He looked out of the window and snapped. "Look, you j.....just don't understand. Women, well we, we simply don't go together."

Hartless was out of the car before I could say another word. He marched a few yards down the foreshore until there was a gap in the railing wide enough for him to rest his frame and look out over the beach.

He was upset. Two months ago I would have danced naked on top of a lighthouse in order to celebrate having upset a journalist. Now it bothered me.

I got out of the car and went over to him. For a moment we listened to the sound of kids screaming, waves crashing, along with the bings and bongs from the amusement arcades and the wasps whizzing round the waste bins that overdosed on fast food leftovers and wrappings.

"Sorry if I got to you Eddie,"

"It's OK."

"I was just trying to, you know, help."

"But it's like I said, y....you just wouldn't understand."

"I can guess."

The reporter shot me a glance.

"You don't like the idea of rejection," I started. "Jo Envy was the girl at school who knew most of the answers, more than you anyway but she wasn't pretty, not pretty enough for all the other lads to fancy, but there was something about her, something that attracted you, or rather your lusty, greasy haired, spotty faced schoolboy, urges. You didn't talk to her because you didn't know what to say, and you didn't dream for one second that she'd be the slightest bit interested in you. But one day, horror of horrors, it gets out that you like her and one of her friends comes up to you in the playground and says, Do you fancy Jo? This is it, the moment you've been longing for and dreading ever since you first laid eyes on her. You panic, you shake. Part of you starts to imagine riding your bikes together and snogging behind the bus shelter while the other half dreads the alternative, the fact that maybe she doesn't like you at all. But you have to know. So you nod and smile and the girl replies that her friend thinks you're nice, probably even cute, but unfortunately, she doesn't fancy you. That's what she tells you, but what she's actually doing is reaching into your body, pulling out your heart, squeezing it till every last ounce of blood is laying on the floor and then stamping on it for good measure. Am I right?"

Hartless shook his head. "I went to a, to a boys only school."

"Oh hell, well that explains everything then, you're just gay!"

"I'm not gay!" He yelled and suddenly wished he hadn't, because most of the people nearby stopped and turned and looked in our direction.

"I,...I'm not gay." He repeated a whole lot quieter.

"So what's the problem?" I asked.

"I thought you wanted me here s..., so you could find out why people keep knocking you over the head?" Hartless asked.

"Let me call her for you!"

"No!"

I held out my hand. "Give me your phone."

But Hartless wasn't going to budge. And he was right, I was meant to be here on business.

"So what about Collingwood?" I asked.

"Who?"

"The guy at Saltys. There has to be more to him than G-strings and liposuction?"

Hartless glanced discretely out over the beach.

"Eddie?"

I stepped up close to him.

"There's talk that him and his brother are, running, some under-aged sex scam, the, they get a lot of big business people at the club, I guess they call it c..., catering for all needs."

"His brother?"

"Yeah, he died the other week, fell off a roof, it was in the papers."

I pressed my back to the railing and let out a sigh.

"Somehow April's mixed up in all this. But what am I meant to do about it?" I moaned. "All I was meant to do was find a girl and now somebody else has got her, so all these other people are going to want to know where she is and me telling them, 'I don't know' isn't going to wash."

Hartless looked at me. "What about Preacher?"

I propped myself back up against the railing.

"I don't know," I admitted. "My gut feeling tells me he's being set up. He upset a lot of people when he turned his club into a no go area for drugs. But, then again, my guts have been wrong before, lots of times."

"So what are you going to do now?"

It was a good question, but in truth, I didn't have a clue. So I decided to be selfish for once.

"What time is it?" I asked.

Hartless checked his watch. "Nearly six."

I glanced at my watch. For the next minute it was actually going to show the right time for once.

"W...why, what are you going to do?" Hartless asked.

"Keep a very important date."

Chapter Sixty-three

I had just over an hour to shower, dress and worry about how the evening with Trish was going to go. I went through a couple of conversations but they both ended up with her storming off and leaving me with the bill.

Thankfully Ricks rang and disturbed my train of thought. He wanted to see me. He said it was important, urgent in fact. The easiest option was to give in and offer him five minutes outside in my best shirt and tie.

"I've been looking through those names and cuttings," he said, waving his lighter at me. "And I think there's a connection."

I watched Ricks plonk his lighter into a coat pocket and take out the filo-fax. He patted it with the back of his hand like he was expecting it to start screaming.

And all the while I wondered if I'd be half as intrigued as he sounded excited. He opened one page in particular and handed it to me.

"It's a list of names," he said.

"I can see that."

"At first, they just appear random, but I looked into them and, it turns out, they are all linked."

"How?"

He stretched his lips. Maybe it was a form of exercise? Maybe he'd never get any laughter lines?

"They were all, suspected of some crime or another but, get this, none of them were ever convicted. On each occasion, the press ran a piece about the injustice of it all, just like with those cuttings you gave me."

Ricks was still whispering but he was speaking at ninety-miles an hour.

"Lent you," I corrected.

Ricks nodded.

"So what was Reece doing with a list like that?" I asked.

"I'm not sure, but every one of these people have since died."

"Died?"

"Yeah, and pretty suspiciously at that, you know, like a drug overdose, or a hit and run."

"And nobody said anything?"

"Well no," he continued waving his hands across the page. "Like I said, they're just random names. On their own, they're nobodies. It's only when you put them together, that you start to see the connection."

I looked at Ricks and realised that everything he'd said had stopped me from thinking about Trish and I wondered if that was a good thing.

"So are you suggesting that somebody killed these people?" Ricks shrugged his shoulders and half laughed. "What do I know? I'm not a policeman!"

"Well I'll see what Walker has to say?"

"Walker?"

"Yeah. These people might have been murdered, you said so yourself. I think that makes it a job for the cops don't you?"

Ricks started to panic. "But they'll just file it away somewhere, you know they will. There's not enough there for them to go on. I need, more proof."

"But if somebody's going around killing people, they're not going to want some small time reporter sticking his nose in where it doesn't belong."

Suddenly Ricks appeared all hurt and stretched his lips still further.

"I haven't done, too badly up to now for a small time reporter!" he snapped.

"That may all depend on how close you get!"

Ricks blew out a mouthful of fresh air then looked back at me.

"I know what I'm doing, Mr Mahoney."

"Maybe you do, but that still doesn't explain why you don't want the cops involved."

He gave me a sideways glance before staring out down the street.

"What is it, Ricks. What is it you're not telling me?"

"Nothing!"

"I know it's nothing, that's what's bothering me! Look, I let you in on this because you wanted to help, but cutting me out of the loop wasn't part of the plan!"

Ricks shifted his gaze a couple of times.

"OK OK," he said, holding up his hands defensively. "But it's just a rumour OK. You probably, wouldn't believe me anyway."

"Try me."

Ricks stepped back into the shadow of the wall for some reason and lowered his voice still further. "Have you ever heard of someone called, The Cleaner?"

I checked Ricks for a moment. "Yeah, of course I have, she does the office twice a week, but we're on first name terms now!"

Ricks flicked his head back but he was too polite to

swear at me. "Do you want me to go on?"

I nodded.

"For a while now, the press have tried to latch on to this figure, The Cleaner, someone who is meant to take care of business, so to speak."

"What kind of business?"

Ricks glanced down the street a couple of times.

"People," he whispered. "who have committed a crime, but for some reason or another got away with it, he, The Cleaner, takes care of them."

"You mean, he's a vigilante?"

"That's a pretty crude term," he moaned.

"You got a better one for someone who takes the law into his own hands?"

"He's only doing what he thinks is right."

"Well personally I don't think its right what the landlord charges me for a pint but that doesn't give me an excuse to pin him to the wall and threaten to kill him!"

"But these people deserved what they got!"

It became clear that Ricks had been taken in by the rumour. Maybe he had posters of Batman above his bed. And I wondered if that was a good or a dangerous thing?

"And how does this Cleaner person go round deciding who to knock off next?" I asked. "I mean, does he stand outside the courts with a clip board or maybe somebody illuminates the sky with a giant Hoover?"

Ricks became agitated. "I don't know, do I."

"And why does he do it?" I asked.

The reporter hunched his shoulders. "It's certainly not for credit. Nobody has any idea what he looks like, or where he operates, other than it would appear to be mainly in the North Yorkshire area. Perhaps, it's the money, I don't know. But I think Reece was onto him."

"You think?"

"It's possible."

"So this is your meal ticket?" I mocked. "You want to write an article based on what probably comes down to either just scare tactics or an old wives tale. I don't know about you, but I've seen a red sky at night and it actually turned out to be somebody's house burning down!"

"This is much more than that!" Ricks argued.

"Why? All you've got so far is an ex-cop who may have been following some guy who may or may not exist, who may or may not wipe people out and who've you no idea if, or where, he'll turn up next."

My dismissive tone deserved a slap round the face. Fortunately Ricks wasn't in a position to oblige

"Come to think of it," I quickly added. "Who's to say this man isn't even a woman?"

Suddenly Ricks didn't look so sure of himself anymore.

"You hadn't thought of that had you?"

He looked down at his homework as if he'd suddenly resigned himself to the fact that he might not go straight to the top of the class after all. I started to leave.

"There's something going on here, Mr Mahoney and you know it, why else would Reece be following Preacher?"

"Nobody said he was!" I argued.

"But that's not what the cops think is it!"

He had a point.

"Oh so now you think Preacher's The Cleaner?"

"I didn't say that."

"But?"

"I just want to know what's going on, and I think you do to."

"Maybe," I agreed.

"So give me a little more time."

I handed the notes back to Ricks. "Somebody's going to a lot of trouble to keep things covered up Ricks, and they're not going to think twice about making sure it stays that way. So just make sure you're not next on the list."

"Thanks."

"By the way," I shouted after him. "Have you any idea why Preacher would want to take an old lady for a ride out to Blakey Ridge?"

"Blakey Ridge?"

"Yeah, it's some pub out in the middle of nowhere."

Ricks dipped his head and put on an exaggerated frown. "No, but I'll find out for you."

Chapter Sixty-four

I drove out to Ayton. I could well have been heading to my last supper, so I was determined to enjoy myself.

In truth I wasn't really sure what I expected to find when I got there, a one-horse town without so much as the horse? Time itself may have stood still. Electricity, perhaps just a rumour. Locals sitting outside their homes patiently awaiting the sight of a passing car before rushing to report the incident, only to be met with a disbelieving glance that suggested they'd had one too many.

Perhaps I would enter The Lodge and the music would come to a sudden halt. People would stare up at me from under their cloth caps and someone, playing at the dartboard, would scowl across at me and suggest, in no uncertain terms, that I'd made him miss. I'd be advised not to sit in Harold's chair, even though he died eleven years before. And finally, on leaving, some caring soul, with a face like a bucket and a figure to match, would remind me not to stray too far from the road.

And, of course, there'd be a full moon.

* * *

I reached the top of Jacob's Mount and watched as the Vale of York stretched out before me in all its green and yellow glory. Tiny fields edged by trees and hedgerows were shrouded in a low evening mist below a dark blue sky.

I flicked the car into fourth and cruised down the hill and into Ayton.

In truth I couldn't have been more wrong. A *Welcome* sign signalled the start of colourful houses set back from the main road behind blooming gardens. Two old men sat on a corner bench happily recalling the good old days. Hedges had been primed, lawns trimmed, flowers pruned and walls graffiti-less. I took a right at the school with its windows intact and drove up towards the restaurant.

The Lodge was a U-shaped building with ivy covered walls adjoining neat brick cottages.

It looked a nice place to stay the night, and not alone.

The hallway led me to an open lounge with comfortable chairs to the left, and a bar on the right. A few people sat in front of an unlit fire, looking relaxed and wishing they hadn't eaten quite so much. Trish was nowhere to be seen, but that didn't surprise me. She was a woman. She'd be late, that was her prerogative. I checked out the brightly lit pumps behind the bar and ordered something I'd never heard of before.

The barmaid didn't even bother trying to place me. She probably assumed I was just passing through. She didn't even bother to make small talk and that pleased me, I was saving all my words for Trish, even though I didn't have a clue what I was going to say.

The beer tasted good, nobody stared at me and nobody complained when I made myself comfortable in one of the leather chairs.

Trish arrived twenty minutes later. She was dressed like a woman ready to impress someone, a short skirt over black leggings above ankle length boots. A roller neck sweater and a thin leather jacket. Her make-up was soft, a little eyeliner and lipstick. I just hoped that someone was me, because she made me start to wonder just how much they charged for a room.

"Hi." She smiled.

"Hi." I replied.

I ordered her a drink and we settled into a couple of chairs next to the window. The reflection of the room stared back at us.

"You look good." I said.

"You sound surprised." She answered.

"A little."

She raised an eyebrow. "So how did you expect me to look?"

I took my turn with the jumping eyebrows routine

"To be honest, I wasn't even sure you'd show, so I didn't give it that much thought."

"Why wouldn't I turn up?"

"You ask a lot of questions!"

"You leave a lot of blanks!"

"Is your drink all right?"

"It's fine."

"Do you come here often?" I asked.

"Not often," she replied with a quick glance around the room as if she might have forgotten where she was. "Just sometimes. Does it meet with your approval?"

"I've been in worse!"

"A simple yes or no would have sufficed."

"Yes."

Trish picked up a menu. "Have you eaten?"

"Yes."

She put the menu down.

"And are you working on another case?"

"Yes."

She smiled across at me. "OK, a simple yes or no will only suffice every now and again, all right?"

"Right."

I told her everything, not only because she'd asked but because she listened, and because I enjoyed telling her. I'd lost count of the times I'd come face to face with a woman I liked only to run out of words simply because of who I was and what I did. And most of the time it never seemed to add up to anything more interesting than a spot on the horizon.

We ordered more drinks as darkness fell and the room grew quieter. Trish had her hands pressed out on the table. I noticed her fingers, slender and ring-less and I couldn't help thinking how they'd go a long way to warming my senses on a cold winter's night.

"So who's baby sitting?" I asked.

"Is that a roundabout way of asking if I'm seeing somebody else?"

I shook my head. "Would you be here if you were?"

"That might depend."

"On?" I asked.

"On what you thought I was doing here?"

"Having a social drink with an intriguing Private Investigator, a likeable hero who you happen to share something in common with."

"Writing?" she assumed.

I nodded. "So?"

"So?"

"Are you seeing anybody else?"

A look came over Trish, it wasn't a very polite look and, although it didn't appear to be aimed at me, I took it personally. After all, I'd asked the damn question.

She twisted a fork between her fingers as she stared down at the table. "No."

Somehow I was expecting a little more.

"You don't say much do you?"

Trish looked across at me. "Neither do you!"

"That's because I know all about me."

"So it's not a case of trying to live up to your reputation as a Private Investigator then, a man of mystery perhaps?"

"I didn't know I had a reputation!" I smiled.

"Yes, and it's one of confusion."

"Confusion?"

She nodded.

"And how do you work that out?"

"Well, for starters, most people don't seem to know your real name or if you're meant to be a writer or a Private Investigator."

I looked at the fork nestling in Trish's hand.

"Does it matter?" I asked. "I mean, I've been working for a guy who doesn't know what his real name is either. He's lost his memory. But that doesn't make him any less important to me."

I was trying to make a point but Trish had an answer. She always had an answer.

"But he didn't forget his name out of choice did he? He's not trying to hide anything!"

"I didn't know I was." I replied, sounding a touch alarmed.

"Only you can answer that."

Trish looked across at me. Her eyes searched deep and long into mine.

"What kind of thing could I be hiding?" I tried to laugh.

"I don't know, perhaps there's a girl you've left behind broken hearted in Manchester, or wherever it is you're meant to come from."

"Actually it's Sheffield, I'd only just moved to Manchester when I got the chance to meet Ronnie."

"That can't have been easy?"

I shrugged my shoulders. "It's not so bad, I mean, I wasn't settled or anything."

"But that still doesn't answer the question does it?"

"No," I replied, eventually. "No I didn't leave a girl behind, not broken hearted anyway."

She raised an eyebrow but I didn't have a clue why.

"What?" I asked.

"What?" she replied.

"That look, what was that look for? What's on your mind?"

"I was just thinking, you might not always know when you've left someone behind."

"Are you suggesting I'm a typical insensitive male?"

"No. I'm simply saying that, sometimes, we just don't know."

Chapter Sixty-five

I walked Trish home. It wasn't far, because Ayton wasn't all that big. She enjoyed describing to me how it only had the one church, two pubs, a chip shop, a hairdresser, a supermarket you could pack inside a telephone box, two telephone boxes, a boarded up Post Office, a café, a garage and Bill, the only Joiner in the village. It also had two bridges, side by side, a flat one that led out into the country, and a humped one that brought people back again.

We took a right by the stream and followed a row of daffodils and sleeping ducks till Trish came to a halt. She'd rented a couple of rooms in a cottage that overlooked the water.

I liked Ayton. I liked Ayton a lot.

Trish glanced her head towards the cottage.

"Would you like to come in for a coffee?"

If I'd started the night with a plan I would now be congratulating myself on how well it gone, right up until the point my mouth took over from my hormones.

"I'd better not."

She smiled politely as the rest of my body fought desperately to separate itself from my tongue.

I stammered on an explanation. "I er.....,"

"It's OK."

"No, I mean, I'd like to but,"

"You're busy."

"Yeah." I said and thought how ridiculous that sounded.

Life in Ayton suddenly came to a halt. Paint dried and grass grew as the two of us stood like cardboard cut-outs staring back at one another. In the silence I listened to frogs croak along the stream and to the lowering of gears as cars reached the hump in the bridge.

And I knew right there and then that this would never go down as one of the most romantic moments ever.

Eventually Trish leaned forward and kissed my cheek.

"Maybe next time then," she whispered.

I felt the touch of her lips on my skin and couldn't believe I was walking away.

"Yeah." I replied. "Maybe next time."

Chapter Sixty-six

I opened the office door and stepped inside. The room was dusky with just about enough brightness from the landing light and street lamps to enable me to make my way safely over to the cabinet without stepping into the wastebin.

I pulled back the bottom drawer and reached inside for the bottle of whisky. It was only then I remembered that I'd promoted it to the top drawer.

I took the bottle out and picked up a mug and sat at my desk. I poured a little whisky and listened to the trickle, it was a sweet sound, so innocent, so captivating, like a river diligently winding its way to somewhere far away, some place nicer than here. I thought of the river in Ayton and standing face to face with Trish and the smell of summer in the air. And I wondered what the hell I was doing here and not drinking coffee with her in her room.

I put my feet on the desk and stared out into the darkness. I liked being alone at times, but I didn't like being alone with my thoughts, there were too many memories and too many questions that I didn't have the answers to.

I decided to scribble the names of possible suspects onto a piece of paper and then pinned them to the wall. I stepped back and looked at them. There was Jenny (Car crash) Preacher (Club Owner) Storey/Machin (lost memory) O'Riley (ice-cream man) Collingwood (Saltys owner) and Helen Fitzsimmons. I couldn't leave out Helen Fitzsimmons. I also jotted down the gang who wanted Storey to deliver April and Lucas and Warne. Lots of names but not one good reason behind them that I could think of.

I took another sip of whisky and the world slowly started to appear a little more obscure than usual.

The door downstairs opened and closed again. I held my breath as the stairs creaked. A silhouette appeared in the frosted glass panelled door. I sat up in my chair. It was times like this when I wish I carried a gun. The door opened. Walker stepped inside and flashed a frown into the office.

"You enjoy working in the dark?" he moaned.

"It's how I work best."

He switched on a light and stepped over to the desk. I shielded my eyes.

Walker pulled up a chair and pointed at the whisky bottle. "You going to keep that all to yourself?"

"Aren't you on duty?"

"I'll get O'Neal to drive me home."

I poured the Inspector a cup. He looked tired. All that paperwork and staring at a computer had finally caught up with him. But I would never tell him that. It can't be easy knowing that, closing one case, merely opened up another.

"How did you know I was here?" I asked.

He sipped some whisky before waving a thumb back towards the door. "I saw your car outside and the landing light on."

I nodded.

"What are you up to?"

I aimed a finger at the wall. "Figured I'd try and make some sense of all this mess. I've seen them do it on the telly, but all I ended up with was a lot names and a few holes in the wall."

"Ronnie won't be happy."

"I doubt he'd ever notice."

"So where have you been? I called round earlier. I even tried your mobile."

"Are you checking up on me?"

"Just wondering. I thought you might want to take a look at this."

Walker pulled out a clear plastic A4 sized wallet and passed it to me. Staring back at me on neatly typed paper was the opening page of my novel.

"Wow," I whistled. "It looks so professional. If only it was as good as it looks."

"I didn't think it was that bad."

I glared at Walker. "You've read it?"

"Just the opening chapter. I thought it was good."

I'm not sure Walker had any idea just how good his words sounded to me.

"Good?"

"Yeah," he shrugged. "Good. Like I said, my wife enjoys a good murder mystery."

"And you?"

Walker started to roll in his seat like someone had filled his pants with itching powder. It was always the same when somebody had something to say but they weren't too sure how to say it.

"It's just that….."

"What?" I asked.

"Well, you don't seem to like Scarborough very much, do you. You put it in a very bad light."

"Not me, the narrator," I argued.

"But it's your book."

I got to my feet. It helped to focus my mind on my first literary criticism. Normally I just turned my back when somebody had a go at me or poked them in the eye. But this was important.

"For one thing it's not how I remember Scarborough as a kid, that's all. And for another, It's my way of trying to recreate the novels of the forties and fifties. It's how I imagine Chandler would have written it if he'd ever spent some time here."

"But he didn't did he! You did. And like I said, this is your book, not Chandler's. If this is what you really feel then fine, but don't go trying to recreate somebody else. It's probably been done a million times already anyway."

Bloody hell! I had no idea Walker was so profound. I knew he was obviously good at his job. He was probably a very good father and a nice husband, but now he was constructively criticising my book, was there no end to his talents?

"So, is it finished?"

"Nearly."

"Then what?"

"Then I spend the rest of my life trying to get it published."

"Pity," Walker sighed as he got to his feet. "I was looking forward to reading it!"

He strolled over to the names on the wall and stuck his hands into his trouser pockets.

"So where have you been?" he asked, without looking back at me.

"For a drive," I replied.

Walker looked sideways at me.

"What?" I asked.

"Do you always put a shirt and tie on and dive into a bottle of aftershave when you just go for a drive?"

I felt my face blush. "You don't give up do you?"

"It's my job." He replied.

It was like sitting in the interrogation room without so much as a breath of fresh air the way Walker grilled people.

"So?"

"I've been out....., for a drink.........., with Trish."

"Trish?"

"Yeah, the girl from the Writer's Circle."

"Right."

Walker returned to the desk and picked up his whisky. "Obviously you don't have to tell me any details."

"Good," I replied. "Because there's nothing to tell."

"Right."

The office fell silent for a moment as the two of us continued sipping our drinks and making discrete glances around the room.

"So how come there's nothing to tell?"

I looked at Walker. "I thought you said....."

"I was only asking!" He insisted. "I mean, you had a nice time right?"

He wasn't going to go away, that much was obvious, because his work never left him.

I stared into my glass and recalled Trish entering the bar, pressing her hand on the table, wondering how much they charged for a room and leaving her alone outside the cottage with the frogs still croaking in the background.

"Yes. Yes we had a nice time," I eventually replied.

"Where'd you go?"

"The Lodge."

"Oh nice," he said, gently nodding his head. "Very romantic."

He sat back down and placed his empty glass in the middle of the desk. "So when are you seeing her again?"

"I'm not." I snapped.

"Oh."

Silence. And it was killing me.

"So things didn't work out then?"

I got to my feet and went back to the wall. "Yes, things worked out fine!" I moaned.

I tried to focus on the names but thoughts of Trish and Walker's relentless questioning weren't helping.

"So how come you're not seeing her again."

"Who?"

"Trish."

I shot him a glance but I couldn't honestly tell him why. I wasn't even sure how the night had ended, apart from me walking off.

"I don't know," I said, quietly.

"You don't know?"

"No!" I snapped.

"But you like her right?"

"She's got a daughter."

"Is that a problem?"

"I don't know. I mean, I'd never even thought about it until now. I don't even know why I mentioned it."

"But you did!"

I tried to avoid Walker's glare. I didn't want to be questioned. I was an abandoned island and I wanted to remain that way. There were plenty of others to discover, islands full of hope and fraught with danger. I just wanted to be left alone.

"Do you like her?"

It seemed like such a stupid question. But then, if it was so stupid, why couldn't I answer him?

"I don't know."

"You don't know?"

"I don't know."

Walker started to laugh.

"What's so funny?"

"Well for most people it's quite a straightforward question."

"I'm not like a lot of people."

"So you don't know if you like her, love her even?"

"I don't believe in love." I said, matter-of-factly, as if such a philosophy might yet save the day.

Walker raised an eyebrow and tilted his head to one side.

"So what do you believe in?"

"Scooby-Doo, but I don't think that's relevant right now."

"You like to avoid the issue don't you, especially when it concerns you."

"I just don't believe in love that's all."

Walker stood up. "Then I should keep away from her if I were you!"

His comment took me completely by surprise. I had no idea what angle he was coming from. Surely he wasn't trying to protect Trish. He didn't know her. And he couldn't be ordering me to keep my distance. He wouldn't dare. It was none of his business. I sat back down.

"Why?" I asked.

"Because I think you're scared Mahoney."

My eyes followed Walker across the office. The whisky blurred my image and closed in on my senses like a thick fog creeping in on me.

"Scared?" I whispered.

"You hide behind smart remarks and other people's problems," he continued. "But you're scared to face your own."

"Maybe I like to put other people first." I said, as I reached for the bottle, but it was hard to find. The room was spinning and the fog was everywhere, covering everything. Even my hand was slowly fading out of view. I would have got to my feet and taken a walk but I was worried I might fall off the edge of the world.

"You don't want to know how you feel about Trish because you're worried it might scare you too much."

I wanted to laugh at Walker but he'd disappeared from view. The office was completely engulfed in fog. The world had disappeared and everybody in it. All that was left was me, a voice and a half empty bottle of whisky.

"Why would I be frightened of that?" I said, but my attempt at a laugh got stuck somewhere in my throat.

"Think about it, Mahoney, think about how you are. Think about what you say, how you think and how you write."

"Hey, slow down, I'm running out of mind!"

"You run people down, you run places down."

"Maybe because I don't like what they've become!"

"But this isn't about them!"

"It isn't?"

"No. This is about you. You like Trish, you probably like her a lot, but what frightens you is that she just might feel the same way about you, and then what?"

"I don't know, and then what?"

"And then you'd have a reason to smile, Mahoney. You'd have a reason to think that the world's not such a bad place after all. You'd have one less reason to feel so bitter and I'm not sure you can handle that."

Chapter Sixty-seven

I fell asleep at the desk. Maybe, if I was lucky, I would wake up that very next morning when I'd first arrived in Scarborough. Maybe, I wouldn't have to answer the phone and speak to Helen Fitzsimmons. Maybe Ronnie would stroll in and offer to take me on a case that I could piece together in novel form and ultimately publish.

But, as my senses adjusted to the room, I could see the plant on the window sill and I could smell the promise of another day. I could feel my neatly printed novel pressed up against the side of my face. And I could taste the bitter pill of failure.

The walls were lilac, the tap didn't leak and I had a hangover from hell. I didn't even know what day it was.

I rinsed my face a couple of times in the sink and clicked on the kettle. It still didn't work.

Any moment now the men who wanted April would call and there was nothing I could do. I was supposed to be following Preacher. I'd let everybody down.

I pulled back the curtains. The world was too bright.

I closed them again. I needed coffee. I shuffled across the floor just as the phone rang. I thought about letting it ring a little longer, but the sound hurt my head.

It was Ricks.

"That advert you put in the paper."

"What about it?" I squeaked.

"Has it got anything to do with a girl called April?"

His question momentarily forced my brain to trigger some response other than, I wanted to be sick.

"Why?"

"Because some geezer was asking about it that's all."

"Who?"

"He didn't say, he rang the office, said he wanted to know about a reward."

"What did you tell him?"

"That I'd look into it. Then he said, if I wanted to know where April was he'd show me. But I can't afford the reward."

I pressed a hand to my head and tried to muster some thoughts.

"All right, look, what did you tell him? I mean, did you arrange to meet him?"

"Yes."

"Where?"

"On the Coronia."

"The what?"

The Coronia. It's a boat that runs between here and Whitby."

"When?"

"Most days."

"No, you idiot! I mean when did you arrange to meet this geezer?"

"Tonight."

* * *

I picked up the phone and called Envy. She didn't answer. I left a message and told her that, if she wasn't busy, could she meet me down at the harbour.

I could do with all the muscle I could get, just in case.

Chapter Sixty-eight

The foreshore was humming. Everyone was taking advantage of the warm clear night and business was booming. Queues formed outside the shellfish stalls, doughnut racks and chip shops.

Darkness was taking its time to fall and allowing just a sprinkling of stars. All in all, it seemed a bit too nice for anything horrible to happen. No thunder, no lightening, no screechy violin.

Ricks was late and there was no sign of Envy. I checked my phone, but no one had called.

I waited at the entrance to the pier. But, twenty minutes later there was still no sign of either of them.

I set off down the pier.

A line had formed outside a small wooden hut. One good sneeze and there would be timber flying everywhere. Inside a man sold tickets for a trip on the Regal Lady.

A billboard advertising the 'Firework display of the year' was propped up against the hut. It was going to get noisy.

There was still no sign of Ricks.

A blind man stood playing guitar nearby. There was a dog sleeping at his feet and a tin filled with silver coins. But no doubt the dog growled every time somebody threatened the tin with copper. I dropped a fifty pence piece. The dog twitched its ear. Relief.

* * *

The crowd dwindled in numbers the further I walked until I was left on my own.

A few yards away the Coronia rocked in darkness. I called out to Ricks. There was no reply.

Like an idiot I checked my watch. I really had to buy another one.

A gangplank stretched across to the deck. It shook in front of me.

I was about to take a step when a loud blast from the Regal Lady froze my momentum and pumped my heartbeat. I watched it pull away from the harbour wall.

People waved as it passed close by. People who wouldn't have waved if they passed you in the street, but for some reason, this was different.

I watched the ship gracefully arc past the lighthouse and out to sea.

* * *

The gangplank continued to sway from left to right as I made my way over. I gripped the railing like a child being lead to the dentist. The waves slapped the bottom of the boat.

The deck was bare but the engine was running.

"Ricks!" I shouted out. "Is anybody there?"

There was no answer.

I searched the top deck as a firework zipped across the night sky. It made me jump and lose my breath. I looked to the horizon as a loud bang descended into a thousands bright lights. People cheered and roared as a dozen more fireworks suddenly ripped from the castle walls and out across the harbour.

* * *

I looked down towards the lower deck and yelled 'Ricks' above the noise of the engine below. There was no reply.

* * *

The crackle and pop of fireworks continued over head. It was loud and disturbing like gunfire.

* * *

There was nobody here and nothing to see. The deck was empty. I stood at the bar as the boat heaved and my stomach churned. The whisky urn looked so appealing. I caught my reflection in the mirror. 'Go ahead' a voice whispered from somewhere inside my head.

I poured a glass and sunk it down. I searched my pocket for some change. I wanted to leave something on the till. And that's when I noticed a foot wedging the door open just behind the bar. I pulled it further open. Another body was lying on the floor. I'd hardly had time to gasp when I caught sight of a figure in the mirror stepping towards me.

The ship rocked, the fireworks crackled and there was a sharp blow to the back of my head and I fell to the floor.

This was becoming an annoying habit.

Chapter Sixty-nine

"The next thing I knew I was lying here in bed with a nurse trying to poke my eye out."

"That's a very interesting storey Mr Mahoney," declared Matthews, but in a tone that suggested he didn't find it very interesting at all. "Unfortunately it doesn't explain how you and Preacher were the only one's who got off that boat alive."

"What about Ricks?" I asked.

"Ricks?" The two of them asked in unison.

"The kid from the evening paper.

"That must be the figure we couldn't recognise on CCTV," Walker announced to Matthews.

The Superintendent looked at him. "Let's look into that, Inspector."

Walker nodded.

"You've got the whole thing on camera?" I asked.

Matthews scratched his jaw and looked back at me. "Which is how we know nobody else came off that boat alive, not until the police turned up and found Preacher with a gun in his hand."

"Why?" I asked.

"Why what?"

"Why were your boys there in the first place?"

"Because we were following Preacher right, and because somebody reported hearing gunfire."

"That could have been the fireworks!"

"I only wish it was," Matthews moaned.

* * *

The three of us had moved to a picnic table just outside the ward. Walker couldn't have gone any longer without a drag on his cigar.

It was a warm afternoon and the surroundings were a whole lot nicer.

Matthews took a short stroll towards where Walker was standing blowing smoke into the fresh air and turned to look at me.

"So Ricks rings you up out of the blue and informs you that the girl you've been looking for is on this boat, The Coronia."

I wasn't sure if I was supposed to be listening or if the Superintendent was just thinking out loud.

"But, naturally, when you arrive, there is no sign of the girl," he continued.

"Naturally?" I questioned.

"Well come on, Mahoney, if I'd arranged to meet a complete stranger in order to exchange this girl, presumably for money, I don't think I'd have picked such an isolated location. What's to stop, whoever, just taking the girl, dumping me over the side, keeping the money and leaving nobody any the wiser?"

I had to admit, dumping Matthews over the side did seem like a good idea.

"Well maybe this guy isn't as smart as you!" I suggested.

Matthews smiled. "And then again, maybe this person never even existed!"

"I don't get you!"

"Maybe the whole thing was simply a set up. There was never a girl, you said yourself, she was dead."

"That was never confirmed," I argued "And what about the girl at the chalet?"

"You don't know it was her!"

I thought back to the moment prior to getting the other bump on my head. I'd heard a voice, it could have been anyone's. And even though I'd seen her tired face, I couldn't have sworn it was April.

"The point is," Matthews continued. "Preacher was using her to get those people down to the harbour so he could kill them!"

"Why? Why would Preacher want to ice anybody?"

Matthews took a moment to sit back down and glance, across at Walker.

"Because Preacher is, this Cleaner thing you've been going on about!" Matthews replied, quietly and very matter–of–factly.

I shot him a disbelieving glance "You don't believe that?"

"Four people are dead, Mr Mahoney, I'm prepared to believe anything right now."

"But...."

Matthews raised his chin. "We all know this bloke is supposed to bear a grudge against people who get away with crimes of one kind or another, that's how he's supposed to have got started in the first place, it was something personal."

I stared back in silence.

"Like how Preacher's dad was killed," Matthews continued. "Two of the three boys thought to be involved in his death both died under suspicious circumstances less than a year later. Nobody gave it much thought at the time, they were just two dossers who were missed by nobody but other dossers, until, that is, a retired cop came along and started to piece matters together."

"I know, Ricks told me."

"The net was closing in on Preacher, so he had to do something."

I stood up for a moment. All this thinking wasn't doing my head any good. I also felt I was letting Preacher down again. Everybody was taking a pop at him, including the cops, how was that for justice?

"But if he is The Cleaner," I started. "And let's not forget, we don't know if this person even exists, then what's supposed to make him, or her so successful?"

Walker and Matthews looked at one another before shrugging their shoulders at me.

"The fact that he always manages to pass the murders off as either a complete accident, or he pins it on somebody else," I explained."

Personally I thought I'd raised a good point, but then it all went quiet as Walker and Matthews kept looking at one another. And suddenly I got worried.

I sat back down. "What?"

"That's just we keep coming back to why you're still alive Mahoney," Walker said, as diplomatically as he could.

"Wait a minute, you think Preacher's out to set me up?"

Nobody answered.

"But why, I wasn't even supposed to be there remember!"

But that didn't seem to cut much ice with either of them.

"All that matters is that you were there and he didn't kill you. Maybe he had somebody else in mind, but you just happen to turn up. Or maybe you just got lucky."

I rolled a hand gently over the lump in my head. "I don't feel particularly lucky!" I snapped

Matthews stepped up close to me. "Right now, I'd be more concerned with, if or what, Preacher might have on you," he said quietly.

"What do you mean?"

"I mean, if he wants to 'pin' these murders on you!"

"The only one who seems to be pinning anything on anybody is you! Jesus, we don't even know this Cleaner person exists, but that doesn't seem to stop you from throwing somebody in the slammer anyway."

I didn't want to get angry, it just increased the pressure on my head, but Matthews was making me feel that way. It wasn't that he was an unreasonable man or that there was anything particularly unlikeable about him, nothing that stood out anyway. The trouble was, as he stared back at me, all I could think of was him selling his soul to Helen Fitzsimmons and me ending up in a tunnel and nearly drowning. Perhaps that's why I said what I said next;

"Or maybe you don't need a reason, just as long as you appear to be doing your job then everybody will be happy, because that's what it's all about isn't it, ticking the right boxes! Making sure you reach your targets."

Matthews offered me a stare before picking up his cup and heading off down the corridor. He wasn't happy, not that I cared. He would have loved to have slammed a door or two just for effect. But he couldn't.

"You really know how to make friends don't you, Mahoney!" Walker mumbled as he stubbed out his cigar in an ashtray.

"I don't like Matthews!" I growled.

"You don't say!"

"I don't like his stupid bow tie and I don't like the way he lied to me about some book advance I'd been offered in order to make me think I could kill somebody."

"What advance?"

"Something about being offered five hundred grand for chasing Hebden. They seemed to think it was a good enough reason for me to go round killing people. And it might have been, if they'd been telling the truth."

"There wasn't an advance?"

I shook my head. "If there had have been I wouldn't be lying here in hospital with a bedpan for company.

Walker nodded.

"I also don't like the way Helen Fitzsimmons played him for a sucker," I added.

"What's Helen Fitzsimmons got to do with anything?" Walker asked.

I looked across at the Inspector. It's possible he had no idea what I was talking about and, quite honestly, I preferred it that way. It meant he hadn't been involved.

"She told me she was behind the whole Frank Hebden affair. She reckons she's got your Superintendent round her little finger."

Walker tried to let out a disbelieving laugh but it got stuck somewhere in his throat.

"You don't believe that?" he eventually managed to say.

"What's it matter what I believe? What's more important is that this town is either stuck with a Superintendent who's a sucker for large brown eyes and a pair of long legs or a Mayoress with delusions of grandeur."

Walker stifled a yawn and stretched his back. "Well it hasn't helped him, if what you say is true."

I frowned at the Inspector.

"Fitzsimmons is all over The Super like a rash. She wants this mess cleaned up as quickly and as effectively as possible."

"But I'd have thought she'd enjoy all the media attention!"

"Actually she's fed up with the bad publicity. It's difficult enough when the sun doesn't shine and hotels fall into the sea, but now we've got four dead bodies all over the harbour, including two policemen."

Walker tucked what remained of his cigar back into his top pocket and stood up.

"Why don't you get some rest?" he said quietly.

"Because I want to know what happened!"

Walker nodded and then he looked at me like someone with a lot to say but wasn't too sure how to say it.

"What?" I asked.

"Maybe you ought to think about what the Super was saying, about you just getting knocked over the head."

"Maybe Preacher just ran out of bullets," I suggested.

"Or maybe he does have something on you?"

"Like what?"

"I don't know, but if he does, then he's going to want some payback. All you have to do is worry about what that something might be."

Chapter Seventy

The hospital ceiling had become far too familiar. I could identify every crack and cobweb. Life was sinking into a routine. Breakfast, thermometer, blood pressure, lunch, check my chart, force a frown, dinner, thermometer, blood pressure, sleep. I was ready to discharge myself even if they weren't. Then again, maybe that was the plan. The monotony would drive me away to free up a much needed bed. Simple and so cost effective.

But this was the big test, this was life's big test. You try your damndest, you go to work, you make friends, you try to earn an honest living, you pay your bills, you smile and say 'hello' to people in the street. But is it all worth it, if you're left alone in a hospital bed staring back at nothing but your dreams?

* * *

I'd tried ringing Envy a couple of times but I kept getting told her phone was out of order. Such valuable things these mobiles, until they don't work.

I was straining my neck in an effort to read the newspaper headline being viewed by a man in the next bed when Trish suddenly appeared by my bedside. She looked nice. She always looked nice. I sat up quickly.

My head still hurt so this wasn't a dream.

"Hi," I said.

"Hi," She replied.

"I, what, how did you know?" I stumbled.

"The Inspector told me."

"Walker?"

She nodded.

Damn, that was nice of him.

I pointed to a chair. "Have a seat."

Trish shook her head. "I can't stop. I'm picking up Amy."

Ah, clever, very clever. Always have an escape plan just in case things don't quite work out. I always used to make that all important call from the phone box so that, if and when things got awkward, I could always say, I'd run out of money.

"I just wanted to see how you were." She continued.

I pressed a hand to my bandage. "The doctor said it was lucky it was my head."

Trish smiled politely.

"But I need to get out, this place is driving me nuts."

She cast a quick glance around the ward. "I hate hospitals."

I nodded. "So how are you?"

"Fine.

A man in a grey overcoat pushed a trolley nearby and offered us a coffee. But we declined and he was glad.

A moments silence followed until we both started to speak at the same time. There was polite laughter followed by a tug of war over who should go first. Trish insisted I should.

"Well I was just going to say, how much I enjoyed the other night."

I waited for her reaction, but I must have blinked, because I'm sure statues were prone to more expression.

"So I was thinking that, maybe, you know, perhaps we could meet up again sometime, when I get out?"

Trish looked awkwardly from one side to another and then at me.

"I don't think that'll be possible." She said quietly.

"Oh," I replied.

"I'm leaving," She explained.

"Leaving?"

She nodded.

"Leaving what?"

"Scarborough. I'm moving to Cheltenham."

I sat up further in my bed. It shot a pain through my head but it wasn't as bad as hearing that Trish was leaving Scarborough.

"Cheltenham?"

Trish suddenly looked like someone who'd arrived for a Cats audition dressed as a dog.

"Look," I began. "I know I say some horrible things about this place but hell, Cheltenham! Where on earth is it anyway?"

"South-west, just below Birmingham."

"Is that possible? Can anything be lower than Birmingham?"

Trish let out a faint smile and decided to sit down after all.

"It's where I'm from. I only moved here to be with someone, but that didn't work out and I don't really know anybody else here. So....,"

"You know me!" I blurted out before realising that nothing was further from the truth. She didn't know me, she had no idea who I was and that much was reflected in her soft smile.

"You're really going?"

She nodded.

"When?"

"Sunday."

"Sunday? This Sunday?"

She nodded again.

I had no idea what day it was. I looked out of the window but I couldn't tell if it was winter or if darkness was falling.

"What day is it?"

"Wednesday," she smiled.

Just a few days in which to find the courage to tell her she was making the biggest mistake of her life. And then to some how prove it.

Trish checked her watch and stood up. "Look, I've got to go."

"I'll call you, before you leave!"

She smiled and nodded and left.

For what felt like an eternity I wondered what I could do or say to make her stay. All I knew was, I had to try something. The ache in my stomach had returned. Only Trish made me feel that way. Only she had ever made me feel that way.

Chapter Seventy-one

The following morning I waited outside the main entrance with all the other patients busy chewing on a cigarette and breathing what fresh air had been left behind.

Hartless had said he'd come and fetch me which was really nice. The surprise was, he came in a taxi.

I got in the back seat next to him. He was already chewing his lip.

"Where's your car?" I asked.

"I don't er, have one."

"You're a reporter and you don't have a car? What do you do, ask people to remain in the accident position till you catch a bus?"

"I d....do pre-arranged features," he replied casually. "So I don't exactly have to rush anywhere."

I nodded. Point taken.

"So how are you?" he asked, as we weaved our way through the over-crowded car park.

"Tired and full of tablets. They took my temperature so often I felt like a weather gage. Have the police been talking to you?"

"What about?"

"About what happened?"

"W....why would they?"

We came to a halt at a junction. Hartless plucked a copy of the evening paper from his lap and handed it to me.

"It looks like they already have their man."

The headline read; *Nightclub owner to be charged over harbour deaths.*

I scanned the report written by Eddie Hartless. It was brief and to the point. It came with two pictures, a large colour shot of Preacher taken sometime ago before he'd lost all his hair and bought a tan. The other of Superintendent Matthews in uniform. There was also a small black and white shot of a man going by the name of Paul Rickson, or 'Ricks' as he preferred to be known, and a brief request asking if anybody had seen him. And if so, to telephone the helpline number.

I looked up from the paper and gazed out of the window as images of Scarborough hurried by.

"W....what's the matter?" Hartless asked.

"I'm not sure Preacher did it." I mumbled.

"But he's the only one who, he's the only one who was there, apart from........,"

Hartless stopped short of adding my name to the incredibly short list of suspects. So I did it for him.

"Me."

He gulped some fresh air and said quietly. "I was, wasn't going to say that."

"But that's exactly what the police want to know and, to be honest, it's what I'd like to know."

"What?"

"Why I'm still alive?"

"You should be glad!"

"I am, but why?"

"W....why are you glad?"

"No, why wasn't I killed like everybody else?"

"Maybe he, or they were about to, b....but something happened?"

"What? Like they ran out of bullets?"

"I don't know!"

"So they bumped me over the head instead?"

Hartless's appearance suddenly took on that of someone who'd wished they'd kept their mouth shut.

"S, so what do the police think?" he asked.

"They think Preacher's got something on me."

"Like what?"

"I don't know. But they seem to think he's The Cleaner."

"The Cleaner?"

I nodded.

"I wasn't even sure he existed."

"I'm still not sure he does," I added. "All the cops have is a few flimsy coincidences. But that seems to be enough to pin everything on Preacher and put him away."

"But he's confessed," Hartless explained as he pointed a finger back to the report.

Adam 'Preacher' Keatley today confessed to the murder of Collingwood, one of his sidekicks and two policemen, Sergeant Lucas and Warne. He will be charged later.

I looked up from the paper as the taxi slipped into a queue at the lights. If Preacher had confessed to the murders then what was the point of having anything on me? Maybe he hadn't killed me because he liked me? Maybe it just came down to something as simple as that.

But then nothing was as ever as simple as that.

I handed the paper back to Hartless as we reached the town centre. The reporter paid without leaving a tip. The driver moaned something that neither of us cared about and left.

"What about Ricks?" I asked. "Has there been any sign of him?"

Hartless shook his head. "You don't think he's involved do you?"

I sighed. "It could be the cast from the Muppets for all I know. That's what happens when you're left with nothing but guesses."

"And w....what about Jo?" he asked.

"What about her?"

"Has she been in touch?"

I shook my head, but then it dawned on me that she hadn't been in touch. Everybody else had; The cops, although it was official business, even Trish. But there was no sign of Envy. Did that make her a suspect?

"You don't think," But Hartless couldn't even contemplate finishing his sentence.

"I don't know what to think Eddie," I conceded. "Except I normally look at what somebody's got to gain from committing a crime, and to be honest, I can't think of anything either Ricks or Envy would have to gain."

Hartless nodded and almost forced a smile.

"But then again," I continued. "I can't think what Preacher has to gain either, especially if he's supposed to be this Cleaner."

"Apart from w....wiping nasty people off the streets?"

"But he's supposed to pin the blame on somebody else!" I added.

Hartless chewed his lip. "So what are you going to go now?"

To be honest it didn't really seem to matter because, wherever I ended up there were always more questions than answers.

"Do you know where Ricks lives?"

"Ricks?"

I nodded.

"I'm not sure. I could find out if you like. W....why?"

"I stepped over to Hartless so I didn't have to shout out all over the street. "Ricks was asking a lot of people a lot of questions."

"Right."

"So maybe one of those people didn't like what he was asking," I continued.

"S... so, how does knowing where he lives help?"

"Because hopefully there might be a clue there as to who that person is, or what that question was."

"B..., but isn't that for the police to find out?"

"Only if it comes up on one of their computers!"

Chapter Seventy-two

Hartless wasn't happy with what we were about to do, but, then again, Hartless never seemed happy about doing anything. All he had to was get Ricks's address, but that was enough for him to start paddling up and down the street a number of times, chewing his lip, scratching his head and mumbling 'oh dear, oh dear'.

I went back to the office before picking up the car. I thought about ringing Trish. She was leaving for Cheltenham, and it just didn't seem right to let her go without saying something other than, 'did you remember to pack a flask?'

I should have gone straight to wherever it is she was, but time and time again I managed to talk myself into doing something for somebody else instead. It wasn't anything heroic, not even considerate, just plain cowardly. When the cavalry finally charged, you'd find me somewhere at the back asking if my horse wanted another sack of oats.

* * *

A large brown envelope lay sealed on the desk next to a packet of chocolate éclairs. My smile at Barbara's kindness quickly gave way when I picked up the envelope. There was no stamp on it, just my name. Presumably somebody had stuck it through the letterbox. I opened the éclairs, popped one into my mouth, pulled up a chair and opened the envelope. A thought, not so deep at the back of my mind, suggested it might have been from Trish and, for a second, I was excited. That's all it took to open the envelope and read the note inside.

If you want to see April again get ten thousand pounds and wait in your office. 5 o'clock today you'll get further instructions.

The note was made up from newspaper and magazine cuttings. I lobbed it onto the desk and finished my éclairs.

Somebody had April.

I checked the time on the answer machine. It had just gone eleven. That gave me plenty of time to pace the floor and decide where the hell I was going to get that kind of money from. Ten minutes later, my only hope appeared to be in robbing a bank. It was only when I got to the window, that my options suddenly doubled.

On a bench in the park sat an elderly couple eating an ice-cream.

Bingo.

Chapter Seventy-three

O'Riley was resting in his office chair appearing totally oblivious to the unbearably hot atmosphere. It made me want to throw up.

He pressed the tips of his fingers together and casually said;

"You see, I told you our paths would cross again, Mr Mahoney?"

He pointed to a chair. I remained standing. He sniffed.

"So what can I do for you?"

I'd never been in a situation like this, therefore I wasn't sure what to do, so I just blurted the words right out.

"I need ten thousand pounds."

It came out as though I was merely asking to borrow a hammer.

O'Riley studied me for a moment. I wasn't sure if he was waiting for a 'please' or, if I was meant to get down on my knees and beg.

"Is that all?" He finally asked.

I shook my head. "I need it now!"

His reaction baffled me because he didn't laugh or dismiss me out of sight. Indeed, he seemed totally intrigued, like I had challenged him to a duel, and O'Riley was never one to back down from a challenge.

"That's a lot of money." He said, quietly.

I looked at the cat, lying lifeless on the cabinet and said. "I already knew that."

O'Riley got to his feet and waddled around to the front of the desk. He was starting to sweat again. He took out a handkerchief and mopped his brow. He propped his frame up against the desk.

"May I ask what you need it for?"

"Sure you can," I replied.

He flicked an eyebrow at me.

"The girl I was looking for?" I continued.

O'Riley nodded.

"Somebody's got her, they're holding her to ransom."

"Do you know who?"

I shook my head.

"They know you're desperate."

I nodded.

"Are you desperate?"

"I'm working for a guy with no memory, I've seen more dead bodies these past two days than I care to remember, there's a goon with large fists wanting to break my bones and I'm asking a man who keeps dead cats in his office for money, so yeah, you could say I'm desperate!"

"And what makes you think I want to lend you the money?"

"I never said anything about lending it."

O'Riley suddenly caught on to what I'd just said. There was a moment's silence that eventually gave way to laughter as he started to rock on the desk. His torso rippled with blubber.

He wiped his brow and retreated back to the other side of the desk. "Oh, Mr Mahoney, you do amuse me!"

"I wasn't joking." I said, defiantly.

But that didn't stop him from smiling.

"Oh I believe you. And that's what I admire about you, your front, you actually have the gall to come into my office and demand money from me," he started to laugh again, "nobody's ever done anything like that before, well nobody who could walk the streets again without a limp, anyway. I wonder would you consider working for me?"

I pulled on my ear.

"I didn't come here for a job, I came here for the money."

"But why me?"

"Because you're the only person I know who comes close to having anything like that amount of dough. And besides, you said you'd liked to help."

O'Riley nodded as he wiped his brow.

"Help, yes," he agreed. "But not give money away."

"Call it doing your piece for charity!"

He cut me a sideways glance. "I'm not a fan of charity Mr Mahoney. I believe there's enough money in the world without having people give it away for nothing."

"So what's your answer?"

O'Riley tipped his fingers together and said defiantly; "I'm afraid I can't help."

"You mean you haven't got the money?"

"I mean, I'm not going to give it to you, not even lend it to you."

"That's a pity," I said, as I walked to the window.

I looked out across the road towards the crowded beach until I could see a figure sitting on a railing opposite, innocently watching the world go by.

"There's a man out here I think you should take a look at," I said.

O'Riley heaved his frame out of the chair and shuffled over to where I was standing. He stopped to look at me before peering through the window.

I pointed my finger. "The man sitting on the railing wearing the overcoat and pork pie hat?"

O'Riley leaned forward on his toes and squinted into the sunlight. "What about him?"

"He's a Health Inspector."

"A Health Inspector?"

"And that brown envelope he's holding is a report he's just spent half an hour compiling on your establishment."

I squared a glance at O'Riley. "And he found some very disturbing facts."

"Such as?"

"Oh I don't know, I just watched him put pen to paper. Seemed very thorough though. He tutted a lot, that's never a good sign, is it."

O'Riley looked at me. This was the moment of truth.

"How do you know who he is?"

"Because I invited him!"

O'Riley smiled like a frozen haddock. "You're bluffing!"

I tapped on the window and waved a couple of times. Thankfully the man in the hat eventually looked up and waved at me.

"Are you sure?" I asked.

I was almost to the door, and that was a whole lot further than I'd wanted to be, before O'Riley spoke again.

"So how come he hasn't shown me the report, that's what normally happens in these circumstance?"

"And what else normally happens?" I said to the door.

I turned to see O'Riley shrug his large shoulders.

"Money gets conveniently handed over," I continued. "And suddenly the report goes missing, which is good for business but not for health and safety. So we decided to do things by the book this time."

The sweat on O'Riley's forehead was practically a tidal wave. But that didn't seem to bother him half as much as I did.

"I thought you were supposed to be the good guy!" he moaned.

"It's not me holding the girl to ransom!"

He shuffled back to his desk and picked up the cat. "So why don't you let me take care of this little matter and it won't cost me any money, or put you in any danger?"

I stared at O'Riley and pictured the bullets flying, April screaming and things not working out exactly as they should have done. Which is why you should always listen to your mother when she says, if you want a job doing properly, do it yourself.

"Because it's my responsibility to get her back and because I'm the one calling the shots!"

O'Riley put the cat down and made his way over to his cabinet to get a drink. He patted his forehead with the handkerchief and poured a large gin. He downed it in one, poured another one and held up a glass for me. I shook my head.

"You know you're walking on very thin ice, Mr Mahoney."

"At least it's still ice, and at least I'm still walking."

"You realise I could make you disappear just like that," he said, with a snap of his fingers. "And nobody would be any the wiser!"

It was only then that I realised just how intimidating O'Riley could be. All I'd ever seen was a sweaty fat man who you'd never want to be stuck in a lift with after a curry and three pints of lager. What I'd foolishly overlooked was the street-fighter, a kid raised from nothing, someone who'd stab a guy in the back before they could so much as blink, just because he could.

But I had to take that chance.

"Why don't you cut the macho stuff O'Riley cos I'm not in the mood. Now you either give me the money or that report goes where it's meant to go and you'll be closed first thing in the morning. I'm not a businessman, but that doesn't sound a very good proposition considering it's a Bank Holiday weekend!"

O'Riley finished his drink.

"When?"

"When what?"

"When do you want the money?"

"I'll call you."

I turned to leave.

"Oh Mr Mahoney?"

I stopped in my tracks without looking back at O'Riley, but I listened intently.

"When this is done, don't ever cross my path again!".

* * *

I stepped out into the hot afternoon air and let the sun warm my face for a moment. Then I crossed the road to where Hartless sat waiting.

"H..., how did it go?" he asked.

"I'm getting the money tonight."

"Just like that?"

"I called his bluff."

"What did you say?"

"You don't want to know!"

Hartless stepped off the fence and handed me my large brown envelope.

"So do we er, do we still have to go to Rick's place?" he asked.

"Unless you have a better way of finding out what happened to him?"

Chapter Seventy-four

Ricks lived in a flat on the edge of town. Four bells lit up the panel on the front door. I pressed the buzzer next to Ricks' name. There was no answer.

Hartless managed to stop chewing long enough to announce. "He, he's not in."

I rang another button. I half expected to hear someone's voice asking who I was, and what I wanted, but all that happened was a buzzer sounded and the door opened. So much for security.

The flat was on the ground floor. We headed down the corridor.

"W....what if he's not in?"

"Then we'll improvise."

Hartless pulled me back by the arm.

"I hope you don't intend breaking in?"

"What would you rather we do, sit around twiddling our thumbs?"

"At least t...., twiddling our thumbs isn't against the law!"

I walked on. "It is where I come from!"

But when we reached the door we found that it was already open. The glass panel had been smashed.

I looked at Hartless. "Do you reckon he forgot his key?"

He shook his head. I stepped inside. Hartless followed.

The flat consisted of a large open room with two doors to the right, leading to a bedroom and a bathroom, and a kitchen at the far end.

"Why don't you check out the bedroom?"

"Why me?"

"Cos you're the one who's used to dealing with people's dirty laundry."

"The, that's supposed to be funny isn't it!"

"It's the best I can do right now."

Probably everything there was to know about Ricks had been chucked across the floor. It was difficult putting one foot in front of the other without treading on a CD, DVD or piece of clothing. It reminded me of Smudge's room, and that wasn't a good omen.

I made my way over to an empty desk in the corner of the room on which sat a computer and a printer. Jagged pieces of paper had been ripped from a notice board hanging from the wall behind. Whoever it was didn't want to leave anything to chance.

Hartless entered the room. "N....nothing in there but an unmade bed and some er, smelly socks," he declared.

"Looks like they took everything."

Hartless pointed a finger towards the computer. "Even the hard-drive."

"The what?"

He ran the same finger across a section of the desk that wasn't covered in dust. "The hard-drive, it's what powers the computer."

"What good would that do?"

Hartless wiped his finger down the side of his trousers and shrugged his shoulders. "They'd be able to work out what was on the computer."

Clever.

Suddenly my chest started to vibrate. I pulled out the phone.

"Yeah."

It was Walker.

"What are you up to?" he asked.

What a choice I had, should I tell him about blackmailing O'Riley or the bit about entering Ricks' apartment without a warrant?

"Nothing," I eventually replied. "Why?"

"Something's come up, or rather somebody."

"What? Or rather, who?"

"Where are you?"

"Ricks's place on Falsgrave. You might want to send some of your boys over, it looks like there's been a break-in."

"Right. I'll pick you up outside the Chinese in five."

I hung up and looked at Hartless. "I've got to meet Walker."

His eyes couldn't have got any larger if I'd blown them up with a bicycle pump. "That was the police?"

"Don't worry, it's not a video-phone. I'll catch up with you later."

Chapter Seventy-five

Walker drove me out along a coastal route south of Scarborough. He had his foot down but there were no sirens and no flashing blue light. The road twisted between the sea and a field full of holiday homes.

At a set of lights, The Inspector swung the car left and down a dipping slipway towards the sea. Policemen in uniform were dotted along the road, each cautiously waving the Inspector through. We stopped on a ridge just above the beach and walked the rest of the way.

A group of people, some in uniform were huddled around an ambulance. They looked towards us as we approached. Walker was frowning. I stopped just short of the group and watched as The Inspector waved a hand and one of the Paramedics immediately pulled a sheet back to reveal a lifeless body.

I wasn't in the mood for anymore dead people, not if I could help it.

Walker studied the figure closely. There was a mumbled conversation, a little pointing towards the sea, a nod and then the body was loaded into the ambulance.

Walker returned to where I stood waiting.

"It's Ricks," he said quietly.

The young reporter wasn't having a good day. He'd had his home broken into and now he'd finally bought his meal ticket out of town. Unfortunately it had only got him as far as Cayton, all washed up on a beach and with the shadow of Scarborough castle still looming in the distance.

He was finally going to make the headlines but not in the way he would have wanted.

"He's been stabbed, twice in the back," Walker announced. "But whether it was that, or the two tons of salt water he swallowed that finally killed him, we'll have to wait and see."

I tried to understand how I felt. There was something in the pit of my stomach that made me feel uncomfortable. It wasn't a pain, more of an ache, the kind of ache I felt whenever I saw pictures of the war and all those bodies lying in the middle of nowhere, far from home. And then somebody somewhere, safe and secure, proudly announces that they had died for a reason.

But dying never seemed a good enough reason to me.

"At least Matthews will be pleased," I said.

"How's that?"

"Presumably this'll give him more ammunition to nail Preacher."

Walker stuffed his hands in his trouser pockets as we made our way back up to the car.

"Do you believe in all this Cleaner stuff?" I asked.

The Inspector looked up, but not to take in the view, more to contemplate what he had to say next.

"I've told you before, I only deal in facts."

"Meaning?"

"Meaning The Super doesn't like this idea of some kind of vigilante running around the town, bumping off who he wants. Whereas I tend to go with the fact that Preacher has confessed to killing four men."

"But not Ricks?"

Walker stopped to frown at me.

"Why would he not confess to killing Ricks?" I asked.

"Could be he thought he'd get a lighter sentence," he shrugged.

But somehow that didn't sit right and Walker knew it.

"Did he confess to being The Cleaner?"

"No."

"No?" I questioned. "So what's his reason for killing everybody?"

"It turns out Preacher had run up quite a debt at the Casino," Walker sighed. "He was on a losing streak. It got so bad that he ended up borrowing money from Collingwood to pay it back."

"Borrowing from Peter to pay Paul?"

The Inspector nodded.

"But that doesn't make sense."

"Gambling, full-stop doesn't make sense, Mahoney. But I guess that's the risk you take."

"But how was he going to pay Collingwood back?"

Walker shrugged his shoulders and carried on walking. "I don't know, perhaps he thought his luck would change but when it didn't, he got desperate. The fact is, you don't owe somebody like Collingwood for too long, it can be bad for your health."

"But that still doesn't explain why he killed Ricks!" I argued.

"It does if Ricks had done his homework. Maybe he found out about the debt, leaving Preacher with no choice but to silence him."

I held out my hands and pretended to look as though I was working on something quiet specific. It was enough to grab the Inspector's attention.

"What are you doing?" he asked.

"Wondering whether to stick this square peg into this round hole or this round hole into this square peg!

The Inspector ignored me.

When we finally reached the car, Walker saw it as an ideal opportunity to take out a cigar.

It gave me the time to consider what he'd said about Preacher being a loser and why it hadn't crossed my mind before. I thought back to one of the sessions at the casino.

Walker got into the car and started the engine. I sat down next to him and buckled up.

"What makes you so sure Preacher's a loser?" I asked.

"What?"

"Preacher, he couldn't have lost every time."

Walker looked across at me.

"The last time I saw him there, he put all his chips on number twenty-six and walked out without seeing what came up."

"And what came up?"

"Green zero!"

Walker slammed the car into gear. "Well there you are then."

"But he walked away without knowing. He didn't even wait to see where the ball landed. Hell, if my life was riding on a number I'm damn sure I'd wait to see what happened."

"While others can't bear to see what does," Walker argued. "That's what makes us all different."

"The point is, what if it had come up?" I continued.

"But it didn't!"

"Just play along for a minute, amuse me. Let's pretend Preacher puts all his money on number twenty-six and it comes up."

Walker was playing along but that didn't mean he had to say anything. It didn't even mean he could look like he was enjoying himself, which he wasn't. I was on my own.

"But he's left the room," I continued. "Nobody's going to chase after him yelling, 'oh Mr Keatley, you forgot your thousand pound winnings' are they!"

We pulled out onto the main road. There was a massive construction taking place. A by-pass into the town centre. It was supposed to help. But all it meant in reality was that the traffic would be squeezed into a bottle neck sooner, rather than later.

"So what's your point?" Walker moaned.

"My point is, maybe Preacher had an account at the Casino?"

"So?"

It didn't take long for us to catch up with a line of traffic heading into town that sometimes crawled but mainly stopped. Walker's patience finally snapped as he let out a loud blast on the car horn.

"Are you allowed to do that?" I asked.

"I'm a policeman aren't I!"

His mood was getting worse by the second.

"But we're not exactly rushing to the scene of a crime are we!"

"We're not bloody rushing anywhere, are we!" he moaned and took another breath on his cigar.

Something was troubling him, but Walker wasn't the kind of person to discuss it, probably not even with his wife.

He pressed a button and all four windows buzzed down.

"Would it help clear things up in that head of yours if we found out whether or not Preacher had an account at the Casino?" he eventually asked.

I looked across at him. "Yes, yes, I think it would."

"Great," he replied, as he stubbed out his cigar and reached for something under his seat.

"Why?" I asked.

"Because now it means I can do this."

In an instant, Walker had placed a blue light on top of the car roof and set off down the road at the speed of sound. The car scattered all in front of us and left a trail of diving bodies and shaking fists. I gripped a handle above the passenger window and frowned at him. Despite hitting almost sixty miles an hour Walker looked back at me and grinned; "Sometimes I just love my job."

Chapter Seventy-six

It took a moment for me to prise my fingers from the dashboard when we finally arrived at the casino. My knuckles were whiter than snow and my head still span with images of construction workers ducking and diving all over the place.

Walker was quickly up the steps and pushing on the glass door. I rushed after him.

The Inspector flashed his badge at the young receptionist sitting behind her desk. "Do any of your members have an account with you?"

It was obvious from her reaction that this wasn't the kind of question she was trained for. For thirty long seconds she flicked her fringe with a finger, said 'erm' a couple of times, glanced at her screen and then at Walker. When she went to toy with her hair for the third time, I feared for her safety. Thankfully a man appeared from the back office.

He looked down his nose at the two of us and asked; "Can I help you?"

"Only if you can tell me if any of your customers have an account with you?" Walker said.

The man frowned at the question and squeaked a 'yes'

"So you'd know if somebody owed you money?"

"Possibly. May I ask why you need to know?"

"I don't, but my friend here does," Walker replied, pointing a thumb at me. "I only came here for the drive."

"I'll have to check with the manager."

"You do that!"

The man stood staring at Walker until the Inspector raised his arm and checked his watch. "And the clock's ticking."

He hurried away. I looked at Walker.

"What?" he snapped.

"Why are you always so charming?"

"I'm getting you what you wanted aren't I!"

"He'd have done what you asked even if you'd leant him a smile."

I was half expecting Walker to snap back. That's what he did, that's what he was good at, defending himself, sticking up for his principles. But all he did was raise an eyebrow and step away from the reception point.

I walked over to where he stood, in the middle of the foyer, staring out into the distance.

He let out a sigh. "I just get fed up with peoples' attitude sometimes, Mahoney. If there was some beer filled yob kicking his weight around they'd expect me here in a flash. But when I want a bit of help, nobody seems to want to know. It's always the same."

I put a hand on his shoulder.

"I wasn't asking you to change your approach, Walker," I explained. "I'd just like you to do it with a smile on your face from time to time!"

* * *

Five minutes later we were lead to the manager's office. A brightly lit room splashed with Ikea furniture and a window overlooking the casino. A silver nameplate glowed up from the desk with the name, Steven Mason, Casino Manager, in bold blue letters on it.

Walker stood legs astride in the middle of the room like an extra from High Noon. He flipped open a jacket button and eased his hands into his trouser pockets.

"So you're Inspector Walker," Mason casually remarked.

"That's very observant of you," Walker replied. "And what gave that away, my forthright nature or my damn good looks?"

Mason flipped a copy of the evening paper across the desk. "Your picture in the paper."

It landed face up with a mug shot of Walker next to a report on the arrest of Preacher.

Walker picked it up and studied the article closely. "Never seem to get me in a good light."

"Why doesn't that surprise me!" Mason replied.

Walker dropped the paper back onto the desk and looked at Mason. He had bright white hair, dark grey eyebrows and a suit sharp enough to trim pencils.

"I need to know if Preacher owed the Casino money," said Walker.

"You do?"

"Yes."

"Why?"

"Because I'm a policeman!"

Mason took a gulp of fresh air and cleared his throat. "As a matter of fact he did."

"A lot?"

"Yes."

"How much?" I asked.

Mason looked at Walker.

"The man asked you a question!" Walker snapped.

"Is it important?"

"I wouldn't be here and he wouldn't have asked if it wasn't!"

"I'm afraid I can't tell you."

"You can't?"

"Data Protection," he replied smugly. "It's the rules."

He was a very brave man because from that moment on, I knew there was going to be trouble. Walker pressed his knuckles onto the desk and leant across the table towards where Mason sat desperately trying to hold onto a relaxed expression.

"You don't want to know what I think about data protection, Mr Mason, because I've had it up to here with all that crap," the Inspector briefly pressed his left hand to the side of his nose. "That and the bloody Health and Safety idiots. All they do is delay nice men like me from doing a damn good job and, when that happens, you have no idea what I might do next. Do you understand?"

"Are you threatening me, Inspector?"

"I'm simply offering you a piece of friendly advice, and guess what? I'm smiling!"

Walker turned to show me a fleeting glance of his pearly whites before glaring back at Mason. It probably crossed his mind that the Inspector didn't have a leg to stand on. But, when you run a casino, it helps to keep the law on your side.

"Two hundred and forty-one pounds," he said quietly.

Walker stood tall and frowned. "What?"

"Two hundred and forty one pounds."

"Are you sure?" I asked.

Mason turned the computer screen to face us. There in bold white letters against a bright blue background was the figure 'Two hundred and forty one pounds.'

"That's it?" I asked.

Mason nodded.

"When did he pay the rest off?"

Mason turned his nod into a frown. "The rest?"

"Preacher told us he owed you thousands!" Walker explained.

Mason looked up at Walker and shook his head.

"I can assure you, Inspector, that has never been the case."

* * *

"Why would he lie?" I asked as we strode out through the lobby.

"Who?"

"Preacher."

"About what?"

"About owing the casino all that money."

Walker shrugged his shoulders as if he didn't care one way or another.

"Doesn't it bother you?"

"Not really."

"You don't mean that?"

The Inspector came to a halt. "Look, Preacher's confessed to killing those people in the harbour, and maybe even Ricks, that's what matters to me, not why he lied about owing some money to the casino."

I continued to stare at Walker until he finally snapped. "What?

"What time is it?" I asked.

Walker checked his watch. "Nearly two. Why?"

"I need to talk to him."

"Who?"

"Preacher."

"Why?"

I don't know…., because….., it just doesn't make sense,

that's all. I just want to talk to him."

"He's going down!"

"Then what have you got to worry about?"

Walker shook off his scowl and pushed open the large glass doors. "Where you're concerned, almost everything!"

Chapter Seventy-seven

Like a gargoyle with toothache on Halloween night, things were getting pretty ugly.

Preacher just about managed to lift his head and raise a smile as I opened the door and walked in. He was sitting at a table in the middle of the room. I grabbed a chair and swung it over to the opposite side of the desk and sat down.

"Mr Mahoney," he said. "What a surprise!"

He appeared calm, relaxed and not like somebody who was about to be charged with murder. All right, so nobody got the chair anymore but anything had to be better than going to jail, with the exception of daytime television!

"Well I couldn't just let you go to jail without thanking you for bashing me over the head the other night!"

Preacher tipped his head to one side and smiled.

"Thing is," I continued. "It's been kind of bothering me and the cops ever since."

"What has?"

"Why all those other people ended up dead and I only

got knocked out."

"Are you complaining?"

"No, just curious."

"Why would I want to kill you?"

"Why would you want to kill anybody?"

"Haven't the police told you?"

"Well that all depends on which version they're offering."

Suddenly Preacher appeared surprised. "Version?"

"Yeah, you see, the unofficial story is that, they seem to think you're somebody who goes under the alias of 'The Cleaner'."

Through a frown Preacher slowly managed a not very convincing laugh. "The who?"

"You heard."

"I've never heard of him."

"Well, he's developed quite a reputation among the press for someone who goes around wiping out people he thinks should have done some time, people like those kids who killed your old man."

Preacher struggled to hold back a wince.

"And Collingwood of course," I continued. "He never seemed to get what he deserved either, not until you shot him anyway. That would seem like justice for a guy who operated dodgy loan scams don't you think."

"Not to mention having young girls romping round his club with dirty old men," Preacher added. "Girls he'd sold down the river, girls with no where else to go, girls like Alana.

I stared at Preacher and, in the stony silence, I tried to work out if what he'd said had bothered me and if that was his intention.

"She didn't tell you?" he asked.

I remained silent as Preacher took a short walk to the other side of the room.

"She has her reasons no doubt," he continued "Like she trusted you, maybe even liked you, so she wouldn't want you to think she was just some cheap call girl. How does that make you feel about Collingwood now, Mr Mahoney?"

My hand had rolled up tight into ball under the desk. I wanted to punch something, someone, but that's not why I was here.

"Alana's dead," I announced.

"I'm sorry to hear that."

"But to answer your question, I still don't think that's a good enough reason to kill Collingwood. Slap him around a bit, but not kill him."

"Then you're a better man than me because, personally, I think he got off lightly."

"You should have gone to the cops," I suggested.

It seemed like a good idea to me, but I had second thoughts the moment Preacher started to laugh.

"People like Collingwood don't go to jail, they don't even stand trial. Hell, I'm not sure the police don't get pay-offs in order to protect what's going on there."

I was so naïve at times.

"Even so," I muttered. "I still can't help thinking there had to be a better way than this."

"People always do, but most of the time they don't have a solution, which means scum like Collingwood go on doing what they're doing and getting away with it, and that just shouldn't happen."

"But then again, that's not the real reason why you killed him is it," I suggested.

Preacher stared back at me with a challenging look.

"I mean, you've known all along what Collingwood was up to, if it meant that much to you, you could have killed him any time, anywhere, especially as you're not too bothered about going to jail."

Preacher tilted his head to one side and waited for whatever was coming next.

"So it has to be the official reason, it has to be about the money you lost at the Casino and borrowed from Collingwood. That's what you'd have the cops believe you killed them for isn't it"

Preacher was slow to nod his head, as though he already figured that I had something up my sleeve other than a cuff. He leant across the table towards me.

"That's exactly what it is, Mr Mahoney, because, let me tell you this, you don't owe people like Collingwood money for too long. Eventually they want it back, and if they don't get it back then they look for retri, ret, revenge, not on you, but on your family or your friends, the people you love, the people you'll do anything for."

"Like your brother?"

Preacher nodded. "I wasn't going to have that."

"So you killed them?"

Preacher stared back at me.

"For the money you'd lost at the Casino!"

He continued to stare as I searched my pockets and placed a receipt on the table between us.

"What's that?" Preacher asked.

"It's what you owed the Casino, it's the bill you put on your tab for that meal you had the other night, along with a couple of drinks.

Preacher looked up.

"Now I'm not one to put a price on somebody's life but I can't help thinking that four grown men are worth slightly more than two hundred and forty one pounds."

"They weren't men, they were scum!" Preacher snapped.

"So this was personal?"

"Of course!"

"Even so, it's still not worth killing for!"

Preacher looked down at the desk.

"So why lie about the money?" I asked.

He looked at me for a moment before getting to his feet and rubbing his bald head with the palm of his hand.

All of a sudden there was something about him that didn't seem right. He appeared troubled, like somebody who was about to go on a long journey but couldn't remember if he'd turned the oven off.

"What's all this about? The police have got what they wanted!"

I stood up and snapped; "It matters to me!"

"Why?"

I stood toe to toe with Preacher. "Because I don't like being lied to and I don't like being bashed over the head without a good reason!"

Preacher turned to pace the room a couple of times before walking over to me again. And then for some strange reason he asked; "Are you wearing a wire?"

"Jesus, Preacher, I'm a small town Private Investigator not the bloody FBI!"

He checked the door with a quick glance then sat down.

"Strictly between you and me?" He whispered.

I nodded.

"I did borrow money from Collingwood but no, I didn't owe the Casino anything."

He paused, then whispered. "I gave it to the church, my brother's church."

For a split second I really thought I was about to crack Preacher round the head but something told me that, he might actually be telling the truth.

"The church?"

Preacher nodded.

"My brother's been running up enormous bills trying

to keep the place going, that and all his other ventures. But it was crippling him, so much so that there was talk of selling up the church and building a supermarket there. Collingwood's pals had already got the contract and the church leaders were ready to take whatever they could. Naturally Peter was distraught, after all he'd done, they were ready to sell him off, just like that. It was my idea to come up with the fund raising activities. He never thought we would reach the target but, then again, he didn't know what I had planned."

"You didn't tell him where the money came from?"

"It was anonymous. And he's never going to find out Mahoney," Preacher added with a finger aimed in my direction.

"He wouldn't be able to live with himself if he knew that his church had survived on the money laundered from a crook like Collingwood. And how do you think the congregation would react? He'd lose it all."

"But how did you ever expect to pay Collingwood back?"

Preacher smiled and sat back. "I didn't. At least, I hadn't thought it through that far. I just wanted to save my brother's work. After all, he's saved me often enough."

I sat back in my seat.

"So why the cops?"

"What?"

"Why did you have to ice the cops?"

Preacher lowered his eyes. "They knew what was going on. They were out to blackmail either me or my brother."

It all seemed to make sense, except for one thing.

"Did that apply to Ricks?" I asked.

Preacher frowned. "Who?"

"The reporter."

"Oh him."

"We found his body washed up in Cayton Bay this morning."

Preacher was staring back at me with a glazed look in his eye, both eyes.

"He'd been shot," I suggested.

Preacher didn't react.

"Twice, in the head," I added.

"Yeah well, I'm sorry about that, but obviously he'd been snooping around like reporters do, you know, I guess he had some information on what I'd been up to. I didn't want it getting out, like I said, it wouldn't have looked good."

I checked Preacher for a moment. It was true, all the words were coming out, but not necessarily in the right order, and none of it made any sense.

"Why twenty-six anyway?" I asked.

"What?"

"Twenty-six, you always put your money on twenty-six."

Preacher raised his chin and smiled. "June the second. It's when I met Julie, my wife. She told me that would always be our lucky number."

I nodded and headed for the door. Why wasn't everything that straightforward?

"By the way," Preacher started. "What I said about this going no further Mr Mahoney!"

I looked back at him over my shoulder.

"I meant it. I've killed for my brother and I'll kill again. I owe him that much. You understand don't you."

I nodded at Preacher and tried to work him out, but it was like staring at a Picasso with the lights off and a fork in my eye.

"What were you doing at the harbour anyway?" he asked.

"I got a call about the missing girl."

Preacher frowned. "April?"

I nodded again.

"But I thought you said she was dead?"

"I did."

Preachers frown grew even deeper.

"Did?" he challenged.

"Somebody wanted to hand her over in the harbour, it could be the same somebody who left me a note asking me to pay a small ransom to get her back."

Preacher stepped over towards me "Who?"

"Well, that's the funny thing, they didn't leave their name!"

"It could be a trick."

"You don't say! Enjoy your porridge."

Chapter Seventy-eight

There had been no announcement about Ricks in the paper, Walker wanted it that way. The official reason was that everything had to be kept on ice until his relatives had been informed. The unofficial reason was that I wanted twenty-four hours to see what I could come up with, other than the same old nothing.

I called in to the Press office. All the staff were there, crammed into a tiny room, diligently tapping on their computer keyboards while the world, in all its glory, flashed past the window.

Hartless took me into the canteen. I told him about Ricks and I told him that nobody else could know until Walker said so.

He let out a faint sigh. "How did it happen?"

"He was stabbed."

For a moment there was silence but I'm not sure if that was because neither of us really knew how to follow up that sentence, or if we were both observing etiquette.

Eventually Hartless asked; "I s..., suppose the police think it's Preacher?"

"They haven't got much else to go on."

"But why s....shoot the other four, stab Ricks and hit you over the head?"

It was good to hear he was becoming as sceptical as I was.

"That's only the start," I said.

Hartless raised an eyebrow.

"I told Preacher that Ricks had been shot and he never batted an eyelid. He just said that he was in the wrong place at the wrong time."

"He didn't do it?"

"Either that or he's made such a habit of killing people that he can't remember how he does it now!"

"But w....why would he lie?"

"Good question."

Hartless sat back and chewed his lip.

"What are you nervous about?" I asked.

He quickly straightened his face as though he hadn't realised what he'd been doing. "All t....these people dying and now you're suggesting the police m.....might not have the right person, that's something to get nervous about isn't it?"

I nodded and thought about chewing my lip as well.

"The, they said that Preacher had borrowed money off Collingwood, money he'd lost at the Casino, that's why he killed him?"

"He was lying," I quietly informed Hartless.

"L....lying?"

"We checked. Preacher didn't owe the Casino anything more than a dinner bill."

"So he didn't owe Collingwood?"

I looked at Hartless and considered what Preacher had told me about not telling anybody. But I felt that, in what was left of my heart, I could trust Hartless. And if I couldn't, then what the hell was I doing here in the first place?

"He'd borrowed money from Collingwood but only to bail out his brother's church. Apparently the authorities were looking to sell the place off and replace it with a supermarket."

"Y..., yes, I remember that."

"But that's off the record. As Preacher told me, it wouldn't look good if people knew that the church had been saved with the money from a heel like Collingwood."

Hartless nodded.

"But that still doesn't explain why Ricks was killed, or even, who killed him."

"Or why Preacher's lying about everything," I added.

The two of us stared at the floor, hoping and praying that, any second, our under worked brains would spring into action and find a solution.

When I realised that wasn't going to happen I got to my feet. Hartless looked up at me. "Did you know that Collingwood had made quite a subs..., substantial withdrawal from his account the morning he was killed?"

I sat back down. "How much?"

Hartless shook his head. "The....they're not giving out a figure just yet, but the rumour is, it would probably cover a minister's expenses f.....for the week."

I had no idea how much that was but I figured it had to be more than I'd see in any one year.

"Why would he need to draw out a large sum of money if he was expecting Preacher to pay him back?" I asked.

Hartless shrugged his shoulders. Somehow I knew he was going to do that.

"So that's it," I moaned. "Still more questions than answers."

A woman stepped into the room and handed Hartless an envelope.

"This just arrived for you," she said and disappeared again.

It was a small padded envelope. Hartless looked at it as though a seagull had just crapped on his tie.

I got to my feet as he ripped the envelope open.

"It's from Ricks," he announced.

I stopped in my tracks and watched as Hartless pulled out a small silver object.

"It's his lighter," I said.

Ricks shook his head. "It's not a lighter, it's a memory stick."

"Is that like a hearing aid?"

Hartless smiled but I wasn't joking. He took me to a room and pressed the silver object into the back of a computer.

A little box appeared on the screen. Hartless clicked it. Another two boxes came up, one was highlighted, 'work', the other 'The Cleaner.'

Hartless looked at me.

"Well go on!" I insisted.

He clicked on 'The Cleaner' and we both sat down. A paragraph came into view with an introduction into Scarborough, a seaside town with sandy beaches, Victorian buildings and breathtaking views. That was followed by a description of Richard Mahoney, a stereotypical whisky drinking, wise cracking, under sexed Private Investigator.

Hartless turned to me and smiled. "G....got you down to a T hasn't he!"

"Well I hardly have time for sex after all that drinking and wise-cracking, do I!"

He continued to scan down the page. It was mainly bullet points about Collingwood's activities including how he'd hired two cops to look into his brother's death. Then a photograph appeared of Warne and Lucas talking to a man in a deserted car park. Hartless took a closer look.

"That's Collingwood," he declared.

"And that's the two cops, Lucas and Warne who were killed on the boat."

"The..., that might explain why Collingwood was carrying all that money, but I don't understand why he wanted to pay two policemen to look into his brother's death if it was an accident?"

"Because maybe it wasn't an accident!"

Hartless let out a quiet groan. "Oh Mr Mahoney, you really don't want to go saying things like that."

"It wasn't by choice."

I got to my feet and pulled on my ear as Hartless sat chewing his lip ten to the dozen.

"These cops," I said, pointing at the screen. "They were up to something else."

"What?"

"They were asking me about a girl called Alana, who's now dead. They were also checking up on two other girls, who've since gone missing. What's worse is that all these girls knew Jenny, the girl killed in the car crash."

"S..., somebody's going around killing all the..., these people?"

"Or at least making them disappear." I nodded.

"But w...., we don't know who and we don't know why."

I shook my head.

"M...,maybe it's better that way."

"How come?" I asked.

"B...because the more people seem to know, the more chance they have of ending up dead."

pter Seventy-nine

I reached the office ten minutes before the call was due. I sat in my chair and stared at the phone.

It gave me time to wonder about Envy. All I knew about her was her name, her qualifications and that she liked working out. Then it dawned on me that, all I really knew, was that she liked working out, the rest she could have made up. This town was full of people who didn't go by their proper name, including me.

I searched my desk for her mobile number. It rang a couple of times and then the answer machine clicked on.

"Yeah, it's me, Mahoney, give me a call when you get a chance would you."

I couldn't believe I was allowing myself to think that somehow Envy might be involved. But she'd been there right from the start. She'd practically arm-wrestled me for the case. But that was to find April? It had nothing to do with Preacher. Unless, somehow, they were linked and I was either too blind, or stupid to see how.

My head hurt. I reached for a couple of paracetemols just as the phone rang.

A muffled voice told me where to go and when to be there. I wanted to do say more or less the same thing, but he hung up. Besides, I needed to find April. I had no idea why, other than, it might provide some answers, and God, I could really do with some answers.

I downed the tablets and checked the clock on the wall.

It was time for a whisky.

Chapter Eighty

I arrived at the car park ten minutes early in my Morris Minor. A dark limousine with blacked out windows pulled up five minutes later. A man got out of the driver's seat and glanced around the car park. I recognised him from O'Rileys office. He was wearing his customary shades and suit. I drove over to the car, turned off the engine and got out. The driver frisked me, it was getting to be a routine.

He tapped on a window. It hummed slowly open until O'Riley's fat face came into view.

"He's clean, Mr O'Riley."

"I showered especially." I said.

O'Riley's stared out beyond me and towards the car.

"I see being a Private Investigator has its rewards," he said, with a patronising smile.

"Yeah," I replied. "I get to meet all these bloody comedians! Now have you got the money?"

O'Riley nodded at the driver. He reached into his inside coat pocket and revealed the top half of an envelope.

"What about the report?" O'Riley asked.

"I told you, you don't have to worry about that. I just want the money."

O'Riley stared at me for what felt like an age, certainly long enough for me to fear he was going to pull out. And I had nothing else to fall back on if he did, other than robbing a bank.

"So?" I asked.

"Paul will keep the money. He's going to go with you," O'Riley stated.

"I have to go alone," I argued.

"Not with my money. People will think I'm going soft," he smiled. "And a man in my position can't afford that, you understand!"

Chapter Eighty-one

I was concerned because the message had insisted on me going alone. But it was O'Riley's money after all, so there wasn't much I could do about it. At least we got to go in one of his cars because, as I argued, driving up in a blue and white Morris Minor might have looked a little conspicuous.

* * *

The sun had dropped from the sky some time ago, but Paul still insisted on wearing his shades. He didn't talk a whole lot either and that suited me just fine. I watched the heather swoop across the hills as we made the journey north and wondered what the next hour would bring just as I had wondered what the last hour would bring. Life was one big wonder being a Private Investigator.

* * *

With Whitby Abbey appearing in the distance we took a right down a narrow dirt track road. Dust clouds rose up all around and suspended the view. We bounced along for three minutes like two kids on a space hopper until finally coming to a halt.

"Is this it?" he asked.

I waited till the dust settled and looked out through the window. A deserted farmhouse slowly appeared. There was nothing else for miles around.

"I guess so."

Paul started to get out of the car. I grabbed his arm. He aimed his shades at me.

"I have to go in there alone," I insisted.

"But Mr........."

"I know what O'Riley said, but there's a girl's life at stake here, so you sit tight and take it easy. Besides," I said, squaring a glance at the miles of nothing that surrounded us. "Where the hell am I going to go?"

I held out my hand and waited for Paul to reluctantly hand me the envelope.

"No tricks Mahoney!"

"Do I look like a magician?"

* * *

I stepped out of the car and looked towards the house. It was only then that I started to wonder if I'd made the right decision. I wonder that a lot. It had become a bit of a bad habit. Maybe I needed to think things through a bit more instead of marching in and seeing what happens next.

The wind whistled through the long grass as I made my way towards the battered remains of the house. I really had to think things through more.

The window panes were smashed, the paint work peeled and the front door hung at an angle. I stepped across a pile of red tiles that had rained down from the roof and carpeted the dirt.

I pushed gently on the door.

Dust rose up in the sunlight and filled the hallway. I let out a cough to clear my throat and offered the customary greeting.

"Hello. Is anybody here?"

Nobody answered.

There was a large room to my left. I went inside. Rubble sprinkled the floor. A pile of papers was stacked in a corner of the room with their pages torn and ripped.

I wasn't expecting a cheery welcome and colourful balloons, but I was expecting something.

I looked out of the window at where Paul sat waiting a hundred or so yards down the road. I offered him a wave just as a hand pushed me in the back and a voice said; "Up against the wall, Mahoney!"

I did as I was told. A hand patted my left and then my right side.

"I thought I told you to come alone!" The voice said.

"I needed a lift! Besides, it's his money."

"Who's?"

"A man called O'Riley."

The voice panicked. "Who's O'Riley?"

"The big 'Ninety-nine', so if anything happens to me, Storey, you're in real trouble."

A hand spun me round till I was looking face to face with Storey.

"How did you know it was me?"

"Who else would go to the trouble of piecing together a note in newspaper cuttings and sticking it to letter headed paper from the Delmont Hotel?"

Storeys face slightly reddened. He tried to wipe it off with the back of his hand but it didn't work.

"Were you followed?" he asked.

"Most of the way."

His jaw dropped as he glanced out of the window. He

couldn't have looked more scared. "Who by?"

"I'm not sure, but most of them carried on up to Whitby."

"This isn't funny!" he snapped.

"Have you ever been to Whitby?"

"Don't be a smart mouth Mahoney, I've got a gun!"

"I can see!"

"You have no idea who you're dealing with here!"

Storey was behaving as though somebody had stuck a packet of drawing pins in his shoes. I would have loved to have nailed him to the floor because all his jumping around was wearing me out. Most of the time he aimed the gun towards the ceiling. I'm not sure he even knew where the trigger was but, the way my day was going, he'd probably get lucky and fire a bullet somewhere where it would hurt me most. It was best to bide my time.

"Are you talking about the mad man jumping up and down in front of me with the pea-shooter or somebody else?"

"Some people came by the hotel," he sweated. "They were looking for me."

"Who?"

"I don't know. I didn't get to look at them. The receptionist tipped me off that somebody was waiting to see me. I just legged it. I haven't been back since."

Storey's breath was short and sharp like most people's when they get in a panic.

"It could have been anybody." I suggested, while knowing it was probably Collingwood's men.

"But nobody knew I was there remember!"

"Well chances are those men are dead now."

"Dead?"

"Didn't you hear what happened down at the harbour?"

Storey's eyes tweaked at me like he was trying to read

my lips. He appeared more insane than ever. He shook his head like someone with a twitch and I wondered if he'd been laid up here since bumping me over the head.

"Where's April?" I asked.

"Have you got the money?"

"Be a hell of a time to admit I'd forgotten it."

"So where is it?"

I took out the envelope and held it up for Storey to see. But when he went to reach for it I pulled it back.

"What are you up to?" I asked.

"What do you mean?"

"This is probably only half of what you'd have got if you'd have delivered her properly!"

"I realise that. But….."

"But, what?"

"But I'd rather take my chances with you," he said, aiming the gun and tapping his temple. "Like I said, we have no idea who we were dealing with. Who's to say they wouldn't have taken the money and killed me anyway?"

"What makes you think I won't?"

Storey smiled at the gun in his hand. "This."

"You going to carry that around with you for the rest of your life?"

He got all nervous. "All you want is the girl, that's all you want. You don't care about the money."

"How things have changed!" I moaned.

"What do you mean?"

"It was you who wanted her in the first place, that's the only reason I'm in this mess."

"But I didn't know why did I!"

"And I suppose you've got bills to pay!"

"That's right," he snarled.

"If only you could remember who to pay them to!"

Storey raised the gun to my face. "That's not funny, Mahoney!"

"So where is she?" I snapped.

Storey flicked his head and pushed me towards another door. I was tired of being ordered around. I just wanted to turn and beat the crap out of him, but I had to think of April. He pushed me into the next room where I could see a young girl kneeling on the floor and chained to a broken radiator. She looked nothing like the angel I'd first seen in the photograph. She was wafer thin with blood shot eyes and matted hair. I could have been wrong but it was like she hadn't had a bath in a week. If she had walked into the office I wouldn't have had a clue who she was.

"April?"

She stared back at me without answering. That didn't surprise me, I was just another stranger who'd walked into her life. "What the hell have you done to her?"

But Storey was too busy checking the window to answer.

"Who the hell followed you Mahoney?"

"I told you...," I started, as I followed him back across the room and looked out of the window.

That's when I noticed another car travelling up the track and kicking up a cloud of dust.

"Maybe they've come to view the house?" I suggested.

But like a kid firing a bazooka at a fly while travelling backwards on a pair of skis, it was a wild and not very close shot.

"I can't believe you let them follow you here!"

Storey was up and down the room like a man who thought he knew where he was supposed to be going but couldn't remember why.

"Who?"

"They're going to kill us!"

I grabbed him by the collar. "There's nobody left to kill us you idiot, Collingwood's dead and Preacher's in jail!"

The slamming of a car door averted my eyes from Storey's fearful gaze. Paul got out of his car and stood blocking the road. The other vehicle came to a halt. Words were exchanged before a shot rang out and Paul slumped to the floor.

"What did I tell you, Mahoney."

"Who are they?"

Storey tugged at the envelope in my hand.

"Give me the money!" he demanded.

"Let the girl go first!"

Storey fumbled with a key, then slapped the whole bunch into my hand.

"The money!"

Two men in suits headed towards the house.

I tipped the envelope upside down and scattered the notes all over the floor. Storey fell to his knees and frantically started to gather them up.

I raced over to April. My first three attempts to open the lock failed miserably. My hands were sweating.

"My name's Mahoney," I said."I'm here to help you. I'm not doing a very good job, I know, but it's the best I can do. Are you OK?"

She nodded.

The fourth key freed the lock. I pulled April to her feet as a shot fired across the room and splattered against the wall above us. Storey stopped picking up the money for a moment to fire back. I hoped it would be enough to keep them at bay.

"Can you run?" I asked.

April nodded.

"Good, cos we'd better get going."

"Wait," she insisted and hurried back to where a coat was lying on a pile of bricks. She picked out a phone and shoved it into her pocket.

"We're getting shot at and you're stealing phones!"

Another shot rang out across the room as we hurried out of the back door. Storey stood alone firing back at them. I wanted to wish him luck but, although I was many things, I wasn't a hypocrite.

* * *

The two of us headed up a steep slope towards a pale blue horizon. At first I led April, pulling her by the hand as we raced clear of the house. The shots grew fainter as did my breath, and my legs started to give way. Hell of a rescue this was turning out to be. All I could hear was Envy's words ringing in my ear, something about how keeping healthy might one day save my life. Bloody women!

"Ha, have you any idea where this goes?" I panted.

"No."

And why would she, who on earth would ever wander this far away from civilisation?

There was a deserted railway line at the top of the hill that overlooked the North Sea. It was probably a lovely view but I needed to press my hands to my knees for a moment in an attempt to recover my breath. April appeared OK.

Out in the distance I could just make out Scarborough Castle perched in the sunlight. It looked so far away.

"What happened to the track?" I moaned.

April looked at me.

"Why would anybody want to dig up a bloody railway line!"

"Look!" shouted April.

I followed the direction of her finger back down the slope and towards the house. One of the men was running towards us and it wasn't Storey.

We had a choice, we could either wait here and get shot or we could run and I'd have a heart attack. One was certainly quicker than the other, but I decided to take my chances on the longer solution.

"Let's go," I said.

* * *

The track slipped down between a sweep of fields on one side and a deep lush valley filled with trees and bushes on the other. On any other day I might have enjoyed such surroundings, unfortunately those days seemed few and far between right now.

* * *

We followed the meandering track forever until April came to a sudden halt.

"I can't go on," she moaned.

She sank to her knees. I knew how she felt, I was also dead on my feet, but I didn't want to give up, because I didn't want to get shot.

I took a couple of deep breaths and glanced back up the track. The man could have appeared at any moment, and I wasn't sure I could talk my way out of this one.

I pulled April to her feet. "We have to go on."

"I thought you were supposed to be rescuing me?"

She was talking much louder than I would have liked. Her voice echoed through the trees.

"I am. I mean I'm trying."

"Don't you have a gun? You could hide somewhere and shoot him."

"No I don't have a gun."

"Why not?" she shouted.

I pressed my hand across her mouth and clenched my teeth; "Because I'm a Private Investigator not a bloody sniper!"

I looked back up the track and wondered why I

bothered. Bloody conscience. How I hated myself sometimes. I'd been shot at, chased all over the place, had my teeth drilled, whacked in the kidneys, and I didn't even know who these people were from Adam! There was only one thing for sure, I didn't want to die, not here anyway.

I took April by the arm and dragged her along with me. She wasn't happy but, then again, neither was I

"Isn't there somebody you could ring?" She moaned.

"I don't have a phone."

"I do," she said, pulling me to a halt and holding out a mobile.

"That's Storey's."

"No it's not it's mine. He took it from me! She argued.

"He took your phone?"

She nodded.

"Why?"

"I do not know. He didn't say. He didn't say much to me at all. I hope he's dead."

"Yeah well, we'll soon be following him if we don't get a move on."

She stood still and powered up the phone.

"Who can we call?" She asked.

"The police would seem like the obvious answer."

"No!" she screamed.

I wanted to gag her, but I didn't have the time, nor did I have any tape.

"Will you keep your voice down!"

"Not the police," she whispered

It would have been nice to know why, but I figured I could leave that till later.

"I don't know who else to ring."

"Don't you know anybody?"

"Yes, but most of them are either dead or missing."

"You are not very lucky!"

"It's the only luck I get!"

"So," she said, pushing the phone out at me.

The only names that came to mind were Hartless and Trish and Hartless didn't even have a car. Then again, I could hardly justify inviting Trish to a gun fight at the OK Coral. She had a kid to think of. It had to be Hartless.

"There's one guy I know but I don't have his number"

"Does he work?"

"Yes."

"Where?"

"The evening paper."

"Good," she said.

I watched her press some buttons that set off a noise and highlighted some pictures and then she read out a number.

"What's that?" I asked.

"The number for the evening paper."

I looked at the phone, and there it was in black and white, the telephone number for the evening paper.

"How the hell did you do that?"

"Internet," she replied as if I had just asked her to spell, Wally.

"That gets the internet? What is it, a phone or a computer?"

"Everything. Now ring your friend."

* * *

It was going to sound like a dirty phone call the way I was panting, but I had no choice. The phone rang a couple of times and was answered by a girl on reception. She sounded like the one I'd spoken to the other day. She told me that Hartless wasn't in. That's not what I wanted to hear.

"Do you happen to know his mobile number? I'm a

friend of his, Richard Mahoney, the Private Investigator"

The line went quiet.

"I know you're not supposed to give it out but this really is a matter of life and death. If you don't put me through, you could be printing my obituary tomorrow."

"One minute," she said.

I heard the ringing of a phone and Hartless answered. She explained who I was and immediately he told her to put me through.

"Mr Mahoney?"

"Yeah, look Hartless, we're in trouble. I need you to get a car here as quickly as possible."

"W..., where's here?"

"Well that's the problem, I have no idea. I took a ride out to a broken down farmhouse north of Scarborough and now we're on some deserted track."

"A cinder track?"

"Maybe. I never was much good at Geology."

"How far from town are you?"

"I have no idea."

"Did you get as far as Robin Hoods Bay?"

"No."

"Then keep walking, you should come to a pub very soon."

"Are you joking or just reading my mind?"

"Seriously, about eight miles from town you'll come to a deserted railway station on your right, a few yards after that, on your left, is a pub. I'll meet you there."

* * *

Much sooner than either of us had anticipated, a deserted railway station came into view, and then the pub, like an oasis, just as Hartless had said.

It must have looked odd to the dozen or so locals sitting in the dim light to see a thirty seven year old man walk into a pub with a young girl, both sweating profusely and with lungs at bursting point. What went through their minds, I have no idea, but I'm sure they'd recount the tale for years to come.

We crossed the room to the bar and I ordered two cokes.

"I'd rather have an orange and water," April said.

It sounded a lot healthier

"Two orange and waters please."

Screw it, I thought.

"And a whisky, no ice please."

I checked the window as the barmaid mixed the drinks. There was no sign of the man. Hopefully he'd given up I looked at the menu board. It had been scrubbed clean.

"Are we too late for food? I asked.

"I can see if there's any leftovers if you like."

"That's good because she's starving and I'm famished."

The woman handed us our drinks with a curious look in her eye. It crossed my mind to explain what was going on exactly, but revealing that I was a Private Investigator and that this young girl was in trouble and that there was a goon chasing us with a gun who might appear any moment, but not to worry because a man from the evening paper would arrive very soon, in a taxi, just didn't seem to cut it.

* * *

They brought us some sandwiches, made up of leftovers and warmed up chips. All the while we ate I kept staring out of the window across the car park, not only for Hartless but just in case the man with the gun appeared. I wasn't sure what he'd do if he found us here. I doubt he had enough bullets to kill everybody but it could have made things a little awkward.

"Why is that man following us?" April eventually asked.

"I was hoping you'd tell me."

"I don't know," she shrugged and carried on eating.

"Well, a not very nice man is willing to pay ten thousand pounds for you and," I said, pointing back in the direction of the farmhouse, "some other goon is chasing us with a gun, that doesn't usually happen because you don't know anything!"

April stared back at me like someone not really sure what day it was.

"Didn't Storey say anything to you?"

"Who's Storey?"

"The guy who tied you to a radiator."

She shook her head. "He kept calling me April."

"Why wouldn't he, that's your name isn't it?"

She shook her head again.

"My name is Anna."

She spoke like Alana with that hint of somewhere foreign in her accent.

"Anna?" I questioned.

She nodded.

"Anna?" I said again.

But this time she didn't nod.

"You're not April?"

She shook her head as I pulled out the photograph and showed it to her.

"That's not you?"

"It is not like me at all." She said, sounding like I'd just compared her to a wild boar.

But that wasn't quite true. I studied the picture closely. It was very much like her. Trouble was, I couldn't convince myself it actually was her. Maybe Storey had made a mistake. I tucked the picture away. Now I had to get used to calling her Anna.

"So where are you from? I asked.

"Romania."

"What are you doing here, in England I mean?"

"Working.

"Where?"

"In London."

"Doing what?"

"I don't like the way you speak to me."

"I'm sorry but I'm hungry and tired and I've just run a marathon. What were you doing in London?"

"I am a waitress."

"So how did you end up here?"

The girl sighed and dropped her fork onto the plate and looked out across the room.

"One night, I am walking home, and this man, this Storey, comes up behind me and puts something over my mouth. The next thing I know I am in the boot of a car. I am tied up. The car is moving. After a while it stops. The boot opens and the man gives me a sip of water, there is a small hole in the tape over my mouth. I try to scream but he shuts the boot and we move again."

"How did you get away?"

"I hear a loud bang and the car crashes, we roll over, like we went down a hill."

I nodded.

"The car is damaged but I am able to kick the boot open. We are in some woods. I cut the rope on some broken glass. I can't see the man. I run away."

"Where to?"

Anna frowned at me.

"Where did you run to?

"Scarborough."

"Why?"

"It is the first place I come to"

"Why didn't you go to the police," I asked.

She avoided my gaze.

"Funny that. You're kidnapped, driven miles from home, involved in a car crash that might have killed some one, I think I'd have gone to the police."

"You don't believe me?"

"What about your friends?"

"What friends?"

"Smudge, your boyfriend, and the people you used to know in Scarborough?"

The girl frowned back at me. "Scarborough? But I don't know anybody in Scarborough."

I watched as she picked up her drink and finished it off. We'd got the wrong girl. People had been shot, tortured, threatened, and all for the wrong bloody girl

"Why didn't you go to the cops, police?" I asked again.

The girl fixed a look on me, like somebody at the end of a zip line suddenly having second thoughts. Then she looked away.

I checked my watch, but I don't know why.

"Who is coming to fetch us? She asked.

"What does it matter?"

"Please, not the police."

She was really nervous.

"Don't believe everything you hear about the cops, they're not all bad."

Her anxiety increased. "I don't want the police!"

She made an attempt to get to her feet. I'm not sure if she intended running, and I wasn't in the mood to find out, so I gripped her hand and held it tight.

"Tell me why you don't want to see the cops!"

She settled down.

"I don't have a visa. I am not supposed to be here anymore," she whispered. "I only came here on holiday."

Everyday the papers were filled with the number of illegal immigrants slipping into the country and how the government struggled to do anything about it. Handing one of them on a plate might have been appreciated, but then again, they'd got us into this mess, it wasn't down to me to help them out.

"Look," I said. "The cops aren't coming, it's a friend of mine, and he won't say anything to anyone. OK"

* * *

Ten minutes after getting absolutely nowhere with Anna, Hartless appeared in a taxi. The girl fell asleep in the back seat before we'd reached the main road. It prevented us from talking at all on the way back.

We stopped at Hartless's flat. Anna was still fast asleep and looked like she would be for the rest of the week. We laid her on a bed and covered her with a blanket.

The two of us watched her sleeping for a moment.

"You think she's the er, the wrong girl?" Hartless whispered.

"Either that or she's hiding something," I replied. "And If I were a betting man, I'd put your house on her hiding something."

Hartless glanced at me. "M.. my house?" he asked.

I nodded.

"Why my house?"

I looked at him. "Because I haven't got one!"

Anna stirred slightly but not enough to wake. We retreated to the front room. I stretched out on the sofa while Hartless settled into a chair. The lights were soft and I was sleepy.

Hartless took a pause from chewing his lip. "S, s... she could actually be who she says she is," he suggested.

I nodded a couple of times, but too many things were bothering me.

"M...maybe Storey got the wrong girl, a lookalike? Hartless continued. "We don't know what he had to go on, apart from the photograph and she doesn't look all that much like her."

"It was taken a while ago," I said, my eyes feeling heavy. "Besides, why didn't she go to the cops?"

"L...like she said, she's not meant to be in this country. The police station's t.... the last place I'd have gone."

"So you hide out in a chalet?" I mumbled.

"I don't know," Hartless sighed. "I, I've never been dragged to somewhere I didn't want to go and left alone without any money."

Hartless may have had a point worth pursuing, but his words drifted off into a dream, as I slowly fell asleep.

* * *

Hartless didn't sleep well. He wasn't used to sleeping upright in a chair. So he was up very early fixing us both a coffee. I, on the other hand, hadn't slept so well in a long time.

Anna was still in the land of nod. I drank my coffee and got ready to leave.

Hartless panicked. "W...where are you going?"

"I need to find out who she is."

"B..., but you can't leave her here, I mean....."

"What do you want me to do, carry her around in a rucksack?"

Eddie's eyes started to spin like plates on a stick. "But, I've got to go to work."

I pressed a hand onto his left shoulder. "Tell them you'll be late. You know this is important!"

"But, ..."

I held up a finger. "She's got nowhere else to stay."

"W...., what about your place?" He asked.

"Don't be silly, I've had practically every heel in town

knocking my door down, it's not safe."

"That makes, that makes me f.... feel really good!"

"Nobody will ever suspect she's with you."

"Who's to suspect, Collingwood's d...dead and Preacher's in jail?"

"I know, "I said, quietly. "But just to be on the safe side."

"You keep mentioning that word, s, safe."

"It'll be all right Eddie."

"You don't know that. N...nobody ever knows that, look at Ricks."

"I won't be long."

Hartless started to chew his lip as he watched me leave.

"You'd better not be!"

Chapter Eighty-two

A large black limo was parked on double yellow lines outside the office. A suit in shades was pressed up against the passenger door. He tapped on the window when he saw me approach.

I stood and watched the electric window slowly open.

"I was rather hoping to have heard from you by now, Mr Mahoney,"

"Yeah, well there's been a problem," I muttered.

"Concerning my money or Paul?"

"Both."

O'Riley raised an eyebrow at me.

"Paul's dead."

The eyebrow somehow got even higher. "Dead?"

"A car just pulled up from nowhere," I explained. "And these people started shooting up the place."

"Who?"

"I didn't stick around to find out."

O'Riley lowered his gaze as he took in what he'd just heard.

"And what about the money?" he said to the floor.

"I left it there."

For a moment the fat man sat quietly grimacing. A lot was going through his mind and none of it was nice.

"I take it you got the girl?" he asked eventually.

I nodded.

"Where is she?"

"Safe."

"Safe?"

Did he expect me to tell him where she was?

"Yeah, safe," I repeated.

"Very well," he said and tapped on the window.

The driver retreated to the car and started up the engine. O'Riley looked at me one last time before he disappeared behind the blackened window.

The car pulled away.

Somehow I was expecting a whole lot more than what had just happened. O'Riley had just lost ten thousand pounds and one of his suits. Maybe he could claim it all back on a tax return. Maybe he wasn't all that bothered, or maybe he was just biding his time.

Chapter Eighty-three

Barbara was catching a cigarette outside the front door.

"Nice car," she observed as the limo pulled away

"Somehow I took you more for a motor-bike kind of girl?"

Her bottom lip curled into a smile. "Kawasaki 125," she mused. "Those were the days."

"Any messages?" I asked.

"Nothing I'm afraid, just a telephone bill."

"I'll see to it when I get back. Oh, and thanks for the Eclairs."

"Anytime."

* * *

As I'd suspected, the walk to the chalet was quicker than driving. Major repairs were taking place at the Rotunda Museum just below the Cliff Bridge. It was causing traffic delays in all directions.

A stiff sea breeze chilled the hot afternoon. Children with nets toyed on the rocks just in front of the Spa, while older people in deckchairs sheltered under handkerchiefs.

* * *

I reached the chalets and pulled open the one where I'd first seen April, or at least, where I thought I'd seen April.

The place was cramped but there was nothing to see. It was almost as if somebody had cleaned the place up, and I don't mean the Council. There was absolutely nothing for me to go on. Somebody was covering their tracks and making it hard for me to prove who April was.

Chapter Eighty-four

"Would you like a coffee?" Barbara asked as I made my way upstairs to the office.

"Every minute of the day."

I sat at my desk and studied the two photographs I had of April. Neither one of them carried enough evidence for me to force the issue. If April denied it was her, what could I do?

The doorbell rang downstairs and I could hear Barbara talking to somebody, a man.

The floorboards creaked as the two of them made their way upstairs. I braced myself for a very large man carrying a gun and making me an offer I couldn't refuse. The door opened and Barbara poked her head inside.

"There's a man here to see you Mr Mahoney," she whispered.

"Who?"

"A Mr Holding, he's very well dressed."

I wanted to ask if he was carrying a gun, but instead I just stood up.

"Shall I show him in? It would look very professional."

It would have been rude not to allow Barbara her moment of glory. So I nodded and quickly tried to decide what I should be doing when they entered. Should I stand or sit? If I stand, do I lean casually against the wall, or professionally, with my hands behind my back? If I sit, do I look like I'm finishing off some important paperwork, or musing over a case? I should have bought a pipe!

By the time the door opened again I was halfway across the floor having decided nothing at all. Barbara entered first.

"Mr Holding," she said.

The sight of Mr Holding immediately banished any and all preconceptions. I'd imagined somebody tall, well built with a belly full of conference meals and takeaways, somebody with a swagger, somebody who knew full well he wouldn't be leaving empty handed.

In reality, Holding was tall, thin, well tanned and had incredibly large ears. He was holding a briefcase in his right hand. About the only thing I'd got right was the suit, although I'd missed the waistcoat.

"Please call me, Vince," he insisted.

We shook hands. His grip was lightweight, if he had been clinging to life, he'd already be on borrowed time.

"Maybe I could fetch some coffee, or tea?"

We both looked at Barbara. She was hell bent on keeping up appearances.

"Not for me, thank you." Said Holding.

"Nothing at all?"

Barbara tried not to appear as though her world had suddenly caved in. "Perhaps a glass of water then?"

She was persistent if nothing else. Holding eventually nodded.

"And a coffee for you, Mr Mahoney." She added,

recovering her smile.

I nodded and Barbara hurried away closing the door behind her.

"So what can I do for you, Vince?" I asked as we made our way over to the desk.

"Actually, Mr Mahoney, it's what we can do for you."

I stopped dead in my tracks and looked across at Holding. He twisted his neck a couple of degrees and straightened his tie, like people do when they've just invited somebody to take their best shot.

"I hate it when people say that."

"I'm sorry?" he asked

"Well it usually means me putting my foot in where it doesn't belong, or having to dodge a bullet or two."

Holding smiled politely and placed his briefcase gently onto the desk. He held up his hands and pressed the palms towards me.

"I can assure you, Mr Mahoney, you won't be dodging any bullets."

We both sat down.

"We?" I said

"I'm sorry?"

"You said, we."

"Ah yes, you see, I am acting on behalf of my client."

"You're client?"

Holding sat back and nodded at me.

"And does he, or she, have a name?"

He waved a hand as if to dismiss my intrigue. "My client's name is inconsequential."

"Well that'll stand out in the directory!"

Holding paused to cast a curious glance in my direction. "Well anyway, the matter in hand concerns the fact that you seem to have something that my client wants."

I tried not to smile too brightly. "Well I'm wondering,

would that be my dashing good looks or roguish charm?"

Holding reached for the briefcase and I wondered if he was about to pull out a lot of money, a stack of cucumber sandwiches or something that went bang when you pulled the trigger. But I was wrong on all three counts. He placed a photograph of April on the desk in front of me.

I took a quick look as though I'd never seen her before. "Seems like a nice girl."

Holding put a hand over his mouth and cleared his throat with a faint cough. He had all the appeal of a dried prune.

"You know her of course!" he said.

"I do?"

"Somebody asked you to locate her and last night you took a lot of Jack O'Riley's money to pay for her retrieval."

"Is that a fact?"

Suddenly Holding had become interesting. But that intrigue was put on hold as the door opened and Barbara returned carrying a tray with a cup of coffee and a glass of water. She placed the tray on the desk next to the briefcase and smiled at our client.

"I found a slice of lemon," she said, pointing at his glass. "I hope you don't mind."

"That's very efficient of you," Holding said softly.

Barbara hunched her shoulders and beamed a smile behind his back. I could be wrong, and I very much hope that I was, but this could have been the best day of her life.

She practically skipped out of the room. I looked back at Holding.

"You've done your homework," I said.

Holding held out his hands in an act of modesty. "It is merely information that's been forwarded to me."

"So what's the game, Mr...., Vince?"

"Game?"

"What are, Mr or Mrs Inconsequential up to?"

Holding pressed the middle finger of both hands together in front of his lips. "It's rather a delicate situation as I'm sure you're aware, Mr Mahoney, but my client needs to see," he pointed a finger towards the picture. "this young girl."

I stared at Holding and watched as he reached for the water and took a couple of sips. It was obvious what he wanted me to say next, so I didn't disappoint him.

"So why are you asking me?"

Holding took out a handkerchief, wiped his lips a couple of times and said; "My client would like you to bring the young lady to a certain meeting place."

"What if I don't have her?"

"Then perhaps you know where she is!"

Now he was bullshitting, but he was good at it. If he had been born a Red Indian they'd have christened him, Talking Bull.

"Even if I did, why would I want to put her life at risk?"

"Who said anything about putting her at risk?"

"I'm sorry, it's just something about the underhand way you come in here with your polite threatening tone," I said as my eyes momentarily strayed back to the briefcase and my mind wondered how much he might try to bribe me with.

"Naturally I apologise for my tone if it has offended you in any way, but I can assure you, the young girl's life is not at risk."

I stood up. "Then we've got nothing more to say,"

"That might depend," Holding replied casually.

"On?"

"How much you want to see Miss Envy again."

He was so cool and calculating, so much so that it made me wonder if he was for real.

"What?" I asked.

"Miss Envy, when was the last time you saw her, I wonder?"

I started to think, one, maybe two days ago, but it didn't matter, they had her now, whoever they were. But she was tough, tough enough to look after herself, wasn't she?

I took a slow stroll around the desk towards where Holding sat, legs crossed.

I gritted my teeth "And why would you wonder something like that?"

"I see her welfare is of some concern to you!"

Suddenly I felt myself torn in two. One part wanted to continue this discussion in a polite and professional manner, while the rest wanted to pin Holding to the wall and beat his brains out.

"What the hell's that got to do with you?"? I asked.

Holding picked up his glass but I reached out and stopped him from taking another sip.

"I said......."

Holding smiled. "I presume she's, what you might call, insurance."

"Against what?"

"Against you refusing to fulfil my client's wishes."

That was it, my patience finally tipped its hat and left the building. It didn't want anything to do with what was going to happen next. I grabbed Holding by the lapel and pulled him up from the chair.

"You'd better start talking!" I demanded.

"About what?"

"About where Envy is?"

"As I have already informed you, on a number of occasions, Mr Mahoney, I am only working for my client,

I don't even know who Miss Envy is, let alone where she is."

I was doing my best tough act, but Holding wasn't even sweating, and the room was as hot as hell. He just looked at me as though the whole situation was nothing more than a slight inconvenience.

His voice was calm and he was never short of an answer.

"So let me speak to the monkey instead of the organ grinder."

"Is that part of your job?"

"What?"

"Insulting people!"

I almost laughed. "I find it helps keep my head above the filth and don't forget, I'm not the one playing with people's lives."

"I'm only doing my job!"

"So go work for somebody else!"

I let go of Holdings lapel and pushed him to one side. He did his best to straighten his collar a couple of times and reached for his briefcase.

"Well I've said all I was sent to say."

He started to leave the room, but I blocked his way.

"How do I know you're not all talk?"

Holding looked at me out of the corner of his eye. "You don't."

I waited for him to explain.

"But are you willing to risk your partner's life on a bluff?"

I pressed Holding up against the wall. My reputation could take a battering because it wouldn't have made a great deal of difference one way or another anyway, but Envy didn't deserve this.

"You really think you can come into my office and threaten me?"

"On the contrary Mr Mahoney, all I have done is pass on information."

"I don't like your fancy talk!"

"I'm sorry to hear that."

"What makes you think that I won't beat the crap out of you here and now?"

"Well for one thing, Mr Mahoney, beating the crap out of me, as you so eloquently put it, isn't going to help find your colleague."

"Perhaps, but it might make me feel a whole lot better.

"And for another, as I've already told you, I'm only the messenger, so you can beat me all you want, but I won't tell you anything, because I don't know anything."

"You know who your client is!"

"Actually no, no I don't. I work for a firm, I simply follow instructions. I'm told what to say and when to say it."

"How do I know you're telling the truth?"

"About your partner?"

"About anything."

Holding looked me straight in the eye. "I don't think I'm in a position to answer that. But let me assure you of this, my client isn't looking to waste anybody's time. He, she, or even they, will do whatever is necessary."

"Even if it means killing my partner?"

"I repeat, whatever is necessary."

"So what happens next?"

"You have four hours in which to get the girl, then we'll call you and tell you where to meet my client."

Holding stepped past me. I took hold of his arm and gripped it tight.

"When this is over," I said, quietly. "I'd leave town if I were you!"

Chapter Eighty-five

Walker was pulling on his coat, when I tapped on the door and entered his office.

He didn't look happy to see me. But then again, he never looked happy to see me.

"There's been some developments," I announced.

"Well they'll have to wait," he moaned. "I've just finished a long shift and I'm very tired."

"There's a deserted cottage off the Whitby Road and just before you get to Robin Hoods Bay, you might want your boys to check it out."

Walker stopped doing up his coat and looked at me. "I really don't want to ask why do I!"

"The girl I was looking for, she was being held to ransom there by Storey."

"Storey? But I thought he was the one looking for her?"

"He was, but when he realised that all this other muscle was involved, he went for the safe option of demanding money from me and then legging it"

"How much money?"

"Ten grand"

Walker whistled. "Where on earth did you get that from?"

"O'Riley."

"That was nice of him!"

"He............," I started to explain but Walker held up his hand and declared.

"I just want to know what happened to Storey."

"Well, I was about to give him the money when some cowboys came out of nowhere and started shooting up the place. I left the money there and grabbed April. The last thing I saw was Storey and these guys shooting at one another. So, like I said, you might want to check it out."

Walker stared at me for a moment before yelling out through the door and ordering a couple of cars to the area.

"There, that wasn't so bad," he half smiled, doing up the rest of his coat. "So what happened to the girl?"

"She's safe." I replied.

"That means you're not going to tell me?"

"Not unless I have to."

Walker shrugged his shoulders. "I thought we were on the same side."

"She just wants to lay low. The thing is, she might not be the girl we're looking for."

Walker frowned.

"She reckons her name's Anna and that she's never set foot in Scarborough before."

"Do you believe her?"

"I'm not sure how I can prove otherwise."

The Inspector looked at me for a moment in the same way he might have looked at a beggar in the street. There were plenty of poor people in the world so why should he give his money to this particular person?

"Have you still got that photograph of her?" he asked.

I handed him the one Storey had given me, and the one I'd taken from Smudge's room. He studied them closely, but nothing seemed to be coming to mind. He pressed them back into my hand.

"Have the lab boys do some enhancements, there might be something there. Anything else?" He asked.

It came across as more of a dare. I mean, he was already halfway out the door. He wanted to go home. It was somebody else's turn to guard the computers and keep the press at bay but, but I hit him with the bombshell anyway.

"It looks like Collingwood was paying two of your boys to find out what happened to his brother," I hurriedly said.

Walker looked back at me for what felt like an eternity. He stepped back inside the office and slammed the door shut.

"Two of my boys?"

I nodded.

"Warne and Lucas. That's why they were on the boat. They were going to sell some information to him. "

The Inspector pressed a hand across his lips.

"The same two cops who were asking about the girls at the flat," I continued.

Walker sat in his chair without taking off his coat.

"There could be a connection!" I suggested.

"How do you know all this?"

"Ricks had some info on him that he sent to Hartless, just in case something happened to him."

"Does this information happen to include what Lucas and Warne were selling to Collingwood?" Walker frowned.

I shook my head. Walker got to his feet again and headed for the door.

"Well it's just my luck that there might be someone who does. He held the door open for me.

"Let's go."

Chapter Eighty-six

The Inspector left the photographs of April with the first policeman he came across, telling him to get them enhanced and see what he could come up with as soon as possible. Then he rounded up a posse and we headed downtown at breakneck speed, ducking red lights and dodging pedestrians.

A policeman was already hammering on the front door to Saltys and getting nowhere, when we arrived.

He turned to the Inspector. "They won't open up sir."

"Then we'd better give them a hand!"

Walker nodded at a couple of uniforms who picked up, what appeared to be a miniature battering ram. The door gave way in one sharp swoop. I followed Walker, O'Neal and a couple of other cops inside.

A guy in a suit was waving his arms about like a puppet caught in a food mixer. "We're not open!" he shouted.

"You are now!" Walker declared as he came to a halt in the middle of the room and looked round.

The place was dark and stank of furniture polish and spirits.

"You just can't barge in here like that!" the man continued.

He was very brave, but only because he probably didn't know who Walker was, or perhaps he'd heard somewhere that not all coppers were alike.

Walker stepped up to him and pointed a finger into his lapel.

"I'm a Police Inspector, and I'm very tired and late for my dinner, so I can do what I want. Now, where's Malone?"

Another figure staggered down the stairs, doing up the final button on his jacket and letting out a yawn. It was the same guy who'd given me a hard time here the other night.

"What's all the fuss?" He asked.

He finally cleared the sleep from his eyes and spied Walker blocking the view of what was left of the club door.

"Oh sh….."

"….we need to talk." Walker cut in.

"About what?"

"Sergeant, would you get everybody else out of the room, I need a little heart to heart. Mahoney, pull up a chair for our friend here."

"I don't want to talk!" Malone argued.

"It wasn't a request!" Walker snapped.

Within seconds the room was as the Inspector had demanded. Everybody had left leaving me resting my shoulder on a pillar watching Walker circle the chair on which Malone sat scratching his head and appearing more than a little worried.

"Now," Walker began. "Why was Collingwood paying two of my men to find out what happened to his brother?"

"I don't know."

Walker gripped Malone's left ear and gave it a polite tug.

"Don't lie to me Malone. You were Collingwood's right hand man he didn't so much as sneeze without you holding out a handkerchief, so don't give me the 'I don't know' crap."

"He just did that's all, what's wrong with wanting to know what happened to his brother?"

"Nothing, in unusual circumstances, but this was very usual, a straightforward case, the bloke fell, fractured his skull and died, end of story. It was an accident and, accidents happen. Except that Collingwood didn't seem to think it was an accident did he. So he hires two of my men to find out what did happen, and now those men are dead and that leaves me very unhappy."

"I'm sorry to hear it!"

"Oh you haven't begun to be sorry for anything yet, if you continue playing the dumb arse."

"I still don't know anything!"

"Well contrary to public opinion I happen to be a very nice man and to prove it, I'm going to give you two options."

Malone arched his neck to get a quick view of the Inspector as he walked behind him.

"The first option is very simple and straightforward and one that I personally recommend, it's that, by the time I've counted to three, you've told me what made Collingwood get so suspicious....."

"I told you......."

"..... The second," Walker interrupted with a finger in Malone's face. "Is for you to keep quiet and leave me with no choice but to have you locked up in Wakey prison and throw away the key."

I looked at Walker and wondered just how serious he was being and, more importantly, how far beyond the law he had stepped.

"On what charge?" Malone asked.

"Illegal loans."

"You can't prove that."

"So how about assisting in a sex trafficking operation for under-aged girls."

Walker stopped in front of Malone and lowered his head until they were face to face.

"Any idea what they do to people like that in jail? One…"

"They were only foreign! Nobody gives a damn about foreigners!"

"Then maybe I'll leave off the bit about where they came from and just include how old they were. Two…"

"You wouldn't do that!"

"Three."

Malone remained silent.

Walker turned away and called out to O'Neal. The Sergeant hurried back inside.

"Yes, sir."

"Book Malone and stick him inside. I want a van here first thing in the morning ready to take him to Wakefield."

O'Neal hurried over to Malone and stood him up. "What's the charge sir?"

"Oh anything horrible. It doesn't really matter, nobody's going to miss him anyway."

Walker did up his coat and looked at me. "Sorry about that Mahoney, just thought we might have been onto something that's all. But at least I can go home now and get my tea. I'm starving."

It was only as they were halfway across the room that Malone started to wonder if perhaps Walker could actually do what he was threatening.

"You can't do this," he moaned.

Walker scratched his ear. "Strange buzzing sound, in my ear!"

"Walker!"

"Did I mention how hungry I was by the way?"

"I've got my rights!" Malone yelled.

"Not since you crossed my path you haven't!" Walker snapped.

"All right, all right," Malone cried out.

He pulled his arm free of O'Neal.

"But you'll drop the charges against me right," he said, stabbing himself with a thumb.

"I don't make deals with scum bags."

"So what's the point in telling you anything?"

Walker strode over to Malone and swiftly kneed him in the groin. "Because you don't want someone like me as an enemy and," he continued raising Malone's head so that he could see the Inspector through the pain, "you'll finally have something good to put on your gravestone."

Suddenly Malone could see he was in a no win situation. He rubbed his groin and recovered his breath.

"There was a couple of things," he said reluctantly.

"Go on."

"The fall from the garage, Mr Collingwood knew something was wrong."

"Let me guess," Walker interrupted. "He didn't like heights?"

Malone nodded. "He would never have been up there in the first place."

"What's the second thing?"

"He didn't have his phone on him."

"His phone," I questioned.

Malone glanced at me until Walker gripped him by the chin.

"What about the phone?" The Inspector asked through clenched teeth.

"He carried it everywhere with him, he was never without it, it had everything that was ever important to him, appointments, collections, but when we went to collect his belongings it wasn't there."

"Maybe he'd lost it!"

"Well it wasn't on the garage roof!" Malone snapped.

"When was the last time anybody heard from him?" Walker asked.

"About an hour before he died. He said he needed to talk to one of the girls about a complaint he'd had. After that he was going to meet us for a drink."

"What girls?" I asked.

Malone was slow to answer

"Answer the man Malone," Walker insisted as he gripped his jaw even tighter.

"I don't know," he muttered through a taut upright mouth.

"You mean to tell me Collingwood didn't know what girls were working for him?"

"It wasn't his show. He just ran the club and the loans. It was his brother who did the prostitution stuff. All we knew was that they were young and foreign."

Walker snapped his hand free from Malone's jaw.

"What about a girl called Jenny?" I asked, right out of the blue.

"Who?"

"Jenny Munro, she was killed in a car crash a few days ago."

Malone was too busy massaging his jaw to bother replying, so Walker gave him a helping hand by aiming a punch to his stomach.

"Answer the question!"

Malone bent double and took an age to straighten himself.

"I don't know anything about a girl called Jenny," He moaned.

Walker looked him straight in the eye and snarled;

"You're lying!"

"Seriously, I don't know about the girl!"

Walker remained in Malone's face. He was really worried now.

"So who did?" The Inspector asked.

Malone's eyes darted from left to right a dozen times like somebody watching a high speed tennis rally.

"The two cops," he eventually answered.

"Go on."

"All I know is, they went to question some girls, see if they knew anything, but apparently they'd legged it, one of them had died. They tried to track them down. They caught up with somebody, one of their friends, they were only supposed to ask a few questions but I guess they didn't want to leave any tracks."

"So they killed her!" I said.

Malone looked across at me like someone who might regret what he'd been involved in, if there had been an ounce of decency in him anyway.

"What else did my men find out?" Walker asked.

"Something, we don't know what, that's why they were on the boat."

"How come you weren't on it?"

"Mr Collingwood asked me to look after the club, guess I got lucky."

"Well not anymore," The Inspector smiled and signalled O'Neal to lead Malone away.

"What do you mean? What about the charges Inspector?"

"Don't worry," Walker yelled. "I'll make sure they stick!"

We watched O'Neal drag Malone away kicking and screaming.

"I didn't think you were allowed to do that intimidation thing anymore?" I asked.

"Well, not at the station, too many cameras and do-gooders. But out here, among friends," Walker glanced up and around the building. "Could become quite useful."

* * *

We stepped outside into the cool afternoon air.

"Do you think that did any good?" I asked.

"Well I feel better," Walker announced as he massaged his knuckles.

"But we're still nowhere nearer finding out what happened."

"Oh, I wouldn't say that."

"What do you mean?"

"Well how about Preacher killed Collingwood's brother but he made it out to look like an accident, Collingwood knew it wasn't, got two of my men to find out what really happened, Preacher got scared and bumped them off. Ricks found out and so he had to go as well."

"Only Preacher said the cops were already dead?" I questioned.

"Well he would wouldn't he, anybody with any sense wouldn't admit to being a cop killer, even if they had been moonlighting!"

"And what about Ricks? Preacher said he'd shot him when he'd been stabbed?"

Walker yawned and checked his watch.

"A minor glitch, but not enough to stall my tea."

"If only we knew what those two cops had found out."

Walker nodded as his phone started to ring.

"Yeah,……..and? Is he dead?……… right, ………..
How much?……….. right. Yeah."

He hung up and looked at me. "There's two bodies at the cottage."

"Storey and O'Rileys sidekick I presume?"

"And a lot of money scattered around that nobody else seemed particularly interested in."

"They just wanted the girl."

"Why?"

A car pulled up and a woman in uniform got out and handed Walker a couple of enlarged photographs.

"You wanted these, Sir?"

"Bloody hell! I'll have to get me holiday snaps done at work!"

"You wanted to know if there were any distinguishing features?" she confirmed.

Walker nodded and followed her finger down one of the enlargements of April. I shuffled over to get a closer look.

"At first it wasn't easy with all the cuts and bruises, but we came across this," she said, pointing at the young girl's neck.

"We thought it was a love-bite at first, but when we got closer, it turns out to be....,"

"A birth mark," Walker interrupted.

The woman nodded. Walker handed me the photographs.

"Good work, ..."

"Lorraine, sir."

"Lorraine."

The woman nodded and stepped aside.

"Does that ring any bells?" Walker asked.

I was already running every image I had of April through my head, but nothing came to mind.

"I'll have to check."

"Be careful."

"She's just a girl."

I didn't mean that to sound like it did, but it did.

"If she's lying, she's lying for a reason and that same reason has got a lot of people killed," Walker said with a rub of his chin. "She's either protecting herself or somebody else. ".

"She is or she was?" I asked.

"I don't know. Maybe I ought to come with you."

"No!" I said.

Walker looked at me wide-eyed as if nobody would ever dare disobey him

"Her life could be in danger, Mahoney."

"I know," I agreed. "But let's not scare her. Let me make sure it's her first of all. Then I'll talk to her. Tell her we're going to get her somewhere safe."

Walker nodded at me and tapped his watch.

"You've got half an hour!"

Chapter Eighty-seven

Hartless was preparing some lunch when I got back. A thick vegetable soup was stirring in a saucepan. It looked as bad as it smelt. I took a moment to catch my breath. All this rushing about was going to give me a heart attack!

"Want some?" he asked, raising some up to my face in a spoon.

I shook my head and went into the front room to find April or Anna, or whatever her bloody name was. She was sitting on the sofa and staring at the television. She was dressed in the same clothes as she had on yesterday, but at least she didn't look so tired, just concerned.

"You all right?" I asked.

She nodded.

Hartless carried a tray in behind me, and handed the girl a bowl of soup. She uncrossed her legs and sat it on her lap. Hartless parked his rear into a seat nearby and spooned his own soup.

"You two getting on all right?" I asked.

"J.. just fine," Hartless replied with a nod.

But the girl just ate her soup and glanced at the TV from the corner of her eye.

I decided to turn it off. She offered me a challenging look, not that I cared.

I sat down next to her, close enough to view her neck. Every so often the scarf she was wearing, slipped just enough to reveal the top of a mark.

"So you've no idea who Smudge is?" I asked.

"I have told you, I do not know this person!"

"Funny, cos he was just saying how much he loved you!"

It was a cruel blow, but one I felt, was worth the risk. The girl cut me a glance. She started to mouth something, but I never got to hear what she said, because Hartless butted in at just the wrong time.

"I the...thought you said he, ..."

I quickly looked across at him.

"He must have the wrong girl," the girl said eventually.

"Well he wouldn't be the first bloke to fall in love with the wrong girl now would he!"

"W.... what's all this about Mr Mahoney?" Hartless asked.

"That's what I'd like to know," I replied, looking back at the girl. "Because Smudge just happened to describe you to a tea, right down to that birthmark on your neck."

I dropped the two photo enhancements, that Walker had handed me, on the sofa next to her. She stopped short of taking another mouthful and looked at them. She sat in silence for a moment and pulled on the scarf.

Hartless hurried over. "What is it?"

I picked up one of the photographs and handed it to him.

"A couple of enhancements the cops made for me," I explained. The boy's name is Alex 'Smudge' Smith and,

I'm betting the mark you can see on the young girl's neck, is the same as on Anna's."

Hartless studied the picture for a moment before cautiously leaning forward and lowering Anna's scarf to reveal exactly the same mark as in the picture, and Anna didn't bother trying to stop him.

"Does that mean I can go back to calling you April again? All these different names are killing me!"

The girl didn't answer.

"W….why did you lie to us?" Hartless asked.

April lowered the tray onto the floor and looked back at Hartless without saying anything.

"April w…we're trying to help you. The, there are people who are ready to kill for you, maybe even kill you!"

She continued to avoid his gaze. She pressed a finger to her lip and tried to keep it from trembling.

I got to my feet and walked to the other side of the room. Hartless sat down beside her. "You trust us d… don't you?"

She looked at him and started to speak in barely a whisper.

"Collingwood's brother, he said he wanted to see me, he wasn't happy. A man had complained about me but I didn't care. I didn't want to do it anymore, but he threatened us, said he would beat us if we didn't do as we were told."

"How d…, did you get into this, this mess? Hartless asked.

I was a student but I got a job at the club. I worked behind the bar. One day Mr Collingwood asked me if I wanted to earn some more money. He said it was just looking after the customers, keeping them company, nothing bad. And that is how it is for a long time and the money is very good. Then he asked me if I would do more. I said, 'what?' he said, 'you know' But I said, 'no'. I was frightened but he did not do anything. Then one day some people say they have found drugs in my flat. They said we will be arrested. It is like the end of the world. I did not want to go home. But Mr Collingwood said he would help me if I wanted."

"But that meant going one step further with the customers?" I assumed.

April slowly nodded. "What could I do?"

"You couldn't run away?" Hartless asked.

April shook her head. "They were watching us all the time. We could not leave the town. He held our passport. We did not even have a telephone."

"But something happened?" I suggested.

April looked at me. "Collingwood's brother was angry when the man complained. He started to shout at me, he hit me lots of times. I fell. He must have knocked me out. When I wake up he is gone."

"Gone?" Hartless repeated.

April nodded.

"You didn't see what happened to him?"

"The first thing I know is when this man tells me I have to leave Scarborough. He says a man is dead. He gives me, and some other girls, money."

"Natalie and Petra?" I assumed.

April toyed with a fingernail and nodded.

"He says our lives are in danger," she continued. "That Collingwood will come looking to see who killed his brother. I tell him that I do not know anything about this, but he says it does not matter."

"Collingwood would have beaten the crap out of you just to make sure you weren't lying," I confirmed.

"W..., why did the other girls have to leave?"

"I don't know," she shrugged. "I think because we are friends, because we live in the same place and they know me."

"But why pretend you'd died?" I questioned.

"The man said it would be safer that way because, if I was dead, nobody would come looking for me."

Clever, I thought to myself.

"He gave us new names and told us we were not allowed to come back to Scarborough or keep in touch with anyone."

"Except Smudge?" I suggested.

April looked up at me. "They said they'd take care of him."

"That's how they found out where you were," I said, trying to fill in the blanks.

April looked back at her fingernail.

"You know he's dead don't you!"

She didn't answer. She didn't have to, her sad expression said everything.

Hartless wondered over to me and asked: "Who do you think paid these girls to leave town?"

"I don't know," I replied. "But I doubt it was the cops. They'd have kept her somewhere safe till they knew what was going on. Apart from that, they haven't got that kind of cash to splash around."

"Well anyway, it d...., doesn't matter anymore because Collingwood's dead. She should be all right!" Hartless assumed.

"Except that Collingwood was dead before we got chased into town by a man with a gun, and before someone threatened to do away with Envy if we didn't give April to them."

"B..., but she doesn't know anything," he protested.

"It's not what she's knows," I suggested. "It what she has."

April offered me a startled look. She was trying to mask a guilty expression. But it didn't work.

"The man who attacked you, you took his phone didn't you!"

April continued to stare at me without answering. Hartless went back to the sofa and sat down next to her.

"It's one of the reasons why Collingwood knew something had happened to his brother," I continued. "When they found his body he didn't have his phone on him and he always had his phone on him."

"Well maybe the man who killed him took it?" Hartless suggested.

"Possibly," I agreed, looking back at April. "Except you told us you weren't allowed phones but you took that one from Storey because you said it was yours. You stole it!"

"He was hurting me!" she cried. "I felt it in his pocket. I just wanted to call somebody. But I did not get any chance to use it."

Hartless put his arm around April in an attempt to stop her from crying.

"It's OK," he said softly. "N..., nobody's blaming you."

April took a moment to blow her nose and wipe her eyes before taking out the phone and holding it in the palm of her hand.

We all looked at it as though it was the Lost Ark.

"You think there's a clue on it?" Hartless asked.

"There's only one way to find out," I replied.

"But Smudge deleted all the names and numbers," April moaned.

"Are you sure," Hartless asked.

We both looked at him.

"I mean, what about the Sim card?"

"The what?" I frowned.

Hartless looked up at me. "It's a er, memory card in the phone, it keeps a record of everything even w...., when the other details have been deleted."

"So we can take a look and see what's on it," I suggested.

"Not without a code," Hartless replied. "Although we could take it to the police station and see if they can crack it."

April got all worried again. "No!"

"This is more important than you just being here illegally April. We might even find an MP who can fastrack a visa for you if we offer them enough! But in the meantime we have to get that phone to Inspector Walker.

"I do not have to come?"

I nodded. "They're going to want to find you somewhere safe to stay."

April looked at Hartless. He nodded back at her.

"All right, let's go," I said.

An outside door suddenly slammed shut and the three of us looked at one another in turn.

"D... did you lock the door?" Hartless asked me.

"Why would I lock the door?"

"Because we're supposed to be k..., keeping the place safe remember!"

I couldn't remember locking the door.

A shadow slid across the wall. My money was on O'Riley, except the shadow only took up half the wall! Only our breath and beating hearts disturbed the silence. The shadow loomed closer. The only escape was out over the balcony and a forty foot drop to the floor.

A gun and then an arm slowly entered the room, followed by a figure I wasn't expecting.

"Surprised?" said the man with the gun.

"Try disappointed!" I moaned.

"But I thought you had it all worked out?"

"Maybe I didn't have a big enough pencil."

"It seems I over-estimated you!"

"People do, it's a common mistake."

Preacher scanned the three of us slowly in turn.

"I the...,thought you were in custody?" Hartless mentioned.

"My brother bailed me out. I'm afraid he had to the moment Mahoney told me April was still alive."

"Holding told me I had four hours?" I moaned.

Preacher shrugged his shoulders. "I couldn't trust you!"

"You just wanted me to lead you to her!"

He smiled.

"You...., you're not taking her!" Hartless said, stepping in front of April.

"I don't intend taking her. All I want is the phone and I promise, nobody'll get hurt."

"So why the gun?" I snapped.

Preacher briefly looked at the gun and then at me. "Just to make sure things get done! I really don't intend using it, not unless I have to."

"You killed Collingwood's brother!"

"You make it sound like a bad thing!"

"Murder usually is!" I insisted.

"He was using young girls for sex and selling drugs to kids. He got what he deserved." Preacher argued.

"So now you're judge and jury rolled into one?"

Preacher started to laugh. "You know as well as I do, that people like him never get caught. And even if they did, nobody would ever give evidence against him. Besides, what happened was an accident, there was a fight, he fell. Couldn't have happened to a nicer bloke!"

"And y..., you expect us to believe that we simply hand you the phone and y..., you let us walk out of here without anything happening to us?"

"Absolutely."

"How come?" I asked.

"Because without the phone you have nothing."

Preacher made it sound simple. Too simple. I quickly tried to retrace the whole conversation because it was as though I'd fallen asleep just at the most important moment. Nothing made sense. Preacher had a gun but he wasn't going to use it. All he wanted was the phone. But he knew, even if he got away today, we'd come after him, we had to, he'd just admitted to killing somebody.

"What about the money y..., you took from Collingwood's brother?" Hartless asked.

Preacher smiled. "It went to a good cause."

"And what about the money Collingwood was carrying when you iced him on the boat?"

Preacher squared me a glance, it was as though he hadn't got a clue what I was talking about.

"Look, enough of the small talk," he said, waving the gun at me. "Just give me the phone."

"If you really mean what you say," I started. "Then, let these two go and I'll give you the phone!"

Hartless got all worried. "Mr Mahoney!"

I waved a hand at him and let Preacher slowly survey the scene. Eventually he nodded.

I stepped over to April and held out my hand.

"Give me the phone."

"But........"

"I'll get you another one with internet and television and satellite dishes and whatever bloody else you want on it."

She slowly placed the phone in my hand.

"Now the two of you get out of here."

April made her way towards the door but Hartless hesitated.

"Why don't y..., you just leave the phone and all three of us walk out of here like he said?"

"Because," said Preacher. "I need to check it's the right phone and Mahoney wants to know where Envy is."

I took a step towards Preacher. He raised the gun at me. I stood still.

"What have you done with her?"

"She's fine, just as long as you get to her in the next," he paused to check his watch, "forty minutes. Now, are you two leaving?"

I nodded at Hartless. "Write me a good column in the paper."

He forced a smile and followed April out of the room.

I looked at Preacher. "Well here comes the bit where I fall into cliché, but you know you're never going to get away with this!"

"I don't intend to," he smiled.

The situation was becoming irritating. Like when you armwrestle someone. You put all your strength behind the move and slowly start to press their arm to the desk. You think you have them exactly where you want them, but all they do is smile back at you.

"Now, give me the phone!" He demanded with a flick of the gun.

I stretched my arm out towards Preacher. He held out an empty hand and, like the fool I was, I lobbed the phone into the air. Preacher watched it cartwheel as I made my move.

I rugby tackled his frame to the floor and managed to get on top of him. I reached for the gun but, as I did, I laid myself open to a hook across the chops. My lip split open and blood flew out across the floor. I retaliated with a crack across his jaw, it jarred my knuckles, but hurt him more. He lifted his knee and caught me in the gonads, I screamed with pain and fell forwards. Preacher rolled me to one side. I jumped to my feet, but just as he crashed into my ribs and barged me through the open double-doors. I was pressed up against the balcony. Preacher gripped my jaw and bent my back over the railing. I thought my spine was going to snap.

"I don't want to hurt you Mahoney," he said.

"You've got a funny way of showing it."

Out of the corner of my eye I could see a crowd gathering below and I had nothing to cling to. I could feel my toes slowly leave the floor and my body start to slip over the edge. What a mess. It wasn't a particularly big drop but the ground would hurt like hell.

In the distance I could hear a siren, but I couldn't tell if it was an ambulance, police car or a fire engine, and whether or not it was even heading this way.

I steadied myself for one last crack at Preacher, but just as I curled my fist, he aimed at punch at my face. I dropped to my knees dazed and confused. I could see a blurred figure hurry back into the room. He picked something from the floor and rushed out through the front door.

I staggered to my feet, cursing and crashing into tables and chairs and door frames as I followed him.

The sunlight scorched my eyes as I stepped outside. Hartless ran over to me.

"Where'd he go?" I asked.

"It's OK Mahoney, the police are on their way."

"I need to know where Envy is, where did he go?"

"He's heading for Jackson Point."

Thankfully Hartless waved a finger in the air because I had no idea where Jackson Point was. I could see Preacher running over a narrow footbridge next to a pub. I hurried down the road and across the bridge and followed Preacher up a set of steep narrow steps. He bundled a couple of ramblers to one side.

I apologised. "Don't worry I'll get him."

The summit opened out into a plateau of spiky grass. Further along the coastline I could see a couple of blue flashing lights. The cavalry was on its way. A few more cop cars screeched to a halt outside the pub below.

Preacher continued along the footpath high above the cliff. But he was no longer running. There was nowhere to run to. I caught up to him quite easily. He stopped and turned the gun on me.

"You're surrounded Preacher. there's nowhere else to go. Give yourself up."

"Stay where you are Mahoney!" he insisted.

A bright yellow Air Ambulance helicopter picked it's way along the North Bay to where we stood, and a dozen or so armed cops crouched and aimed their rifles in our direction. I hoped they were good shots.

The helicopter hovered lower bringing with it a gale from the whooshing blades.

"Drop the gun Preacher and put your hands in the air," beamed a voice from the helicopter. It was Walker.

"It's over Preacher," I said. "Just do as they say."

Preacher lowered his arm but he didn't drop the gun. He left it pointing at the floor.

"I'll talk to Walker, we'll sort this out."

"He'll ask too many questions."

"That's his job," I argued.

"I can't let that happen."

"But you don't want to die!"

Preacher smiled. He was making me nervous.

"What happens to me isn't important. Always look at the bigger picture Mr Mahoney."

And with that, he took something from the phone pressed it to a rock on the floor and banged it with the butt of the gun a couple of times. He looked pleased with his work. Then he hurled it, and the phone, as far out to sea as he could.

"I don't understand." I said.

"Preacher this is your final warning, throw the gun down and put your hands in the air!"

"This is the way it has to be, Mahoney."

Preacher looked down at the gun. The helicopter blades flapped behind him. The noise was deafening. He struggled to stand straight.

"Preacher, I'm warning you!" Walker yelled.

"You'll be a hero, Mahoney, you'll probably even make the papers, the local one at least, the man who caught The Cleaner."

"I don't believe that, I know you didn't kill Ricks, he wasn't shot he was stabbed."

"I know, he was dead when I got there. I think somebody was trying to set me up."

"Who?" I yelled.

"It doesn't matter."

"It does to me!"

Preacher shook his head. "Like I said before, I was merely serving a purpose, whoever set me up was doing me a favour."

He slowly raised the gun.

"Preacher!" I shouted.

I prayed he wouldn't point it at me. I considered the possibility he might even aim it at himself, instead he took the third option and held it towards the helicopter. He didn't get the chance to squeeze the trigger. Preacher's body jolted twice as he slumped to the floor and onto his knees. He looked up at me.

"It's been nice knowing you, Mahoney."

Like a falling oak, Preacher slumped face down on the ground. I fought the gush from the helicopter blades and struggled towards him. His legs slipped over the edge slowly pulling the rest of his body with them. I threw myself to the floor and reached out. I caught him by his jacket. He was heavy. I should have worked out more. I should have worked out!

"Where the hell's Envy?" I yelled.

Preacher dangled from my hand, he already looked dead. The helicopter closed in above us.

"Preacher, where's Envy?" I shouted again. "She doesn't have to die!"

He slowly opened his eyes.

"Where's Envy?"

The jacket started to rip in my hand.

"An unmarked grave at my brother's church, you'll………." The jacket ripped completely and Preacher slipped from my grasp. I watched him fall through the sky and bounce off the rocks and into the sea.

I turned to see a crowd of uniforms engulf the scene. The helicopter landed. Walker got out and waited for it to take off again. He strode over to me with his usual look of concern.

"I hate those bloody things," he moaned as the helicopter circled above. "You all right?"

I nodded.

Everybody staggered against the cut of the blades as the helicopter dipped to retrieve Preacher from the water.

Walker glanced over the edge. "What was all that about?"

"I'll tell you on the way."

He helped me to my feet. "Where are we going?"

"To the church in Cloughton and quickly."

Walker nodded. "We'll take my car."

"Inspector!" somebody shouted.

We turned to see one of the uniforms holding up Preacher's gun.

"What's the matter?" Walker asked.

"This gun," the man explained. "It's not even real."

Chapter Eighty-eight

Walker radioed ahead, and it was a good job he did, because Preachers calculations had left a lot to be desired. He'd told me that we had forty minutes to save Envy, but by the time the first police car had arrived, she was already on her last breath.

Preacher had buried her in a coffin with enough food, water and air to last twenty-four hours, at least that's what Fletcher had estimated. Trouble was, Preacher hadn't taken into account that she would panic as people tend to do when they realise they're being buried alive. There were scratch marks on the inside of the lid where Envy had ripped her nails. Suddenly I didn't feel so sorry for Preacher.

When we finally arrived, she was laying on a stretcher in the ambulance with an oxygen mask over her face. I went to speak to her, but Fletcher stopped me short.

"We've sedated her," he calmly explained. "She was in a state of shock. She'll be OK, but she needs a lot of rest."

I looked at her lying still on the stretcher.

"She's a strong girl," he assured me.

"I know."

"That's probably what saved her."

That's what she'd told me. Look, after yourself Mahoney, because you never know when you'll have to go that one step further.

I stepped back and allowed the Paramedics to close the door and pull away.

All around me the police where busy sealing this and searching that. They'd fenced off the unmarked grave, but all they found was proof of what I'd known all along, Preacher had buried Envy. That was his get out of jail card. He'd needed me to lead him to April and, just in case I didn't play ball, he would hold Envy hostage.

"Something on your mind, Mahoney?" Walker asked.

"There's always something on my mind Walker, that's the trouble with being me!"

Walker nodded and almost smiled. "So would you like to share it with me?"

"I just don't understand what Preacher was up to that's all. He didn't have an escape plan, the gun wasn't even real. It was almost as if he wanted to die."

"Maybe he missed his wife?" O'Neal suggested.

The three of us looked in turn at the grave in which Preacher's wife lay buried, but, deep down, I don't think any of us were convinced about that.

"He congratulated me." I said, with a sense of shock.

"On what?" Neal asked.

"Capturing The Cleaner."

"Is that what he said?"

I nodded.

"He said he was The Cleaner?"

I nodded again.

"But you don't believe that?" The Sergeant asked.

"I don't know," I sighed. "All I do know is that somebody went to a lot of trouble to kill a lot of people, but Preacher wouldn't tell me why."

"Maybe that why he bottled it," Walker suggested. "He didn't want us knowing for sure."

"Yeah," O'Neal agreed. "Because, if he really was this Cleaner, then it's the perfect end. We can't question him, we can't prove anything one way or another. People will have to make up their own minds. There'll be those who assume he's dead and those who'll believe the myth lives on."

Walker looked at me and put a hand on my shoulder.

"And what do you think Mahoney, do you think the myth lives on or is The Cleaner really dead?"

Chapter Eighty-nine

I was back in the office alone. I was studying some case notes Ricks had put together, and that Hartless had kindly printed off for me. I was hoping something, somewhere would rise from the pages and smack me right between the eyes. That was the only way I was ever going to find out anything.

I was still searching for the missing link, not to anything as dramatic as; did man really descend from apes? – that much was obvious every Saturday night, in the town centre, after a few beers. What I wanted to know was why Preacher would want to take on death with just a plastic gun?

But all I found was what Preacher had been up to that Sunday night out at Blakey Ridge. It's where he'd proposed to his wife, and where he'd scattered her ashes. It had become something of a ritual, the first Sunday of every month, Preacher would pick up his mother and drive out to the monument. They'd lay some flowers and stay for a meal. It was just something else that suggested Preacher wasn't a killer.

* * *

And the whisky wasn't helping. I knew it wouldn't, but that didn't stop me from drinking it.

Not knowing what really happened, not knowing the truth, bothered the hell out of me, bothered me so much, I poured another glass.

Five minutes later a figure appeared at the door and pushed it open. Either I'd lost my hearing or they hadn't knocked.

I focussed my eyes, as best I could, and saw Debbie glaring down at the glass in my hand.

"I thought you said that stuff was like, poisonous?"

That was all I needed, another female ready to nag me in my hour of darkness.

I took another sip. "Maybe I did."

"So why are you trying to kill yourself?"

"I figured I'd save somebody else the trouble!" I moaned.

"Is somebody trying to kill you?"

"I was speaking metaphorically."

"I know what that means," she beamed.

"I'm happy for you!"

"You should be happy."

"Why?"

"You're in the paper and stuff."

"And stuff?"

"Yeah."

"You've been reading the papers again?"

Debbie placed a copy of last nights evening paper on my desk, with the headline; N*ight Club Killer nailed on the beach,* staring straight back at me.

"You're like famous. You caught a bad man."

"Actually I didn't catch him, I let him slip through my fingers."

"Is that why you're unhappy? You think you should have saved him or something?"

"No, I'm unhappy because I've been shot at, knocked over the head, twice, had my teeth drilled and I still don't know why. And the only person who could have told me, decided to go and get himself killed."

I drank some more whisky.

"Why were you chasing him?"

"Because he had a phone that didn't belong to him and he had my partner."

"You've got a partner?"

"I told you I did"

"No, you never!"

I looked at Debbie. I could have sworn I had. But then again, I've told lots of people lots of things. I can't remember everything. I couldn't be sure about anything anymore. I was getting old!

"Well I have," I finally said.

"Is she better than me?"

"She's better than the both of us"

"So how come he had her?"

Good question.

"I don't know, she was sedated the moment they pulled her from the grave."

"She's dead?"

"No, Preacher hid her there. Anyway I'll ask her what happened when she comes round."

Debbie wandered over to the window and studied my plant.

"Nice plant."

"Would be if it flowered."

"It's got a flower," she declared and held it up for me to see.

A white flower bloomed from one of the stems.

"Well how about that!."

She took it to the sink and ran some water over it. Then she picked off a few dead leaves. Nurture, that's all it took.

She replaced the plant back on the window ledge and returned to the desk. She picked up my glass and took a short sharp sniff. It nearly blew her head off.

She coughed and sat down and took a moment to recover her breath.

"The paper said this Preacher bloke killed all those people," she said.

"That's because that's what they do."

"What?"

"They wrap things up in neat little stories so they can sell their neat little papers."

"But it's what the police said as well."

I looked at Debbie. She'd made herself comfortable in a seat, and three things occurred to me; who'd invited her in here in the first place? Why the hell was I discussing anything with her? And, how drunk I was getting.

"That's because they've got targets to meet and, as long as somebody takes the fall, everybody ends up happy, because it looks like they're doing their job."

"Did he kill all those people?" she asked, aiming a finger at the names I'd pinned to the wall.

"Not all of them, no."

"So who are they?"

I took my glass for a slow walk across the room and stood in front of the wall. Slowly the names came into focus.

"Collingwood and his sidekick were loan sharks who ran Saltys. They were killed on the boat by Preacher. He admitted that. Warne and Lucas were two cops who had been hired by Collingwood, they were also killed on the boat. Preacher told the cops he'd killed them, but he told me a different story."

"He didn't kill them?"

"He said they were already dead. He didn't kill a reporter by the name of Ricks either, because I told him that Ricks had been shot when, in fact, he'd been stabbed."

"So if Preacher didn't like, kill them all, then who did?"

I raised a finger into the air. "Good point. Because, according to the CCTV footage, apart from Ricks, who was later found washed up in Cayton, nobody else got on the boat."

"Except you?"

I managed a frown at Debbie. "Yeah, except me."

"And the police!"

"The what?"

"The police," she said, striding towards me. "They found you knocked out and Preacher holding the gun."

I nodded, but I was yet to convince myself I knew what she was talking about.

"Who's to say the police didn't kill Ricks?"

The room fell silent. I couldn't believe what I'd heard and I wished I hadn't drunk so much.

"There was nobody else, you said so yourself!" she continued.

I dropped my glass onto the desk and hurried to the sink. I filled it with cold water and sunk my face inside.

"If you're so convinced Preacher didn't do it, and you know you didn't do it, then it must be them!"

I towelled my face and looked at Debbie. She was accusing someone in the police force of murder, but there was nothing I could think of to change her view, or mine.

I looked at the wall again.

"There's been somebody else involved in all this right from the very start," I mumbled.

"Who?"

"Somebody who was paying a man to bring April to Scarborough, I think they wanted the phone, they were paying him a lot of money. I presumed it was Collingwood, but Collingwood took me to see a dentist and asked me a load of questions. They weren't the same men."

I looked back at Debbie. "And one of them's still out there."

"Are you sure?"

"It would help explain where the money went," I continued.

"What money?"

"Money that Collingwood had drawn out to pay the cops."

"For what?"

"He wanted to know what had happened to his brother. He was supposed to have died in a fall from his garage roof, but it turns out he'd probably been killed sometime before. That's what the cops were meant to have looked into."

"And how would they have found that out?" she asked.

I pulled on my ear. "What?"

"How he'd died. How would they have found out how he really died?"

"I'm not sure." I paused. "But I know a man who might."

I picked up my coat and headed for the door. Debbie stepped in front of me.

"Where are you going?"

"To the police station."

"I want to come."

I help up my hand. "No."

"But,"

"Look, you've been a great help Debbie, but too many people have died asking questions I don't know the answers to, and I don't want you to be the next."

Her lip quivered, not because she was frightened of dying but because she didn't like being told, 'no'.

"But what about you?" she asked.

"If I'm lucky, I'll just get hit over the head."

"And if you're not?"

I pressed my hand to the side of her face and smiled. "Then maybe you can talk Ronnie into being his new partner."

Chapter Ninety

Fletcher was sitting at a computer when I arrived at the lab. His was holding his glasses in one hand and tapping to the beat of a song on the radio with his other. He looked like a man deep in thought.

I stood near the desk and cleared my throat.

He looked up with a start. "Mr Mahoney!"

I nodded.

"Come for a job?"

"Not particularly."

"Just as well, we're only taking on skeleton staff at the moment!" he said sincerely. Then he let out a laugh, loud enough to wake the dead. I started to laugh as well, but I couldn't be sure if I was laughing at him laughing or at the joke itself.

"Ah, the old ones are the best," he said, slowly calming himself. "So what can I do for you?"

"The two cops who were killed in the harbour the other night. Lucas and Warne."

"What about them?"

"Did they ask anything about Collingwood's brother?"

Fletcher got to his feet and tipped his glasses back across the bridge of his nose.

"Such as?"

"Such as how, when and where he died perhaps?"

I watched as he loosened his cravat with a finger and stared back at me for a moment.

"He fell from a garage roof!"

"I know that's not true, and Walker knows it too."

"Does the Inspector know you're here now?"

Suddenly it occurred to me that I didn't know who the hell was involved in all this, except it could have been someone from the police force. Someone with access to all the details, someone like Fletcher. And I was all alone in a morgue with him and nobody else knew I was here. He could shoot me between the eyes and lock me away in one of the drawers and nobody would have been any the wiser. I had to call his bluff.

I reached across the desk and held out the phone.

"Why don't you ask him for yourself?"

Walker had no idea where I was. I couldn't find him, but I didn't think he'd mind. I needed some answers and I needed them now.

Thankfully Fletcher waved the phone away. "Why do you ask?"

"You know they were probably feeding information back to Collingwood?"

He nodded.

"I was just wondering what that information might have been that's all."

"But the case is closed and Preacher was charged, or would have been anyway."

"So, just humour me."

Fletcher sat back down and put on his glasses. "Warne

did ask me if I'd taken a look at the body, yes."

"And what did you tell him?"

"That I had. He asked if I'd noticed anything out of order. He was being very cagey about it all, and I told him that if he really wanted to know anything, then he'd have to go through the proper channels. He wasn't happy."

I looked at Fletcher. "Collingwood's brother had died well before the fall from the garage."

"I know. I'm a Pathologist," he beamed. "It's my job to know."

I raised an eyebrow. "So, do I have to go through the proper channels to find out how and when?"

"Strictly speaking, yes."

I let out a sigh.

"But off the record, no. Basically because I no longer have any records!"

Fletcher was confusing me and he could tell as much as I followed him round the desk.

"Does that mean you can't tell me?"

"Why are you asking?"

I looked at Fletcher and realised everything I said from now on could get me killed. He was standing behind his desk. Maybe he had a gun in one of the drawers. My palms started to sweat. Fletcher didn't look like a killer, but then, what the hell was a killer supposed to look like? What about all that stick for being the way he was? Maybe this was his time for revenge?

All the same, I had to ask, because getting killed seemed a whole lot better than never knowing what the answer was.

"Because I don't think Preacher did it," I eventually declared. "I mean, I don't think he killed Collingwood's brother."

"I see."

Fletcher paused like a man deep in contemplation. Was

this it? Was he about to pull a gun from the drawer and save me from my agony?

"So?" I asked.

He lowered his right hand to the desk. I followed it closely. He turned down the radio. I breathed a sigh of relief.

"I estimated that the fall from the garage roof occurred at approximately 9am," he began in his telephone voice. "Whereas I later discovered a number of cuts and bruises, including the blow to the head that had actually caused his death, had been delivered some twelve, thirteen hours before."

"Which would have made it?"

"Around eight or nine p.m."

I took a slow walk round the desk and pulled on my ear. "Nine o'clock Sunday?"

Fletcher nodded.

"Any idea what the date was?"

He quickly picked his way though a diary on the desk.

"June the 2nd," he replied.

"The first Sunday of the month," I mumbled.

Fletcher removed his glasses. "Does that help at all?"

"And you can prove all this?"

"Actually no."

I frowned at him.

"Because when I said I could tell you, off the record, that's precisely what I meant. I no longer have any records."

My frown increased.

"Somebody took them," he casually explained. "Along with the clothes they'd found the body in. Otherwise I'm damn sure I would have discovered, in due course, exactly where he'd been killed and who had done the killing."

"You're that good?"

"Oh you have no idea how damn good I am!"

He was right and I'm sure he would have loved the chance to show Sergeant O'Neal.

"What about the computer?" I asked, pointing at the desk.

"Oh, I'm afraid, whoever it is, was smart enough to delete my files as well, including who killed Reece. I can't tell you how angry that makes me."

"I'm sure."

"So what now? I mean, now that you have no proof?"

"It's never stopped me being a pain in the arse before!"

Fletcher did his laugh again and then followed it with a cautious expression.

"I hope you know what you're doing Mr Mahoney."

I still couldn't be sure Fletcher wasn't involved but, then again, that included anybody and everybody else.

"It's never stopped me before!" I said again.

"No, I'm being serious," he said, opening his arms out wide. "Whatever rogue went to all this trouble has an admirable amount of influence and some incredibly powerful friends."

"You're only saying that because it's got a lot of 'r's in it aren't you?" I suggested.

Fletcher shook his head and softly replied; "No, I'm saying it because somebody is willing to go to extraordinary lengths to cover up what really happened."

I turned my back on Fletcher and headed for the door. The volume increased on the radio. The door was still too far away. I wondered how it would feel being shot in the back? You'd never know. There'd just be a sharp pain and that would be that. Only then would you know if all that praise on a Sunday morning had been worthwhile.

Fletcher started to sing. Nobody would sing and fire a

gun at the same time, would they?

I reached the door and pulled it open. I hurried outside, and didn't look back.

Chapter Ninety-one

It was a busy day at the church, The Archbishop himself was here. He'd come all the way from York to tip his toe into the sea, and then confirm the Reverend Keatley as Bishop. It's what the whole town had been talking about for weeks, and it was turning out to be quite some occasion. Street parties lined the village, banners hung from rooftops, and the smell of sausages, chicken and freshly baked bread filled the air.

A television crew took up part of the main street with a van and lines of thick cable. Cameras zoomed in on every angle and reporters readied themselves for one last brush and polish. Scarborough was well and truly back on the map.

Who would want to spoil such a day?

A bright sun lit up the blue sky and shone down on a crowd of people gathered across the road from the church. Young, middle-aged and elderly people prepared to wave their flags. It was all so bright and cheerful, like we'd just won a war, or were about to crown a monarch.

Every car that came to a halt was greeted with loud cheers, because anybody who was anyone was going to be here today. Which probably explained why I hadn't got an invitation.

Not that that was going to stop me from taking a moment to pay the Rev. Keatley my sincere condolences and congratulations at the same time.

I avoided most of the crowd by taking a back route through the graveyard. The bells started to ring out as I passed between a gathering of people in expensive suits and dresses, braving the sun and showing off their jewellery.

I was halfway to the vestry, when a pair of sun glasses and long legs blocked my path.

I stood quite still, unsure of whether to laugh, cry or pretend to faint. Helen Fitzsimmons was flanked by her entourage, two bulky young men dressed with trademark frowns plus a token female, who seemed to spend most of the time, checking her watch and inspecting a clipboard.

Fitzsimmons lowered her glasses and offered me a challenging smile. "I didn't know you were a religious man, Mr Mahoney?"

"I figured this omnipotent stuff might come in handy in my line of work, you never seem to know what's going on behind your back."

"I agree."

"So is that the reason for all the muscle?"

"Muscle?" she questioned.

I nodded towards her entourage. "They here to stop people from stabbing you in the back?"

"Why, are people looking to stab me in the back?"

"I'm not sure."

"Are you?"

"Actually I prefer the full frontal approach!"

"I remember," she smiled. "But keeping it up seemed a

bit of a problem!"

A low blow and one I should have been prepared for, after all, Fitzsimmons was smarter than your average Mayor, a lot smarter, and I'd made the mistake of underestimating her. Round one to the woman in the neck-chain.

"I hear you were a very brave boy the other day," she continued in a fresh tone.

"Brave?"

"Chasing that Preacher chap."

"Hardly brave," I reasoned. "His gun wasn't even real!"

"But you weren't to know that."

"I just wanted to know what he'd done with Envy."

"Your partner."

I nodded.

"And how is she?"

"She'll be OK."

"I'm glad to hear it."

A couple of press guys appeared from nowhere and flashed their lenses in Fitzsimmons's direction. She offered them a casual pose, before taking me by the arm and leading me a few yards down the path, and out of earshot.

"Listen Mahoney, I know we had a little spat the other night, but I really would like to put all that behind us."

"You would?"

"Yes. I feel it's important that the two of us work together. I'm attracting a lot of investment into this town, not only the Sands development, but other projects as well. And part of that deal is to make the streets safe again."

"Is that, officially or unofficially?"

Fitzsimmons did her best not to glare at me. "I'm not sure I know what you mean."

"Well, you were the one bragging about having the

Superintendent round your little finger!"

Her eyes practically glowed. "Can I help it if he falls for my charms?"

"That's because he doesn't know how dangerous you are."

"Dangerous?" she sounded shocked, but appeared to be complimented at the same time.

We stopped twenty or so yards further down the pebbled path. Fitzsimmons looked at me. "What's important is that we show the likes of Collingwood and Preacher that the bad guys can't win anymore."

"I understand where you're coming from with Collingwood, but what's your beef with Preacher?"

Fitzsimmons stretched a disbelieving smile and displayed her ring of confidence. "Aren't you forgetting, he killed all those people!"

I shook my head. "At best he killed two people. He certainly didn't kill Ricks, and I'm not convinced he killed those two cops."

"If that's the case, then why did he get himself killed?"

I shrugged my shoulders. "I'm not a mind reader. I can only guess he was trying to protect somebody. Somebody he thought enough of to take a bullet for, and then fall two hundred feet down a cliff."

Fitzsimmons's eyes inadvertently flicked towards the church and then back at me.

"Surely you're not suggesting......" she began.

I cut her off. "The harbour killings weren't about who owed who what, they were about how Collingwood's brother had died."

"He fell off a roof!"

I shook my head. "He was killed the night before, but not by Preacher, he was laying flowers at his wife's monument and having dinner with his old lady. I know, because I checked it out."

A group of people passed close by. The Mayoress forced a smile, but not in her normal relaxed pose. They all shook hands and then moved on.

Fitzsimmons shot me a look. "And you can prove all this?"

"Unfortunately no,"

"No?"

"No, because my guess is, whoever set up Preacher, is somebody powerful enough to ice the reporter who'd got too close to the truth, and then delete a load of valuable police files."

"The Cleaner?"

"Perhaps, if you believe in such a thing."

Fitzsimmons studied me for a moment.

"You said, guess."

"What?"

"You said, guess," she repeated. "You said your 'guess' is whoever set up Preacher."

"I know." I nodded.

"So, what you actually believe all comes down to a guess?"

"It's all I have."

She half laughed. "And what do you intend doing with your guess?"

"Taking a poke at the truth."

"By doing what?"

I looked towards the church. "Going in there and giving Keatley a piece of my mind. Then grabbing one of those cameras and sharing that same piece of mind with whoever else might listen."

Fitzsimmons gripped my elbow. "Is that why you're here?"

"Would it bother you if I was?" I snapped.

"Don't be a fool Mahoney!"

"It wouldn't be the first time."

The bells suddenly stopped ringing.

"But without any proof you'll have a lynch mob on your hands. Most of the people here worship Keatley, they sit on his every word. He's saved some of them from deaths door, others he's simply given a reason to believe again. If you want to ruin all that, then I think you're going to need a lot more than just a guess."

"Like I said, it's all I've got."

She gripped my elbow even tighter. "But I can't let you do that"

I glanced down at her fingers eating into my elbow. Then I looked her in the eye. She was trying to be as diplomatic as possible.

"Not today anyway," she said quietly. "Not with all this attention. Damn it, Mahoney, all this town gets is bad news. I'm afraid I'm not going to let you rain on this parade!"

"Are you threatening me?"

The smart looking woman with the clipboard stepped over to Fitzsimmons and bravely suggested that they ought to get a move on. But, right now, her Ladyship had more pressing matters. She raised a finger and the woman retreated.

Fitzsimmons turned and smiled at me. She brushed my face, softly, with the side of her hand. "I'm simply suggesting, for your own sake, that you don't go anywhere near that church!"

"Or what?" I asked.

"There isn't an alternative!"

* * *

I stood alone in the graveyard, as the church organ enticed a mass of voices to sing something nice about somebody they hoped would one day welcome them with open arms.

Otherwise, all they'd done was dress up once a week, smile meekly at a familiar face and shake their hand in a passing moment of politeness.

Up in the window Jesus appeared just as unhappy as ever.

I started towards the gate and back from where I'd come from. Another wasted journey.

I had my thoughts, my hunches, my list of possibilities, but as Fitzsimmons had rightly declared, without any proof, I didn't have a leg to stand on.

Whoever was controlling matters had covered every angle. I either had to swallow my pride and walk away, or wait for a better opportunity.

The voices in the church reached a crescendo. It was a nice hymn, with the kind of tune that made the hairs on the back of my neck stand up. Who was I to take all that happiness away?

I opened the gate and took one final look at the church. The whole thing was beyond me, the hope, the faith, the charity, the scaffolding, the steeple, the clock, Shit, it was ten past twelve! Trish!

* * *

I had my car, but I needed to get back into town at the speed of light.

Walker was leaning up against an unmarked car with his arms folded and looking like a man who'd been dragged to the shops when all he wanted was a pint.

"Do you have to be here?" I asked.

"Not if I can help it, why?"

"I need to be somewhere in a hurry."

"Is this official business?"

"It gets you out of here!"

"Good. Sergeant!" Walker shouted to a group of cops standing on the roadside. "Take care of the God botherers,

I'm just popping into town."

O'Neal nodded at the Inspector as the two of us hurried into his car.

Walker lit up his cigar. "So where are we going?"

"I need to be at the coach station."

"Pity. I was hoping you were offering to buy me a drink!"

"Maybe afterwards," I suggested.

We pulled away through the crowd, but nobody waved.

All this way just to run into one more dead-end, I thought to myself. I wanted to talk to Walker. I wanted to trust him. But something told me to wait. I had no idea what was going on or who was behind it all. And, until I did, it wasn't worth putting my life at risk.

"Something on your mind?" Walker asked, out of the blue.

I looked across at him. He glanced back.

"I was just wondering if this thing went any faster that's all!"

"I'm glad you asked," he replied, lowering his window.

"Better buckle up!"

He popped the blue light onto the roof and I gripped the handle above the passenger window tighter than I'd ever gripped anything before in my life.

Did this mean I was ready to die for somebody?

Chapter Ninety-two

The station was full of coaches, faces and luggage. It was hard to imagine so many people leaving at once. Maybe they knew something I didn't.

I checked a dozen busses before I found the one with *Cheltenham* marked on the front. Most of the passengers were already on board. Some watched their luggage being loaded. Others shared farewells. Trish was nowhere to be seen. Perhaps she'd changed her mind. I searched the bus. She was sitting near the front with Amy.

"Hi." I said.

"Hi." She replied.

"I thought I'd missed you!"

She checked her watch. "Another five minutes and you would have done."

"I was wondering......"

A loud bang threw me off track as one of the loading bays was slammed shut.

I looked down at Trish. "Can I have a quick word?"

She waited for me to continue.

"In private."

After reassuring Amy that she wasn't about to make the three hundred mile journey on her own, the two of us stepped outside, and found a square yard of space.

"I was hoping you might have changed your mind." I said.

"Why?"

I shrugged my shoulders, it was a good question after all. Maybe I should have thought this through before ploughing headlong into yet another disaster.

"Are you going for good?"

Trish nodded.

"What about holidays? I hear Scarborough's a lovely place to visit!"

She couldn't help smiling, it was as though she never thought she'd live to hear me say something like that.

"So what's in Cheltenham?" I asked.

"My family. Some friends."

"But I bet it hasn't got a beach, a sea or a castle? I was just thinking of Amy, that's all!" I lied, and she knew it.

"It's where I was born, it's where I feel at home. It's where I belong."

Suddenly a vision of Humphrey Bogart stepped out of the shadows and whispered in my ear, '*step up close to her kid, look her straight in the eye and tell her that, where she really belongs is here with you, in your arms, then kiss her on the chops.*'"

The last of the suitcases entered the coach and the door slammed shut.

"I think you're making a mistake!"

"It wouldn't be my first," she said, with a smile. "And I doubt it'll be the last."

"But..."

"But what?"

'if she gets on that bus, you're going to regret it, maybe not today, maybe not tomorrow, but one day'

"You know I like you."

She smiled and nodded. "But this is about Amy. I only came to Scarborough to see how things might work out, but they didn't. Now it's her turn. She's the only thing that matters to me now."

I glanced up at the coach. Amy was at the window staring back at us, and I wondered just how far she'd get, if Trish stayed with me. There were a lot of people on the bus who could have taken care of her!

The driver pulled on his sun glasses and heaved his pot bellied white shirt up the steps and yelled. "All aboard for Cheltenham!"

Trish pressed a hand against my cheek and whispered the words I never wanted to hear. "Goodbye Tony, Richard."

I was a writer, I was meant to have a head full of words, so why couldn't I find something to say that would make her stay, or at least force her to have second thoughts?

My heart was aching and my stomach churned, but my brain was empty. Another blank page.

I looked to the sky as she kissed my cheek. I even considered praying for the first time in my life. What did I have to lose? God, is it too late to join the club? If not, can I ask a favour? I don't want Trish to leave, but I can't find the words to make her stay. Maybe you can. Maybe you could blow a tyre for me?

But what if she did stay, would that mean I'd have to go to church every week, or would every now and then be OK?

I walked her to the door. "Maybe I could come and visit?"

"Why?" she asked.

"Look, would you stop asking why!"

"Final call!"

I pointed a finger up at the driver. "Stall the engine for a moment would you!"

"I've got a schedule to keep to!" he argued.

"I'll get you a police escort."

He held up his hands and sat back.

I looked at Trish. I didn't want it to be the last time I ever saw those green eyes.

"Look, I don't have all the answers, maybe that's why I try and help people, maybe I figure that by helping them I'm helping myself. I don't know. All I know is, I've never done anything worthwhile in my life and, I have this feeling, I don't know what it is because I've never felt it before, but I didn't have it until I first saw you, and now it won't go away. Actually, I'm not sure if I ever want it to go away."

Her eyes started to water. Maybe she had something in them? Or maybe I'd said something nice and meaningful, for the first time in my life?

I held her hand. "I'd really like it if you stayed here."

"I'm not sure that's enough," she croaked.

"So then tell me what is.............., please."

THE END